What People Are Saying About *Leaving An-nalise*, *Saving Grace* and the *Saving Annalise* series:

"[*Saving Grace* is] a riveting dram...... with plenty of twists and turns for an ex-citing read, highly recommended." Small Press Bookwatch

"...an exciting tale that combines twisting investigative and legal subplots with a character seeking redemption...an exhilarating mystery with a touch of voodoo." Midwest Book Review MBR Bookwatch

"[*Saving Grace* is] a lively romantic mystery that will likely leave readers ea-gerly awaiting a sequel." Kirkus Reviews

"Katie is the first character I have absolutely fallen in love with since Steph-anie Plum!" Stephanie Swindell, bookstore owner

"Could not put [*Leaving Annalise*] down and did not want it to end!" Rebec-ca Weiss, attorney and reader

"As much as I loved *Saving Grace*, I love *Leaving Annalise* even more." Rhon-da Erb, editor

"Living through Katie is at times nerve-wracking, embarrassing, exciting, frightening, but most of all, it was really funny." Heidi D., librarian

AUG - - 2016

Leaving Annalise

Katie & Annalise Series, #2

Pamela Fagan Hutchins

Farmers Branch Manske Library
13613 Webb Chapel
Farmers Branch, TX 75234-3756

Leaving Annalise Copyright © 2013 by Pamela Fagan Hutchins. All rights reserved. Printed in the United States of America. No part of this book may be used or reproduced in any manner whatsoever without written permission except in the case of brief quotations embodied in critical articles and reviews. For information, address SkipJack Publishing, P.O.B. 31160 Houston, TX 77231.

SkipJack Publishing books may be purchased for educational, business, or sales promotional use. For information, please write: Sales, SkipJack Publishing, P.O.B. 31160 Houston, TX 77231.

First U.S. Edition
Hutchins, Pamela Fagan

Leaving Annalise/by Pamela Fagan Hutchins
ISBN: 1939889014
ISBN-13: 978-1-939889-01-0 (SkipJack Publishing)

Foreword

Leaving Annalise is a work of fiction. Period. Any resemblance to actual persons, places, things, or events is just a lucky coincidence.

To Eric
(again)

Acknowledgments

Heartfelt appreciation to my editor Meghan Pinson, who managed to keep my ego intact without sacrificing her editorial integrity. I can't imagine this book without her. Thanks of generous proportions to my beta readers (Rhonda, Nan, Vidya, Rebecca, Susie, Allison, Stephanie, Deborah, and Gigi). I am grateful for your honesty, opinions, and eagle eyes. The biggest thanks go to my Cruzans: husband Eric, friend Natalie, and house Annaly. They are the ones who inspired me to dream up stories in the islands. Eric gets an extra helping of thanks for plotting, critiquing, editing, listening, holding, encouraging, supporting, browbeating, and miscellaneous other roles, some of which aren't appropriate for publication.

Thanks also to princess of the universe Heidi Dorey for fantastic cover art.

Table of Contents

Chapter One

I don't know why on God's green earth I said yes to it.

I was taking my star turn as master of ceremonies for the Mrs. St. Marcos pageant. That's right, I said Miss<u>us</u>, not Miss. I had the honor of hosting the old married ladies' pageant. Forgive me for saying so, but I've never been much of a pageant person in general—despite my dear friend Emily's insistence that her Miss Amarillo title helped pay for her degree from Texas Tech University—and these Mrs. pageants took me to a whole new level of "huh?"

Yet there I was. Half of the population of the island came, too. The rowdy half. I was sure that the object of my unreturned and supposedly buried affections, a guy back in Texas named Nick, would have said they were acting like they were at a tractor pull, not a beauty pageant. Or so I imagined, as we hadn't spoken in many moons.

Jackie, the pageant director, hiked her low-slung blue-camouflage pants up over her considerable bana, almost covering her two-inch thong-panty-T, and gushed, "I can't believe we so lucky someone as talented as you gonna do our pageant." In her island lilt, *can't* sounded like *cyahnt* and grammar took on a much simpler and present-tense-oriented role.

I nodded at her, but she couldn't fool me. She was just relieved to have found a big enough sucker to do the gig at all. She had tried to book my singing partner, the sultry Ava Butler, after seeing us perform together one night at The Lighthouse on the boardwalk downtown. Jackie liked our banter and stage presence, but she preferred Ava's status as a bahn yah (born here) local to mine as a continental transplant. Ava, wisely, had found an excuse not to do the pageant, and recommended me. I would make her pay for that.

The pageant officials were holding the event in an "open-air" theater, which was a genteel way of saying un-air-conditioned. The wooden doors and shuttered windows were propped open, but no discernible light or breeze penetrated the interior. The event was running on island time. Warm bodies sardined too long together were making for a stifling environment, even backstage. Living on St. Marcos, I had learned to appreciate the cleansing properties of sweat, but the other things heat brought, like flies and ripe body odor, not so much. I swatted at a fly.

My sort-of-boyfriend Bart, head chef at and one of the owners of the popular Fortuna's Restaurant in Town, was sitting somewhere out there in that people soup, whether I wanted him to or not. A girl could only eat so much of his signature mango-drenched Chilean sea bass before growing gills. I wasn't even sure why he'd come, since he'd found his new kitchen manager dead that morning. I would have thought he'd have things to do, but apparently not.

Lately it felt like I never quite got outside his field of vision, and I was going to have to fix that. Like right away. I wanted to time travel into the next day, past the part of the evening where I told him that he wasn't Prince Charming and my life was no fairy tale. Maybe. If I got my courage up.

I parted the red velvet stage curtains half an inch and peeked through, but I couldn't find him. I let the slit in the curtain close.

Jackie spoke again. "Move your things over there, mind." She was tugging at her black tank top, which clung to the individual rolls around her middle and the indentations carved by her bra. Her tugging better revealed her lacy bra straps, but at least they matched her shirt. Her red doo rag didn't.

It was hard to take her seriously looking like she did, but I tried. I lugged my overstuffed wardrobe bag across the plank floor to the back corner, sweating my makeup off within those twenty seconds. My bag held the many outfits I had brought at Jackie's explicit instructions. She decreed that we would change clothes each time the contestants did, to "keep it interesting." That meant five changes, Lord help me.

Jackie walked toward a dressing room marked with a glittered aluminum-foil-covered star with one cardboard point exposed. Her flip-flops slapped the floor with each step. I checked my watch. We were now officially thirty minutes beyond the announced start time. Jackie blamed her delay on the day's drama, which she had inserted herself into. The dead kitchen manager, she had informed me, was her third cousin on her mother's ex-husband's side.

As she entered the dressing room, Jackie turned back to me and said, "If the police come to talk to me about Tarah, I'll just be in here," then closed the door.

Lord Harry.

The crowd out front grew noisier. I could hear their bodies shifting in the rows of wooden fold-down seats, their makeshift fans swishing back and forth, as small feet ran up and down the narrow aisles of the dark theater. A baby shrieked and I winced. My thirty-sixth birthday was fast approaching, but my biological clock wasn't keeping pace.

I busied myself arranging my dresses, shoes, and jewelry in order of their upcoming appearances until Jackie emerged from the dressing room. Somehow she had managed to one-up her last stunning ensemble by sausaging herself into a ruffly, too-tight, too-short tangerine number. A toothy smile split her ebony face. "I wore this dress to my own crowning. It still fits."

"Wow," I said, and sucked in my stomach.

Jackie was a former Mrs. St. Marcos herself, a tall, beautiful woman, but she had put on forty pounds since her pageant days two years before. Some memories just aren't made for reliving.

And then it was time to begin. Jackie took the podium and welcomed the audience, calling out attendees' names individually, starting with the most important people in the room.

"Good evening, Honorable Senator Popo, Senator Nelson, he lovely wife, and they three beautiful chirruns dem," she said. When she had made it through her list ten minutes later, she finished with "And a pleasant good evening to all the rest of you ladies and gentlemen."

I was used to this pompous circumstance by now, after moving to St. Marcos in search of serenity all of nine months before—which I had found, thanks mostly to the half-finished jumbie house I'd bought.

Jumbie as in voodoo spirit.

Yeah, that kind of jumbie.

That may sound wacky if you don't live in the tropics, but everyday life interwoven with the supernatural was something else I'd gotten used to. Estate Annalise was quite famous on island, and between my gigs as half a singing duo with Ava and my association with my house, apparently so was I.

Finally, Jackie moved on to introduce me, and I took the stage feeling awkward without Ava there to validate me. I regretted my long black spaghetti-strapped dress as soon as the thigh-high slit exposed my skinny white gam and got me the first wolf whistle of the night. Not what I'd aimed for. Still, the rest of the crowd laughed good-naturedly at the whistler, and it felt like I was off to a good start.

The contest itself was painful. There were only three contestants, which I found surprising. After the first segment, evening gown, Jackie and I did a quick change together in the dressing room.

"Why aren't there any more contestants?" I asked as I finger-combed my long red hair and held it up in a twisting fall. Nah. I dropped it and the waves resettled against the middle of my back.

Jackie struggled with the side zip of her asymmetrical dress. The gap seemed insurmountable and the tune to "The River's Too Wide" sprang into my mind. "It hard to find a Local married woman on St. Marcos," she said.

I couldn't argue with that.

Her voice rose, and with it, her index finger. "My cousin Tarah never gone be married now, and all because she give everything to her job."

The recently deceased Tarah already had her halo and wings.

I went onstage to introduce the fashion segment, then stood to one side. The first contestant strutted out in a long-sleeved cropped top that was completely open in the front. I didn't close my mouth the entire time she was on stage. The crowd lustily cheered her on. We'd gone from tractor pull to strip club.

Bart's blond head stood out against the sea of black hair. He caught my eye and pumped his fist in the air.

God, please make this evening end soon, I begged.

Jackie motioned me in for another wardrobe change, but when I emerged in my next outfit, she stopped midstride and put her hands on her hips.

"Katie, change that dress," she barked. "It too much like what I wearing."

My, how things had changed since the judges named this woman Mrs. Congeniality. I was hot. I was sweaty. I was reluctantly channeling Nicole Kidman with my red hair and "couture." I was not happy to be there, and I don't like people to boss me around. Plus, my Michael Kors slate-blue Grecian dress was my absolute favorite garment, and this was the only foreseeable opportunity I'd have to wear it on island. She was not going to rob me of my one small joy of the night.

"Change yours," I retorted. "Mine fits perfectly, and your back seam just split." I turned on my heel and walked to the mirror, stretching to make the most of my five foot nine inches plus three of heel. I stole a glance back at her in the glass.

Jackie was gaping open-mouthed and craning her head toward the guilty seam. Everyone in earshot backstage flashed thumbs-up and OK signs. Katie, the instant hero.

I strode straight to the stage to launch the intellect portion of the competition. First up, one of the contestants used her allotted time to speak on the importance of breastfeeding.

"Sagging is a misguided fear," she explained to the rapt crowd. "I still breastfeeding my eight-month-old boy, and I no think I saggy, wah you think?"

The audience loved this, and shouted back their high opinions of her breasts (or was that "opinions of her high breasts"?). Whatever it was, it was torture to behold. Not as bad, say, as when I crumbled to the floor and mewled like a kitten during my last trial in Dallas, a moment captured for generations to come on YouTube, but it was still pretty bad. I projected myself to my happy place, imagining the soothing rush of water across the rocks at Horseshoe Bay.

Somehow time passed. We were nearing the end of the pageant after four exhausting hours. I had sweated less in steam rooms. I calculated the small fortune I'd spend on dry cleaning while I waited backstage for the judges' final tabulations. I changed back into my Michael Kors dress just to torment Jackie and was retrieving my lipstick for a touchup when my iPhone buzzed from the depths of my purse. I picked it up and took a look.

The text read, "I vote for the MC."

Weird message. Was it from Bart? I looked at the number. Nope. One of the judges? Couldn't be. It was from the 214 area code, my old Dallas stomping grounds. I looked at the number again, and my stomach lurched.

"Who is this?" I replied, knowing the answer.

"Nick."

I lost my breath and couldn't catch it.

Chapter Two

Truth be told, the serenity I'd sought on St. Marcos was in no small part to escape my feelings for Nick—the ones he had made clear he did not share— and the soggy, drunken mess I'd made of myself over him. I'd buried my phone's old SIM card only a few months before with great solemnity and purpose so Nick couldn't reach me even if he wanted to. I hadn't just buried the SIM card, either. I'd put my dead mother's heirloom ring and an empty bottle of Cruzan Rum under the dirt, too. Release. Closure. Moving on from the pains that bound me. But apparently I'd failed. How did he have my new number? And what the hell did "I vote for the MC" mean, anyway?

Jackie hissed at me, "You're on."

"Can you take over for me? I'm feeling ill." I put the back of my hand to my forehead. Was that a fever? Or was I just delirious?

Miraculously, Jackie didn't give me any lip. She just nodded, put on a wide pageant smile, and hit the stage. The way she shouldered on through her grief was an inspiration.

Alone, I texted back to Nick. "?"

"For Mrs. St. M. I vote for you. Great outfits."

I felt my face scrunch like a Sharpei in confusion. "What? Me? Where are you?"

"Back row, far left."

"St. M???"

"Couldn't be watching you at this pageant from anywhere else."

My hands started shaking so badly I could barely type. Holy guacamole, this couldn't be happening. In the middle of the already surreal Mrs. St. Marcos contest, in the middle of my five ridiculous wardrobe changes, here was Nick. Had he come to the island to see me? I clasped my hands together for a few seconds until they stopped shaking.

I typed another message to him. "What are you doing here?"

"We need to talk."

Ha. Those were practically the last civil words he had spoken to me, a lifetime of humiliation ago in Shreveport, Louisiana, before I threw myself at him and he opted not to catch.

Well. Truth be told, there was a little blame on my side of the cosmic ledger. Details.

He sent another text. "I even brought the damn bar napkin. May I have another chance?"

Oh, no, and here were the details, whether I wanted them or not. The bar napkin. The one he'd held in a tight grip in my hotel room in Shreveport when I lied about my feelings for him and he erased me from his life. The napkin he'd made notes on to talk to me about, the napkin I had ridiculed, along with him. My bad. Someone needed to inform my emotions that burying a SIM card was an act of finality, because they hadn't gotten the memo.

The room was spinning. It was all too much. I had to get out of there. I turned off my phone, grabbed my purse, and left the theater in my blue wake with not a thought in my head but the need to escape to Annalise.

Chapter Three

I didn't make it far in my strappy high-heeled sprint. My dress weighed a thousand pounds and I'd only stuck to my New Year's resolution of thrice-weekly karate workouts for one-third of a week. I burst out the back door of the theater, clippety-clopped up the sidewalk, and turned the corner that would take me past the front doors to the parking lot, my truck, and my house. Except as I hit the front sidewalk, I ran pell-mell into Nick himself.

Somehow I managed to bounce back and remain upright, and to keep from voicing the "Oh shit" that sprang to my lips. But I still mouthed the words.

"I had a feeling you'd bolt," he said.

He looked exactly as I remembered him—gorgeous, angular, and dark, thanks to his gypsy ancestors—but he was *smiling* down at me. That was a change. He'd done a damn good impersonation of Heathcliff on the moors last time I'd seen him.

Traitorous tears spilled from my eyes.

Nick stepped close and wiped them away. My face burned under his fingers, then cooled as soon as he pulled back. It was the first time he'd ever touched me, other than shaking my hand when we met over a year and a half before. The sound of beetles buzzing in the outdoor lighting was the only sound until he spoke again.

"So, this is what lawyers do for fun on St. Marcos?"

That made me laugh. I dried my tears with the back of my forearm and tried to remember to hate him. "It was awful, wasn't it?" I asked.

He grinned. "You look the best I've ever seen you. You're so tan and . . . fashionable."

Heat rushed to my cheeks. "What are you doing here, anyway?"

He leaned back against the wall of the theater and crossed his arms. "I came to talk to you. And to see you."

I looked around us. Nothing to see but the roach coach that served snacks at intermission. I busied myself with putting my phone away in my pocketbook, then held the purse with both hands in front of me. "You missed a lot of those opportunities, even when I was still in Texas."

"I did. I'm sorry. Can you forgive me and let me tell you what I came to say?"

"How'd you know where I was?"

"I'm a professional investigator."

He was, but he didn't look like it right now in his khaki cargo shorts, red Texas Surf Camp t-shirt, and thong sandals.

"So Emily told you." Emily, Nick, and I had made a formidable litigation team—paralegal, investigator, and attorney—back at Hailey & Hart in Dallas.

"I had to buy her a very expensive lunch at Del Frisco's first."

I stared at the ground, thinking. Could I forgive him? I wasn't sure yet. Could I listen? I couldn't exactly say no when he'd come halfway around the world—and I didn't want to. Sweat was dripping down my chest to my stomach, following a trail I had imagined his tongue making many times.

Stop it, I told myself.

"OK, I'll listen. At lunch tomorrow."

Nick's lips compressed into a line. The front doors to the theater swung open and people started exiting around us. I got a steady stream of congratulations and atta-girls, which I responded to with nods and hand lifts.

"Katie?"

Bart's voice brought me to attention and I swiveled my head toward him. Bart. My not-yet-ex-boyfriend. He wasn't alone, either. An unfamiliar too-cool forty-something guy in skinny jeans and dark sunglasses leaned in and said something to him. The man's dark head was a contrast to Bart's light one, and Bart's de rigueur outfit of plaid shorts, collared shirt, and brown boat shoes completed the inverse image. Bart nodded and I lip-read his reply: "Everything is fine. I'll talk to you later." The hipster headed toward the parking lot with a blonde Amazon encased in spandex right behind him.

Bart shouted to me over the tops of people's heads. "I didn't know you'd stepped out. Are we still on for dinner?"

And then he noticed Nick. Bart's brow furrowed as Nick locked eyes with him and didn't flinch. It had the potential to go bad in a hurry. I took two giant steps toward Bart and grabbed his arm like it was a life preserver, hoping he couldn't feel the tremors racking my body.

"Absolutely. If you're up for it, with what happened to Tarah and all." I pressed my paper-dry lips against a thin sheen of sweat on his cheek.

"I am." Bart exhaled audibly and swiveled his head toward Nick for an introduction, but I gave him a push toward the parking lot. He stopped on the way to greet a covey of customers, ever the sociable restaurateur.

Hurry, Bart, I thought. Before I lose my willpower.

I looked over my shoulder and Nick straightened up from his slouch against the wall, silent and unhappy, which served him right. Sort of.

"Tomorrow, then," he said.

I nodded.

Bart returned his attention to me and took my arm. As we couple-walked off to my truck, I could feel the heat of Nick's eyes on us.

"Tomorrow what?" Bart asked.

"Lunch," I said, hoping brevity would do the trick.

"Who is he?"

I scrambled for a good lie and couldn't find one, so I stalled until I came up with a bad partial truth and delivered it casually. "He's an investigator I knew in the states, down here on a case. We ran into each other after the pageant. It'll be nice to catch up with an old friend."

Our feet crunched the gravel as we moved beyond the lights around the theater into the dark parking lot. Bart pulled me closer to him, weaving even more than I was in my heels. He was bulkier than Nick. The thick blond hair on his arms rubbed against my skin and the heat of his body, the nearness of him, suddenly was too much. He smelled like rum.

Dammit. He knew I'd given up alcohol, that I couldn't drink, that I mustn't drink. The endless wine-tasting parties with his high-living clientele were hard enough for me. He'd promised not to drink around me anymore.

More sweat, this time beading my upper lip. My pre-pageant sushi lunch no longer sat well in my stomach, and in a wave of certainty, I knew I needed away from him that very second. For good.

"Bart."

"Yes?"

We stopped beside my ancient red Ford pickup, the replacement for the one that went off a cliff without me months ago. "I'll have to pass on dinner. I feel sick." It was as true as when I'd said it to Jackie earlier, but I left out the why. And the "not just tonight but forever" part.

"Really?"

He sounded suspicious, but I couldn't see him in the dark.

"It just came over me. I'm sorry."

"Let me drive you home."

No, I thought, panicked. "No, thank you. Sweet of you. Gotta go." I feared I would throw up on him.

He deposited me in my truck and I pulled the door shut without giving him a chance to kiss me goodbye. He stood there staring in at me, then knocked on the window.

"Aren't you going to leave?" he asked, his voice raised so I could hear him through the glass.

I yelled back, "In a minute. I just want to call Ava. Safety first." I retrieved my phone from my handbag and held it aloft. "See you later."

He hesitated. I waved goodbye. He walked over to his car and looked at me again. I put my phone to my face and pretended to talk to Ava, acting my little heart out. He opened the door to his black Pathfinder, turned to me one last time, then got in and slowly drove away.

I was a total shit.

Chapter Four

I put the phone down, drew in a ragged breath, and wondered if I was developing adult-onset asthma. Why was it so hard to breathe? I watched the digital clock on my dash count forward the minutes. Time dragged by. Breathing didn't get easier. I sat there in the dark.

Tap tap tap. A noise in my left ear, on the window.

Of course. This is what I had expected. But when I peered out, I got a big surprise.

A puffy black face was staring at me from four inches away. A not-so-attractive oversized male face, but one I knew well. It was Officer Darren Jacoby, a longtime admirer of Ava's and a short-term non-admirer of me, with a Caribe version of Ichabod Crane looming behind him. Jacoby rotated his hand, pantomiming rolling my window down, old school. I turned my key halfway in the ignition and used the button to lower the window.

"I looking for Bart," Jacoby said.

"He's not here."

"Can you pass the message to him?"

Ichabod pulled at the waist of his pants and smoothed his shirt over his stomach.

"If I talk to him, I will."

"You not keeping company with him anymore?"

"Not really."

Jacoby nodded, looking like I'd said something smart. Then he walked away. Ichabod turned and followed him. I rolled up my window.

The whole thing was odd bordering on a little bit terrifying. It hadn't helped with my breathing issue. I put my head in my hands.

Tap tap tap.

Not again. I looked up to give Jacoby an OK sign and saw the face I'd expected the first time.

"Let me in?" Nick asked.

His question spun my dial from wrecked to enraged. I started the truck and hit the window button again. It started its descent. I yelled out the slowly widening gap.

"You think you can just hop in my car, when you treated me like I didn't exist for months? Now you show up where I live, where I work, where I have a life, like I'm just going to put out the welcome mat for you. I already gave you my friendship and my dignity. What else do you want, Nick?"

I thwonked my head down on my steering wheel once, twice, then turned on him again. "Who am I kidding? I gave you my heart, you asshole. So how about my wallet? Or would you just like me to cut off my arm instead?"

I wasn't so much screaming as drilling my words into the thick night air in a high-pitched rush, and then I couldn't catch my breath. I tried—I gasped—I blew out oxygen to make room for more, and none was coming back in.

Nick spoke but I couldn't hear him over the buzzing noise in my ears. I turned the air conditioner on my face full blast and felt the warm air cooling as it hit my sweat. After a few seconds, I could draw in a deep, shuddering breath. As soon as the air came into my lungs, I sobbed it back out again. Over and over.

I flapped my hand at Nick, who was still talking. "Go away. Go back to Texas. I don't want anything to do with you. I don't want to be friends or pretend to be nice. Just go away."

Nick's hand grabbed mine as I shooed him with it, and his calloused grip was strong but gentle. A real man's hands, my father would have said. Nick leaned his head into the truck.

"Katie, listen to me. I'm sorry," he said, but I cut him off.

"For what? Because you wasted your money coming here?"

"God, no. But I only have forty-eight hours until I have to leave. Are you going to make me stand out here that whole time, or could you let me in where you can yell at me from close range?"

Forty-eight hours?

Shit.

I did want to talk to him. I wanted to rip his head off first, but afterwards, I wanted to hear what he had to say. My sobs turned to sniffles. A car drove slowly past us in the parking lot. Great. I probably looked like a drunk prom queen fighting with her date.

"Can I please get in the car with you?" he pressed as a black Pathfinder jerked to a stop beside me, skidding the last few feet.

Oh, yes, I knew that car. And it was driven by someone who was about to be very mad at me. A door slammed. Feet crunched on gravel. But it wasn't Bart who appeared at my window.

Ava came up beside Nick, looking incredibly Ava-like in a stretchy red dress with off-the-shoulder sleeves and voluminous black hair billowing behind her in the night wind. Ava, whom I had supposedly called from my truck. Oops.

"Girl, got an angry man over there who come and get me." She stabbed an index finger toward Nick. "That the one you not s'posed to pine for?"

I instantly regretted that I had vomited up the whole story about Nick to my new friend. Not exactly what I wanted him to hear, but oh well. "Correct," I said.

"Thought so," she said. "I think the one in my car expect you to choose between the two of them real quick." *Thought* sounded like *taught* and *think* like *tink*. *Them* like *dem*.

"He sent you over here to tell me that instead of coming himself?" The heat rose in my face and settled over my cheekbones.

Ava shrugged and she had the grace to look apologetic. But it wasn't Ava I was upset with. I remembered Bart's liquored-up breath from earlier and I added that sin to this new one. I pulled my gearshift forward and slammed it down into drive, but kept my foot on the brake.

"Tell him he just made it pretty easy," I told her. I unlocked the doors. "Get in," I said to Nick. Letting him in didn't mean I had to be through letting him have it.

Ava got back in Bart's Pathfinder. Nick went around and climbed into the passenger seat. I punched the accelerator and enjoyed the sensation of my big tires throwing rocks ten feet into the air behind me. I hoped a few of them made contact with something shiny and black with four wheels.

"Don't get the wrong idea," I said to Nick. "I'm just mad at him."

He didn't answer, but he pulled his seatbelt across his body and snapped it into place. I turned the wheel hard to the left, barely slowing down for the turn out of the parking lot. I mashed the pedal to the floor and an enormous pressure I hadn't known I'd borne lifted from me, floated in the air above my head, and then was gone.

Wow. What was that?

"Where are we going?" Nick asked. His body was angled toward me and his dark eyes bore into me.

"Scared?" I asked him.

"No, curious."

I put both hands on the wheel, ten and two, and drummed the fingers of my right hand. A tingling sensation had started somewhere deep inside me. Excitement. Something I hadn't felt since the last time I'd been in Nick's personal space. I knew I'd better hurry if I had a prayer of continuing this ass-chewing. I kept driving.

We crested Mabry Hill, the highest point at the center of the island, and I didn't even tap the brakes as we changed trajectory for a downward plunge. I felt crazy alive. As we approached the first turn, I slowed the truck to a nearly reasonable speed and snuck a glance at Nick. He was still staring at me.

"What?" I asked.

"I'm just waiting for you to answer my question."

We rounded the bend and the Caribbean Sea spread out before us under the spotlight of the full moon. The moonlight turned the night sky from black to a blue suede. The trees on either side of us were ghostly in its light, but I knew them by their silhouettes. A stately kapok. A cluster of giant mahoganies. The spidery arms of a flamboyant, and the deceptively smooth-looking tourist tree that by day flaked like a sunburn.

"We're going to my house," I said.

"The one you live in or the one you bought?"

"Emily didn't miss a detail, did she? No, we're not going to Ava's." That's where I was living until my contractor finished the work at Annalise. Crazy Grove had promised to have me in before summer, and it appeared he'd just make it.

"Em told me about your boyfriend," Nick prodded.

Ex-boyfriend, as far as I was concerned. It was none of his business, though, so I didn't respond.

"Are you in love with him?"

"How about we play the quiet game? First one to break the silence is the loser," I replied.

Nick appeared to roll his eyes, but with only my peripheral vision I couldn't be sure.

I drove on, swinging left again onto Centerline Road. Just for fun, I gave the truck a little more gas and reveled in the sight of Nick bouncing up and down. Fifteen sadistically perfect minutes later, we pulled up the dark driveway to Annalise with the moon's beacon pointing the way to the most beautiful place in the world.

"Jesus, is this your house? It's amazing," Nick said.

"You lose," I said.

Five of my dogs met us in the side yard, barking joyfully. The sixth, my German shepherd and personal protector, Poco Oso, was back at Ava's place. Nick rolled down his window and talked to them, which drove them into a fever pitch. "Highly suspicious new person," they announced. I parked my truck under the immense mango tree on the near side of the house.

Now what?

My flight had seemed like a great plan until we landed at our destination. I felt a little airsick. Nick wasn't suffering, though.

"Here," he said, handing me a Kleenex.

Mortified that my mascara had run, I started to mop at my face.

"Don't do that!" Nick shouted.

I jerked back. "What?! What did I do?"

"That's not for your face. It's for you to read."

My forehead formed its familiar pattern of a bazillion furrowed lines and I consciously tried to erase them before they became permanent. "What is it?"

Nick searched with his fingers for the dome light and punched it on. "Read it, Katie."

It wasn't a Kleenex. It was a crumpled cocktail napkin with writing on it.

Oh.

The napkin.

I couldn't believe he had kept the damn thing. My mouth fell open. Fly-catching position, I realized. I shut it.

Nick ran his hand back through his hair.

Ah, the hair scrub, I thought. He was nervous.

I read the words written in blue ballpoint pen above, below, and around the Eldorado Hotel & Casino's logo.

Can't happen now/you stop my heart

I want to do this right

Wait for me

I smoothed the soft bar napkin and tried to take it in. When we'd talked last summer in Shreveport, he had only gotten through the "can't happen" part before I launched a defense in my weapons-of-mass-destruction mode. My brain struggled to process the new information.

"Stop my heart"—that was good, right?

Mine felt like it had just stopped, as a matter of fact. I searched his face for information.

He said, "Can I tell you what I should have said in Shreveport, Katie? What I meant to say?"

I nodded, because I didn't think I could even speak. Strong fingers of emotion were wrapped around my throat and were squeezing it shut. From past experience, I knew this was probably for the best.

He cleared his throat. "There were three things I was going to say to you," he said, gesturing at the worn paper. "What I didn't get out after the 'this can't happen' part, at least before you got upset, was the word YET, and . . ." Here he stopped and muttered, "You can do this, Kovacs," so softly that I wasn't sure if I'd heard him or if it was only the wind.

My words broke through the grip around my throat. "And what?"

He laughed, breaking the tension. "Slow down, this is important."

He closed his eyes for a moment and then looked straight into mine. "That my heart stops whenever you walk into a room."

He waited. Here was the part where I was supposed to say something.

I sat still as granite. I didn't want to mess this up with the wrong words, and I couldn't find the right ones. But in my confusion over what to say, I left a silence that I didn't mean. Nick frowned slightly, but he went on.

"And so the second thing was that I wanted to do this right. I wanted a real relationship with you, not just a wild weekend."

Again, he waited for my response, and again I sat stricken mute.

He dragged his hand back through his hair. "But my third point was that I needed to ask you to wait, because things were too crazy in my life right then. I needed time because I didn't want the beginning of us ruined by all of that."

Finally, I could speak.

"Oh, my," I said in a squeaky whisper.

That was it. But what I felt? I would have crawled on my belly across hot broken glass to hear those words from him.

The little voice in my head chimed in. "But he hurt you. He was cold and mean. He could have said these words to you one thousand times over before now."

Shut up, I said back. This is the good part. Where was the voice to cheer me on and wish me happiness?

Nick spoke. "But that night, everything went to hell. I got so angry at you that—"

I found my breath. I had to get something out before I did something foolish, like listen to the little voice that wanted to sabotage this for me. "Nick, stop. I have to tell you before you say another word: I am so sorry. I lied to you. You were right, I did tell Emily I was in love with you, and I knew you'd overheard us on the phone. But when you started with 'this can't happen,' I was mortified. I got defensive and I was . . . I was . . . well, I was awful. And I was wrong."

Nick released a giant breath. "It's OK. I know I blew what you said out of proportion. I wasn't as mad at you as I was at myself for messing it up—my life and that conversation—but I blamed it all on you. I was a shit to you, and I know I hurt you. What happened is my fault. You coming to St. Marcos is my fault. That damn McMillan trial fiasco was my fault. It's taken me months to get up the courage to come here. But I had to say all this just one time. I had to try."

Those. Those were the words I needed to hear.

Chapter Five

I didn't exactly want to be reminded about the humiliation of losing the rape trial of basketball superstar Zane McMillan, but other than that, his words were perfect. Bart's face flashed through my mind again, but I refused to feel the guilt I knew would come. I'd deal with it later.

"Come on," I said, jumping out of the truck. My heels sank into the ground, so I took them off and tossed them into the bed of the pickup.

Nick was standing beside me trying to soothe the dogs. Sheila, a rottweiler, hung back. Cowboy, the alpha male, muttered in dog-speak under his breath. He gave Nick a thorough sniff-over before he let the others check him out. Nick stood his ground and I let the dogs do their thing. If he didn't pass their muster, I'd rethink this.

The night air was singing its song of coqui frogs and leaf-rustling breezes, brushing my cheeks with its soft, damp kiss. I put out my hand to Nick, and he tucked it into his. He leaned in toward my face, which prompted a whine from Sheila. I ducked away from him, lifted the side of my long, voluminous skirt and flipped it over my arm, then loped toward the house, tugging him behind me.

We ran lightfooted, Nick trusting me to lead the way, the dogs all around us. When we came to the door of my big yellow house, I pulled Nick inside and the dogs stayed on the front step. The electricity wouldn't be on until Crazy got one last permit, but I knew my way around even in the dark and I didn't hesitate. I shut the door behind us, closing out the night-blooming jasmine and keeping in the sawdust and paint. Now the only sound was our panting breath.

I pulled Nick through the kitchen, where there was enough moonlight streaming through the windows that I could make out the hulking, unfinished cabinetry and appliances.

"Kitchen," I said without slowing down.

Onward we ran into the great room, where the ceilings opened up into a towering cavern thirty-five feet high. The moon was brighter there, shining through the second-story windows onto the tongue-in-groove cypress and mahogany ceiling and the rock and brick fireplace the original owner had installed for God knows what reason in the tropics.

"Great room," I announced. "Watch out for the scaffolding."

I ducked between the steel supports and made a sharp right down a short, dark hall to an empty bedroom whose magnificence echoed that of the great room. The moon beckoned through the glass panels in the back door. I stood in the middle of the room and dropped Nick's hand and my dress to wave my hand over my head.

"My room."

I took a step toward the balcony door, but Nick grabbed my arm and swung me back around to him, creating a collision reminiscent of the one outside the bizarre beauty pageant two hours earlier. Only this time, I didn't bounce back from him. I stuck. Like glue.

He slid his hands from the base of my neck up into my hair on both sides and leaned his face down to mine, his dark eyes intense. "Slow down."

I put my hands around his wrists and stood on tiptoe to whisper, breath-distance from his lips, "We're almost there."

He closed the millimeters between us and pressed his warm, soft lips against mine.

Oh, my merciful God in heaven.

We stood there, lips clinging to each other as the seconds passed, until I disengaged. I pulled his hands down gently and backed toward the door without letting go of him. I reached behind me and turned the knob, pulling the door inward and hooking it open.

"Watch your step," I said, moving out onto the ten-foot-long red-tiled balcony. Someday soon it would have a black metal railing.

"Whoa," Nick said as I hung right and sat down at the far end of the narrow platform, my knees up and my back against the wall. It felt like sitting on thin air, except that thin air probably wouldn't be quite as tough on the tush. Below, and beyond the patio tiled in pavers that matched the balcony's, the pool shimmered, the moon dancing upon it like it was the pot of gold at the end of a rainbow. The moonlight was so bright that I could make out the brilliance of the dark turquoise pool tiles underwater.

The earth fell away fifteen feet past the pool, sloping dramatically into the valley that surrounded Annalise. It was like we were encircled by a moat of treetops. Rooftops off to the west marked the end of developed land on the island, and beyond them the moon glinted on white sand and the silver-streaked, undulating navy-blue sea. Three large ships dotted the horizon, one a cruise ship ringed with lights and two others, dark and lumbering.

Movement caught my eye closer in. I looked down. A tall black woman was standing on the far edge of the pool. She wore a mid-calf plaid skirt, faded but full. She lifted it with both hands and swung one foot through the water with her toe pointed, as if to test its temperature. The young woman cut her eyes up at me and did something she'd never done before. She smiled at me, then covered her mouth to hide it.

I glanced up at Nick. He hadn't moved, nor did it appear as if he had seen my friend. He just stood staring into the distance. I looked back at the pool, but I already knew she would be gone.

"What do you think?" I asked Nick.

He came over and sank down beside me. "Wow. Just wow." He reached for my hand and squeezed it. "You've got the train back on the tracks, for sure." He brought my hand to his lips and kissed it. "I was worried about you."

"You mean when I had my complete and utter booze-fueled meltdown in court in front of the whole city of Dallas and tucked my tail between my legs and ran to hide in the islands?"

He kissed my hand again, then two more times in quick succession. "Yes, then."

I sighed. "I haven't had a drop of alcohol in two hundred and nine days." I pursed my lips, thinking about all of Bart's parties and how hard it was to abstain in that environment.

"Good for you." Nick was playing with my fingers, bending them, straightening them, kissing each one. It was pleasantly distracting.

"Thank you."

"I quit the firm," he said. "Opened my own investigations business."

"So I heard. Congratulations."

"My divorce is final." He kissed the inside of my wrist.

"I heard that, too. So it sounds like you have all those messy details in your life straightened out."

He leaned his head back against the wall and I admired his profile. Nick is not small of nose, but it works for him. He sighed. "Not exactly."

I curled my toes in hard, then released them. "Meaning what?"

"Meaning—well, wait a second. I don't want to get this in the wrong order. I need to tell you something else first."

"Ohhhhh kayyyyyy . . ." I said. Prickles ran up my neck.

"When I heard what happened to you, how you were nearly killed by the same guy that killed your parents, it knocked some sense into me. I was letting my pride get in the way before. So I got here as fast I could."

Not very damn fast, I thought. "That was more than six months ago."

"Yes. Unfortunately, I have challenging personal circumstances," he said.

"Get to the point, Nick," I said. Which sounds harsher than it came out. I swear.

"I couldn't come because of Taylor," he said.

My heart sank.

Chapter Six

My mind conjured up a young blonde with an acoustic guitar. No, I knew he didn't mean Taylor Swift. But who the hell was Nick's Taylor? I spoke through my clenched jaw. "Taylor," I repeated.

"Yes. Taylor. He's fifteen months old." Nick squeezed my hand.

Not a woman. A baby. Only a slight improvement. I had an instant headache.

"A baby."

"Teresa is with me, too."

Teresa. This just got better and better.

"Really."

What the hell was he doing here with me, then? I tried to pull my hand away, but he wouldn't release it.

"Katie, let me finish."

He had divorced recently, and I thought I knew it was because he and his wife didn't like each other, but I had always wondered if there was more. A baby would definitely be more. "Go on."

"He's my nephew. His mom, Teresa, is my little sister. Didn't I ever tell you about her?"

"No." The relief made me lightheaded. Taylor was neither a woman nor his baby. "That's great!"

"The father, Derek, is a loser, a spoiled rich kid who went from rehab to dealing to prison right after he knocked my sister up, and now he's on parole. Teresa was living with my parents in Port Aransas, but the loser was too close to them, less than an hour away in Corpus Christi, and he kept showing up, so she and Taylor came to stay with me when he was about three months old."

I pondered Nick as a big brother with a troubled little sister. I got the loyalty part. My older brother exemplifies apple pie and baseball. If anything, I'm the cross he bears, especially after our parents died. Little sisters can be hell. I hadn't expected a baby in Nick's life, though, no matter whose it was.

"So?" Nick asked. "Any thoughts?"

I counted to ten.

I didn't know what to say.

My dreams of Nick involved sexy times and happily ever after, not him an ocean away with a little sister and a toddler in tow. I restarted my count.

My hair had long since come loose, and I tucked it behind my ears. I licked my lips. I kept counting.

A gust of wind tore across the balcony so strongly that I grabbed Nick to anchor myself. Dirt whirled up from the bare earth beyond the pool and shot into the air like a dancing geyser. When the wind changed direction and spun the funnel across the yard to the patio below us, it pushed me back against the wall.

"What the hell?" Nick yelled, jumping up and pulling me to my feet. He stepped in front of me and a smile broke across my face.

Yes, Annalise, exactly. That's just how I feel inside.

"I think my jumbie says it way better than I can," I said.

The funnel backed off slightly and spun on the patio, the top of its cone just out of arm's reach. I looked down into its dirtless core and my hair floated up like I was underwater.

"Your jumbie? Like a ghost? Yer shittin me, right?"

"Nick, meet Annalise. Annalise, this is my charming friend, Nick." I let go of Nick and put my hands on my hips. "She must like you at least a little, or she'd have sucked you in there by now."

I turned toward the wall and put my face and hands on her yellow stucco. "I think he gets it," I said. "Thank you."

The funnel stopped spinning and the dirt dropped to the patio with barely a whisper. The gentle breeze resumed. The night was eerily quiet and the smell of dust lingered. Annalise's display had energized me, excited me. If this was all I got of Nick, so be it. I'd make the most of it.

Nick was staring at me. "That was wild. And you," he said, and his voice grew rough, "you are the jumbie."

I put my hands on his chest and rubbed up and out, across his collarbones, over his shoulders.

His eyes gleamed in the dark. "That was friendly."

I slid my hands up the dark skin of his neck, then pulled it down just enough that I could bite the base of it where it angled down into his broad, chiseled shoulders. I nudged the neck of his t-shirt aside to get just the right spot. And another, and another, up and around the back. I had wanted to do this since the first time I saw him, and it was even better than I'd imagined.

"Holy shit, you're not a jumbie, you're a vampire."

And then he pushed me against the wall, his hands following a path on me much like the one mine had on him. When he reached my neck, he grasped my face under my jaw and around the back of my head and held me still while he kissed me like it was a contact sport. If it was, I'd started it—and as far as I was concerned, I was winning.

Mother Goose and Grimm, I wanted to eat this man alive.

"Katie? Is that you?" a voice called out.

And just when we were getting to the good part.

Chapter Seven

I jumped, colliding teeth with Nick and biting his tongue. "Ow!" he said.

"Sorry about that," I whispered. I wiped a drop of blood from his lip.

I yelled, "It's me, Rashidi. I'm on the balcony outside my bedroom."

"Who the hell is Rashidi?" Nick said, pressing his fingers against his mouth.

I came up on my toes and kissed Nick one last time, sucking his lip as I lowered myself down, pulling his head with me, which had the effect of starting the whole oral-gymnastics exercise over again. Nick pushed his body against mine, hard, dragging himself against me.

I pulled my mouth away and his followed mine. "We have to stop."

"I don't like this Rashidi," Nick said against my mouth.

"Good evening, Katie, Bart," I heard from somewhere down below.

Woopsie. "Hi, Rashidi." I wriggled out from between Nick and the wall and reached for Nick's hand. I peered down at Rashidi. "But this isn't Bart."

Rashidi John and my five dogs were standing on the side patio between the pool and the hill leading up along the back of the house and out to the driveway. His long dreadlocks were tied back neatly in a tail, his skin darker than the night sky around him. He craned his head up toward us, and the five dogs did too, six dominoes in a row.

"Hello, Not-Bart," he said.

I winced. "This is Nick. From Dallas. Nick, Rashidi."

Rashidi was one of my best friends, a University of the Virgin Islands botany professor, and the one who had introduced me to Annalise in the first place when he was moonlighting as a rainforest tour guide. Now he was house-sitting until she was ready for me to move in. I had forgotten to expect him. There were other things on my mind.

"Nice to meet you," Nick said.

"We were just leaving," I added. "We'll meet you by the garage."

I squeezed around Nick on the narrow balcony and he followed me through the house. In the kitchen, he slipped his arms around me from behind and stopped me for a few last kisses, but we made it out to the driveway without too much delay. We found Rashidi sitting on the hood of his red Jeep, chewing on a stalk of sugar cane.

"Hey," I said. "I'll introduce you properly tomorrow. We're in kind of a hurry."

Rashidi's smile was all teeth. "Yah mon. I got what I came for," he said, pinching the front of his shirt and giving it a shake, "so I off to town for now." He hopped off the hood and got in the Jeep. Just before he put it in gear, he rolled down the window and called out, "Have fun, Katie and Not-Bart," then drove away.

Nick shook his head and laughed. The dogs settled by the garage door in the dirt, their usual sleeping spot. We walked the fifteen yards to my truck, hands entwined, my skin tingling where it met his. We were leaving, but where would we go—back to his hotel? I shivered and hoped he didn't notice. He didn't release my hand until momentum forced our hands apart when we went our separate ways to get into the truck.

I climbed in and reached to turn the keys in the ignition, but they weren't there. Nick got in and scooched toward me as I turned on the dome light and scanned the seat.

"I can't find my keys. I thought for sure I left them in here. I always do."

"Oh, no. I don't have them."

I searched inside and Nick searched outside, to no avail. I perched on the seat, half in and half out of the truck, facing Nick. "I guess we need to retrace our steps," I said.

"Nah, I have a better idea."

"What's that?"

"Let's go parking."

Before I could answer, he was crawling into the truck and on top of me, lowering me onto my back on the bench seat. I let out an involuntary but surely quite sexy "oomph." A few wriggling, grasping minutes later, I broke lip lock. "Not here."

Nick mumbled, "What's wrong with here?" and reattached his lips to mine.

I thought of the five dogs outside the truck and Rashidi showing up again with us behind nothing but clear glass. I spoke without detaching this time. "Somewhere else, somewhere more private."

Nick lifted his head a fraction of an inch and I could feel him thinking.

"Have you ever hotwired a car before?" he asked.

"Of course not. My dad was the Dallas chief of police. I didn't run around with bad boys."

"Well, you do now. Or at least a good boy who can hotwire your car."

"And you know this how?"

He grinned. "It's better if you don't ask that. I need something with a small, flat tip to use as a lever, like a knife or something, and a couple of bobby pins." He leaned back down and kissed the breath out of me. "And I think we should hurry."

I hurried. The bobby pin was easy. They were scattered all over the floor of the truck. But a flat-tipped object to use as a lever? I reached down and pulled out the machete Ava had instructed me to keep beneath my seat. "How about this?"

Nick slid down me, in a very nice way, and to his feet outside the door. "Now that's what I call a knife," he said in a bad Australian accent. "A little big, though. Do you have a flathead screwdriver?"

I pointed to the giant toolbox I had in my truck bed, because that is how a butt-kicking goddess in the St. Marcos rainforest rolls. "Back there," I said. "But, really, shouldn't we search the house first?"

Nick winked. "Who knows where they could be, and we're in a hurry. A very, very big hurry."

He pulled his phone out of his pocket and used it as a flashlight. I heard my tools tumbling around as he made a shamble out of my organizational system, but he was back in seconds with a screwdriver. I moved aside to let him in and he set to work quickly.

"In these old trucks like yours, it's easy," he said, removing screws one by one from the steering wheel cover until it fell onto the floorboard with a plop. Every nerve in my body tingled with anticipation. The whole slightly-criminal-past thing was unexpected, and hot. I wondered how my father would have felt about Nick. And how my kindergarten-teacher mother would have, for that matter.

"You have to pull the wire harness out of the steering wheel, like so. This is the female end, with openings for each wire that comes in the back."

"Cool," I said, and leaned in to kiss the dark skin below his ear. If he thought I was paying any attention, he was mistaken, but I liked the rumble of his voice from his chest.

"That's going to slow me down," he said, but he didn't sound upset about it. "I need to find the wires for the power supply, the starter, and the dashboard. Power is usually red, the dashboard normally has some yellow, and the starter is generally green."

"Um hmmm," I said. My hand snaked its way to his nicely defined chest somehow. Not on purpose, of course.

"You're being very bad." He turned his head just enough that I could catch his lips in mine for a moment, then pulled away. "Focus, Kovacs, focus. OK, I'll stick one end of the bobby pin into the yellow wire's dashboard hole like so. Then I'll stick the other end of the bobby pin into the red power hole. Ouch!"

I stopped. "What's wrong?"

"Old thing gave me a little shock. Not bad, though. It's only twelve volts." He tried again. The dashboard lit up, and I lit up with it. This was almost better than sex.

"Now we leave the bobby pin in here like this until we want to turn the car off. Then we just pull it out."

I was pretty sure I was going to start rubbing against him like a cat if he didn't finish soon.

"Now we stick a second bobby pin in the red power hole, and the other end into the hole with the green starter wire, and leave it there until the engine engages."

The engine started to crank, then caught.

My stomach flipped with the engine. One step closer to wherever we were going and whatever we would do there. Nick jumped out and ran around to the passenger seat and I crawled into the driving position.

"You make that look awfully easy," I said as I put the truck in drive and pressed the accelerator.

"Years of practice," he admitted. "But it's not so easy if you don't have bobby pins. Then you have to rip the wires out of the harness and twist the right ones together. Or if you have a new car with one of those electronic anti-theft devices, then you're SOL unless you're a semi-pro thief." He put his hand on my leg a few inches above my knee and gently squeezed. It tickled just enough for me to jump a little.

"Where are we going?" I asked.

"I'm staying at Stoper's Reef. How about we go there?"

I held myself to a smile that I hoped didn't look easy. "I think that would be all right."

The Reef was on the near side of Taino, which was better known as just "Town." In fact, it was only five minutes away from Ava's house, so I was driving a route I knew well. Clouds had gathered in front of the moon and the road was dark. The trees closed in on both sides, leaving a narrow path that blended with its surroundings except for the tunnel of light beamed ahead of us by my truck. We barreled through the black corridor.

I curled my fingers around Nick's, which were still curled around my thigh. He flipped his hand and took mine, then started stroking my fingers with his. Twenty agonizingly long minutes later, we reached Nick's hotel and parked next to the building. I jumped barefooted out of the truck.

"This way," he said, and I followed.

Chapter Eight

Nick opened the door to his hotel room and flipped on the light switch. My mouth went dry and I froze, feeling exposed in the garish light. I had waited so long for this, imagined it so many times. Hell, I'd already had more orgasms than I could count with this man, none of which had required his actual presence. What was wrong with me?

He turned to look back at me. "Are you OK?"

I nodded.

I would be so much better with a rum punch. Or a Bloody Mary. Anything with alcohol in it would work, would take the edge off, would make me less me and more sexy.

Nick smiled at me and my hot face burst into flames.

"Come on in," he said. He reached out for my hand and pulled me to him, kicked the door shut with one foot, and slid the other hand around my waist, drawing me in and saying those last words with our lips touching, which ended up as much nibbling as speaking, and resulted in a free-falling kiss.

Oh. My. God.

Kissing had never seemed like a big deal to me. With Bart, I'd gotten to the point where I would rather we did the deed and skipped the kissing part. I thought it was invasive and animalistic. But I was so wrong—I just hadn't been kissing the right guy.

With Nick, my insides swirled and my hands moved of their own accord. Oh, the lean, hard shape of him under my palms, the too-good-to-be-true sensation of his skin under my fingertips as my hands found their way under his shirt. His fingers floated up my arms and across my shoulders, down my chest and up my sides, sliding in and out of the edges of my dress to tease my breasts. Somehow, without me even realizing it, Nick found his way under my skirt and his fingers walked up my thighs and across the front of my panties. I gasped and he shoved his hands under the bodice and sent the dress over my head and onto the floor.

"You are so beautiful," he said.

He held me away from him and his eyes burned as they roamed over me. He skimmed his palms down my arms and caught my hands in his. I closed my eyes.

"Katie?"

It was so much easier to feel sexy in a blue Michael Kors dress than standing naked under a hotel light. I prayed that he wouldn't notice the dimpled parts of me. I prayed that I could keep my mouth shut about the lights.

"The lights," I said, failing.

"I'll close my eyes."

"But Nick," I said.

He kissed my nose. "No problem."

I exhaled and opened my eyes. Nick had his back to me as he pulled his shirt off. Muscles rippled under his brown skin. He flicked off the light switch and as soon as the room darkened, I felt a wave of released tension. I heard the rustle of his shorts as he unbuttoned them and kicked them off. Then his body met mine, full contact from knee to shoulders, and his skin warmed the places where mine had cooled as soon as he moved away.

"Thank you," I whispered.

"Of course," he said.

He started moving me slowly backwards by my shoulders. When the backs of my knees met the edge of the bed, he pressed one hand into the small of my back, then slid his other hand around to cradle my neck. He lowered me onto the bed and moved above me so smoothly that our lips never broke contact. He reached down and removed my last article of clothing, and I did the same for him.

But even as the front of me enjoyed Nick, the back of me realized I was naked on a hotel bedspread, with God knows what kind of ground-in awfulness rubbing against my skin.

"The bedspread," I said, choking on the words and hating myself for not holding them in, for not being a wanton sex kitten who could make whoopie on a filthy unwashed hotel comforter and think nothing of it. He was going to think I was an even bigger disaster than he already did.

But he laughed.

"I'm sorry," I blurted out.

"Damn, Katie, I've missed you."

He pulled the bedspread back, then the top sheet. I rolled onto the bottom sheet and he pulled the offending linens underneath him and tossed them to the floor.

"No bedbugs now. Are we good?"

"I swear that's it," I said, and I could feel the blush in my cheeks. I knew I needed therapy, and a lot of it, but that was a problem for another day. Now, I was here, and I was not going to screw this moment up any further. I channeled my inner sex goddess. "Come ravage me senseless."

He lowered his lips to mine and I could still feel the smile on his lips when he kissed me. A happy warmth caught fire somewhere above my feet and below my head, somewhere nice.

"You have to hold perfectly still now while I get to know you," he said.

I wriggled my toes and the warmth grew. "Hi, Nick, I'm Katie," I said, and he cut me off with a kiss so deep I felt like I was falling backwards into a cloud. And then he kept his word and explored all of me, slowly, bit by bit and part by part, finally surfing his olive-skinned body up the length of mine until I shivered and bit into his shoulder. My wriggling spread from my toes up my body, and he seemed to like it.

"OK, you can move now," he said.

An explosion went off in my brain, and I transformed into someone I had never been before, someone carnal and sensual, someone brazen. "I can't believe how gorgeous you—" I started to say, but I never finished my thought, as Nick's hand found just the right spot. I managed a gasp, and then his mouth was on mine, rough and urgent this time, and mine was, too. I began to touch him again, and his entire body stiffened.

"What about, you know," he managed to say.

"I've got it covered."

"Thank God."

And he was inside me, and it was simply everything. It was everything, and everything else was nothing, nothing but the two of us in that bed. It was tender, then barely restrained, then desperate, wild, and needful. And it was us, together, and we knew, we both knew, that this was not the way it was for the rest of the world. This was for us alone. The world stopped spinning and hung suspended in the sky while we came, together, long, and hard. How could sex be *this?*

In the trembling moments afterward, joined together and holding on as tightly as we could, I spoke first.

"That was . . . different . . . better . . . remarkable. Oh God, I sound like an idiot who's never had sex before. Not that I have sex all the time. But I have had sex, of course, and, oh, I think I'll shut up now." I held my breath as he pressed his nose against mine, his lips against mine, and all the rest of him against me as well.

"That was the most amazing thing ever. Ev-er," he said. He pulled his head back and I could see the shine of his eyes even in the dark.

"You are awfully good at this," I said.

He kissed me on the tip of the nose. "We are. We are awfully good at this together."

"Imagine if we practiced."

"Oh, I plan for us to practice. A lot."

I really, really liked the sound of that.

Chapter Nine

I tingled and jangled my way out of sleep, my body reliving the night before, and opened my eyes to find Nick looking at me.

"Hello, beautiful."

"Good morning." My voice rasped as it tried to wake up.

"I watched you sleep half the night."

"I hope I didn't snore," I said. I had gotten up once to go to the bathroom, and I remembered that he had snored, but in an unguarded way that was kind of nice.

"Un poquito."

I groaned and put my face in his chest, then turned my head so I could speak. "I had the oddest dream right before I woke up." My words came out slowly as I yawned and stretched without sacrificing body contact. "I dreamed you and I were on a beach, with my dogs, and an old West Indian woman walked up, and . . ."

Nick interrupted me. "Read your palm."

"Yeeeessssssss. How did you know that?"

He shook his head and shrugged. "You aren't going to believe this, but I was having the exact same dream when I woke up."

"That's crazy."

"Yet it's true." He rubbed his cheek against mine.

"She said I was an empress. What do you think it means?"

"I don't know, but I think it's cool." He lifted his head back up and I put my hands carefully on his familiar yet new face. I closed my eyes and let the energy fill me up. I could get so used to this.

Nick's phone buzzed and he blew air out between his closed lips. I pulled my hands away from his cheeks. He rolled over and fumbled his hand around on the floor until he found his shorts and pulled the phone out of his pocket.

"Son of a bitch."

My stomach tightened. "What is it?"

"Texts from my sister. Her stalker boyfriend found my condo."

Shit. Shit shit shit. I edited myself before I spoke. "Are they OK?"

His thumbs flew as he texted. "I'm not sure." He pulled on his underwear and stood up, then dialed the phone and began to speak intensely to the agitated female voice that answered on the other end.

I stacked pillows against the headboard, wrapped the sheet around me, and sat with my arms around my knees, watching him as he paced. When Nick gets upset, his face takes on a "harbinger of death come to claim your soul" look. In such a sexy way that it occurred to me that the interruption would probably hurt less with my clothes off. But they were already off, and it hurt plenty.

I slithered out of bed with the sheet around me and retrieved my heap of a dress from the floor. I tiptoed into the bathroom and stared at myself in the mirror. The woman looking back at me had a fright wig of crunchy red hair that screamed "I stayed up all night having Animal Planet sex." My repeated applications of Emily-inspired Aqua Net during the pageant the night before had seemed like a good idea at the time, but now it was time for a bucket of water over the head. That would take care of the wandering eyeliner and stage-mascara'd eyelashes, too.

I looked away from the horror in the mirror and shimmied into my evening gown, then turned back to my image. Holy shit. There was a transvestite hooker in Nick's bathroom. The walk of shame through the parking lot was going to be harrowing. The Reef wasn't the nicest hotel on St. Marcos by any stretch, but it had done its budget-conscious best imitation of Caribbean-vacation chic. The walls were an innocent yellow, the cabinetry a crisp white. Hibiscus blossoms floated in a glass bowl on the vanity, matching the hibiscus-print shower curtain. I wrinkled my nose. Too matchy-matchy. But one look back in the mirror and I knew I was no one to judge.

I could still hear Nick talking, but I needed some toiletries, pronto. I snuck a glance out the door at him as I rummaged through his shaving kit for tooth-paste with one eye on his reflection in the mirror. I finger-scrubbed the last twelve hours out of my mouth, then doused my face with cold water and got to work on it with a scratchy bath rag. Then I swiped on some Right Guard, straightened my long blue dress, shut the door, and tried to tinkle.

The sound of my pee hitting the water was only slightly quieter than the sound of Niagara Falls in the middle of a thunderstorm. No, no, no. I squeezed in vain, trying to exercise some volume control. But it was no good. I stopped altogether.

What to use as a noisemaker? There was no fan in the bathroom, no radio, no telephone upon which I could fake a loud conversation with Ava. Desperate, I stretched over to the bathtub and threw back the curtain. I couldn't reach the faucet handles, though.

I did an audio check on Nick. Still engrossed. I lifted my left foot. Just short. I scooted my butt to the edge of the toilet seat and tried again. Toe met chrome. Hallelujah! I scrunched my toes and applied clockwise pressure, and the sound of the water pouring into that tub was sweet music to my ears.

Thank you, God, I whispered.

Nick poked his head in the door. "Are you getting in the bathtub?"

"Wait! I'm using the potty," I said, and my voice squelched like feedback between a speaker and a microphone. I dropped my dress around me and assumed what I hoped was a dignified pose.

"But you turned on the water," he said.

"A little privacy here, please?" I hoped I sounded airy and confident.

"You're beet red."

"I really don't want to pee in front of you on our first date. Our first whatever that was."

Nick grinned, put his hands in the air, and backed out. "I could still hear you, you know."

"Shut uuuu-up," I yelled as he closed the door.

When I emerged from the bathroom, Nick was leaning back in bed with his eyes closed, wearing only his silver boxer briefs. Holy crap, he was sexy. I'd known he'd look good, and he'd *felt* pretty damn good the night before, but seeing his dark skin and smoothly defined body in the light of day hurtled over my expectations.

I needed to show an interest in his sister and her baby.

"So, is your sister OK?"

He pursed his lips. "Not really. She's kind of come unglued."

"What happened?"

"She posted a picture on Facebook of her and Taylor by the pool in front of a sign that had the name of the condos on it. Derek showed up this morning, pounding on the door and screaming at her. He's gone now."

"Sounds awful."

"Yeah." He patted the bed beside him, in the middle. I looked for a graceful way to get from where I was to where he was, but there didn't seem to be any way to accomplish that in an evening gown. I stepped around the pile of red bedspread on the floor and crawled across the bed on all fours to him, trying not to look like a really bad eighties rock video. I plopped down near him and wiggled closer. He slipped an arm around my shoulders and kissed my awful hair. "I'm sorry, I hate ignoring you, but I've got to help my sister right now."

By force of will, I kept my lower lip from extending. "I understand." I didn't, though. Why didn't she just call the police? What could Nick do from here? This was our first morning together, a morning for room service and nakedness.

No, that wasn't fair. I could understand. I just didn't like it.

I stared past my feet over the end of the bed at the tan low-nap carpet. Practical. Sensible. Like I needed to try to be.

"I'm sorry," Nick said again. The red light on his Blackberry started blinking. New message. New message. Read me now. READ ME NOW, it screamed. Or maybe it didn't, but it might as well have. I hated that phone.

"That's fine," I said. "Really. I need to run back to Ava's anyway. Shower. Change clothes. That kind of thing." Immediately, I wished I hadn't said it. What if he didn't want me to come back? What if he got on a plane and went home and I never heard from him again?

He might tell his friends he'd always wondered what Katie would be like in bed.

"How was it?" they'd ask.

"Meh," he'd answer.

He interrupted my nosedive. "Can't you stay here? Hopefully this won't take long."

That was better.

I really did need to re-beautify, though. Nick might not be ready for too much of the real Katie. I shook my head. "Could you call me when you're done?"

"Yes, and then will you come back? I don't want to lose any more time with you than I have to."

My heart danced a crazy love dance. He wanted to spend all his time with me. This was really happening. He pulled me to him and kissed my lips long and hard.

"Absolutely," I said.

"That's settled, then." He held up his phone with his thumb set to press the speed dial. "She's waiting for me to call back. So I'll see you soon."

"Soon."

Chapter Ten

I stepped out into the brightness of midmorning in the Caribbean. The sun bathed the world in light not unlike but a million times better than the yellow walls in Nick's hotel room. Along the side of the building hibiscus clamored, the source of the cuttings in the bathroom, no doubt. I shielded my eyes and tried to make my Shoeless Joe Jackson walk of shame as quickly as I could. Damn, it was a long way to my truck. I started trotting across the parking lot. Just as I reached the truck, my phone rang. It was Ava. I didn't bother saying hello.

"Don't start with me," I said. I crawled in and remembered I had no keys. Shit. But I knew how to hotwire a truck now, didn't I? I hadn't paid close attention, but it wasn't rocket science.

Ava's island accent danced across the phone line. "Wah? I just checking on you, that's all. So, talk to me. What happen?"

Nick had left the bobby pins attached to the yellow and green wires. Green for go, yellow for something else. Both of them needed to be connected to the power. Power was red. I knew that whatever yellow was, it came before go. I stuck the opposite leg of the bobby pin with the yellow wire into the red wire. The dashboard lights came on. Ah, yes. Yellow for dash lights. I connected the green to the red with the ends of the other bobby pin. The engine turned and caught. Hot damn.

"Sorry, Mom, but I couldn't come home because I spent the night with a boy. Am I grounded?"

I maneuvered the truck out of the parking lot onto the short stretch of road that passed Columbus Cove on the way to Ava's place. A flotilla of kayaks paddled by on my left, creating a neon rainbow across the flat water.

"It seem I a bad influence on you. Lah, he a sexy one."

"Keep your eyes off him, woman." Ava was supposedly dating Rashidi, but she didn't do exclusive very well. "So, tell me, how bad is it going to be with Bart?"

"Bart? He already forget all about you. Heard he dating the recently di-vorced former Mrs. St. Marcos. I think you know her." I laughed again. "Speaking of Jackie, you hear her cousin die?"

"I think it's a stretch to call her a cousin, but she told me. I already knew, though. She was the kitchen manager at Fortuna's."

"Yah, bad stuff happening, mon."

"I just pulled up in the driveway. I'm hanging up now."

Ava's small house was white and boxy, without a stick or stem of landscap-ing to soften its edges, but it had plenty of personality inside. The front door opened onto a miniature great room whose rattan furniture and Formica-topped table overlooked Columbus Cove far below. To the right were a balcony, a cheery galley kitchen, and the bathroom, and to the left were our bedrooms.

"Honey, I'm home," I yelled as I patted the bouncing head of Poco Oso, then made a sharp right into the tiny blue bathroom. Entering it was like diving into a tiny bay surrounded by a coral reef. The whole room was decorated with seashells. Shells in bowls, shells in box frames, even shells inset into the stucco walls, or "masonry," as the Locals called it.

I turned on the shower and stripped down.

Ava rattled the knob, then rapped on the door. "Don't lock me out of there. I need details, and I need 'em now."

I turned the knob to unlock the door and ducked inside the shower stall as my friend threw the door open.

"That why they call it mooning. You need sun on that bana. I take you to Old Man's Bay soon and we tan you up."

"My tush is going to stay as white as God made it, thank you very much."

"Enough about your flat ole white-girl ass. Spill it," she said, and planted herself on the toilet seat. "And don't leave out the good parts."

I squirted Pantene conditioner into my hand and rubbed it into my hair, only noticing my mistake when it didn't lather. I stuck my head under the water. "Oh my God, Ava, he came to see me and he's really sorry and the only reason it took so long is because of the baby, but maybe it will be different whenever he can get rid of it—"

"Baby? Somebody getting rid of his baby?" Ava shrieked.

"No, not getting rid of like *getting rid of.* I meant when the baby *leaves,* because right now the baby is living with him." I rubbed shampoo into my brillo-pad hair and started scrubbing.

Ava ripped the shower curtain open. She was still in the hot pink silk teddy that she wore like a housedress. Her voice shot up an octave. "You pining over this man who make a brand new baby with another woman and that OK with you? What wrong with you, Katie?" She planted her small hands on her hips and cocked her head.

I snapped the shower curtain shut. "No, you've got it all wrong."

"I only got what you tell me."

"Let me try again."

"I listening."

"Nick's little sister and her baby moved in with him last year to get away from the baby's dad, because he had just gotten out of jail. So Nick's life was really complicated, and it still is, but he said his heart stops when I walk in a room, so he had to come."

Silence from outside the shower. I took advantage of the break in Ava's inquisition to rinse out the shampoo and try the conditioner again.

Finally, Ava spoke, her voice lower. "You believe him?"

"Yes, of course. What, you think he's lying to me?"

"I don't know the man. That's why I asking you." She opened the shower curtain again and I realized I was not going to win a battle over my modesty with Ava. She leaned so close the water beaded on her face. "You got it bad for him. He hurt you once. What make you think he won't again, and here you go throwing a perfectly good fish back in the sea only to end up with one that rotten in the head."

"Nick is not a rotten-headed fish, Ava."

"You know what I mean."

"I do. And he's not. And, besides," I said as I turned my face away and squirted shaving cream on my leg, "I have had six orgasms since I saw you last night, and that has to count for something."

I'd just *thought* Ava was shrieking before.

"Six? Six? That man give you six orgasms? Where he staying? What his room number?"

I threw a handful of shaving cream at her, then switched legs. "I'm considering never letting the two of you meet again."

"What you doing here, then? Hurry, hurry."

"So, now that you know what the emergency is, could you please help me pack a just-in-case overnight bag and quit badgering me?"

"I got just the thing for you to wear," she said, and sprinted out of the room, muttering, "I never had six. Six? Six?"

I finished my shower and threw on a robe, then packed overnight essentials and padded wet-footed into my bedroom. Ava had already thrown every garment I owned onto my bed, and most of her stuff, too. Poco Oso was running in and out of the closet, feeding off the excitement in the air. Ava rattled off outfit advice that was nearly as worthless as Oso's help.

"This one work real well for me," she said, holding up a black mesh body stocking. I shook my head violently. She shrugged, wadded it in a ball, and tossed it toward her room. It landed ten feet short of her door.

I held up a zebra tube top and shirred black satin miniskirt accusingly. "I couldn't pull this off in a million years. On you, it shoots sparks. On me, it's just awkward."

She harrumphed and threw it on the floor. By the time we'd agreed on my clothes and sleepwear, my canvas overnight bag was bulging. I'd have to hide it in the toolbox, as it screamed "desperate woman making premature assumptions."

I slipped on my favorite pair of tan linen shorts and a lime-green tank and looked around my room. I felt like I was forgetting something. I patted my pockets. No keys. I went to my bedside table and grabbed the spares.

My phone dinged with a text. Nick. "Ready when you are. Hurry back." My heart fluttered like a new butterfly with wings heavy and wet, hopeful, vulnerable. I prayed we were done with the sister-mama drama as I stuffed my bathroom case in the top of my bag and slung the straps over my shoulder.

Ava stood in the doorway and studied her long French-manicured nails. "Try not to run into Bart. He may be more upset than I tell you earlier."

I stood at the door with my suitcase and my dog. "Be a pal. Let me live in denial."

"All right. Hey, before you go, I met a man last night. He a big-shot music producer, new on island. I invite him to our gig this weekend. So don't bail on me."

"We be gigging. I be seeing you later."

She narrowed her eyes and jutted her chin. "Be careful, now."

"Yes, ma'am."

I gave her a smacky kiss on the cheek and headed out the door. I stuffed my bag into the toolbox then got inside to un-hotwire the truck.

After I reconnected the wires and steering column cover and turned the spare key, the truck started with a powerful roar. I kind of hated using keys anymore. It felt so safe and boring, although it occurred to me that Ava and I really should change our locks if my house keys didn't show up soon. I'd have to call Rashidi later and ask him to keep an eye out for them. I hit speed dial for Emily, and drove as fast as I dared.

"Hello?" A three-syllable word, ending in oh-oh. So Emily.

"He's here."

"You're gonna have to do better than that." Emily's voice was so loud that I moved the phone an inch away from my ear.

"He's here and it's awesome."

"Thank GAWD," she said. "I was having second thoughts, but the horse was already out of the barn."

"It's going to be OK. Bart is pissed, though."

"I expect he is. But I wouldn't have told Nick where you were if I didn't think he was for real. Still, you be careful."

Ava first, and now Emily? I needed a sign around my neck that said, "I have it together, really."

"Love you, Emily. Gotta go."

"Love you, too."

We hung up. I really missed that woman. Ava was my best on-island friend, but Emily was my bestest best friend in the world.

I pulled into the Reef's parking lot and found a spot outside Nick's oceanside room, right up next to the hibiscus and under one of the coconut palms that ringed the pink stucco hotel. Pink stucco against blue ocean always works.

I strolled toward Nick's room, trying for nonchalance, but my heart was jackhammering. Less than twenty-four hours ago I had thought I'd never see this man again, and that he liked it that way. Was I supposed to play it cool now, or give in to my urge to leap into his arms and wrap my legs around his waist?

Nick opened the door. I smiled, but it felt stiff on my face. I tried again.

"Hi," I said.

"Hey, beautiful," he replied. He leaned toward me and kissed my cheek. "And you smell good."

"You do, too." I huffed his scent. Heady stuff. "You really, really do."

I'm not sure how it started, but at some point I realized that I was totally making out with Nick in broad daylight, and that my hands were desperately seeking skin. My God, I was a cat in heat.

Suddenly my peripheral vision caught unexpected movement in the parking lot and prickles raced up my neck. I peeled myself off of Nick over his mumbled protests and searched out the source. Nick followed my gaze and our eyes settled on a black Pathfinder.

"Looks like your boyfriend's car," he said.

It was definitely Bart's car. He wasn't in it, but the movement I'd seen had come from that direction.

"Ex-*sort-of*-boyfriend," I said. I tried not to move my head as I cast panicked glances far and wide. I didn't see him. Maybe he was here on restaurant business. A girl could hope.

And then I realized I had forgotten to ask about Nick's sister and nephew. He was going to think I was completely self-absorbed. Make that still completely self-absorbed. I hoped I'd come a long way since the days of shopping Neiman Marcus at lunch and drinking my free time away, but even the thought of that old Katie brought back feelings of deep humiliation. I would not be her.

I put my hand on his chest. "How's your sister?" I asked. "Are she and the baby OK?"

He put his hand over mine and curled his fingers around it. "She's at the police department and a buddy of mine is helping her with a protective order."

"Did they get Derek?"

"No, he was gone by the time the cops arrived. My friend is taking her to stay in a hotel until I get home."

"I'm glad. Derek sounds scary."

"He is. He really is."

"Do you need to be there, Nick?" I said it because I needed to. I tried to sound sincere.

He shook his head vigorously. "No, my friend has it under control. I need to be here." He held up his phone and turned it off. "With a Do Not Disturb sign on the door."

Meow. Time for lucky number seven.

Chapter Eleven

By the next morning, I was at the point where Nick could practically just look at me and I'd have to add one to my running total, and I'd completely lost count of what number we were on.

We ordered room service early—for some reason I was ravenously hungry, God *knows* why—and then dressed for the day. Three cheers for the just-in-case bag. We brushed our teeth side by side in the bathroom and Nick retrieved a bottle of Estee Lauder moisturizer from the depths of his shaving kit. I took it from him and raised my eyebrows.

He shrugged. "Years of surfing with no sunscreen."

"Kind of a girly brand, isn't it?"

"Show me where it says 'for women only.'" He held it out for my inspection. "Just because I'm a man shouldn't mean I can't use the good stuff. And you weren't calling me girly an hour ago."

Good point. "Here, let me put it on for you."

I stood nose to nose with him and massaged the lotion into his face. His eyes closed. I kissed each temple, his nose, his chin, his forehead.

"You are the perfect woman, you know."

"And it only took you this long to notice."

He swiped his nose against mine Eskimo-style, then grabbed a hibiscus blossom from the bowl on the bathroom counter. He smoothed my hair behind my ear with one hand and slipped the hibiscus behind it with the other. My heart thudded in my ears. I didn't ever want to leave that room, but we had to check out soon. Our plan was to visit Annalise in the daylight before grabbing lunch at the must-see Pig Bar, where Local swine guzzled nonalcoholic beer. Then we'd head to the airport at the last possible second to make it in time for his midafternoon flight. After that, there was no plan, and I didn't want to think about it.

Nick walked back into the room and packed his bag while I unfolded the *St. Marcos Source* that had come with our breakfast. The headline read "Police Rule Fortuna's Death Bad Luck." Apparently, they theorized, Tarah Gant had slipped and hit her head in some freak-accident way when she was closing things up the night before she was found. I cringed and read further. "Ms. Gant's family expressed outrage at the quick closure of the case. 'Something not right about how Tarah die. Her baby's daddy fight dogs, bring the wrong kind of people dem around. Police not even questioning him. She deserve justice.' Bart Lassiter, executive chef and one of the owners of Fortuna's, declined to comment other than to wish the family and friends of Ms. Gant his condolences." The overwrought "family" quote had Jackie written all over it. I was glad to disassociate from the whole scene.

"You ready?" Nick asked.

I dropped the paper. To leave this room, and him? Never. But I said, "I am."

He opened the door and I crept out into the sun, blinking like a mole. We walked to the truck and Nick threw his bag in the back. I got in the driver's seat, where a surprise was waiting for me: a single red rose tied with a white ribbon. I picked it up and the sharp thorns bit into my flesh. "Ow," I said as Nick got into the passenger side.

"What is it?"

I held the flower out to him and he took it. "I had a visitor." I turned on the ignition.

"Didn't you lock the doors?" He rolled down the window and tossed it out, his jaw set.

Had I? I thought so. But I'd never given Bart keys. "I must not have."

"I'm becoming less fond of Bart," Nick said.

I felt guilty and a little sorry for Bart. Breaking up is a bitch, and even bitchier if you're the one being broken up with.

Nick reached for my hand. "I can understand why he wouldn't want to let you go."

I sure wished he would, though.

We talked all the way from the Reef to Annalise, stopping by Ava's house – she wasn't home – to pick up Oso on the way. I told Nick more about Annalise and the spirit that had lured me out of my old life and into this new one. "Tell me the truth. Do you think I'm nuts?"

I twisted my hair around my finger and remembered how I used to get my finger stuck in it. My mother's scolding echoed in my mind: "If you need something to do with your hands, put them to work, but get them out of your hair, Katie Connell." Unfortunately, I had no work to put one of them to.

Well, I could . . .

But even thinking about that made me blush.

Nick's answer pulled me out of the rabbit hole I had fallen into, and surprised me. "Nope. I believe there's more out there than we can pick up with our five senses. Maybe it's because I grew up near the water. It gives you a sense of this incredible power, of the existence of things we can't see." He gave my hand a squeeze. "Like mini tornadoes in the middle of the night on a back porch. Or identical dreams of palm readers."

"Exactly." God, I loved that man. As we drove up the center-island road on the edge of Town, I pulled the truck to a stop to let a line of schoolchildren march across the road to their bus stop, a row of daffodils in yellow shirts and green skirts and shorts. "I want to hear more about your business. What do you call it?"

"Remember I told you about my college band?"

"Stingray?"

"Right. I named the company Stingray Investigations, like a sting operation and as a nod to the other me. People seem to like it and remember it."

"That's brilliant." A passing truck honked at me. It was one of my contractors. I honked back like a Local.

"Thanks," Nick said. "My work is internet intensive—well, that and phone—and I can do most of it from anywhere. My assistant, LuLu, is trustworthy, and even better, likes being trusted with responsibility. Our offices are modest and we have low overhead, which has been key. It took a lot of careful planning, but it's working out."

"I'll bet you planned for half an eternity," I said, and punched him lightly on the arm.

"Hey, I think things through. When the situation demands action, I act."

"I just wish you'd acted a little sooner about us."

"Well, you did tell me I was a foolish boy for thinking you would be interested in me last time I saw you."

I scrunched my face. "I don't think I called you a foolish boy, but point taken." I changed lanes to avoid a rooster escorting two hens across the road and was careful to avoid the goats grazing on the other side.

He laughed and shook his head. "Unfortunately, there's a difference between emotions and emergencies for me."

Not to me, there isn't, I thought. Oh, well. "You're here now."

"I am. And I'm sorry. I wish I had gotten here faster."

We drove up the last section of winding road toward Annalise. Tarzan vines hung from the branches of the trees that grew over us in a closed canopy. Elephant ears climbed their trunks. The vines knocked into my windshield in a crazy drum solo as we drove under them. I turned in the gate and we passed through a forest of towering mango and soursop trees with avocado and papaya trees in their shade. Passion fruit vines crawled up the tree trunks.

"This is like something out of a movie," Nick said, shaking his head, a smile growing on his lips. He rolled down his window and we breathed in the scents of bay leaves and fermenting mangoes. The smell was intoxicating.

We pulled up the driveway between the bright beds of crotons I'd planted the week before. The bushes alternated orange and yellow, then pink and green, one after another. In the center of the beds by the kitchen window stood my new little banana tree. I parked beside Crazy's multi-colored pick-up truck, which was behind Rashidi's Jeep.

"Look," I said, pointing to the base of the tree. A green iguana stood there chewing, like I'd posed him.

"That's so cool," Nick said.

We hopped out, and so did Oso. The other dogs clustered around to inspect him. Crazy, also known as Grove or William Wingrove, was stalking around behind his workers, hurling abuse at them in a way no continental ever could have gotten away with. I shouted a greeting and he walked over to us. If Crazy found it odd that I was holding hands with someone new, he didn't say anything, for which I was grateful. I made introductions.

Crazy wiped his dusty hand on his jeans and stuck it out. "Good morning."

Nick shook Crazy's hand. "Nice to meet you, sir."

Crazy shook his head. "Only Mrs. Wingrove call me sir. Crazy will do." He turned to me. "Railings dem going up on balconies today. Gonna finish the kitchen, too. Three weeks, Ms. Katie, three weeks."

"Thanks, Crazy. That's great. Hey, you haven't seen my keys, have you? I might have lost them here last night."

"No, but I tell men dem. We all watch for them." He went back to berating his crew.

Rather than retrace our steps from the pitch-dark tour through the side door the night before, I wanted to start Nick at the front of the house. He looped his arm around my shoulders and squeezed me as we made our way there. I slipped my arm around his waist. We fit together so perfectly that I moved carefully so as not to break the connection. We stayed melded together as we walked up the stone and red-paver steps.

The front entrance was regal, with island-traditional mahogany double doors that I had commissioned from a local carpenter. A mahogany-framed hurricane-proof window crowned the entrance. I stopped at the top step and slipped out of Nick's arms so I could press my face against the pillar and breathe in the air. The trade winds were blowing briskly from the east and the sun-drenched porch felt almost cold. Nick leaned into me from behind with his arms raised over our heads and pressed his hands and face to the pillar as well.

"She's magnificent."

At his words, I felt a soundless hum. Annalise. Hopefully it meant she would be a supportive friend, rather than a jealous lover. "She likes you, too."

Nick turned his face so his mouth touched my ear. "I'm glad. Very, very glad." The current from the house was growing so strong that my body vibrated. "I can feel her through you," he whispered.

Damn.

"Ms. Katie, where you want to put the—oh, didn't mean to interrupt, sorry," Crazy said, coming through the front door.

Reluctantly, I peeled myself out from between the pillar and Nick. I was out of breath and pretty certain I was flushed, but I was too high on the experience to care.

Crazy stared at me, then said, "No rush. I talk to you later," and walked back into the house.

Nick lifted my hair and kissed the nape of my neck. "I don't think he's going to look you in the eye for a week."

I opened the door and we stepped into the foyer. Our voices laughing together filled the high ceiling, making a new sound altogether, like an enchantment. Adding Nick to the chemistry with Annalise was magical so far.

I steered him left. "Office, with great views." We went to the south window to look out on the stone ruins of the sugar mill for a few minutes until I led him out the other side of the office to the next room, a half bath. "Company potty, sans actual potty."

"Details," Nick said, and winked. We walked back to the master bedroom, painted a cool mud-mask green. He grinned. "I recognize this room." It was the most completed room in the house, except for the kitchen. Nick marveled at the compact bathroom. "What a good use of space."

"I couldn't move the walls, so I did the best I could with the footprint I had," I said, standing with my hands on the edge of my beloved six-foot-long claw-footed jet tub. "The tub was too expensive and takes up too much space, but I love it, so I left everything really open to make up for it."

"I think it was a great purchase. Full of possibilities."

I could think of a few myself, possibilities that had never occurred to me with Bart. But Nick? Hubba hubba.

"Come see my closet," I said, and took him by the hand.

I had made a dressing room and closet out of a long rectangular space that, oddly, was open to windows all along one side. I'd install curtains soon. I didn't know what the original builder had planned to do with it, but I liked the idea of choosing my clothes in natural light.

"What's this hole?" he asked, pointing to the base of a corner.

I knelt down to look. A five-inch-square hole three inches deep marred the surface of the wall. It looked like someone had chiseled it out with a screwdriver. "How strange. I have no idea. I'll have to ask Crazy."

I stood and brushed the concrete dust off my knees. We left the master suite, and I walked to the center of the great room and tried to paint a picture of the original Annalise for him. "Except for the tongue-in-groove cypress and mahogany ceilings, it was all concrete. And really dirty. Imagine a whole lot of poo. Horse, bat, insect, you name it."

"I can't believe you came in here, much less bought her."

I laughed. "It has been difficult at times."

He looked over my shoulder into the kitchen, then walked in and grabbed a box of Clorox Wipes off the brown and green granite countertop. "I knew I'd find these somewhere in here, Helen," he said.

Helen, as in Helen of Troy. My heart felt like it would explode with happy.

"Busted," I said, then, "Good morning," to the three men installing my new stainless steel appliances. In the islands, it's customary to call out a greeting upon entering a room, or even just a building.

"Good morning, miss," they rang back in chorus.

"You sound like an island girl," Nick said.

"Yah mon," I replied. "Except that Rashidi and Ava would beg to differ." I stood in the center of the action in the kitchen admiring the subzero refrigerator. "Looks great, guys," I said.

"Thanks, miss. We working hard, so tell Crazy, now," one said.

"I will, Egg." I really liked Egbert. He'd been the only bright spot of working with my original contractor, Junior, whom I'd had to fire after less than a week. Luckily, Crazy picked up Egg for his crew. Unluckily, Junior still claimed I owed him money. I disagreed.

Nick turned around in a circle, taking in the details of the cherry cabinetry and the gaps where appliances would soon be installed. He stopped. "I want to get my hands on her. I want to be part of this."

Jealousy tugged at me when I realized he was referring to Annalise. "We want to let you." I was referring to her and me. "She was abandoned, you know. The old owner is in prison. I think she likes all the attention now."

I showed Nick my music room next, a smallish room in the front corner of the house off the kitchen. It was the perfect size for my grandmother's piano and a few more instruments, a couple of microphone stands and some sound equipment. I had painted it a cool aqua and the windows gave it an abundance of eastern morning light. Tall, narrow cathedral windows lined two sides of the room and a big flamboyant tree right outside the front windows provided shade. The peacock flower was the best tree in the yard, and the view out the window was through its leaves and orangish-pink fronds into the valley beyond. Ava and I had tested the acoustics in the room and found them perfect. I could picture Nick and me there, instruments around us, hand-written music and lyrics on a yellow pad in front of us.

"You've got room for my bass stand in this corner," he said. "We could write some music together, you know. Are you any good with lyrics? Because I'm hopeless."

Now my heart did explode, shooting out millions of sparks that became yellow butterflies descending into lazy circles in my stomach. I threw my arms around him.

"Was that a hug or a tackle?"

"Both. I have to make sure you don't run away."

"I'm not planning on it." He hugged me even tighter, but I didn't complain. This is what John Mellenkamp meant, I thought. Hurt so good, for real. But it got better when Nick said, "I can't even tell you how all of this amazes me, how you amaze me. I can see the mark of you everywhere in here. And it's not just that, Katie. I can see what you've done with yourself. I've always had a thing for you, you know that," which I hadn't ever been sure of, but was really glad to hear, "but still, you've surprised me. In a good way."

I had no words. I just tried not to cry as I said, "Thank you."

"You're welcome."

I soaked him in, the setting, our connection, the universe spread out around us, and the sensation of my heart so large and buoyant it was floating above us like the sun. It was pretty darn wonderful. Day one of the rest of our lives. I inhaled with my eyes closed, memorizing the moment, and prayed nothing would come along to screw it up.

Chapter Twelve

We walked back into the kitchen just as Rashidi entered it from top of the stairs to the basement, where he kept up a temporary bedroom.

"Good morning," he said.

"Good morning, Rashidi. Did you find my keys?"

"No, sorry."

"Rats. Well, do you remember Nick?"

"Yah mon," he said.

To Nick, I said, "That's how it sounds when someone from the islands says it."

Rashidi walked toward Nick with his open hand raised outward at chest height and chimed in, "Not-Bart, you sure you know what you getting into with this one? She got a smart mouth on her and she known to do some crazy things."

I cringed at the "Not-Bart," but Nick didn't. He raised his hand and he and Rashidi clasped them and leaned in for a chest bump, some kind of secret man-bro handshake ritual. Having no testicles myself, I have never had the urge to greet someone by pretending I'm about to wrestle them to the ground.

"What she needs is a strong man and a firm hand," Nick said, and he ducked before my swat even came near his head.

"Good luck with that, meh son," Rashidi said.

Everybody was laughing when a BOOM rocked the house. It literally shook the walls, which was a mighty trick since they were an eight-inch-thick mass of cement poured into concrete blocks. Dust flew. I heard the flapping of wings and saw through the rear window hundreds of bats take flight in broad daylight from under the eaves.

In the aftermath, I saw that everyone had crouched to take cover but me. I'd run and put my ear to the wall. Annalise's wail was unmistakable, and painful to hear. What in the hell was happening?

"Everyone all right?" Rashidi asked from the floor.

In the background, I heard male voices answering him, but I blocked them out. Nick's face appeared close in front of mine, and I held up one finger. I put my forehead against the wall and felt waves of anguish shoot through me.

"What is it, Annalise?" I whispered.

Movement, on my right. There. There she was. I turned to follow her through the great room, catching a glimpse of a flash of skirt and the bottom of a bare and dusty foot as she ran out the open front door. I ran, too. Footsteps pounded behind me, but I didn't look to see who they belonged to. I stumbled at the threshold and caught myself just before I tumbled headfirst down the steps—hands to the ground in a bear crawl—then resumed my flight.

At the bottom of the front steps, I searched for her. She was halfway up the entrance lane to my left, her white blouse sailing behind her. I kicked my flip-flops off and tried to match her pace, but she was as fleet as one of the tiny island deer. The distance between us increased. The scarf she wore over her hair flew off and tumbled in the air through the avocado trees on the side of the road and into the brambly tan-tan beyond, and she stopped and turned to look back at me. She motioned with her arm toward the gate and pointed. I looked ahead a hundred feet and saw sparks shooting from the utility pole by the entrance. I looked back at her for confirmation, but she was gone.

I ran again, harder, toward the entrance, a yellow masonry structure with no metal spindles yet where metal spindles one day soon would be. And, for that matter, there was no actual gate across the opening where one day soon a gate would be. A work in progress, like the rest of Annalise.

"What is it?" Nick's voice, right behind me.

"I don't know," I panted, and pointed ahead.

We were almost there. Nick outpaced me now and Rashidi outran him. Rashidi reached the pole first. By then, I could see Crazy's old patchwork pickup truck parked outside the fence. A green quarter panel here, a maroon tailgate there, and a black hood; a tribute to his thrift and resourcefulness. Beside his truck was a white truck with a decal that said Water and Power Authority, better known as WAPA.

Two blue-uniformed men were kneeling between the pole and the trucks, looking down into the tall grass on the side of the road. WAPA employees. Rashidi was with them, and now Nick. I was only yards away. Rashidi was crouching with his hands outstretched. Finally, finally, I was there, too. Crazy lay in the tall grass with his right arm twitching and his index finger pointing. His mouth was moving.

"Crazy!" I cried, throwing myself down beside him and grabbing his left hand. "Did someone call an ambulance?"

The WAPA men looked at each other.

Rashidi pulled out his phone. "No signal. I run back to the house and call." We had cell reception at Annalise, but only at the house. It was fifteen minutes to get back within range once you left her hilltop.

"Hang in there, Crazy Grove," I said, squeezing his hand.

"What happened?" Nick asked the workers.

The heavier one spoke. "We start to connect the electrixity for the house. Mr. Wingrove stand at the pole with us. The transformer blow. He fall to the ground."

I looked at his name tag. "Did he get electrocuted, Mr. Nelson?" I asked. I put the cool backside of my hand on Crazy's brow. His eyes locked onto mine as he continued to work his lips and jaw. If he was trying to speak, I couldn't make out the words.

Nelson said, "I don't think so. We standing right here, too, and we feel no shock. He just fall."

My mind raced through the possibilities, but my medical knowledge was limited to back episodes of *Grey's Anatomy*. I looked up at Nick. "A heart attack?"

"Maybe. Or a stroke, or an aneurysm." He closed his eyes, then rubbed his hand through his hair.

Rashidi was back. "I call for help. They say an hour to get here."

"An hour? He can't wait an hour," I said. I looked up at Nick. "Can you bring my truck? We'll take him to the hospital ourselves."

He nodded. "Keys?"

"In the ignition."

Nick sprinted toward the house. Rashidi knelt beside Crazy and me again. A croaking noise escaped Crazy's lips. I leaned my head closer to his mouth. "Lotta," he rasped.

"Lot of what?" I asked.

Rashidi snapped his fingers. "Not 'lot of.' Lotta. He wife. Carlotta."

Crazy closed his eyes. His right arm stopped twitching. I put my fingers against the inside of his wrist. He still had a pulse. "Do you know her, Rash?"

"Yah. I call her." He leaned over Crazy. "Crazy, mon, I borrow you phone and call Lotta."

Crazy's head moved. Just a tiny nod, but enough. Rashidi gently patted Crazy's front pockets, then reached under his hips to his back pockets. Nothing. He ran to Crazy's truck and climbed inside, then jumped back out holding Crazy's cell phone as Nick pulled up in my truck.

Nelson and his partner, a thin gentleman with a beard and *Graham* embroidered on his chest, gently lifted Crazy as Nick opened the door to the bench seat in back. He got in on his knees and held out his hands for Crazy's shoulders.

Rashidi said, "I meet you at the hospital. I gonna call Lotta from the house, tell men dem what happening."

Nelson and Graham slid Crazy as Nick pulled him into the cab. Crazy groaned.

I shuddered. Poor, poor Crazy. I climbed into the driver's seat and the guys shut the back doors. Nelson leaned in my window.

"We make a report. I pray he OK."

"Thank you," I said.

Nick buckled into the passenger seat and reached for my hand. I let him give it a quick squeeze, but then pulled it back to the steering wheel. Crazy was in for a bumpy ride.

We didn't speak as I navigated the twists and turns of the overgrown rainforest road. I drove as fast as I dared. Cars on St. Marcos are from the US and have left-hand drivers' seats, but they're driven on the left side of the road, and the fast-growing foliage crowds both sides of the road, tending to push drivers toward the center. It's nerve-racking, especially around blind right-hand curves. As I turned the corner to the right past a hilltop outdoor church, an ancient Range Rover barreled down the center of the road at us.

"Look out!" Nick yelled.

I screamed and hit my horn. The Rover didn't flinch or change course. I broke hard to my left and we crashed into the underbrush as I mashed the brake. As we slowed to a stop, the front bumper connected with something solid and low, something impossible to see with the thick undergrowth around it. I put the truck in park. Nick and I looked at each other.

"That was close," he said.

I exhaled. "Hang in there, Crazy. I'm sorry," I said.

I put the truck in reverse and pressed the gas, but softly. The truck whined, unwilling at first to back up the hill. I pressed harder. The passenger's side wheel spun without making contact, but the driver's side bit into the ground and threw us up and over the first large bump. The bumper scraped loudly as it bid the obstacle adieu. Small trees and large bush grabbed at the undercarriage and scratched at the doors. I let off the gas when I judged the back bumper had reached the edge of the road.

"I'll direct you," Nick said. He jumped out and ran into the center of the road. He checked both directions, then signaled with his hand for me to back out. When I had maneuvered into my lane, he hopped back in. Rashidi pulled up behind us and tooted his horn. I waved to him. Explanations could wait.

"That was exciting," I said to Nick as I hit the gas and lurched forward.

Nick's head slammed against the headrest. "Still is." He turned to look back at Crazy.

"Is he OK?"

"Fine. The same."

Five minutes later, we broke out of the rainforest and onto clearer, more level ground. Nick's phone dinged four times in rapid succession. He pulled it out of his back pocket and checked the screen.

"Shit, shit, shit," he said.

I was pretty sure I knew who those messages were from. I gritted my teeth. I could grow to resent the rivals for Nick's attention pretty easily. I forced myself not to let it show. "What is it?"

"I told her not to go to my place, but she didn't listen." He slammed his hand against the dashboard. It wouldn't have taken much more force to activate the airbag.

"What did she say?"

"Derek trashed my condo."

"Oh my God." I heard a groan from the backseat and whipped my head around for a quick glance at Crazy. I changed my tone. "Crazy, you hang in there. I'm getting you to the hospital as fast as I can."

Nick's phone rang. He picked it up on one ring. "Teresa?"

A sneering male voice answered him. Either that or Teresa was awfully masculine.

"Asshole," Nick yelled and clicked off the call.

"What was that?"

"Derek. He said, 'You still think you can hide that bitch from me,' and then I didn't listen to any more."

I immediately felt guilty about my green-eyed envy.

"He was in my place. And if he found my cell number, he probably found a lot more than I want him to. I keep a lot of passwords and numbers in the same file. He could be hacking into my bank accounts for all I know right now. Getting into client confidential files. Changing my alarm codes at the office. Son of a BITCH." His voice cracked and his eyes flashed. He pushed a speed-dial button. "LuLu, I need your help," he said. He explained to his assistant what had happened and set her to work.

We had reached the hospital by this point, and I pulled into the turnout for the emergency room. Nick hung up and ran into the ER entrance. Rashidi was right behind him.

I opened the door by Crazy's head. His eyes were closed. I checked his neck and found his pulse. Still there. I smoothed his wiry hair. Please God, let him be OK, I prayed. Unfortunately, I had to trust God *and* the staff at the hospital to save him. I looked over at the building, which didn't inspire confidence. It looked more like Joliet than a hospital, with walls built of gray cinder blocks no one had bothered to paint and an actual barbed-wire fence around its grounds.

I heard the clatter of wheels behind me as emergency-room attendants rolled a stretcher out to the truck. I joined Nick and Rashidi on the sidewalk. A heavyset woman trotted up to us. Her peppery curls hugged her face under a red Sunday hat that matched her linen dress. Rashidi stepped toward her.

"Oh, Mr. Wingrove, poor Mr. Wingrove" she said in the genteel island way.

"Lotta," Rashidi greeted her, and she fell into his arms. "I so sorry."

The attendants wheeled the stretcher past her toward the ER and she collapsed over it. Crazy lifted his right hand a few inches, and she took it. She righted herself and walked beside him into the emergency room. Rashidi followed with a steadying hand on her shoulder.

I started to go after them, but Nick grasped my arm.

"I am so sorry to do this, Katie, but I have to get to the airport. It's already one o'clock. I was supposed to be there now."

I started to swallow, but my throat closed and stopped the motion midway, giving me a choking sensation. I bore down and forced it to completion. Of course. Nick had to get home.

"Let me tell Rashidi," I said.

"I can take a cab," he said, pointing at a taxi parked at the curb. The driver was talking on his cell phone, the radio blasting "It's car-nee-val" out of the open windows. It struck a chord with me. Every day of my life on St. Marcos had a crazy Carnival feel—one minute a merry-go-round and the next a house of horrors. Today more than ever.

I looked back into the emergency room, then at Nick again. "Rashidi is all the help they need for now. I'll come back here after I drop you. I won't be a second in there."

Nick was already in my truck when I returned a moment later. This time I let him hold my hand while I drove. Halfway to the airport, I spoke.

"Look, I know there's a lot going on, and this is going to sound selfish, but please try to understand. Crazy being sick, it changes everything. Not just for him. For me." A tear welled up and threatened to spill. Don't do it, I ordered. Don't you dare roll down my face.

"I'm sorry," Nick said. "It seemed like the work was going so well. You'll have to find a new general contractor, I guess."

"Maybe. I hope not. Crazy was trying to finish before summer, because all his workers take off weeks at a time then. We won't make it now. This sets us back, way, way back." The tear spilled. Dammit. "Bad things happen to empty houses here. Just last month a property was burglarized and torched when the owners were off island. I invested all my savings, and I've given up my job until I finish the house. I can't afford for things to blow up now." I hated to sound weak, but I blurted out, "I wish you could stay."

Nick frowned and sighed. "I wish I could, too, but I have to get back. Teresa's leaving for basic, and I have to find a safe place for Taylor and me."

The road crossed through a deep cut in the hilltop. Man-carved cliffs of white stone faced us from either side of the road. When we crested the hill, I saw the airport below us on the other side. "What do you mean?"

"For us to live. Taylor and me."

"He's living with you? Why?"

"Because Teresa asked me to keep him."

I was so confused. "Start at the beginning. I don't know what you're talking about. Where is she going to be, and why does she want you to keep him?"

Nick dragged his fingers from the front of his hair across his scalp to the back and sighed. "I'm sorry. I thought I told you the first night I was here."

I thought back. He had talked about Teresa and Taylor, then Annalise had thrown a dust devil at him. That had started some hanky panky, and we had never resumed the conversation. "No."

"Oh, God. OK, well, Teresa signed up for the Marines. She has to go to basic training in California. She asked me to keep Taylor for a few months until she's done."

"Why not your parents?" I asked. I didn't shriek it, but close.

"Because of Derek," he said. "For a lot of reasons. And because I'm his uncle."

I kept my mouth shut by sheer force of will, but only barely. When I trusted myself, I said, "OK."

"I have to keep him available for Teresa to visit while she's in training. It will be a few months before I can leave Dallas."

"It will be a few months before I can leave St. Marcos." I bit my lip to keep him from seeing it tremble.

He put his hand on my leg. "It's going to be OK, Katie. We'll figure this out. I'm all in when it comes to us, I promise."

I turned in the gate to the airport. Too soon. We were already there, and there was so much left to say. Yet I knew he had to hurry, had to leave. I parked at the curb beside his outdoor gate. The line to check in for American stretched to the street under the open-air pavilion. We jumped out of the truck.

Nick hefted his navy Nike carry-on bag out of the back of the truck and dropped it on the sidewalk. He barely had time to open his arms before I lunged into them and smashed my face into the Stingray logo on his shirt. I gulped in the scent of him. I committed the feel of his shoulder blades and back muscles to memory.

"Just a few months. It sounds like a long time, but it's really not," he said.

It sounded like forever to me.

Chapter Thirteen

Things didn't get better any time soon. Work on Annalise ground to a halt for a few days while we all waited and worried about Crazy. Finally, the doctors diagnosed a stroke. They said his right side was partially paralyzed and his recovery would be slow and uncertain. I was torn up about it for the both of us.

To make matters worse, later that week Ava and I had a gig at a bar called Trudy's, which was right next door to Fortuna's. I dressed carefully. The risk of a Bart encounter was high and Ava's producer friend was coming. I donned a white sleeveless dress with a round neck that skimmed my collarbone and a skirt that fell from a nipped waist to below my knees.

Ava was at the bathroom mirror doing her makeup when I wedged in to get my hairspray. She took one look at me and said, "That dress ain't gonna save you, Sandra Dee. You ready?"

What did she know, anyway? She was rocking an eye-popping yellow two-piece outfit, midriff baring and curve-clinging. I couldn't imagine where she found her clothes. Maybe I just needed to shop somewhere besides Nordstrom's online.

"Nearly." I went back to my room and grabbed my keys and purse, but a search for my iPhone bore no fruit. First my keys, now my phone. I needed to Velcro my hands to keep from losing things. I shouted, "Ava, have you seen my phone?"

"No, but we gonna be late. You can live without it for one night. Let we go now."

Um, no, I couldn't. I was a victim of a love so new I hadn't even taken off the price tags yet. I might die if I missed contact. But the iPhone remained unfound, so I had no choice, and away we went.

The bar was packed. We shoved our way through the noticeably white East End crowd to the stage. Trudy's reminded me of a stateside club. It had no water access or even an open area, just a bar and a dance floor enclosed by four walls, with a disco ball and piped-in air conditioning. We had cut it pretty close due to the search for my phone, and the natives were restless. We set up quickly and I started to go for a water, but Ava shook her head. She pointed at my spot beside the microphone. Just to drive her point home, she hit Play on the music for our first number. Not an auspicious beginning.

We made it through our first set with no mishaps. However, when Ava's producer friend hadn't shown up by the time we started the second set, I thought Ava was going to unravel. He still hadn't arrived by our second break. She spent all of it laughing too loud at the unfunny jokes of her bar-side admirers and watching the door.

He finally showed up halfway through the third set. I knew he was there when Ava did a massive hair toss and the sultry in her deep voice kicked into turbo. The only people entering the bar were a middle-aged white guy whose belly was too big for his low-slung skinny jeans and a Slavic woman a head taller and fifteen years younger than him.

I'd seen him somewhere before. He had hair that was only slightly more black than gray, and thinning, which his swoop of wavy bangs didn't do much to hide. He wore black from head to toe and shoulder to wrist. If I'd have worn that outfit, you could have filled a bucket by wringing the sweat out of it. He headed straight for a barstool, where he got busy with his Blackberry.

"That's him," Ava said through her Julia-Roberts smile, like a ventriloquist.

"What's his name?"

"Trevor Weingart. He produce for Slither, you know, the band with that lead singer who carry around a big snake, good-looking guy?"

I knew who she meant. And he was good-looking, in a malnourished, hero-in-addicted, overly-tattooed sort of way. "Joe Slither."

"Yeah, him."

I squinted to see Trevor in the glare of the lights. I would probably tower over him. Short guys usually put on a show for me, but we'd see.

I thought he'd make me nervous, but we launched into our next song, Pink's "Please Don't Leave Me," and I felt solid. I even kept in sync with the drop-beat rhythm of our reggae version of "Don't Stop Thinking About Tomorrow" that a friend of Ava's had mixed for her.

When our set ended, Ava sank a death claw into my upper arm and dragged me to the bar. Before we could get there, Bart materialized. His blue eyes were flat and navy, his mouth set. He was holding a beer in one hand and a Bloody Mary in the other.

"Hooooh no, mister. She have business with me," Ava told him, not relinquishing me. A microgram more pressure and my arm would erupt.

"This will only take a minute," he said.

Ava put her finger up, close to Bart's face. "One minute, Bart, and I mean it. This important."

I considered protesting, but I wanted to get it over with. "One minute, Bart. That's all."

Ava released me and I walked straight to the bartender with Bart behind me.

"Soda water and lime, please," I said.

I didn't look at Bart, and he didn't say a word. He was staring at me, though, and his eyes were heavy on me. The bartender handed me my clear plastic cup.

"Thank you," I said.

I pointed at a table and we sat down. Bart wore black, like Trevor, but different. A black t-shirt, black-and-white plaid shorts with a red stripe, and black laceless tennis shoes. A counterpoint to my white, and a totally different look than his usual blues and yellows.

"How's the investigator?" he asked. Angry red lines spiderwebbed the whites of his blue eyes.

"Fine," I said.

"Is he gone?" He took a sip of his beer. Grolsch. My brother used to collect the nifty green bottles for their permanently attached ceramic stoppers.

"Yes." I should have said "none of your business."

"Good. I forgive you. Just don't let it happen again."

I tried to be gentle. "Bart, I don't want to get back together."

"You think you don't. But I know better. A woman like you shouldn't be alone. Especially on this island."

I raised my eyebrows so high it gave my forehead a nice stretch. "I'm not even sure what that's supposed to mean."

He drained his beer and set it down. Hard. "It means that if you are my woman, I will protect you. And you are my woman."

In my mind, I saw a red rose with a white ribbon on the seat of my truck. I shook my head, looking down. "I'm not." And I didn't need protection. I had a jumbie house, a guard dog, a machete, and Rashidi had given me a flare gun. He'd tried to make me take an unmarked gun, warning me that it was every man and woman for themselves on an island where the cops were often the bad guys and continentals like me got even less help. But his admonishment that I should shoot to kill and lose the body was just too much. The flare gun was enough for me.

"You may not understand it yet, but you are. You'll see."

He was creeping me out. I stood up. "I'm sorry things didn't work out for us. I really am. But it wasn't just because of the investigator. Whose name is Nick, by the way."

He didn't stand, didn't look at me, just stared down into his empty beer bottle. "Oh, I know his name."

I lifted my shoulders and chin high and walked away, careful not to betray my anxiety. What the hell was that about, anyway? I'd always found him a bit controlling, but he was taking it to a whole new level. A delusional level.

I reached Ava, Trevor, and the Eastern European siren in the bar. I tightened my lips into a smile.

Ava didn't hesitate. "Trevor, this is Katie Connell. Katie, Trevor Weingart."

"Nice to meet you," I said.

"Yes," he answered. "Just a moment." He stuck his Blackberry to his ear and walked away from us.

Ava turned away from Trevor's date. "So?" she asked me.

"Don't look at Bart. We need to stay away from him. Both of us. Please."

She put her hand on my shoulder. "I not looking. You OK?"

"Yeah, he didn't touch me, he just, well, said weird stuff. I'll be fine. Let's fake it and sing pretty."

"We good at that," she said.

I smiled, and tried to mean it. "Yes, we are."

We turned back to Trevor's date to make small talk. "So, tell us about you," I said.

She looked down her nose. "I'm from Romania. I work as a gymnast in our national circus."

"Wow, that's interesting."

"Yes," she said, "and usually men show me good time. Trevor promise me fun, but so far we not find it. Where is Mr. Slithers? I expect to party with him, instead we here babysitting chef from Trevor's restaurant. So much for bling-daddy dot com."

Ava and I looked at each other.

"Katie?" Bart's voice said behind me.

Ugh. I rolled my eyes at Ava, then turned around to face him.

"You forgot your drink."

"No, I have it right here," I said.

And he splashed the entire contents of his Bloody Mary onto my pristine white dress.

Chapter Fourteen

Weeks passed and June came. The official start of hurricane season was June first. The trickle of tourist business dried up then, and the whole island population went on vacation. With little to no work going on up at Annalise, I spent my days there, doing dribs and drabs from my own to-do list and trying to discourage unwanted visitors by my presence.

The day I was supposed to meet my tile contractor, I passed the time by staining the mahogany stair treads. Pumpy had said he'd be there "early-ish," but I'd already finished and was scrubbing my hands and knees with turpentine and a soft-bristled brush by noon. I felt very much the DIY goddess, a St. Marcos version of Ty Pennington, if Ty was a redheaded, green-eyed woman.

I used my forearm to brush a strand of hair that had strayed from my pony-tail out of my mouth. I hoped Nick wouldn't pick that moment to call, or I'd ruin my phone. Ever since I found it under my pillow the night of the Bloody Mary fiasco I'd been keeping closer tabs on it. It was my only connection to Nick.

He was back in Dallas with Taylor—in a new condo and new office, with new passwords, codes, and whatnot—and Teresa was visiting them from California as often as she could. The police hadn't been able to make a case for breaking and entering against Derek, so he roamed free. Derek had no legal claim to Taylor since he'd never married Teresa or filed for visitation, but that didn't give Nick any peace. He installed top-of-the-line video security at home and at Stingray.

I heard a vehicle outside on the drive and froze. I recognized the sound of that engine, and it wasn't Pumpy. I snapped my fingers and whistled for Oso. I heard his nails clicking across the main floor to me. "Let's go, boy," I said. We exited the side door onto the driveway and my eyes confirmed what my ears had told me. Bart. "Heel, Oso." He sat beside me.

I hadn't seen Bart since he drenched me with a Scarlet A at Trudy's. By the time Trevor returned from his phone call that night, I was in the bathroom, where I discovered that while water made my white dress see-through, it did not remove the tomato juice or make me stage-worthy for anything but the soft-porn version of *Carrie*. I had slunk to my truck wearing a ratty sweatshirt the bartender found in the storeroom, with Ava as my bodyguard. She was spitting mad about the blown tryout.

"I can't fix this with Trevor," she had fumed. "I not even his type."

Since Ava is every man's type, I had a feeling she could overcome his blonde-giant fetish, but I didn't approve of that method anyway. She'd been itching for Bart to show up again so she could "kick he ass between he teeth," but he hadn't.

Until now. I stayed by the door and took a few centering breaths. I thought through self-defense. My machete was in the truck and my flare gun in my nightstand. Not good. I'd have to rely on Oso and the gang for protection. Unfortunately, they knew Bart as a friend.

Bart turned off his engine and got out. As he walked toward me, he passed the front of his car and I noticed that the driver's side headlight was busted out and the bumper was scratched and dented. Bart loved that Pathfinder and he took obsessively good care of it. I couldn't imagine him driving it with an imperfection, which meant he was highly motivated to see me, although I couldn't imagine why, or what I was going to say to get rid of him. I decided to meet him halfway to keep him outside.

"I'm here to apologize," he said.

I stopped. Far enough. "Really?"

He looked tired in his white L'École Culinaire Academy t-shirt and khaki cargo shorts. I wondered where his trademark plaid was.

"Yes. I was jealous, and I'm over it. I'd like to start again, as friends."

"So you're apologizing for. . ." I prompted. I heard a new vehicle turn into the entrance lane. I turned to look and saw the tile contractor's truck. I rejoiced. Safety in numbers.

"How I acted last time I saw you in Town. At Trudy's. I shouldn't have. Things haven't been going very well for me lately, at the restaurant, I mean. Locals haven't come in as much since the thing with Tarah. I'm under a lot of pressure."

A few other things he could be sorry for came to mind, like following Nick and me, like making Ava speak for him, for leaving spooky flowers in my truck.

Well, I wasn't sure if he had really followed us, and my only proof that he was behind the rose was circumstantial. I stood there, my brain's processor busy but my face blue-screen.

"Katie?"

I stroked Oso's head. His fur was standing on end. "I appreciate the apology."

Pumpy pulled to a stop beside Bart's Pathfinder and got out. The tile man came forward and I greeted him with a lot more cheer than usual.

"Pumpy, it's so good to see you. This is Bart, the chef and owner of Fortuna's."

"Ms. Connell, always a pleasure. Mr. Bart, a pleasant good afternoon to you."

"Good afternoon," Bart replied.

"So, I here to measure your floors and plan out the rest of the tiling. I see myself in and come find you when I done?"

"Yes, fine. Thank you."

I watched Pumpy waddle into my house with a yellow pad in one hand and a tape measure in the other, thinking, *Don't leave me.*

"I brought you something," Bart said, "as a friendship gesture." He walked back to his Pathfinder and retrieved a plastic bag. Instantly, Oso's hair lay down. The traitor smelled food. Within seconds, the rest of the dogs had abandoned their lounging stations around the side yard and were crowding Bart. He held the bag high. "Back," he said to them. "Lunch," he said to me.

I didn't want to eat. I wanted him to leave. But I was raised a Southerner. Telling Bart to take his food and his creepy self away felt like bad manners. Thanks a lot, Mom. I took comfort in knowing that Pumpy was there, and that his departure would make a good excuse to wrap things up with Bart.

I motioned for Bart to follow me into the kitchen, where I pointed at the breakfast bar. He set down the bag beside a package of sussies (my mother's word for "just because" surprises) for Nick. Oso stationed himself as close as he could get to the luscious smell. Bart lifted two Styrofoam containers and a six-pack of Heineken from the bag. I watched his eyes as he read the address on the package.

"Something for your boyfriend?" he asked.

I ignored his question and grabbed the package. I balanced it on my hip. "Smells good," I said. "Let me go wash up and I'll be right back."

While I had no power yet, I did have hose water in the laundry room from a temporary tank. I set Nick's box in the corner and washed my hands in the floor basin.

"Looks like a good idea," Bart said from behind me.

"Excuse me," I said, and he pivoted away, giving me just enough room to pass. He kept his eyes averted, but I couldn't help but brush against him. My skin crawled.

I grabbed one of the Styrofoam containers and a fork and retreated as far as possible from the beer. I leaned against the cabinets beside the partially installed stove and opened the lid to find roasted chicken falling off the bone, home-made barbecue sauce, Caribbean rice, and peas. A deep-fried johnnycake the size of a paperback book. My stomach growled.

"Not Fortuna's fare," I said.

Bart smiled. "Our new kitchen manager recommended it. It's from a barbe-cue shack near my place."

I chewed very thoroughly and studied my food. I'd only made it through three bites when Pumpy—God bless him—showed up again.

"I ready, Ms. Connell."

"Excuse me, Bart. I have to go with Pumpy. Thanks again for the lunch. And for the apology." I snapped my container closed.

Bart's mouth turned down.

"Why don't you see yourself out," I continued as I backed out of the room. Pumpy had already disappeared down the stairs to the lower level. I gave a little wave and ducked into the stairwell behind him.

I tried not to breathe as I waited to hear the sound of Bart's engine. The silent seconds ticked by. I reached the ground floor where Pumpy was waiting for me. Still no engine.

Pumpy called for my attention. "Well, I measure the rooms, and I calculate it up real good, three times. You got enough tile for half the rooms left. You need to get more." He thrust a piece of paper from his yellow pad at me.

I glanced down, but didn't read the numbers. "What? That's impossible," I said. I'd ordered twenty percent too much tile. We couldn't have run out.

"Yah mon, so sorry. I finish what you got. Maybe it come in quick."

"Let me see your tape measure," I said.

He handed it over. I re-measured the rooms, confirming dimensions I already knew by heart. I went outside and inspected the remaining pallets of tile. I counted them up. I calculated square feet. I compared it to the footage of the rooms, and a headache formed behind my left eye. We didn't have enough, but what I didn't know was *why*. I was furious.

Finally, I heard Bart's Pathfinder start, then the sound of his tires on the dirt lane. That at least was good.

I ushered Pumpy's plump figure back to his car. On our way through the bottom floor, I saw a sight that filled me with dread. Another hole, this time in the back of the living room wall. Concrete dust and crumblings littered the floor below it. It looked just like the other: five inches square and three inches deep.

"Did you see this?" I asked Pumpy.

He squinted in the dim light. "No, miss. Why you got a hole in the wall?"

I ignored him and showed him out, then stood in the driveway watching him go. When he had turned out of the gate, I dropped my face into my hands. If every day was this hard, I would need to grow an armadillo shell.

I walked back into the kitchen, fretting, and almost didn't realize what I was looking at until I was a few feet away from it. A giant bush rat was sitting in the middle of my kitchen island, eating my leftover chicken, rice, and beans. I screamed as loud and long as I could.

He hesitated for a moment over his Styrofoam treasure chest, then lifted his tail and ran toward the great room. I ran after him. He scurried up the interior of my unused chimney, and my heart sank. If there was one rat in that chimney, there was probably a whole family of little ratlings.

Gross.

I'm allergic to cats, but it was clear I needed to acquire a few of them, and fast.

My phone buzzed with a text. I picked it up.

"Smile: Nagyon Seretlek," Nick's text said.

Ever since he returned to Dallas, Nick had been sending me daily "Smile" messages. Sometimes they were serious, and sometimes just silly.

I replied. "Nanu nanu?"

"Wrong."

"Live long and prosper?"

"Nope."

"May the force be with you?"

"Wrong again."

"I give up, what does it mean?"

"You're a smart woman. Figure it out."

I googled it on my phone. In seconds, I *did* smile. It meant "I love you" in Hungarian. My clever gypsy lover.

I texted back, "Taim i' ngra leat."

"That's my girl."

"Thanks. I needed that."

My phone rang. It was the real McCoy.

"What's wrong?" Nick asked.

"I have just had an incredibly crappy day, and to top it all off, the grand-daddy of all bush rats just helped himself to my lunch in my kitchen."

"Did he say thank you?"

"No, and he left a mess, too."

"You need a man up at that place."

"Are you applying for the job?"

"Will the position be open in a month?"

"Absolutely."

"Well, kill the fatted calf, baby, I'm coming to your home."

I leaned my head back and closed my eyes. That sounded very good to me.

Chapter Fifteen

Early one morning a few days later, I swung my truck up toward Annalise to check on the previous day's progress, with Oso riding shotgun. I was steering with one hand and holding my precious cup of King's coffee in the other—I had become addicted to my morning dose of the local brew—and cursing Ava with every drop I spilled. She had woken me up at 2:30 a.m. to tell me she'd talked Trevor into a do-over, information that could have waited for a better time, like between dawn and dusk. Oso wagged his tail every time I blurted out an explative.

When we made it up to the house, I found Rashidi cleaning a bowl and spoon in the laundry-room basin.

"Good morning, Rasta man. Do you have the day off?" I asked.

"And a pleasant good morning to you," Rashidi said, ruffling Oso's ears. Rashidi was the one who found my six dogs for me originally, and it was he that selected Oso to act as my protector. They had a special bond. "Yah mon. No tourists, no students. I a free man."

"Want to join me on a mission of stealth?"

"I all about stealth. And missions dem. Me and my good friend Tom Cruise. What this mission, if I choose to accept it?"

"Egg hinted that I should make a trip out to Junior's new job site. Something to do with my missing tile."

"Uh oh. If Junior involved, it gotta be no good."

"My thinking exactly. Just let me check on yesterday's work first."

Fifteen minutes later, we got in the truck and Oso vaulted into the bed, which he was happy about. He loves to feel the breeze on his nose from back there.

"So when Not-Bart coming back on island?" Rashidi asked, as we drove back toward Town down the rainforest road.

"A month. His sister is almost through with basic training, and then Nick hands his nephew off to his parents. He keeps asking me when *I'm* coming *there*, and he's so damn calm about it. I don't think he completely understands why it is impossible for me to leave in the middle of this construction nightmare."

"Not such a bad thing, to have someone what want to see you." He chuptzed low, a rueful rather than a derisive sound, then said, "Ava 'bout through with me."

I didn't know how to respond, so I let silence take over. She hadn't said so, but I'd noticed Ava losing interest in fidelity again. Someday she'd look back and regret tossing Rashidi aside, I was sure. He was not only smart, motivated, and kind, but he was loyal and easy on the eye. He'd just had the misfortune to fall for a girl with a restless heart. Rashidi really liked Ava—the flesh and blood woman, not just the bombshell that every other man on the island liked. The funny, insecure girl with the giving heart.

I turned the radio on and we drove into a one-hundred-percent Local neighborhood in the center of the island, listening to The Jam Band sing "Man Terrible." Rashidi sang along word for word. I had an address for Junior's job site, but there were no street signs in that part of Town. "Good thing I with you," Rashidi said. "You be lost and unwelcome without me."

The most important characteristic of anyone on St. Marcos is whether or not you're bahn yah, and my flaw of birthplace was compounded by my lack of pigmentation. I didn't blend well. Stealth, indeed.

We pulled up to a peach-colored one-story house with rebar sticking up off its flat, sloped roof. Locals tend to leave room for expansion as cash permits, so it's a familiar sight. A truck was parked in the driveway, a big newish midnight-blue Silverado that belonged to none other than Junior.

"Well, we in the right place," Rashidi said.

"Yah mon," I said, and Rashidi laughed. "Let's make us a little less obvious." I pulled past two more rebar-topped houses and turned left at the corner. When I was sure I was out of sight, I parked. "I'll be right back."

I got out, leash in hand, and snapped it to Oso's collar, then let down the tailgate and he jumped out. Rashidi's door opened and shut.

"What are you doing?" I asked.

"Tom Cruise don't wait in the truck."

"Come along then, Tom."

He patted Oso's head. We cut through the side and back yards of the houses between us and Pumpy's place.

"Excellent specimen of frangipani in flower," Rashidi said, pointing at a tree in the yard of the eggshell-blue house on the corner. "Nice avocado tree, almost ready to go to fruit," he said as we stole across the yard of the seafoam-green house next to it. I rolled my eyes. Ever the botanist.

As we slunk up to the peach house's front window, I had a clear view into the living room and eating area. Behind them we could see the kitchen and what would probably become an office. The open floor plan was common, but it wasn't the layout that caught my eye. It was the bright and shiny new eighteen-by-eighteen-inch faux travertine porcelain floor tile throughout that did, tile identical to that which I had purchased for Annalise. Not only that, but there were still a few boxes of it against the living room wall.

Rashidi chuptzed. "He t'iefin' you." When Rashidi gets upset, his accent thickens. This phrasing was near-homicidal for the peaceful Rastafarian.

I stood and gaped at Pumpy and Junior, who were seated side by side at a folding table in the eating area. Junior was wearing his red, green, and yellow Rastafarian winter skullcap so old it had a big patched hole in it. I guess he was ready in case we had a sudden spate of subzero temperatures. I ducked out of their line of vision and peeked around the window just enough to see them. Junior wrote something, whipped his hand from right to left, and handed a rectangular paper to Pumpy—a rectangular paper known the world over by its shape. A check.

Damn the luck.

Pumpy took it, then they stood and shook hands with clasped arms. They walked toward the door.

"Let's get out of here," I whispered, and Rashidi and I sprinted back to the trunk. I didn't bother to put Oso in the bed, just opened my door and said, "Up, boy," and climbed in behind him. Rashidi was already buckled in by the time I got in my seat.

"Well, looks like I have to fire another contractor. Do you think I should make a police report?"

"Nah, cop you get probably Pumpy's first cousin."

"You're right."

Rashidi shook his head. "Girl, you gonna need an awful big piece of paper for the list of enemies dem you makin', and true dat."

True dat, indeed.

Chapter Sixteen

It was my birthday, but I had blocked out the big three six. I'd decided I wasn't doing my birthday that year, so it was as good a day as any to move into Annalise. Luckily I had already moved most of my furniture in, since the entire Caribbean Sea had been falling from the sky for the past twenty-four hours. I'd had to swim upstream just to get there from Ava's that morning. It seemed as if all the forces of nature, including my jumbie house, were conspiring to test my mettle. I stuffed another towel against the threshold to the kitchen door as the wind pushed water over it and ran to change the bowl under the dripping ceiling in the master bedroom.

I wanted help. And a break from everything going wrong that possibly could. I didn't need another island holiday to stop work on my house. I could live without any more mysterious holes appearing in my walls or roses appearing in my truck. And I could stand to see the love of my life, who was still in Texas with a business and a baby while I was stuck in the tropics battling the elements.

I missed Nick. On my worst days it seemed like I'd dreamed his whole visit up. He'd been rock solid every day since then, but still. Absence makes the heart grow fonder and the head grow crazier. I crawled up on the marble countertop with a box of dishes and transferred fiesta plates of three sizes into the glass-fronted dark cherry cabinets.

"Why are you making it so hard, you big dumb house? I thought you wanted me here," I scolded. Annalise had told me we could save each other, right in front of Rashidi on my first visit to the house. Not in so many words, but clear enough that he and I both understood.

I opened a box of utensils and put them in the drawers I'd cleaned and lined with shelf paper the day before. If I expected an answer from my ghostly friend, I didn't get one. Annalise was pouting like a child. A very big, very spoiled child. I hadn't even seen her face since the day we rushed Crazy to the hospital. I bent down to open another box. Crystal wine glasses and big-mouthed margarita glasses from my old drinking life in Dallas. Ugh.

I'd thought I would have an easier time with my alcohol-free lifestyle with Bart out of my life, and it was true that helped, but being lonely didn't. Especially since I spent three nights a week in bars performing. Most club owners tried to ply Ava and me with booze, hoping we'd forget to collect our cash at the end of the night.

I pushed the box of glasses aside and moved on to the next one. Water glasses and coffee cups. Much better. I carried it over to the cabinet next to the sink and moved my large multicolored coffee mugs into the cabinet above the dishwasher with a little too much force. The noise made me feel better, though, and allowed me to take out a little healthy frustration. Between Nick describing his efforts to thwart Derek and every last adorable thing Taylor did, I was getting jealous. I wanted him to be with me, to think about me, and to talk about me. To help me with my house, like a normal boyfriend would. But he wasn't a normal boyfriend. He was Uncle Nick.

Come hell or high water, though, Nick and I were going to see each other in less than four days. He had tickets to the island, hallelujah! But first I had to deal with the house. Alone. Because despite my best efforts, I hadn't found anyone who could—or would—come help me.

I had tried last week to talk my big brother into coming to St. Marcos to help me get the house ready and move in. Lucky Collin is my in loco parentis, but he'd said, "No can do, sis. I'm moving, too."

"What?!?" I shrieked into the phone.

"Thank you, I didn't need that eardrum anyway," my brother said. "I signed on with the New Mexico state police. Gonna be part of their clandestine lab team busting up drug farms, putting the bad guys in the pokey."

"Umm, congratulations. But what the hell am I going to do now? You were my only hope."

"You're the big girl who had to move down to the islands all by yourself and buy that house. You'll figure it out. How come your boyfriend isn't helping you?" There was an edge of sarcasm in his voice that made me wary.

"He can't come."

"Not much of a boyfriend then, is he? But it was him that drove you down there in the first place, after all."

Yeah, more than an edge.

"Collin, he's different than you think. You'll see."

"I still think you're taking a big risk. Speaking of big risks, did I tell you I'm moving into the Taos house?"

"What? That's great."

The house in Taos had belonged to our parents, and it had always been special to Collin. I'd have said good for him any other time. I tried once more. "You haven't even come down here to see me, you know. It's been nearly a year. You could be here to celebrate my birthday with me."

I could almost see his "talk to the hand" gesture as he cut me off. "Happy early birthday, little sis. Find yourself another Huckleberry this time. Or you can come here and help me move."

A tremendously bad idea. We clicked off.

I'd also tried to rope Rashidi into the job, but he was at a hydroponic-farming conference in Florida learning how to fertilize plants with fish poo, nuggets of information gold he could bring back to his students at UVI. Great, but no help.

The only thing Ava had to offer was moral support. She was bad ass with a machete when she chose to be. But she could find almost any excuse to get out of manual labor, and when I asked her to help me move in, she suddenly needed to help her parents in their pool-supply store, serve meals to the homeless, and gather alms for the poor. Ten to one her nails would look fantastic next time I saw her.

I forced my mind back to the present and ripped open a box I hoped held cereal bowls, since it was the very last box and I had yet to come across them. It did. I started stacking them on cabinet shelves until I had done all I could for the time being. I looked out the window at the storm. It was already gloomy, a rainy midafternoon. I prayed to the god of power companies, "Please don't let the WAPA guys flake out." Up until then, the power had been supplied by a portable generator and my shower was courtesy of a water pump connected to it. The light came from drop lamps on long extension cords that I carried around with me. I was more than ready to leave the dark ages.

The next task on my list was a doozie: cistern inspection. I decided to call Nick before I got started. Someone had to know why I was never seen again, just in case.

He answered on the first ring. "Hi, beautiful. Happy birthday."

"Thanks." I skipped the preliminaries and got straight to it. "I have to go down into the cisterns to check that they're filling. I'm a little scared."

"That's nuts. Can't Egg do it?"

"Egg's grandmother passed away, and he won't be back from Trinidad for a week. I can't get any of the guys to do anything other than the work Crazy has on the lists. If one more person says to me 'It not me job, mon' or 'That not what the Crazy boss man tell me to do,' I am going to commit a serious crime."

"Why do you have to check them, anyway? If you've got water, they're working."

"Crazy made me promise. He said we have to check them when they're partway full because it's a big house with a huge swimming pool and we need all five chambers to fill, or I'm not going to have enough water." It was $350 per truckload for water, something I knew because Crazy had made me fill the pool as soon the tile work was finished to protect it. It had taken ten truckloads. "At the rate the rain is falling, they'll be full by dusk. It's now or never."

"I wish I was there."

Him and me both. "It's gonna be OK. All I have to do is go down into the center cistern under the dining room. The other four are connected through openings in each of its walls. I'll stick my measuring stick over into each one, and if it comes back wet, there's water. If you don't hear from me in an hour, call Ava and have her send in the cavalry."

He promised he would.

We hung up. I took several cleansing breaths and traded in my flip-flop sandals for water socks. I jammed a hard hat on my head. It had a snazzy head lamp, and I switched it on. I doused myself with Cutter extra-strength mosquito repellent. I put on an orange lifejacket and tightened the straps, then positioned my drop light near the hatch in the center of the dining room floor.

I kept breathing in through my nose, like Mom taught me to do when I feel panicky. I was almost ready.

I picked up a six-foot-long contractor's measuring stick in one hand and dragged my one-woman inflatable raft to the open hatch. When I looped the raft's side rope around my hand, I ran into my first snag. Too big.

"Spit in a well bucket," I said.

That made me smile. I had no idea what the expression meant, but Dad had always said it when something went wrong. I let air out of the raft until it was small enough to fit through the hole, then I followed it down the ladder and into an incredible roar.

I hadn't expected the noise, but it made sense. Water was cascading from the sky into my rooftop catchments, through the pipes, and falling fifteen feet to the five connected cisterns. My head vibrated with the sound.

I stood with my head one foot below the hole and blew the raft back up until I was light-headed and my breathing was shallow. I didn't want to think about what might be down there with me in the noisy dark. Frogs. Centipedes. The creature from the black lagoon. At least there weren't water moccasins on St. Marcos.

I took another step down the ladder. With each step, the roar grew louder. My feet were now eight feet below the dining room floor, and the raft was dangling another five feet below me. It wasn't like I was plunging to the center of the earth, I reassured myself. I started talking myself through Annalise's floor plan to keep myself calm. The cisterns were level with the basement, which was built into the side of a hill. The basement was half cisterns and half patio rooms that looked out onto the pool and deck. The cisterns were inside the hill, behind the patio rooms. One was under the kitchen, another below the music room, the center one was under the dining room, and two were below the foyer and the office.

The rope to the raft went slack. I took two more steps down the ladder, then three. My feet were under water, cold water.

"Just rainwater," I whispered. "Perfectly clean."

Dark water terrifies me. I focused on the thought of Crazy and his crew bleaching out the cisterns and cleaning them with pressure hoses. Crazy had made me come into the caverns to take a look when they were finished.

"Clean enough to eat from," he'd said.

Not by my standards, I'd thought.

We had kept the cisterns plugged until Crazy was ready. A month ago, he'd given the order to open the intake pipes, and the wait had begun. Only it hadn't rained until this week. So the water was fresh. Just rainwater, I told myself again. That's all.

I eased myself into the raft. I knew I had to do this right. I couldn't fall in and submerge my lamp, or I'd have to find my way out of the depths of hell with only one tiny square of light above me to lead me back to the ladder. If that happened, I wouldn't have to worry about drowning or getting trapped down there, because I would have a massive cardiac infarction and die.

The raft rocked violently as I entered it, but stayed upright. I puffed out a huge exhale and gave myself a push off the cement bottom with my stick. I was Jonah. Or Pinocchio. The roar of water swallowed my nervous laugh. I gave myself another tiny push.

The beam from my headlamp was weak and I couldn't see the walls around me, but I knew they were there. I'd just give myself a few pushes until I came to a wall—assuming I didn't spin myself in endless circles—and then I could feel my way along it. I shuddered. I wasn't touching anything with my hands. I would have to navigate around the room sans feeling.

Bump.

I screamed.

But it was only the raft hitting the first wall. I willed my racing heart to slow. Get a grip, Katie, get a grip. I used the stick to push myself along the wall, looking for a cut in the concrete. I didn't see it until I was practically nose to nose with the gap. If the water had been any higher, I could have floated into the next chamber and never known I'd changed rooms. A huge lump formed in my throat.

"Annalise? Are you there? I could use some company."

Only the roar of the water answered. Anger flickered inside me. I let it rage in me for a few moments, but it was a dangerous emotion. I closed my eyes and red turned from orange to brown and then black. I opened them and the color didn't change.

All right then, time to check for water in the next cistern. I pulled my measuring stick out of the water and suddenly realized I'd made a tactical error. I wasn't going to be able to see a waterline on a wet stick in the near dark.

The gears in my brain froze. A crippling impulse to get the hell out of there came over me. The darkness moved closer in. The space was shrinking.

NO, I thought. It's not, Katie, it's not.

My hands were shaking so much my stick scratched against the raft. I grabbed one hand with the other, still clutching the stick. OK, think. Think think think.

The solution wasn't hard. In fact, it was so easy I felt foolish. I reached the stick across into the other cavern and extended the stick downward sharply. I felt soft resistance when it splashed the water.

My breath came in a rush. I was fine. I was doing this. I *could* do this. I pushed off the bottom again with the stick, keeping the raft against the wall. The scritchy rubbing sensation of stick against floor comforted me.

Bump.

A corner. I maneuvered the raft around it without losing contact with the wall, then started moving forward again. I came to the next opening. I poked my stick over the ledge and smacked it downward.

It connected with water.

Two down. Two to go. I was working this like a boss. A champ. A hoss. A butt-kicking Amazon rainforest goddess. I remembered my palm-reader dream—no, a butt-kicking empress.

I came to the next cavern. Extend, lower, splash. Onward.

I came to the last cavern, the one under the music room, if I'd kept my bearings. Extend, lower, air. Thwack—my stick hit the inside of the wall of the cavern. It took me by surprise and I lost my balance. The raft shifted out as my body shifted in. There was nowhere to catch myself, and I fell across the ledge, hard. The raft shot out from under me and the cold water sucked my legs and torso into its grasp. A surge of water pushed at me, shoving me farther onto the ledge. I screamed, short and shrill. The sound echoed from the cistern in front of me.

I pushed my hands downward against the inside wall of the cavern to keep myself from tumbling over. My stick fell to the dry, sloped floor twelve feet below and I heard it rattle in the empty echo chamber over the roar behind me as it rolled to a stop at the low center.

I lowered my head, gasping, and that's when my hard hat joined the stick. The impact shattered the headlamp, and suddenly it was quite, quite dark.

F-word. Definitely. F-word, f-word, f-word. I held perfectly still, my disorientation so complete that I was sure that if I moved I would tumble into the empty cistern, break both legs, and die of starvation if I wasn't eaten by rats first. Rashidi would find my body when he got back from Florida, and Ava would cry pretty tears. Nick would cash in his tickets to St. Marcos and spend the money on a diamond ring for a new girlfriend.

Long seconds passed, or maybe they were minutes, and my breathing slowed. I inched my body back off the ledge and lowered it carefully into the water. The cold pushed in on my lungs. I held on to the ledge with both hands and turned my head toward the light above me. The top of the ladder was clearly visible, descending from the beautiful square of white. I knew to an absolute certainty that if I stayed there any longer, the Loch Ness monster would come for me. It was only twenty-five feet to the ladder. I could do this. I just had to stay calm.

I let go of the ledge and frantically overhand-crawled my way toward the ladder. No way in hell I was letting my face touch that black water. My lungs burned. My water-shoe-clad feet kicked to no effect. I was splashing so much I couldn't see in front of me. Where was that damn ladder? I kept thrashing forward.

Pain shot through my wrist as my hand had smashed into the ladder. I grabbed hold of salvation with all four limbs.

Thank God.

I pulled myself out of the water step by step. When I was halfway up, the creepy crawlies started. Leeches? Spiders? I slapped at my arms and legs until I realized I wasn't hitting anything but me.

I screamed up the hole. "Were you just going to leave me to die in here on my birthday, you big heartless jumbie?"

No answer.

Halfway up the ladder, I realized that I was leaving a hard hat and a shattered light in my water-storage facility. It wasn't working, though, so I wouldn't be drinking broken glass any time soon. As for the raft, so what. I was out of there.

I pulled myself through the hole and stepped off the ladder into the promised land of my dining room under the beautiful yellow beam of the drop light. My trembling legs dripped a puddle on the floor. Suddenly, my half-finished, dimly lit house looked blessedly civilized. I scrambled for the shower, dragging the drop light with me, and scrubbed liquid soap into a bubbly lather. It occurred to me that I was washing with the same water I had just fallen into, but somehow it was different in the light and after going through carbon and ultraviolet filters. I scrubbed my skin nearly raw toweling off, but with a clean, dry pair of shorts and a tank top, I was a new woman.

Who would never go into a cistern again in her long-legged life.

Chapter Seventeen

Fifteen minutes later, things took a decided turn for the better. Nelson and Graham of WAPA called to let me know they were on their way to connect Annalise's power supply. It was all I could do not to jump up and down and squeal.

I turned off the drop lamps and was enveloped by the false twilight of the storm. All I could hear was the stampede of rain on the roof as I ran through the house in the dark, flipping every light switch into its on position. I walked to the center of the great room and checked the time on my iPhone. I closed my eyes and waited.

Before long, a buzz that turned into a crackling noise filled the house. Oso whined from somewhere across the house and I felt a shock, like waking up from a bad dream. Like defibrillator paddles to the chest. I gasped. The floor beneath me trembled, and for a split second, I wondered if the current had exploded something vital, but there was no acrid scent in the air. No crackle of flames. No tumbling chunks of masonry. I remembered to take a breath, and it came out in a gasp.

Then a light like dawn filled the room and I let my head fall back. My chest heaved. There was a loud popping noise, and then came the light of one thousand suns. It was Christmas, New Year's Eve, and the Fourth of July.

"Oh, Annalise," I said. "Do you like it?"

She didn't answer.

Pouty child, I thought. I know you do.

Light filled every nook and cranny of her space, and I saw her like never before. Cobwebs in the corners. A streak of dust across a window. The deep rusty red rock of her fireplace echoed in flecks in the tile floor.

She was beautiful. I wiped the tears from my cheeks.

I still had a lot of work to do, but I set to it with a joyful heart. And now that we had electricity, I could fill the house with music. I plugged my iPhone dock into the wall and selected a playlist I had made just for this day. U2's "Beautiful Day" came on at max volume and I laughed aloud.

The occupancy inspector was still due to arrive, but it was past five o'clock. What self-respecting citizen of St. Marcos would come out after hours in weather like this? I resolved to occupy Annalise illegally for my first night. So what? Rashidi had for months. Besides, I was born to be a rule-breaking rebel.

I sashayed down the hall to the kitchen, picked up my to-do list, and read my next item, now doing step ball changes in place. "Unpack clothes." I could do that. I got busy putting hang-up clothes into closets. I pulled out a special outfit I had bought for the next time I saw Nick, a teddy made of peach-colored gauze. Not my usual sleeping look, but sleeping wasn't what I had in mind. I counted the days until he'd be back, even though I knew by heart that it was three and change. Only three.

I walked back to the kitchen to get a glass of water yelling, "Only three. Three, three, three, three, threeeee." Oso trotted over to see what the heck was going on, and soon we were barking, singing, leaping, and shaking our groove thing along with Katrina and the Waves to "Walking on Sunshine."

"Good evening," a man's voice called out. "Excuse me, miss?"

My party came to a screeching halt.

Standing in my kitchen was an overweight but not obese black man dressed in a brown uniform and looking like what I hoped Rashidi's cousin's uncle, the permitting inspector, would look like.

"I'm . . ." I fumbled for words.

He grinned. "I knock, but no answer, and I hear the barking and the singing, so I poke me head in. I hope that OK, miss. I from Permitting, and my name Charles."

His uninvited entry was considered normal on the island, even if it's rude bordering on criminal where I'm from. I'd been on St. Marcos long enough to be glad Charles wasn't put out with me for not hearing his arrival. My Southern hospitality kicked in automatically.

"Oh, good evening and welcome, Mr. Charles," I said. "I can't believe you came out in this rain, but what a wonderful sight you are."

Mr. Charles soon set about doing the things he needed to do in a most leisurely fashion and with several breaks, whether he needed them or not, for some cold ginger beer from my cooler. Good manners must have kept him from remarking on the scaffolding in the great room over the tan sofa and rattan coffee table. Hand-washed laundry hung upon the structure to dry, like flags on the tall mast of a sailing ship in a dead calm.

Mr. Charles presented me with a signed copy of the occupancy permit. It wasn't clear whether he'd actually done anything except consume my ginger beer, but I had my permit. Rashidi had come through. That piece of paper entitled me to the honor of spending my first night alone in a large house with a capricious spirit, completely isolated high atop a hill in the midst of a dark rainforest filled with unusual noises.

I showed Mr. Charles out, poured myself a bowl of dry Life cereal, and sat at a barstool to eat. Why hadn't I found a way to get the gate installed before I moved in? Regret coursed through me.

The sun had set and the rain had stopped, leaving a heavy stillness in the air. I wiped dampness from my upper lip. The urge to jump in my truck and rush back into civilization was overpowering. But if I did, there were no streetlights for the drive back up through the rainforest, and I would be returning to a gigantic and—hopefully—empty house. It was a good thing I didn't have rum to go with my fancy crystal glasses, because I couldn't have withstood the craving for a nerve tonic right about then.

I put my bowl in the sink and opened the pantry to put the cereal box away, and saw that Granddaddy Bushrat had returned to chew through a bag of Frito's. He leaped from his perch on the pullout shelf past my left ear and onto the floor.

"Yaaaaaaaaaaaaaaaaaaa," I bellowed in a voice I did not recognize as my own.

I grabbed an extra-large can of Bush's Baked Beans and hurled it at the thief, who was thankfully heading down the hall, otherwise my throw would have smashed the new cabinets. Instead, unbelievably, my wimpy girl-arm achieved a moment of athletic greatness and Señor Raton was muerto.

"Yeeeeaaaaaaaahhhhhh," I whooped.

But "eeewwwwwwwwwww" was the next thing out of my mouth when I realized that someone was going to have to clean up the mess, and I was the only someone around. Gagging, I set to the task with an old spatula, a gallon of bleach, and tattered rags. Rain splattered on my head as I dumped all of it into the outside garbage can and almost included the contents of my stomach. Getting a couple of big cats was definitely at the top of the next day's to-do list.

When I came back in, I stood beside Oso and looked around at my progress. I *was* the butt-kicking empress of the rainforest, and I had taken out a ferocious creature armed with nothing more than my wits and a can of beans. Who needs a big jumbie house, anyway? Bring it, rainforest.

And then my phone rang.

Chapter Eighteen

It was Nick.

"Hi, baby!" I said. "I survived it!"

"That's great, I'm proud of you." His voice sounded strained, even considering the cell connection in a rainstorm. "But we need to talk."

The blood drained out of my face. Oh, no. That's what my law school boyfriend had said just before he told me he'd met someone else. I started to pace around the kitchen. "What is it?"

"Derek—he found us, and he threatened to take Taylor."

"Oh my God, no!" I said, giving myself a mental slap. I was a certified freak. My only problem with Nick was his family, not other women. The poor guy didn't even know he was a victim of my issues, and I needed to keep it that way. I was a total therapy candidate.

"He's a chicken shit. He ran off when I called the police."

"Still, that's scary." My pacing had taken me to my bedroom, and I walked around the bed to the patio door then reversed course.

"Yeah, it is. Especially for Teresa, because she's leaving. I promised her I'd find us a new place."

I stopped in my tracks. "Us? But isn't Taylor moving in with your parents?"

"He was, but Teresa begged me to keep him. I couldn't say no."

Really, how could he say no? He couldn't. I knew that. Somewhere deep inside me I even knew I would have thought less of him if he had. But the ramifications of his yes jumped across the phone line and sucked all the oomph out of me.

"Of course," I said. I lay down on my bed and stared up at the leaky ceiling.

"Let me buy a ticket for you to come here. I miss you," Nick said.

"Oh, Nick." My voice caught on his name. "I miss you, too."

"Then come."

If only it were that easy. I closed my eyes to keep the tears in. We hung up a few minutes later, both of us sad, with nothing resolved. For the next two days, Nick re-asked me to come to Dallas approximately once per hour, and I kept re-explaining why I couldn't go. He didn't understand the gravity of my situation at Annalise.

Early in the evening two days later, Rashidi knocked on my front door.

"Hey, this is a surprise," I said. Normally, the twinkly-eyed, blue-jean- and t-shirt-clad sight of him was cheerful, but now, not so much. I was feeling down-in-the-dumpsy, alone down-in-the-dumpsy.

He raised his eyebrows. "I expect so. I come by to check on you, since you not returning my calls."

I mentally crossed my fingers. "I'm sorry. Cell reception is bad up here today."

"What's this I hear from Ava that Not-Bart can't come and you moping around?"

Ava really did have such a big mouth. I tried to hold back my tears and felt my face turn in on itself. "Oh, Rashidi," I sighed.

He beckoned me outside with one finger and we went down the front steps to the spare carpet of new grass that sprang up after the storm. He patted the ground beside him. It was a lovely evening, if a little warm. In June temperatures over eighty-five are not unusual, although it rarely rose above ninety or dipped below seventy-five. I stripped some leaves from a dangling branch of the flamboyant tree as I passed it, then collapsed beside Rashidi cross-legged, my full pink knit sundress pooling over my legs.

"So why you upset?" he asked.

I tossed my handful of leaves into the air. The ever-present wind caught them and carried them across the yard and down the hill, where I imagined them disappearing in the nearly impenetrable tan-tan bushes interwoven with yellow blossoms of Ginger Thomas. The seedpods on the tan-tan rattled and I pictured the tiny leaves gently bumping the pods and releasing their music. Wind chimes. A melancholy sound.

"Because Nick's not coming. He's going to have Taylor for another six months. At least. And I can't leave Annalise."

Rashidi looked at me through narrowed eyes for a moment. "You love Not-Bart and you tryin' to convince me you can't go because of a house? That crazy. You not worried because you hear the old owner out of prison, are you?"

"What? No, I hadn't even heard that. He's out?"

"Well, he out of jail, but he under the ground, six feet under, so it not a problem." Rashidi grinned. "Ain't no problems up here bad enough to hold you, the way I see it. I stay up here and keep an eye on things." He waved his hand over his head. "What the worst can happen? Someone don't do he job? Pumpy come steal more tile? I bring women in the house and romance them up? None of that gonna kill you."

Jeez, I hate it when logic gets in the way of a good snit. "Even if I do go, the baby will be there." I knew I sounded peevish, and I looked up into the sky dotted with fast-moving white clouds, wishing they'd disappear into the wild blue. Was I this person? Was I?

Rashidi laughed. "Wah, that child got some dread disease, something contagious what gonna kill you?" He slapped his knee and laughed at himself. My palm itched. He needed a smack. Or maybe I did.

"I don't know the first thing about toddlers," I confessed. "They terrify me." I wondered how my mother had done it and why I wasn't more like her.

"Ain't nothing to know. Most everybody figure it out when the time comes they have to. I expect you be the same." He laced his hands behind his head and leaned back on the thin grass with his eyes closed.

I bit my pinky nail to the quick, then attacked another finger. After mauling that fingernail and three others, the logjam inside me broke.

"Well, crap. What are we doing talking? I've gotta go pack."

Rashidi met my eyes. A ghost of a smile swept across his face, then disappeared. I raised one eyebrow, and he nodded, three times, slowly. "And I got to find a woman."

It seemed someone had accepted the inevitability of Ava being Ava.

I ran to get my suitcase.

I stood in line at the ticket counter the next day waiting for my turn. When I reached the counter, the former Mrs. St. Marcos glared down at me, tall and scary in her tight navy-blue uniform. By night, pageant diva. By day, fearsome guardian of American Airlines' gates.

"So, Katie Connell," which she pronounced Con-NELL, "it hot and the line long. State your business."

"Good afternoon, Jackie," I said, and bowed my head forward with a brown nose. "I want to purchase a ticket to Dallas."

"You know you can do that on the computer. Or even the phone if you old school."

"Yes, but I want to go right now. Today. This saves a step."

Her eyes rolled.

Here it comes, I thought.

Jackie let out a loud, five-second-long chuptz. I couldn't generate half the spit on a day's notice that Jackie just had instantaneously. Impressive.

She held out her hand. I stared at it.

"Passport, credit card."

"Right." I dug, found them, and slapped them into her hand.

My phone rang and Jackie withered me with a glare. I admired how seriously she took her job. Really, she wasn't better suited to any role I could think of, except maybe warden of a women's prison. I looked at my phone.

It was Nick. I picked it up.

"Hi, beautiful," he said. "What are you up to?"

"Hi, baby." Had he guessed I was coming? I hadn't told him. "Nothing much. You?"

"I need a ride."

Prickles raced up the back of my neck. Nick could be anywhere in the world, but all of a sudden, I didn't think so.

"Hold on." I put my hand over the mouthpiece. "I changed my mind," I said to Jackie.

I'd just *thought* her earlier chuptz was impressive.

"You for real?" she asked.

"Sorry. Plans changed." I held out my hand for my documents.

"Like I got nothing better to do. Get on with you, then. Tell people dem you sorry and move on out the way."

"Thank you." I turned obediently, gave a little wave, and mouthed the word "Sorry" at the line of people. To a man, woman, and child, they ignored me.

I took my hand off the mouthpiece. "Where are you?" I asked.

I pushed my way through the crowd. A phalanx of big, meaty men was blocking the way between me and the entry gate. Every eye in the ticket area joined mine as we swiveled our heads to catch a glimpse of whoever it was that merited this much muscle.

"Three guesses," Nick said.

I was scared to jinx it. "The grocery store?"

A hollow-cheeked man was strutting behind the behemoths. Aviator shades covered his eyes and his expensively layered black hair hung in strings past his shoulders. Somehow he looked handsome, even as malnourished as he was. His clothes suggested that he'd come straight to the plane from whatever club he had graced with his presence the night before: self-consciously frayed jeans and an untucked shiny gray long-sleeved shirt rolled up at the cuffs and unbuttoned halfway up and halfway down.

"Slither," a teenage girl behind me breathed.

I looked closer. She was right. The singer made it to the curb, where an Escalade with tinted windows was waiting. The passenger's side front door opened and a tall blonde got out, her bones straining against the confines of her spandex dress. She opened the back door and got back in. A face I knew leaned toward the open front door from the driver's side.

Trevor. Of course. Ava had said Trevor produced for Slither. The musician slunk into the passenger seat and closed the door.

Nick said, "Wrong. Next guess."

"Your office."

Excitement over, the walkway cleared. If Nick was here, he was sure to be through the gate already. I trotted toward baggage claim with my rolling suitcase trailing behind me and my carry-on bouncing back and forth against my hip. My back was sweating under my laptop backpack. I tucked my pocketbook under my arm and clutched my iPhone in one hand. I weaved through the surprisingly large throng, wondering who they were and whether they were aware it was hurricane season. I looked around for Nick and couldn't find him. My skin was tingling. My body knew he was there.

"Wrong again," Nick said, but his voice was in stereo. His warm hand touched my shoulder and I smiled. When I turned around, I nearly combusted at the sight of him.

I tried to rein it in. I was no Meg Ryan, and this wasn't Katz's Deli. I threw my arms around his neck and leaned my head back. My eyes loved this face, the sharp cheekbones, the sparkling brown eyes, the crooked nose. I pushed my nose into his chest just to get closer to his smell, a musky-woodsy scent uniquely his.

"You're here," I said. "You're really here."

"I really am."

We beamed, unable to tear our eyes off each other. Until a certain small person interrupted us.

Chapter Nineteen

Strapped into a complicated-looking car-seat/stroller thingy, and yelling that he wanted "down, down, down" (at least that's what I think he was saying) was a large baby. Or a small toddler. I didn't know which. A young boy of some sort, anyway, presumably named Taylor.

I don't know why it surprised me. Nick had told me he had to keep Taylor, but, still, I gaped. Here I was, and here he was. I waited for my maternal instinct to kick in and tell me what to do. Nothing happened.

Taylor flailed his legs and tore at his shirt. The Velcro straps on his sneakers had come undone somehow. He blinked big brown eyes under a tousled mop of hair. There were still crease marks on his cheek, probably from sleeping on the plane.

Nick said, "Taylor, this is Ms. Katie. Can you say hi and blow Ms. Katie a kiss?"

Taylor whipped his face away. This shifted the burden of communication to me. Was it normal to feel nervous about talking to a toddler?

"Hi, Taylor. Welcome to St. Marcos! I'm so glad to meet you."

"DOWN!" he yelled at me.

Nick laughed. "In a minute, buddy." To me, Nick said, "We've got a lot of bags. If I set him free, we're going to have a hard time handling everything."

"How old is he?" I asked.

"Sixteen months. Why?"

I guessed that meant he could walk. "Because I think I can watch him while you get the bags."

I immediately regretted it. Who was I kidding? But I put my game face on.

"If you're sure, that would be great," Nick said. "He's been cooped up all day." He unharnessed Taylor and set him in front of me. Before I could reach down to grab hold of him, Taylor was wobbling full tilt through the crowded baggage claim area. It was shocking how fast he could motor.

"Slow down, Taylor," I called as I chased after him in my stylish yet suddenly impractical strappy sandals.

Taylor toddled on, giggling.

I ran, apologizing. "Excuse me, pardon me." I pushed my untethered waves of hair back and wished for a ponytail holder. "Sorry, oops." Tourists surged back from us like a school of parrotfish. I caught Taylor by one plump arm just as he was about to climb onto the baggage carousel. I scooped him up and he turned his laughing eyes onto me. He smiled beatifically with red bow lips that would have cost a fortune in Hollywood. I wouldn't say my heart melted, but it softened a lot.

"Hey there, speedy. Want to come to my house and meet my doggies?"

His eyes lit up at the word "doggies." "Ruff ruff."

"That's right. Doggies. Ruff ruff. But we have to get your bags and go ride in my truck to get there."

"Vroom, vroom."

"You are such a smart boy. Yes, let's go to the truck with the bags and go see doggies."

I put his feet on the ground, but this time held tightly onto his hand as he continued to chant "ruff ruff" and "vroom vroom." We made our way slowly back to Nick, whose shoulder muscles rippled under his shirt as he hefted a bag from the carousel. My stomach fluttered in response.

Down, girl.

I buckled Taylor back into the stroller with a promise of vroom vrooms and ruff ruffs.

"Cute kid," a deep voice said behind me.

I whipped around and saw a dark blue uniform. I looked above it into a broad and familiar face. Jacoby. Being friendly. I was too startled to reply.

Nick walked up, pulling two rolling suitcases with soft-sided bags perched on top of them.

Jacoby said, "Who your friends?"

"Oh! I'm sorry. Jacoby, this is Nick, and Nick's nephew, Taylor. Nick, this is Jacoby, Officer Darren Jacoby."

"Nice to meet you, Officer Jacoby," Nick said, extending his hand. Jacoby swallowed it whole with his. They shook.

"Nice to meet you. You know, she not half bad," Jacoby said, gesturing at me with his chin. "A good afternoon to you all," he added, then headed toward the ticketing area.

I gaped after him. Jacoby had complimented me. I felt a warmth in the center of my chest.

We started walking to the truck and Nick asked, "So why are you carrying bags? And how did you get here to pick us up so quickly?"

"I was bringing Mohammed to the mountains," I said. "I didn't know the big mountain and the little mountain were en route."

"But what about Annalise?"

"Just a house," I said, and we locked eyes and smiled, until I stumbled over a curb and nearly went down.

"Nice, Lucille Ball."

I curtsied.

Between mine and theirs, there were a lot of bags to load into the back of my truck, but Nick wedged them all in, then put the car seat in the center of the bench seat. "Up you go," he said, lifting Taylor in. Nick and I settled on either side of him.

And baby makes three, I thought. I sucked in a deep breath.

Nick reached over the car seat and took my hand. "Hey, beautiful, how are you over there?"

A lump formed in my throat. "Happy," I said. "Very, very happy." It was not a word people had used to describe me for most of my life, but I realized it was true. I was happy.

"Happy is good. I'm happy, too."

I turned the truck's big red nose up the bumpy road to Annalise. "How long can you stay?"

"Same as we'd planned."

"Are you serious?"

We had planned for Nick to commute virtually and leave his return as open-ended pending never. I felt like bouncing up and down in my seat.

"If you're OK with having us both here."

I tore my eyes off the road for a moment to look at him. "Anything to have you here. Anything." He squeezed my hand. "What does Teresa think about it?"

"Whoa, there," Nick said as I veered toward the center of the road.

Woopsie. I steered us back to the left.

Nick continued. "She thinks it's great I have Taylor out of the reach of his sperm donor."

"Will Derek try to make you bring him back?"

Nick shook his head. "He won't even realize he's gone. He just wanted to control her."

We neared the final turn into the gate, which I'd had installed on a rush job the day after my first night alone at Annalise. "Here we are."

"I can't wait to see your progress," Nick said as I sped up the lane.

I didn't answer. We both saw Bart's car at the same time.

Nick's face darkened. "What the hell is Bart doing here?"

"I have no idea." I parked in the driveway. "I'm sorry, Nick. Give me a second and let me get rid of him."

I walked over to Bart's Pathfinder, but he wasn't in it. I turned back toward Nick, shook my head and raised my hands outward, shrugging. I pointed at myself and then the house, then went to the side door. It was unlocked, but I'd double-checked the locks before I left. I opened the door.

"Hello?" I called into the kitchen. "Is someone here?"

No answer.

My stomach churned. "Bart, I know you're in here. Please answer me."

Silence. I walked through the kitchen. I could feel static emanating from the floors and walls around me. So my moody jumbie had returned, and she didn't like whatever was up. I went into the great room and threw the balcony doors open.

"Bart?" I leaned over the rail and saw Bart below on the backyard patio. He had his feet up on the table next to red roses tied with white ribbon. His profile was to me and he didn't turn my way at first, just sucked hard on a hand-rolled joint. Even from twenty feet above him, I could see that his eyes were blood red and his hair was, frankly, disgusting. Greasy. Dull. Kurt Cobain in his heyday, and I'm not a Nirvana fan.

"Hey," he said, and turned toward me.

I heard the side door open behind me, then Nick's voice, Taylor's happy squeals, and the panting of Oso. Half of me wanted to shout for them to wait outside. The other half wanted to yell for Nick to hurry up. I did neither.

The static from the house intensified. Footfalls sounded behind me.

"You need to leave, right now," I said to Bart.

Nick stopped beside me. He called down to Bart in frighteningly calm voice. "Hey, buddy, why don't you get the hell out of here and never come back."

I felt a tiny thrill. Something about the bad-boy protector in Nick turned on the bad girl in me. Or at least the girl who wanted to help him find the fastest way out of his clothes.

"Who the hell are you?" Bart asked.

"I think you can figure that out."

Bart's face registered the dawning of realization, which only made him look more stoned. "Hey, I thought you weren't coming."

Nick shot me a look.

"I haven't talked to him in weeks," I said. "But it's a small island. Word gets around."

Bart sneered. "Tell him any lie you want, Katie."

He stood up, threw the roses into the pool, and strode toward the driveway. A few moments later I heard his engine start, then tires spinning against the rocks as he drove away.

Chapter Twenty

I turned to Nick, ready to apologize again, but he didn't look upset.

"You forgot to tell me your crazy ex-boyfriend is a stoner," he said, and swiped my nose with his thumb.

I shook my head and sighed. "It's a new development."

"Two words: restraining order."

"You may be right."

And that was the end of it, which totally caught me by surprise. My previous really serious relationship before Nick had been the year after I'd made partner at Hailey & Hart. My boyfriend's ex couldn't get over him, and I couldn't get over her. Eventually, I drove him away, not back to her but on to someone new. Was Nick really that much more centered and rational than me?

I shuddered. The last time I'd gotten all wonky, he'd stayed away for nearly a year. Maybe wonky was bad and unwonky good.

Restraint. I could learn to exercise a little restraint.

We turned around and went back into the great room, where Taylor was running around the legs of the scaffolding.

"This house is named Annalise," I told him.

"Reese," he said, and tumbled to the floor. His head hit the tile with a loud thwack, followed by two beats of silence, then an ear-shattering wail. I felt a keening rise up around me.

"Do you hear that?" I asked Nick.

"Hard to miss," Nick replied. "The boy has some lungs."

"Not Taylor. The other sound."

"Nope. What is it?"

I smiled at him. "Annalise," I said. "She's wailing along with Taylor."

Nick picked up Taylor and was rocking him back and forth as the boy screamed. "Maybe I just can't hear her over this."

Maybe. But I didn't think so. Most people couldn't. Did I care that he couldn't? I let the thought brew for a moment. My own answer surprised me. No, I didn't mind. I kind of liked having Annalise to myself.

When Taylor's cries subsided, Nick said, "I need to feed him some dinner."

"I'm not sure what I have for a little boy."

"No problem. I packed enough for tonight. We'll have to shop tomorrow."

Nick brought the car seat stroller thingy into the kitchen and buckled Taylor in. He pulled out a tray attachment.

"My God, does it play 'Twinkle, Twinkle, Little Star,' too?" I asked.

Nick laughed and spread an assortment of Cheerios, green beans, and bits of string cheese in front of Taylor. I thought the cheese might be a little stale from the trip, but I exercised my newfound restraint and didn't say so. Taylor gobbled it down with Oso stationed close by. Taylor threw a Cheerio on the floor. Oso snapped it up. Taylor laughed and kicked. Another Cheerio hit the floor. Oso wagged his tail and ate it, too. Taylor squealed. A game.

"Uh oh," Nick said. He put his hand over the pile of food. "No, Taylor. This is your food. Oso has his own food."

Taylor stuck out a fat lower lip. Nick held out a Cheerio, but Taylor jerked his head away.

"This will go bad in a hurry," Nick said to me. "Oh well, he's not going to starve to death." He unstrapped the boy and set him down again.

Oso walked up and licked Taylor across the whole face. Taylor lost his frown and lunged for the dog, and I panicked and raced toward them, not sure how Oso would react. But Oso didn't flinch. He wagged his tail as Taylor cruised along his body, using fists full of fur for balance. He'd secured a best friend with two bites of Cheerios and a yummy face. I backed away.

"Can we let him play outside for a little while?" Nick asked. "He'll wind down in an hour or so. Fresh air and exercise will help speed the process." He winked at me and held out his hand.

I crazy love it when he winks. He could ask me to stand on my head and count to ten thousand and the answer will always be the same if he winks.

"Yes. Sounds like a great plan."

We followed Taylor outside to meet the rest of the dogs. After a few sniffs, all of them but Oso wandered off. Nick and I sat side by side on the front steps and watched Taylor lead Oso on a chaotic exploration of the yard. Kitty, the big gray outdoor cat I'd acquired from the animal shelter that week, lifted her tail and ran for the bush.

"Is he always this busy?" I asked as I nestled my head into Nick's shoulder.

He slipped his arm around me. "This is nothing."

Oh, my.

The sun was setting, and a breeze picked up from the east. Nick raised his arm and ran his fingers through my hair. He lifted it up and slipped his face under it, then softly kissed his way up the back of my neck. He hit my just-the-right-spot spot, and my body's constant thrum since his arrival ratcheted up even further.

"Is Taylor looking sleepy to you yet?" I asked.

He chuckled. "Wishful thinking. We can probably give him a bath in about half an hour. After that, I read him a book and sing him to sleep. Estimated crib touchdown in one hour."

He kissed my neck again.

"Wow, that's an awfully long time." I'd always heard that couples had a hard time fitting in sex once they had kids, but I'd thought they just needed to try harder. Taylor was showing me the error of my ways in a hurry.

Nick's phone rang. He looked at the number. "My parents," he said. "Do you mind?"

"Of course not. Go ahead."

He answered the phone and walked out to where Taylor was rolling in the grass, which, unbeknownst to him, was the premier spot for cell reception. I followed and sat down beside Taylor. He rolled into me with a giggle, then rolled away again.

"Slow down, Mom," Nick said. "I can barely hear you. Can you repeat that?" His jaw clenched. "You and Dad need to file a police report. Don't wait. I'm serious."

"I love you guys, too." He hung up and stared out over the tops of the mango trees in the valley before us.

"Nick? What's up?"

He sat down in the grass beside me and his words came out low and fast through chalky lips. "Derek showed up looking for Teresa and Taylor at my parents' place. They told him they didn't know where they were. He said he hoped they were smarter when he came back the next time."

I matched his half-whisper. "Your poor parents."

Nick cupped his hand around the back of my neck. "I'm so glad Taylor is here."

"I'm glad you guys are here, too." And I was. Even if Taylor had taken me by surprise. "Are you OK?"

"I'm great. I'm with you, Taylor is safe, and my parents are OK. Derek won't hurt them. It will all be fine."

I nodded. I hoped so.

Nick stood up. "Taylor, let's go find your bedroom."

I hadn't even thought about a bedroom. We headed through the front door and I led them to the office. "How about here? It's only two doors down from us."

"Looks good."

We moved Taylor's things in. "Watch this, Taylor," Nick said, and he quickly assembled a portable playpen in the center of the floor, then clapped his hands and said, "Yay, Uncle Nick!" Taylor joined in.

I did, too, but it was an uncertain clapping on my part. The pen was pink. I leaned into Nick and whispered, "Isn't Little Mermaid a girl thing?"

He put a finger over his lips, then moved close to my ear. "I left in a hurry. We stopped at Walmart to pick one up. They were out of Buzz Lightyear, and Taylor went nuts for Ariel. I didn't have time to talk him out of it."

I clapped my hand over my mouth to hold in the laugh.

Nick mock-glared at me and said, "Katie, where can we have our B-A-T-H?"

My cheeks filled with heat instantaneously.

Before I could think of an answer, he laughed. "Let me restate that. His, not ours."

"Oh!" I put the backs of my hands on my cheeks. "The only one I trust to be clean is mine. Follow me, boys."

So Nick gave Taylor a bubble bath in my claw-foot tub. He had to stand up and lean in over its tall sides, and it looked painful to me. I'd clean one of the smaller bathtubs between the Jack and Jill bedrooms upstairs in the morning, but Taylor seemed to love my tub. He kept up a constant stream of chatter as he played with his toys, although I couldn't understand a word of it.

Nick looked over his shoulder at me and spoke over Taylor's voice. "My life sure has changed since Taylor moved in. It's nonstop with this little munchkin." He lifted the boy out of the water and wrapped him in a rainbow-striped beach towel, then carried him in to my bed and started dressing him, stopping to blow loud raspberry kisses on his belly. More squealing.

When he was done, he picked up Taylor and a picture book, *Go, Dog. Go,* and asked, "Do you have a chair that rocks?"

I didn't have a true rocking chair, but I did have some outdoor chairs that rocked a little. "Follow me," I said, and led him out to the great room's balcony.

Nick and Taylor took a seat and Taylor squirmed until he found just the right spot in Nick's lap. I sat beside them and Nick gave his chair a little test rock.

"Perfect," he said. "And the view is great, too."

"I love it here, especially at sunset," I said.

"I was talking about you," he said, and smiled at me.

My stomach did a flip-flop, and I smiled back.

I watched the fruit bats, known locally as island sparrows, come out of the eaves and sip from the pool while Nick read to Taylor. When he closed the book, Taylor turned around and put his head on Nick's shoulder. Nick started rocking. I matched their rhythm.

"Oh, say can you see, by the dawn's early light, what so proudly we hailed . . ." Nick sang, off-key.

I covered a smile with the back of my hand. Taylor fell asleep before the rockets' red glare. I followed them in to the makeshift nursery and watched as Nick skillfully transferred Taylor to the playpen and covered him with a crocheted blanket. I held my breath, but Taylor only snuffled as his body settled on the mattress. Nick closed the door with barely a click.

"He goes to sleep really easily," he said.

"You're very good with him."

"Thanks."

We stared at each other. It was our first moment alone since he'd gotten there, and the quiet was abrupt.

I put a hand on a hip and tried for a Mae West voice. "Would you like to see the room where you'll be staying, big boy?"

"Lead the way, beautiful."

As I walked into the bedroom, Nick scooted in close and put his arms around me from behind. I leaned into him and we swayed. "I love you," he whispered in my ear. "I couldn't stay away from you any longer."

My heart swelled. I turned into him and said, "I feel exactly the same way." His lips closed over mine, warm and soft.

"Wait," I said. I switched off the bedroom light.

"Better?" he asked, laughing.

"Much."

"I can still see you, you know."

"I'm going to pretend you didn't say that."

And then his lips found mine again, and I forgot about the light and the little boy down the hall, and was conscious only of Nick, of me, of us, of this.

Afterwards, we lay together in the dark. I held his arm in front of me and kissed all the parts I could reach.

Nick spoke, his voice low. "Are you sure this isn't too much for you, me moving in with my nephew?"

I stopped kissing him and turned so I could see his face. He looked serious, worried.

I reached one hand into his hair. "It will be fine." I ran the hand down his neck and over his shoulders.

Nick put his hand around my wrist. "You cannot imagine how much I've missed you." His voice was suddenly rough. "I don't want to be apart from you, ever."

"Show me," I said.

And he did.

Chapter Twenty-one

My slow-moving island life sped up with Nick and Taylor around. Nick set up the USVI branch of Stingray Investigations next to the headquarters of Connell Construction in a bedroom on the third floor. Our new office had tongue-in-groove ceilings, a wall of windows, and a balcony that looked over the sugar mill ruins and mango forest. The builder had probably designed it to be an alternate master or guest suite, but now that we had commandeered it, I wondered why I hadn't done so in the first place. It was the perfect place to work—Excel, QuickBooks, and TurboTax were a lot less painful with a view like that.

On a typically perfect late June morning, Nick was in the office tracking down a runaway polygamist wife who had left her fourth husband with a mountain of credit card debt and I was downstairs rehearsing with Ava for our upcoming re-gig for Trevor. Taylor was playing in his new high chair in the music room with us.

"So, how it going with your sexy man?" Ava asked. She was almost demure in a strapless black knit romper.

"It's going great," I said, then couldn't help adding, "Although not like I'd envisioned."

"What, he not perfect like you?"

I ignored her. "There's just one more person living here than I'd planned for. It's much harder to be spontaneous, if you know what I mean."

"HUN-GEE," announced Taylor.

"Just a minute, sweetie, and I'll get you some fish sticks," I said.

"You mean harder to go for six orgasms in a day with him around," Ava said.

"HUN-GEE," he insisted.

"Yes, that's exactly what I mean," I said, then turned to Taylor and gave him a crisp salute. "Yes, sir, right away, sir."

"I go make a phone call, then," Ava said. She walked out to the front porch and I went to the kitchen to broil some frozen fish sticks. When I took them to the music room ten minutes later, the high chair was empty. Taylor was gone. In a split second, everything changed.

I called out for him, but there was no answer, and I screamed for Ava and Nick.

"Help! I can't find Taylor! Help!"

Nick's feet hit the floor and I heard him running. My stomach lurched. I ran for the stairs to the ground floor that led out to the pool, and by the time I was halfway down, Nick had caught up with me. I heard Ava's heavy footsteps above us.

Nick and I burst through the open sliding glass door onto the back patio and my heart choked off my breath. I saw the top of Taylor's head in the deep end, a few feet from the ledge.

"No!" I screamed. "No!"

Nick jumped in feet first, but what I saw when I got to the edge of the pool didn't make sense. Taylor's head was out of the water and he was holding onto a ladder that was perched across the corner of the pool.

Ava came running out the back door onto the patio, yelling, "What going on?"

Nick crossed the pool in seconds and gathered Taylor in his arms. The boy didn't make a sound, just looked up into Nick's face as Nick swam the few yards to the shallow end on his back and climbed out. I wiped tears from my cheeks and held out my arms.

"There you are! I was so worried about you," I said.

Nick handed him to me and I squeezed him so hard he kicked, but I didn't let go. All I could think of was Rashidi telling me I'd figure out the kid thing when I needed to, like everybody else. But he was wrong. I hadn't.

I started to cry again, and I handed Taylor back to Nick.

"I'm a failure at this, Nick, I'm so sorry."

"Hush," he said. "It's OK. You're not a failure. You're great."

But I knew I was. How could I have let this happen? What was wrong with me? If Taylor had died, it would have been my fault.

"How that ladder get there?" Ava asked.

Nick said, "I have absolutely no idea. It wasn't there an hour ago when we were swimming."

Ava cocked one hip and folded her arms across her chest. "There nobody even here working today. We the only ones."

I tried to pull myself together. "The dogs knocked it over, maybe?"

Nick shook his head. "Couldn't be. It was leaning up against the back of the house yesterday, over by where the workers were fixing the cistern catchment. Even if the dogs were out here, they couldn't have moved it across the patio and put it over the edge of the pool."

And that's when I heard Annalise. She was singing, "You are my sunshine, my only sunshine," deep inside my head.

It felt like the patio was spinning around me, and I was the only thing anchored. I grabbed a chair to keep myself from falling. And then I felt her. A hand on my shoulder. I jumped and turned. The hand lifted and I saw nothing, but the singing didn't stop.

Nick and Ava were staring at me. Ava's eyebrows had stretched into high peaks. Yeah, it probably did look like I was having a psychotic break.

"She loves him," I said, swallowing hard. "She's singing to him."

Nick nodded. His eyes never left mine.

It's one thing to raise a dust cloud or make a booming noise. It's another thing altogether to save the life of a child. And that's what she had done, I was sure of it.

"Annalise saved him," I said. I was as sure of that as I was that she'd saved me.

That night, Nick and I sat up in bed discussing our domestic arrangements while Taylor ran his favorite plastic dump truck all over our legs.

"Taylor went to day care while I worked back in Dallas," Nick said. "We need help. We're understaffed."

"I agree. And one of us is underskilled."

Nick turned to me and shook his head. "No, one of us isn't. It could have happened to anyone, Katie, and he is my responsibility."

But I knew the truth. I would never, ever let anything happen to Taylor on my watch again, but I also recognized my limitations. "Well, at least we're in agreement on the needing help part." I kissed Nick. "I'm going to wash my face."

Nick snatched up *Go, Dog. Go.* "We're going to read our bedtime story."

Ten minutes, one mud mask, and a Nair job to my legs later, I returned to the bedroom. Nick and Taylor were snuggled up, eyes closed.

I leaned in and whispered, "Are you taking him to his room?"

I got a snore in reply. Taylor's soft snuffles echoed Nick's snores in a way that did something funny to my heart. I lay down beside Nick and snuggled in close.

Chapter Twenty-two

I knew just the person to ask for help, so the next day, Nick and I took Taylor to meet Crazy Grove. The old man sat wrapped in a white crocheted blanket in a threadbare recliner that had probably been red once upon a time. He pointed at Taylor and then at his knee, so I helped the little boy onto Crazy's lap. The rambunctious toddler sat still, gazing into Crazy's wise eyes like a charmed python. I was mesmerized. Why couldn't I do that?

"We need help with Taylor," I said. I explained what had happened the day before.

Crazy shook his head. "Lotta!" he called.

Lotta stuck her head around the kitchen door and I heard loud crackling noises. It smelled like the Wingroves would be eating "fry" chicken, as the Locals called it.

"Yes, Mr. Wingrove?" She wore a bright yellow apron that made her round middle look like a rising sun.

His words were slow and still slurred, but I could understand him. "Your sister need to help them with the boy." He waved his left hand in a "make it so" gesture, then he fell back in his chair, spent.

Lotta nodded. "I send Ruth round tomorrow morning."

Nick and I looked at each other. He grinned and shrugged. "Well, all right, then!" I said. "Thanks!"

A week later, I pulled the sheet over my head and tried to go back to sleep, but the echoes of little boy yells and the barking of my German shepherd begging for Cheerios kept me awake. Theoretically, Nick was letting me sleep in until Ms. Ruth arrived. How did real parents do it? Between the things Nick and I did that robbed us of sleep and the ungodly hour at which Taylor woke up, I'd started to look like a raccoon.

"Katie, quick, in the kitchen," Nick yelled.

"Coming," I mumbled. I dragged myself to a seated position and scrubbed my eyes against the bright sun streaming in through the windows. I searched for clothes. None on me, and none on the floor. They were probably buried under the covers at the foot of the bed. I stumbled to my chest of drawers and pulled a black-and-white striped sundress over my head, then used the potty, freshened up, and hauled my matted red mop into a high ponytail before I shuffled into the kitchen.

"That was quick?" Nick teased. "Happy July Fourth. There's coffee."

I nodded. I rubbed my eyes.

He poured me a cup of black coffee and placed it in my hands, wrapping my hand around it with his. Our overlapped fingers alternated stripes of white and golden tan.

"Ugh," I said.

"You're welcome." He grinned. "I thought we could have breakfast before Ms. Ruth gets here."

I smiled. "Or we could sleep."

"Kay Kay," Taylor yelled from his high chair. Nick had set him up at the breakfast bar.

I walked over and kissed the top of his head. "Good morning, Taylor."

Oso sidled up to me and I scrunched his ears. I took a seat next to Taylor, who held a fistful of Cheerios out to me, the same ones he'd just been rubbing against his drool-covered mouth.

"Yum, yum." I pretended to eat them and tried to prevent contact with the spit. Taylor kicked and squealed. Oso scooched closer to him, looking hopeful.

Nick clanked a plate down in front of me. When had his arm gotten so brown? "Homemade cinnamon rolls."

I looked up and saw the Pillsbury can on the counter.

He saw my gaze. "Home made," he insisted. "Try one."

"Too tired to eat."

Nick shook his head. He handed me a fork. "Eat."

Oso gobbled Cheerios from Taylor's hand. I pretended not to see it and started to cut into my roll with a fork.

"Stop!" Nick yelled.

I froze and glared at him, fork hovering. "Make up your mind, mister."

"Do you notice anything special about it?" he pointed at the cinnamon roll.

I peered at it. It was iced. And not very well iced, at that. I squinted. The icing was squiggly and sparse. "They're really well-done?"

"Read it," Nick said, his tone wry, but also something else. Excited.

"I can make out an M. M, something something something, something something. I can't read the next word at all. Then there's a short word, kind of melted. Starts with an N."

"No, it starts with an M."

I contemplated my breakfast again. I bit my lip.

Nick came over to my side of the breakfast bar, saying, "Taylor, she's making this awfully hard." He rubbed the boy's head, then took my hand in one of his.

"Katie, you complicated, difficult creature, I want to spend the rest of my life with you, and we've wasted too much of it apart already. I'm trying to ask you to marry me."

I studied the cinnamon roll again, looking for it, dazed, stunned. "But what does it say?" I asked.

"Oh, Jesus, Joseph, and the sainted Virgin. It says 'Marry Me.'"

Marry him. Marry him. Marry him. So fast. Yet so not fast. We'd known each other for nearly two years. I'd loved him from the moment I met him. I'd given up on him to protect myself. I had quit hoping. And now . . .

I'd given up on him.

Oh, shit.

I jumped up, knocking the barstool over behind me. "Oh no, Nick, oh no, what have I done?" I wailed.

"I don't know what you're talking about," he said, looking stunned. Stricken, even. A frisson of guilt ripped through me as I realized I'd made a terrible mistake. So I ran.

I flew down the stairs and out the back patio door. I stopped and grabbed a piece of broken tile as Nick ran out the door with Taylor on one hip and Oso on his heels, calling, "What's the matter?"

I didn't answer. Down the sloping side yard I ran, slipping barefoot on the baby grass. When I was about a hundred yards from the house, I stopped and twirled in a slow circle, scanning the ground below me for a flat gray rock.

Nick stood back about ten yards, watching me. Taylor was holding a hand down for Oso's tongue. I saw the rock to Nick's right and fell to my knees beside it. I pushed it aside and dug the edge of the tile into the soil, but it didn't do much of a job, so I dropped it and started digging with my hands. When I'd uncovered two inches of dirt, I shoved my fingers in, probing. Nothing. I dug another inch of dirt out, then probed again. My fingers hit something solid.

I looked up at Nick, who was watching me, bemused.

"I had given up on you," I said.

He came and stood beside me. "Honey, is there some kind of medication you take at a moment like this?"

"I'm serious, Nick. I had given up. And I needed something to make myself let go."

He lowered himself and Taylor to the ground and sat cross-legged, setting Taylor free to play with Oso. "OK, I'm listening."

I took a deep breath. I plunged my hands back into the dirt and walked them along the surface until I found a small square of plastic and smiled. It had only been eight months since I'd buried it, so it was still in pretty good shape. Or maybe old SIM cards never die. I pulled it out and handed it to him.

"What's this?"

"A SIM card."

He pursed his lips. "I give up. Why a SIM card?"

"So I wouldn't wait around for you to call me anymore."

His mouth opened. "Ah. You changed your phone number. Yes. That's why I had to get your number from Emily." He reached out and touched my cheek.

I nodded and started digging again, carefully uncovering the plastic Cruzan Rum bottle on which the SIM card had rested. I pulled it out and held it by its neck.

Nick nodded in appreciation. "A rum bottle." Barks and squeals and dog fur and little boy face flashed by in the background.

"Yes."

I closed my eyes and put my hands back in the hole. Carefully I lifted out handfuls of dirt and sifted them onto the grass between Nick and me. Handful by handful, I excavated the hole as Nick sat like a stone.

And then I found what I was looking for, and tears welled up in my eyes. I grabbed Nick's right hand with my left and pulled a handful of dirt out. I sifted again, and I dropped a ring into his hand. He worked it between his thumb and forefinger until he could see it was a dirty gold band.

"It was my mother's. And her mom gave it to her when she married my dad. She'd always told me that she would give it to me when my time came." A sob welled up in my throat, but I swallowed it. "It never did. And then she was gone. And you were never going to happen. So," I gestured over the hole, "I buried my past so I could move forward."

Nick pulled me to him, into his lap, dirt, wild hair, and all. He hugged me and rocked me. He kissed my forehead. Then he slipped me back to the ground and got down on one knee with my mother's ring clasped between his thumb and forefinger. "Katie Connell, will you please marry me?"

Now it was right. "Yes, of course," I said. "Yes, yes, yes."

Nick put my mother's ring on the third finger of my left hand and leaned his forehead against mine. A cold wet nose poked between our faces, and then a grubby little hand smacked Nick on the cheek.

I started to laugh. Once I started, so did Nick. He grabbed Taylor around the middle and held him against his side. I slipped my hand through his arm and we walked in lockstep back toward the house, the valley echoing behind us.

Chapter Twenty-three

July passed in a blur of happy, of wedding plans, sleepy days, and magical nights under a tropical breeze. Happy. I was happy. Something I'd never been until Nick, and now was to the nth degree. I'd even had a month's break from my deteriorating ex-boyfriend, holes in my house, and thieving contractors. Sure, we worked hard, too, but I've always worked hard, and I didn't mind.

But that didn't mean I'd say no to a day off. When Ms. Ruthie arrived one morning and set about washing the breakfast dishes, Nick whispered to me, "How about we play hooky at the beach today, just you and me?"

"How about yes?" I responded. I turned to go get ready, but I heard Taylor singing, and it stopped me short. "Do you recognize that song?" I asked.

Nick smiled. He always understood Taylor. But it was Ruth who spoke.

"You are my sunshine," she said.

She joined in with Taylor, her soprano voice shaky with age or a delicate vibrato. Either way, their duet sounded lovely.

"What she said." Nick grinned. "And bravo, Ms. Ruth. Very nice, Taylor."

There were plenty of explanations why Taylor would know that song. All kids know it, practically. But still. The possibility was there.

Right after lunch, Ruth and Taylor waved goodbye from the driveway as we drove away. I rolled my window down and stuck my face into the warm breeze, turning it up to catch the sun on my cheeks. I whooped.

Nick was behind the wheel, practicing his left-hand driving. He was getting pretty good at it. "Yah mon," he said, and I laughed.

I navigated Nick down out of the rainforest to the west end of the island, opposite of our normal route to Town, then southward to the secluded entrance to Turtle Beach. We drove another half a mile down the service road to a tiny dirt lot.

"Where's the beach?" Nick asked.

"Through there," I said, pointing through a thick stand of sea grape trees. I grinned at him. "It's kind of remote."

He leaned across and kissed me. "Sounds just right."

A strip of swampy land webbed with mangroves and sea grape trees protects Turtle Beach from vehicles and casual visitors. We threw our bags over our shoulders and each grabbed an end of the cooler and set off down the path, following signs to the turtle nesting sanctuary ahead. Within ten yards, sweat was running down my neck. We rounded a bend that emptied out onto the wide swath of white sands that cover the southwest point of St. Marcos and the sparkling turquoise water beyond.

"Wow," Nick said. "This is the best beach I've seen on the island yet."

"Those sea turtles know how to pick 'em."

We waded through the sand. My calf muscles were burning.

"If you loved me, you'd carry the cooler on your head," I told Nick. He was not only carrying his own beach bag, but also lugging a beach umbrella with a heavy wooden base that kept uncollapsing into the back of his calves.

He raised his eyebrows. "If you loved me, you would have hired me a Sherpa."

"I'm not sure, but I think that's racist," I replied. "I'm an employment lawyer, you know."

Nick laughed. "I didn't suggest you kidnap and enslave him," he said. He stopped. "How about here?"

"Just a few more yards, around that bend. It's perfect there, you'll see."

He grunted and we resumed our sand march. Around the point, the beach widened. One hundred yards of fluffy white sand tapered off to meet an endless turquoise sea. And we were the only ones there.

"Holy shit," Nick said. "I recognize this place."

I looked around us. Of course I recognized it, I'd been there before. But in the months since my last visit, something felt different, yet more familiar. "What do you mean? This is your first time here."

He set down his load. I set mine down, too. He turned in a small-stepped circle. "It looks like someplace I've been before. With you."

I reached for his hand and peered down the beach. Wind rushed past my ears, masking everything but the sound of the waves. Except for one other sound. I closed my eyes to concentrate on the noise. Barking. It was the sound of my dogs on the beach, but it was only in my mind, in a memory. And without opening my eyes I saw the white sand ribbon in front of us, and an old woman walking toward us.

"Our dream," I said.

Nick squeezed my hand. "Yes, that's it. This was the beach in our dream." He stepped in front of me and kissed me on the lips. "Empress."

My lips curved into a smile under his. We were there. In the exact spot we had dreamed about together. My lips and the rest of me lit up like a sparkler. When we broke apart, I was still smiling.

We set up, which was easy since my brightly striped umbrella had popped up again as we rambled the last few yards. I laid my thick white beach towel in its shade, slipped off my yellow Fresh Produce sundress, and stuffed it in the beach bag.

"We're getting married this weekend," I said, looking up at Nick from under the floppy wide brim of my straw hat.

He smiled at me, his eyes obscured by sunglasses but his mouth soft. "This is true."

"Wanna get wet?" I asked.

He dashed off. "Race you!"

"Cheater," I yelled, running after him.

Nick turned around and ran backwards in exaggerated slow mo until I caught and passed him at the water's edge. I splashed out until the water slowed me down, then strode farther until I was in up to my rib cage. Nick slipped his arms around me from behind, and I put my head back under his chin, loving his height, loving his hard body and the way mine molded into it.

"That hat makes it awfully hard to kiss you," he said.

I rolled the brim back with both hands and turned my head up until our lips met. His tasted of sweat and seawater, tangy and salty, and I let mine cling to them for several long beats.

"Better?" I asked.

He moved his mouth to my forehead as I turned until the fronts of our bodies pressed together. "Much. Makes me pretty happy we have a whole beach to ourselves."

Reflexively, I checked the beach. Damn.

"Well, we did. Now we have to share."

He looked, too. "We could drown them."

I laughed. He grabbed my hand and we walked back to shore together. A family of five had set up twenty-five feet from our umbrella. So much for sexy times at the beach. As we neared our spot, I heard the heavy bass opening bars of Queen's "Another One Bites the Dust." Nick's ring tone. I was shocked we had signal.

"Could you answer it? My hands are wet," he said.

I reached deep into the beach bag and pulled out the phone. "Hello?"

"I just leave you a voice mail," Rashidi said. Usually, Rashidi drove me crazy by his very refusal to do just that. It's an island thing.

"What?"

"You and Nick need to come home, straight along."

"Why?"

"Someone been here, and Taylor and Ruth gone."

Chapter Twenty-four

The world froze. I stumbled into Nick and grabbed his arm.

"Rashidi said someone broke into the house, and Taylor is gone."

Nick ripped the umbrella out of the sand and started shoving towels back into bags. I grabbed one end of the cooler as he hoisted the other, and we took off down the beach, his longer legs stretched out and pulling me along. I forced myself to keep running even though my lungs were burning and my legs were turning to lead in the heavy sand. We made it to the truck in half the time it took us to trek out.

"I'll drive," I said.

"Good idea," Nick replied. "I'll call Rashidi."

He pressed Talk and I heard the distinctive sound of a call failing.

"Shit," Nick yelled.

"We may not have good service on this side of the rainforest."

Nick blew an O out of his mouth. "OK."

I reached for his hand and squeezed. "I love you. I'll get us there as fast as I can."

I felt him looking at me, and I turned and met his eyes. The panic in them tore at me. But they focused as we looked at each other, the black centers shrinking. He blinked. "I love you, too. Thank you, Katie."

I sped along the coast and up the winding road through the rainforest to Annalise. We arrived in a cloud of dust with a skidding stop. The dogs circled the truck, barking. Ms. Ruth stood between her old Buick Lacrosse and Rashidi's Jeep.

She ducked her chin back into her neck. "Wah the matter?" she yelled.

Nick reached her in three giant steps. "Where's Taylor? Who's been here? Is everything all right?"

Her hands flew to her bosom. "Lah, you scaring me. Taylor asleep in he car seat." She pointed into her back seat. "I ain't seen nobody, and everything OK. We at Lotta's all day. What wrong?"

Rashidi came out of the side door and stopped behind Ruth. He held up both hands. "I no wanna scare she."

I joined Nick and searched Rashidi's face for clues. "What's going on, Rash?"

"The house unlocked. Somebody do bad things in the office. They left this in the kitchen." He held up a sheet of paper.

"I lock up before I leave," Ruth protested, her hand raised toward the side door.

But I'd never changed my locks after I lost my keys.

Shit.

Nick took the paper from Rashidi and angled his body toward me. I put my head to his shoulder and we read the typed note together.

You took something of mine, and I want it back.

"Who?" I asked. A parade of possibles ran through my mind. Bart, me? Junior, money?

"I don't know," Nick said.

The sun was descending, throwing a glow on Ruth as it sank behind the hills to the west. She shook her fist. "No bad man gonna mess with things round me."

Me either, I thought.

Chapter Twenty-five

Nick and I watched Ruth and Rashidi drive away, his Jeep just behind the dust plume trailing her gold sedan. The rainforest swallowed them one after another.

"That note is creepy," I said.

"Very."

He pulled me into him. I tucked my head down into the nook between the side of his chin and his shoulder. The unyielding edge of his collarbone supported my cheek. I traced his shoulder blade with my finger, the tip dipping off the blade and over his shoulder muscle.

"You OK?" he asked.

Someone had left a really strange note in my kitchen, and Nick and I'd had the bejeebers scared out of us. We were about to face whatever it was that had been done to the office. Yet somehow I wasn't completely freaked out. "I'm fine, baby, I really am."

He squeezed me. "Why don't we put Taylor in bed first? Then we can deal with the rest of it."

"Good idea."

We went together to Taylor's room, Nick carrying the boy in his car seat. I unbuckled him and Nick lifted him gently and placed him in the pink playpen. He sighed and nestled himself against his blue blanket. Nick leaned all the way in and gave him a clean diaper. The boy's dark lashes lay against his cheek, and his back rose and fell in a slow cadence. He usually flung his arms out, but this evening he tucked them around his face.

"You know he'll be up at some ungodly hour," Nick said.

That I knew. "That's all right, this once."

"We'd better go check out the damage."

"Right." I followed Nick up the stairs to the office.

"Oh no," I said. I grabbed the door frame to steady myself.

The room looked like a cyclone had blown through. Paper blanketed the floor. The file cabinet lay on its side. Whoever was in there had swept every item off the desks, including our open laptops. Mine was upended but fine. Nick's screen was shattered. And like the heavens themselves had rained down upon it all, water had pooled over everything. Taylor's dump truck was parked in the middle of the mess with its bed in the unload position.

Nick pushed his hair back. "Tossed. Thoroughly."

"Do you think they were looking for something?"

"Hard to say. Maybe, or maybe they just wanted to send a message. Maybe both."

He stepped into the room and righted the file cabinet. His action mobilized me. I snatched up printouts, matching their corners and stacking them in neat piles on the desk. I gathered up pens and paperclips, file folders and highlighters, and reassembled everything. The process pulled me back together, too, mostly. In fifteen minutes we'd restored a semblance of order.

I said, "If anything was missing, I didn't notice."

"Me either. But we can't assume this is the only room they touched. We're going to have to search the whole house."

"How about you take the basement and we meet in the middle?"

"Sounds like a plan."

Half an hour later, we met back in the great room, which actually functioned as a great room since contractors had finally removed the scaffolding last week. Neither of us had found anything else disturbed, but my unease still lingered. Nick stood with his hands on his hips. "That's all we can do for now. I'm salty and I could really use a shower. Besides, I think it would help," he gestured toward the office, "with this. Will you join me?"

I love to shower with Nick, to feel the hot water trickle around us until it runs cold, forcing us to run to bed to keep warm together. He was right, a shower together would wash the creepy away, but I told him I wanted to feed the dogs and double-check the locks first. "Go ahead and jump in. I'll be right there."

"I can do that for you," he protested.

I stood on tiptoe and kissed him. "I know you can, but I want to. I have to have a do-better with the troops. They should have stopped this and left us a bloody corpse."

I set out Purina and water as dusk fell. Six canines clustered around me, ignoring my lecture and lining up at the food bowls in the garage according to their pecking order. I looked up when I heard an unfamiliar car pulling into the gate. Its lights were off. Not Rashidi. Not Ruth. Not Ava or Crazy. Not even Bart. My intuition screamed a warning at me: *You took something of mine, and I want it back.* Maybe I wasn't as OK as I'd thought. Maybe bad man dem coming.

For a nanosecond, I thought about running into the house and grabbing Nick out of the shower. But I didn't, because my intuition could only be rampant paranoia, and if I ran for help I'd be leaving the ramparts unmanned. Ever since my pitiful failure on the day of the pool incident, I had started coaching myself when I was at a complete loss as to how a normal woman would handle herself. It was like the WWJD bracelet my parents made me wear in middle school, hoping it would keep me away from drugs and maternity wards. What Would Jesus Do? Lately I'd been using WWMD—What Would Mom Do. And W the hell WMD now? The answer came without thinking. She would protect her family.

I ran into the garage and grabbed the flare gun from my truck's glove compartment. I gulped air and stepped out on the driveway. I immediately felt exposed, trapped in the light cast by the motion detector lights. I stepped back into the shadow and hid the flare gun behind me. My dogs gathered around me, warm fur pressing against my legs. Good, reinforcements.

I didn't get a good look at the car until it turned up the driveway in front of me. It was a dark sedan of some sort. Nick would know. It parked fifteen feet down the driveway and idled. Maybe it wasn't a bad man, after all. Maybe it was a roti delivery man gone astray.

The car stopped. The door opened. A man got out. He walked in front of his still-running car, backlit by the headlights. He was roughly my height, average for a guy, but a head shorter than Nick. He was so thin his ribs formed something like a six-pack underside of his tight tank shirt and made his muscles look bigger than they were. His olive skin was covered with elaborate tattoos of women and a Maltese cross. His dark brown hair fell straight across his brown eyes.

"Where's Nick?" he growled. His tone spoke of long-held grudges and dreams of revenge. Definitely not the roti delivery man. Callia started growling.

"Excuse me, who may I say is asking?" But suddenly, I knew. I just knew.

"Just tell me where he is." Five other dogs joined voice with Callia.

"Inside."

"Get him."

I didn't budge. "He's not available right now."

The man yelled, "Nick Kovacs, you got one minute to get out here." He reached into his pocket and pulled something out. I saw a glint of light on a blade as I heard a faint click underneath the sound of the wind. Switchblade? How *West Side Story* of him.

No answer from inside, thank goodness. I shouted, "Ignore him, Nick. I've got the gun." And I pulled it out and pointed it at the man I believed was Taylor's father. I hoped he couldn't tell it was only a flare gun in the dark.

"No need to get hostile."

"Leave."

He put one leg back in the car. "My boy shouldn't be sleeping in some pink-ass crib. He needs to grow up to be a man. Bad enough that bitch gave him a girl name. I'm coming back for him. You be sure to tell him, tell Nick."

I saw rapid movement out of my peripheral vision, on the far side of the car.

It was her. Black, beautiful, and ferocious. Her skirt billowed behind her as she lifted a large flat rock—not unlike the one I'd used to mark my burial spot—which pulled her shirt up and exposed her hard stomach. When she brought the rock down on the sedan's front window, Derek jumped back and fell to the ground. He scrambled away from the car in a crazy crab-walk. The dogs rushed at him, snarling, but stayed well back.

"Son of a bitch. What was that?"

No more rock. No more woman.

"Fate," I said. "Leave."

He stood up, brushed off the seat of his pants, and glared at me. "Shooting out my window doesn't make you tough."

I held the gun steady. "You're next."

Derek climbed into the car and was already accelerating before he threw it in reverse. The engine whined and the transmission clanked, then the car shot backwards down the driveway and its back end swerved into my front yard. He jammed the gas and threw it in drive, digging a hole in my new grass before rocketing forward. His front wheels bit into the gravel lane and the back wheels lost traction. Six dogs ran after him as he fishtailed and then disappeared in the dark. I heard the car turn out of the gate and onto the road back to civilization.

I heard a sound from the house. My adrenaline surge had my heart doing wind sprints. I wheeled with my hands raised to protect my face and torso and flexed my knees. I was ready to fight off the devil himself barehanded. Me and Annalise.

"I gave up on you," came Nick's voice from the kitchen.

"Sorry." I was a goddess. No, scratch that, I was an empress. "We just had a visitor."

Chapter Twenty-six

To say that Nick was upset about Derek showing up is an understatement of gargantuan proportions. He raged, he cursed, and he paced all night long. I listened both to him and for the sound of the dark car in the drive.

By morning, his rage and fear had tempered into resolve and a punchy wryness. I rubbed the last bit of moisturizer into his droopy-eyed face as Taylor sat on the bathmat at our feet, running his dump truck back and forth over Nick's toes. A horn honked outside. Nick and I both jumped.

"I'll see who it is," I said, glad the house was locked up tight. Surely Derek was a creature that didn't come out in the daylight?

"Wait," Nick said, his face grim. He grabbed my robe from the hook on the back of the door and slipped it on over his skivvies. When he cinched the belt, the lavender velour ended two inches below his boxers. Mrs. Doubtfire with a furrowed brow and really good legs.

"That will certainly scare off any bad guys," I said.

Nick snatched Taylor into the air and the boy screamed with laughter.

"What if it's—you know," I said. I inclined my head toward Taylor.

"If it is, one of us will have to take him back to his room. For now, I'll just keep him out of line of sight."

I led the way through the bedroom and great room to the kitchen window and we looked out onto the driveway. Jacoby was leaning against the bumper of a dark SUV. Another man sat in the passenger seat. I felt my eyebrows lift. I looked at Nick.

"One of the good guys," I said, wiping the back of my hand across my forehead.

I walked out to the driveway and raised my hand. "Good morning. What brings you out before the rest of St. Marcos is even awake?"

"Good morning. Ava say you having trouble," Jacoby said. "I swing by to check on you."

I had left Ava a message the night before about what happened. She had never called me back, but clearly she'd gotten my message.

"You could say that. Let me get Nick and we'll tell you all about it."

"I'm right here," Nick said, coming outside with Taylor on one hip. He'd exchanged my bathrobe for khaki cargo shorts and a Texas A&M t-shirt. He and Jacoby exchanged good mornings. Taylor said good morning so much like Ruth that even I understood him. Nick and I laughed.

Jacoby said, "He make a proper island boy one day."

"Who's in the car?" I asked.

"My new partner. Morris. He shy." Jacoby waved Morris out.

Morris unwound himself from the passenger seat and joined us in three strides of his stork-like legs. "Yes, sir," he said to Jacoby. I'd seen him before.

Jacoby sighed. "Morris, we partners. Don't call me sir."

"No sir, I mean OK."

"Katie and Nick, Morris. He learning the ropes. Morris, Katie and Nick."

"Good morning," I said to him. "Nice to meet you." Nick echoed me.

"A pleasant good morning to you." We shook hands. Morris's were clammy. I'd been that scared of Jacoby once upon a time, too. Poor bastard. Morris shifted from one foot to another and crossed his arms. "I see you before," he said to me. "At the theater."

Yes, that was it. In the parking lot outside the theater, months ago, the first night Nick was on island. I smiled at him. He dipped his chin.

"Now, listen and learn," Jacoby ordered him. To me, he said, "Go ahead."

I gave Jacoby the rundown on my Derek encounter.

"Don't sound like he have a gun," Jacoby mused. "That good."

Nick chimed in. "I plan to track down his parole officer and report seeing him here, as soon as Texas wakes up in a couple hours and right after I call a locksmith to come out here and change all the locks."

Jacoby grunted. "Got a picture of him or a license plate number?"

Damn. I'd had the chance to take down his plate number, and I'd whiffed it. Nick said, "No picture, but I can try to print you something from the internet."

"Just email the link." Jacoby pulled a card out of his wallet and handed it to Nick. "I make the call to his parole officer. Mean more, one officer to another. And I keep an eye out for him on island, see if I can get a few of my friends to do the same."

"Thank you, Jacoby," I said.

"Yah mon. You a freshwater West Indian now," he said, calling me by one of the slightly derogatory names the true West Indians gave to continental transplants. But his eyes gave his good humor away.

"I'm singing with Ava tonight at Crystal's," I said. "We're auditioning for that producer who just moved here. Trevor Weingart. You should come."

Ava's name added an inch to Jacoby's height. "I swing by," he said. "But I don't like he."

Jacoby tended not to like anyone Ava did, so to speak, although I wasn't sure about Trevor. We shook hands all around, then Jacoby and Morris drove away.

That night, the sun was setting as Nick, Taylor, and I drove along the winding north-shore road to meet Ava at Crystal Bay for dinner. Horses grazed in the guinea grass on our right. Pelicans dove in the surf on our left. We made a sharp right turn at a thick stand of coconut palms and Crystal Bay opened up before us. The sea was dark below the half ball of orange behind it. The balmy wind blew small whitecaps across the outer reef and pushed the smell of the sea into our open windows.

We pulled into the dirt lot below the restaurant, which had a perfect view of its namesake. Close enough to feel a part of it, high enough to make it a panorama. It was perfect for a lazy Sunday morning of lobster Benedict and surf, but it was Thursday night, and we were running late enough that Ava had beat us here. Nick dropped me at the steps and he and Taylor went to park the truck.

I climbed the stairs to the restaurant, which was an immense covered deck. The stage and bar were nearest the water, a pool table and the enclosed kitchen were on the far side against the hill, and in between was a large open area crowded with wooden tables.

Dark was overcoming dusk outside, and the lights were on in the restaurant. I saw Ava as soon as I reached the top of the steps, and headed to the stage to help her set up. She was pulling at her sequined neckline, coaxing the stretchy purple fabric down to better display her girls. As I got closer, I could hear her muttering under her breath, holding both sides of an animated conversation. I felt my brows rise. She looked up and saw me, and I lifted my hand in a wave. She pointed to the back of the room, where Jacoby raised his hand in greeting to me.

"You late," she said.

"I sorry," I said, Local-style.

She chuptzed. I chuptzed her back.

"That almost passable," she said.

High praise. I pitched in, and together we finished readying the equipment. When we were done, Ava went to the bar and I looked around the rapidly-filling deck for Nick.

He had taken a seat with Jacoby, and Rashidi had joined them, too. Jacoby had Taylor on his knee facing Nick. Nick was opening his mouth when Taylor would pull his right ear and closing it when he pulled the left one. Taylor loved this game. He really was adorable. I knew I would miss him when he went back to Teresa. Still, I was ready to have Nick all to myself. I wasn't afraid to admit it. In two days I would be a bride, and I wanted to be the princess, too.

"No Trevor yet," Ava said in my ear. "He off island all summer and now he late."

I reached down and behind me and caught her hand in mine. She spun me around and tried to adjust my neckline downward. "I don't need a breeze," I said, hauling my turquoise V-neck back up. The front and back plunge of the sleeveless fitted cotton dress made it skimpy enough already.

Ava and I stepped back onto the stage. I looked above the heads of the packed house rumbling with conversation, beyond the lights on the deck and into the dark, into the snaking vines and gnarled and twisted trees of the forest. I listened through the conversations and clinking dishes for the night sounds of the island—frogs, birds, crashing waves. I felt Nick's gaze, and at the touch of his eyes on my skin, I swallowed. Magic.

We kicked off our set with "Rhiannon," a song I love that always makes me wish I had a deeper voice so I could sing the Stevie Nicks part. As the applause died down, we picked up the tempo with Ava's new favorite, "I Kissed a Girl and I Liked It." I didn't like it so much myself, but it usually got the crowd going, which was what I thought was happening at first.

The bouncer was arguing with someone, and that someone wasn't backing down. Ava and I kept singing but I stretched to get a better view. The owner, a burly Local who could have worked the door himself, left his post behind the bar and moved toward the melee. The heads of every patron swiveled to follow him. Ava and I looked at each other and shrugged but kept going. Moments later, the bouncer folded his arms.

The owner pulled a wad of cash out of his bar apron and approached the primo table in the center of the floor. He held it out to one of the men seated there and pointed to the bar. The guy pocketed the money and his whole party strolled over to the bar, laughing and slapping each other high fives.

Then Trevor stepped out of the shadows with his latest delivery from the woman-of-the-week club catwalking behind him in a vinyl outfit that screamed whips and chains. Actually, with hips as thin as hers, it wasn't out of the question that she was a he. Slither and Trevor's date's apparent twin followed them to the vacated table and they all sat down.

I stopped singing. No one noticed, because they were gaping at a rock star so bona fide he'd graced the cover of the *Rolling Stone*. He wasn't the reason I stopped, though. The final member of Trevor's circus troupe was.

Bart.

Ava elbowed me. "Close you jaw. Time to sing."

Luckily, she sang the first verse of "Underneath It All" alone, so I had time to regroup before the chorus. It didn't matter much anyway. Slither was pretending not to play to the crowd, and they were following his every studied sip of his drink and examination of his phone.

But the chorus was as far as I got before Bart walked over to Nick, who was standing at a table towards the back with Taylor perched on his hip. I cringed, waiting for Nick to crash a chair over Bart's head. He didn't. But Jacoby stood up and leaned toward Bart, throwing a shadow over him. Bart took a step back, then turned and walked away quickly.

The crowd was applauding again. I didn't dare look at Ava, because I was pretty sure she'd turn me to stone if I did. Bart had returned to Trevor's table. He leaned in to Trevor and said something, then headed down the stairs to the parking lot.

"If you don't mind, could you not screw up the rest of my life?" Ava said, pinching the back of my waist with considerable strength. "Sing, dammit."

I grabbed the microphone and gave it everything I had in "Travelin' Soldier," which was a good thing since it was my lead. It must have been enough, because Ava didn't pinch me again. After our set, Trevor introduced me to a very bored and distracted Slither—"Nice to meet you, charming show"—and congratulated us on a great performance. I barely registered the words. I nodded and smiled enough to satisfy Ava, but I got the heck away as fast as I could. Nick was already pulling the truck around to pick me up when I got outside.

"What happened with Bart?" I asked, climbing in next to Taylor's car seat.

"He congratulated me on our engagement and said that nothing makes a better alliance than a common enemy."

"What do you think he meant?"

Taylor thrashed in his seat. It was past his bedtime, and he was fighting off sleep with all he had.

"I don't know. Before I could ask, Jacoby jumped in and asked Bart if Tarah's spirit was letting him sleep at night. Bart looked a little spooked, so I told him to kindly get the fuck away from our table."

"Tarah, his old restaurant manager?"

"I assumed so." Nick smoothed the hair back from Taylor's forehead as he drove. "Jacoby said he talked to Derek's parole officer. He's scheduled to check in with her on Saturday. She said she can't do anything until he's been arrested or she has proof he failed to meet the conditions of his parole."

Which we didn't have. "Ugh. I'm sorry."

Nick reached over Taylor and we locked hands across his lap. "No, I'm sorry. I'm the one who dragged you into this mess with Derek."

"No more than I dragged you into mine with Bart."

"We're quite a pair," he said. "Hey, I know. Why don't we get married this Saturday?"

"I can't think of anything I'd rather do."

Chapter Twenty-seven

Nick and I spent most of the next day shuttling our wedding guests from the airport up to Annalise. By late afternoon, we'd all gathered on the patio for a rehearsal and Collin was misbehaving, in typical Collin fashion. He had just quick-stepped me down the aisle to the spot of grass behind the pool where we would hold the ceremony the next day.

Duke Ellis, a local attorney I'd partnered with the year before to defend Ava, would officiate. Kurt, Nick's father and best man, waited with Rashidi and Nick on the groom's side of the aisle, and Emily and Ava waited on mine. Nick's assistant LuLu had her tattooed arms wrapped around Taylor as they waited for their chance to bring the rings, and Nick's mom, Julie, stood to one side trying to keep everyone in their places just long enough that we could call this practice round a success.

Attorney Ellis said, "So then I'll say, 'Who gives this woman to be married to this man?'"

Collin answered, "And I'll say our parents and I do, since it is rumored that the groom has knocked her up."

I slugged Collin in his rather large bicep. He didn't flinch.

"Ignore him. He's always like this, through no fault of my parents," I said, mostly to my new in-laws, whom I had known for less than a day. But Julie was laughing and Kurt was smiling, so I figured we were in the clear. We went through the motions of the rest of the ceremony quickly and cheerfully.

After Duke told Nick to kiss the bride—and my brother wished my almost-husband luck—Nick reached out and pulled me gently to him. My body moved to his like the end of a magnet to its north. He looked down into my eyes and held my gaze as he spoke to our guests.

"Some of you may have wondered why we moved so fast with all of this. But when you know you've found the one, why wait for forever to start?"

Oh, how I adored that man. I could count up all the things I loved about him—the way he made me laugh, his soft spot for kids and dogs, his great butt . . . I could go on and on. But you can't sum for love by adding up good qualities and multiplying by a factor of merit. Love is a prime number. Nick was my one.

Later that evening after a gigantic cookout on the beach, we returned to the patio to hang out while the sun set. We'd rented plenty of tables and chairs and we lit the tiki torches and passed around cans of mosquito repellant. The no-see-ums always attack newcomers first.

LuLu had taken a shine to my brother, who in turn was shining on Emily, which he was prone to do and she was prone to ignore. The three of them sat together drinking painkillers, a pineapple-coconut-orange rum drink that Emily suffered for on her last visit to St. Marcos, which seemed like ages ago. I'd thought she would never touch them again.

LuLu turned to me. "Katie, Nick said you're a singer, but Collin said you're an attorney. I'm so confused."

Ava came over and said, "She both, but I hear she better at lawyering."

"Ouch," I said. Everyone laughed.

Ava still had on her wedding-rehearsal-beach-barbeque-appropriate red spandex tube dress with the keyhole neckline. She pulled a chair up beside me and sat. "I let you practice with me." Lulu clapped with delight.

Emily said, "I've seen them, and they're fabulous."

Ava started snapping her fingers and singing a song from *Grease*.

I jumped right in. "Summer lovin,' happened so fast."

Nick jumped up from the next table and jogged into the house as everyone else joined in and it became a sing-along. We had nearly finished when he reappeared with a Fender bass hanging from his neck and an amplifier in one hand, cord dragging behind him. He bent down and plugged it in.

As we reached the last line, "those su-uh-mer ni-hights" the bass came in, electric and rumbly. Nick fingered the last long note for effect, then did a Pete Townsend jump at the end.

We cheered ourselves madly. Nick said, "With greatest appreciation to my father, who brought my bass from Texas."

"Yup," Kurt said, from his table by the pool. He dipped his head and Julie clapped Taylor's hands together beside him.

It was the first time I'd heard Kurt speak. Nick had told me that his father was from Maine, as if that explained something. I'd never known a Mainer before, but I was willing to bet they didn't talk much.

From there, Ava and I went into an ethereal rendition of the Indigo Girls song "The Wood." I almost didn't make it through, standing there in front of everyone I loved the best, between Nick and Ava in my most favorite place on earth ... it was too much and not enough at the same time. Seeing Nick's parents' clasped hands and Taylor asleep in Julie's lap made my loss so clear. But at the same time, how could one heart take any more joy?

At the end of the night, Nick limped off to make nighttime bed checks and lock the doors and I went to the kitchen for glasses of water. I heard footsteps coming up the stairs and turned around to see Emily peering around the corner, her blonde hair in the lead. Its height and volume after a day of travel and a night of revelry truly amazed me.

"Yoo hoo," she called, coming into the kitchen and putting her arms around me.

"Hi, Em," I said, hugging her back.

"I'm so happy things worked out for you and Nick," she said. "I was worried when you said you were getting back together with Bart. I know I kind of pushed you toward him in the beginning to help you get over Nick, but—"

"Whoa, whoa, whoa," I said. "I never said I was getting back together with Bart. I never even considered it."

Nick appeared in the doorway behind Emily. His jaw was clenched, his eyes wounded. I shook my head no at him.

"But I got a text from you that said that," Emily said, wrinkling her brow.

"I didn't send anything like that." I suddenly had a really sickening feeling.

Emily turned around and saw Nick. "Oh, you're right," she said. "I remember now."

"Do you still have it?" I asked. "Like in a string? I want to see it."

"I don't know." Her eyes were wide.

"Emily, you don't have to pretend for Nick. If you got a text like that, I want to see it. He knows I wouldn't send it. But weird things have happened around here, and this could be one of them."

Emily looked back and forth between Nick and me, then wailed, "Oh, God, I feel terrible."

"Don't," Nick said. He walked in and put his arm around me from behind and his chin on my shoulder. "I'll leave you guys to figure this out. Emily looks traumatized." He kissed the side of my head. "Hurry, though?"

"Of course," I said, and he headed for our bedroom. "Now, Em, show me the text."

We went downstairs to Emily's room for her iPhone and she clicked the button to scroll back through the message string.

"Here," she said. She held the phone out to me.

I read it aloud. "'I wanted you to know I am getting back together with Bart.'"

She had responded, "Wow, that's sudden. Are you OK?"

No reply.

The next text was from me, a day later. "Bart is nuts. What did I ever see in him?" And her reply, "I am so glad to hear you say that." And me, "Team Nick, baby."

"See?" she said.

"Yes. It's very strange."

I looked at the date on the odd text. May seventh. That was right after Nick's first visit. I closed my eyes and took myself back. No doubt I'd sent the "Bart is nuts" text.

Then it started coming to me. White dress. The Boardwalk. Tomato juice. Wanting to tell Nick about what Bart had done, but not able to because I didn't have my phone. I opened my eyes, and found Emily staring at me, and twirling a finger in the ends of her hair.

"I had a gig with Ava that night, and I didn't have my phone with me because I couldn't find it. A few hours later, when I got home, it was under my pillow."

Emily wrinkled her nose. "What do you think happened?"

Bart had creeped in my space, he'd stolen my phone, he'd handled my pillow to put it back. Really, the whole idea of it freaked me out. And I got to find out about it the night before my wedding.

Well, fine. I wasn't letting him—or anyone or anything else—spoil even one iota of my happiness.

I pointed to the text that said Bart is nuts. "That pretty much says it all."

Chapter Twenty-eight

By four o'clock on Saturday, we had transformed Annalise. Emily, Julie, LuLu, and I gathered pink trumpet vines in the forest after breakfast and spent the morning weaving them through a wire arch in the back yard to make an altar. Ava had promised to come after she helped her parents in their store, which I took to mean after she'd rolled out of bed at noon and blown her parents a kiss as she drove by their place. We finished the arch without her and stood back to admire our work.

"Something's missing," Emily said, cocking her head.

LuLu circled the arch. "It looks pretty to me."

"It is pretty," Julie said. "Katie, do you have any tulle? And maybe some glitter?"

"I have glitter. I'm not sure about the tulle."

We went inside and searched my closet and drawers until Julie held up an ivory skirt with a tulle overlay. "Could we use this?"

Emily lifted the bottom of the skirt to display it in all its glory. "How vintage Jessica McClintock of you," she teased. "Where did you wear this?"

I shot her a sideways look.

Lulu said, "You could cut that off and put it with some combat boots and it would be awesome."

I smiled. Lulu's pink hair and nose stud would finish out that look just right. If I didn't already know how smart and capable Nick thought she was, I would have written her off at first glance as a punk kid.

I handed Julie a pair of scissors. "Be my guest."

Thirty minutes later, the arch was fairy-tale ready. We made matching centerpieces for the patio tables out of the leftover tulle and decided that Martha Stewart couldn't have done it any better.

Meanwhile, Nick, Collin, and his father gave the grounds a trim and swabbed the decks out back. When I started getting a wee bit stressed midafternoon, Nick commandeered the men to mop inside the house. My friends foraged for snacks as I stood at the kitchen island and breathed deeply. My pulse slowed down in direct proportion to the concentration of Pine-Sol in the air.

"Your freckles have gotten darker," Emily said as she poured a bag of microwave popcorn into a bowl, "and your pupils are like saucers. Are you OK?"

"Nothing a little sparkling water can't fix," I said as I poured myself one. "I think it's all just hitting me at once."

"Isn't it time for you to beautify?" Emily asked, hooking me by the arm.

"Yes, let's," LuLu said, and slipped her arm through Julie's.

We set up our snacks and beauty camp in the master bedroom. I laid my dress out on the bed and we gathered around it to oooh and aaaah, but before we could do it justice, Nick walked in.

"What's this?" he asked.

LuLu stood in front of the dress with her arms out wide to block his view. "No, no, no," she said.

"Out, mister," Emily ordered. "You won't see her again until she walks out to marry your ass, so be nice and kiss your fiancée goodbye for the last time."

Nick swooped me over backwards and kissed me. When he set me back on my feet, I fanned my face. "Be still my heart."

"See you in a few hours, baby."

I waggled my fingers in a goodbye gesture and Emily and LuLu said, "Goodbye, Nick."

I heard Ava's voice as she approached, singing the Captain & Tennille's *Wedding Song* like a show tune. It was shift change time at the girl party. LuLu and Julie kissed my cheek and left to shower in their own bathrooms, and Ava, bearing a bulging cloth bag, slipped in the door right afterwards. I was alone with my two best friends.

"I promise not to let Emily touch your hair," she said in a stage whisper, unzipping her valise and dumping it on the bed.

"And I promise not to let her dress you," Emily vowed. She looked at the pile of strikingly small outfits and asked Ava, "What are those, anyway?"

Ava grabbed a nail file from my bedside table and flopped down beside her clothes. "After-party options."

Emily and I exchanged a glance. "After party? It's called a reception," she said.

"OK, reception options. What are you going to wear?"

"I was just planning on wearing my bridesmaid dress," Emily said.

Ava raised her eyes from the serious business of her nails to look at me. "Do I have to?"

Unfortunately, I hadn't chosen cheetah-print micro minis, and satin was not Ava's favorite textile. "Only until we finish pictures," I said. "Now, I'm getting in a bubble bath, and I promise, neither of you are going to touch my hair or my dress." I shut myself in the bathroom and rotated the valves on my claw-foot tub to full-blast hot.

Neither of my best friends would have chosen my dress, but I loved it. I ordered it from Nordstrom's: a sequined ivory bodice with a V-neck and spaghetti straps and a wrap-style mid-calf skirt. Much to Ava's chagrin, I was wearing it with her pearled flip-flops. "They for the beach," she'd said. And when Nick put the gold band on my finger—or back on my finger, rather, since I'd been wearing it for an engagement ring for the over a month—I would be wearing something worn by my mother and her mother before her. I slipped into the tub just as Emily walked in.

"You need some smell-good," she said. "Matches?"

"Left-hand drawer."

She got them out and lit the big jasmine candle on the counter, then she pulled out her phone. "Music." She pressed the screen and Patsy Cline started to sing "Always."

"Thank you, Em."

She put a finger over her lips, flipped off the light switch, and shut the door. I sank down into the water up to my smile. The muffled sounds of Emily and Ava chatting outside the door only added another layer to the perfection.

An hour later, the three of us were standing abreast in the bathroom putting on makeup. Time was racing faster and faster. I heard the first cars starting to arrive. Doors slammed. My heart galloped in my chest. I applied eyeliner, mascara, and lipstick as Ava and Emily continued chattering on either side of me, but I barely heard them. I hardly noticed when LuLu and Julie joined us. I was marrying Nick. I had never been more excited about anything in my life. I was ready. Now, now, now, my heartbeat said.

I looked into the mirror and dropped my lipstick to the floor. There were five faces, but none of them was mine. I blinked and gave my head a shake. Impossible. Julie handed me the lipstick and gave me a funny look.

I looked back into the mirror. This time I saw four women and myself. Annalise had disappeared. A knot welled in my throat. I swallowed, but it stayed firmly lodged.

A knock on the bedroom door. "It's time, ladies." Collin. With kisses on my cheek, my friends left the bathroom. I followed them into the bedroom.

As she reached the bedroom door, Julie turned back to me and put her hand on my arm. "I'm really happy you and Nick found each other, Katie. Kurt and I both are."

A tear threatened my mascara. "Thank you, Julie. I'm very lucky."

And then only Collin and I remained. My big brother, the one who would stand in Dad's shoes tonight.

"You're gorgeous, sis. I'm proud of you. Mom and Dad would be, too." The tear in my eye was catching. I used the handkerchief I had wrapped around my bouquet of orchids to wipe his away.

"I love you, Collin. Thanks for being here. For everything."

"I brought you something blue." He pulled a little piece of paper out of his pocket.

"What is it?"

He handed it to me. It was a tiny printed picture of my father in his dress blue uniform when he was the Dallas chief of police. "I thought you could tuck it in your flowers or something. He'd want to be the one to walk down the aisle with you."

I didn't trust myself to speak, just slid the picture under the satin ribbon around my bouquet. I nodded at him, my lips tight. He nodded back. He stuck out his arm, I took it, and its warmth under my hand flooded through me. My family. We were it.

The sound of steel pans playing the wedding march floated up to us from the back yard as we made our way carefully downstairs and out to the patio into the soft yellow August light. It was warm, even though the sun was setting. Down the flower-strewn path between the tables my brother and I walked,

around toward the arch at the far end of the pool, where Nick was waiting for
me.

My eyes met his. The shine in his blinded me to everything but him. He was
simply gorgeous, and I wanted to drop my flowers and run the rest of the way
to him. He had rolled up the sleeves of his white linen shirt, exposing the dark
skin on his arms, the skin I loved to hold next to my own. Behind him, the arch
framed the valley of mangoes and the western shoreline. It was so clear you
could almost see to Vieques, Puerto Rico. I pictured my mother standing there.
I know she would have approved. Of Nick, of the view, of everything.

Words were spoken. Duke's. Collin's. Emily took my orchids and I put my
hand through Nick's arm. I wanted time to slow down, but it wouldn't. The
best I could do was savor it, so I tried to memorize every detail, from the sound
of the macaws in the distance to the feel of the breeze lifting my hair and
teasing my neck.

LuLu carried Taylor forward with our rings and Nick slipped my mother's
ring onto my finger, for good this time. I put the gold band we'd chosen
together in Town on his finger. And then he gathered my face in his hands and
kissed me. I went up on my toes and threw my arms around him and buried my
face in his chest. I let the tears come, and he rocked me back and forth.

"I want to go back and do that all again," I whispered to him.

"I could relive the moment when you and Collin walked out the door over
and over, myself."

I leaned back in the circle of his arms and he kissed me again.

The steel pan band began to play and everyone surged in to hug us, one
after another: Kurt and Julie, LuLu, Rashidi, Ava and her parents, Ruth, Emily,
Crazy and Lotta, my old boss Gino from Dallas I'd had absolutely no idea was
coming. Contractors. Musicians. Neighbors. Friends.

Our biggest guest, Jacoby, waited patiently for his turn at the end of what
had become a long line. He wrapped me in a bear hug and shook Nick's hand.

"I got news," he said.

"Good news only, tonight," I said.

He actually cracked a smile, which I'd never seen him do before. "How
about good news first?"

"Marginally acceptable," I said. But I reminded myself that nothing would bring me down. Not tonight.

"I post Morris at your gate to keep out bad man dem."

"That is good," I said.

"What's the bad news?" Nick asked.

"Derek check in with his parole officer. She say he had a timecard and pay stub for the whole week. She think we confused here in the islands, get the wrong guy."

Nick closed his eyes and sighed. I put my head against his shoulder.

"I sorry about that. Least he not here to spoil the day," Jacoby said.

"True dat," Nick said, and I laughed at his accent, which was worse than mine.

"Go enjoy some food. We have a great mahimahi." I glanced behind him and saw Julie standing in the midst of the steel pan band with a mallet in her hand. Nick claimed she had never met an instrument she couldn't play.

"What you trying to do, kill me? I allergic to fish dem."

"Shellfish, too?"

"Nah, they no problem."

"Well, then stick to the whelk and lobster Rashidi brought."

Jacoby sauntered off to the buffet line. We left the subject of bad man dem and joined our party.

But just after the sun went down, we heard a distant crack and all the lights went out, leaving us in sudden dusk. My pulse surged and I reached for Nick. I knew that sound well after Crazy's stroke. It was a power transformer blowing out by the gate. Amused voices rose around us, but I was worried. What if someone was out there? What if they'd disabled the transformer on purpose?

I heard the squawk of a radio, then Jacoby's voice right in front of us in the dark. "Morris report everything fine."

"Thanks, Jacoby," I said.

Everything was fine except for the fact that we had fifty people in the growing dark at our wedding reception.

Before I could even run for candles, though, all the lights came back on. Applause filled the air. Wow, WAPA's fast tonight, I thought. Then I realized that was impossible. It wasn't WAPA. And magic was the only other way I knew to fix a blown transformer.

"Thank you, Annalise," I whispered. "What a lovely wedding present."

The party continued, and it was fabulous. Nick and I slipped away just past midnight as everyone else danced and drank rum drinks on the patio.

"Wait," Nick said as we neared our room. He stopped me and swept me up into his arms. "I want to carry you across the threshold."

I felt light and incredibly feminine, and I raised my face to rub noses. "My husband. My gorgeous husband, with his erotic nose."

"It's enormous, Katie."

"But your hair balances it out nicely," I said. He bumped me into the doorframe on purpose, and I laughed.

"Yeah, me and Lyle Lovett."

"No comparison, Nick, no comparison."

He settled me on the bed. Fresh hibiscus petals were scattered on the sheets around me. They reminded me of our first night together at the Reef. There was a chilled bottle of sparkling cider in an ice bucket and pieces of the bride's and groom's cakes on the nightstand by a ribbon-wrapped bottle of Nick's fancy face cream and a pale purple bottle of my favorite perfume, Interlude.

"Ah, flower petals and perfume. Nice touch," I said.

"And thank you for taking on the responsibility of keeping my complexion soft and creamy."

I laughed. "You're welcome."

"I love you, my wife."

"I love you, my husband."

And, no surprise, we soon forgot about the cake, sparkling cider, and presents, and all the people gathered outside in our honor, and Taylor in the next room, and world peace, and starving children in India. We entered that special place we went to together, that wild river that we would ride, never knowing what was next, but only that it would catch us helplessly and willingly in its current. We drowned ourselves in each other until we reached that moment of ecstasy and the river threw us onto the beach, joined and panting and alive.

Very, very much alive.

Chapter Twenty-nine

At nine o'clock the next morning, someone was knocking on our bedroom door. I could not imagine what they were thinking. I kept my eyes firmly closed.

Nick moaned, but his hand sneaked out and slipped down to a personal area of mine. I gasped. He pulled me to him and whispered, "Please ignore them."

"Just a minute," I called to whoever was behind the door.

"OK," Nick's mom called in her soft, lovely voice, "but Taylor has breakfast in bed for you two sleepyheads."

This announcement, made on the other side of a thin door with a flimsy thumb lock, did not seem to get through to my new husband. It seemed that a minute really would be all we would both need. I sank my teeth into his shoulder as the spasms ripped through me. He panted and held me so tight that I knew I would have fingerprints amidst the freckles on my pale white skin. Intense and wonderful.

"Mom, can you stall Taylor long enough for us to get decent?" Nick pleaded.

"Make it fast, or he'll probably feed it all to the dog," she said.

Nick raised himself up and smiled at me. "Good morning, beautiful wife."

"Good morning, my love."

"We'll have to save the rest of the indecency for St. John."

Kurt and Julie were staying with Taylor so we could leave for our honeymoon down island that afternoon. I got up and put on pajama pants and a tank top.

Nick got dressed and went to the door. He looked at me and nodded as he called out, "We're starving. I wonder if there's any way to get some breakfast around here."

Giggles pealed behind the door. Nick threw it open, and Julie guided Taylor into the room. He was carrying a basket as big as he was, and Oso was on crumb patrol. Julie lifted Taylor and the basket up onto the bed.

"Taylor, did you do this for us?" I asked.

He nodded proudly.

"Thank you. You are such a sweet boy."

We pulled out a red-and-white-checked tablecloth, a thermos of fresh-squeezed orange juice and two cups, buttery biscuits, bacon, and two of Taylor's plastic bowls with steamed-up snap-on tops that appeared to hold scrambled eggs. I smiled at Taylor, who pointed to his grandmother.

Julie handed us two steaming cups of coffee and said, "We're all out having our breakfast by the pool. Kurt's guarding my food from the dogs until I get back, so I'd better hurry. We need to drop you at the seaplane at one, right?"

"Right," we said in unison.

She picked Taylor back up. "Time for you and Oso to come play out by the pool."

"Thanks, Mom," Nick said.

The next few hours rushed by as we enjoyed our guests, showered, packed, and took Kurt and Julie through the hurricane checklist Rashidi had helped us put together. Running the Annalise household presented a test anytime, but even more so during hurricane season. Nick taught Kurt how to operate the critical systems: the cisterns and pump, the generator, and the solar-powered gate. I took Julie through maps to the gas station, hospital, and grocery store.

It was soon time to leave. Our wedding party walked us to the truck and Collin slapped Nick on the shoulder. "If you ever need anything at all, call."

Emily kissed us both. "I'm taking credit for this, you know. Without me, you guys wouldn't be here. I would accept, as a token of your appreciation, lifetime vacation privileges up here at Annalise."

LuLu chimed in, "Me, too."

"Done!" Nick said. "Collin, can I talk to you a minute?"

"She's already giving you trouble?" Collin asked. I didn't bother to sock him, but I gave him my best eye roll.

The others wandered off, leaving Nick's parents with us and Collin.

Nick leaned toward Collin and said, "Listen, it's really unlikely, but there's a possibility Taylor's father is on island."

"He's on the no-no list," I said.

"My parents are already on the lookout, but I wanted to let you know, since you'll be staying here a few more hours, and my parents will be gone." Nick described Derek to my brother.

"No problem. Might be fun if he does show up while I'm here." Collin grinned. No one will ever accuse him of hiding his light under a bushel basket.

We piled into the truck approximately on time, Kurt behind the wheel to familiarize himself with the route and Nick riding shotgun to issue manly instructions. We pulled to a stop in the parking lot of the seaplane base twenty-five minutes later. After we checked in, Nick's parents hung around to have a snack with us at the café on the dock.

"That's weird," Nick said as we stood in line for beef patties.

"What's weird?" I asked.

He thumbed his phone screen. "I have two missed calls. No voice mails."

"Who from?"

"It says unknown. Maybe a well-wisher. Or a client."

Or maybe it was Derek. There had been time enough for him to fly back to the island after meeting with his parole officer. Could he be calling on his way up to Annalise? But he wouldn't call. Would he?

"They'll call back if it's important," I said.

We settled at a table close to the water with our spicy beef patties and Nick's phone rang again.

"Hello? Hello? Hello?" He shook his head. "The call dropped. Whoever it is, they're persistent."

Nick's parents were talking about their own honeymoon sailing through the islands in Acadia National Park off the coast of Maine. Well, Julie was talking about it, anyway. Kurt mostly nodded, with an occasional "yup." I kept one eye on Nick and his phone.

Our boarding call came over the loudspeaker and Nick's phone rang again at the same time. I hugged and kissed his parents goodbye while he answered it. And then the hair stood up on the back of my neck and tiny prickles of shock raced up my scalp.

I turned to look at my husband. I couldn't read his expression, but he put his hand over his free ear and walked away from us. His body was radiating anguish and channeling it straight to me.

"Katie? Are you all right?" Julie asked.

But I was moving toward Nick. I reached out to touch his back and my hand froze in midair, fearful of what it would receive when it closed our circuit. I laid my hand on him anyway.

He hung up, turned around, and slumped over into me. His face was pale.

"Derek? Taylor?"

"No," he croaked.

"Your sister?"

He nodded into my shoulder.

Chapter Thirty

"Two Marines are at Annalise," Nick said hoarsely. "They asked us to come back up there and if I knew where to find my parents." He raised his eyes to mine. "We're listed as next of kin, Katie. This is very bad. Teresa told us anything short of death is handled with a phone call."

"Oh my God," I whispered. "I'm sorry, Nick, so sorry."

"They said that they weren't authorized to release information to me over the phone."

I struggled to process the news. The timing was gruesome. It seemed to be hovering right outside the bounds of my reality, and if I didn't let it be real, then it might not. But I knew it was.

"Your parents," I said gently.

Kurt and Julie had moved in close to us, and they looked frightened. Nick started talking to them. I saw their lips moving, but I didn't hear a word. It was like I'd tuned into a silent movie halfway through. I had just met Kurt and Julie and I didn't know Teresa at all. I was sad for them, especially Nick, but I wasn't part of their grief. They huddled together on the dock, holding each other as they sobbed. I gripped Nick's hand.

It was a grim drive back to Annalise. When we got there, the Marines delivered the news officially to the Kovacs. Ruth took Taylor to her house and Rashidi shuttled Collin, Emily, and LuLu to the airport. Julie and Kurt retreated upstairs to lie down. I stuck close to Nick, trying to help. His pain was visceral to me. It carried me back to the loss of my parents. He didn't say a word and I just kept holding tight to his hand.

That evening, I sat in the great room with Nick and his parents as they talked about what would happen next. We didn't know much, only that Teresa had died after she stepped on a landmine on the night before our wedding. Obviously, there would be no honeymoon now.

Nick spoke. "One thing is for certain. We can't let Derek get his hands on Taylor."

Kurt responded in his broad Maine accent. "Can't imagine he wants him."

"It would sure cramp his lifestyle," Nick said.

I wasn't so sure they were right, but I stayed out of it. I was too new to the family to make waves.

Julie joined in. Her soft voice was weak, and grief had drawn her face in. "Don't underestimate the influence of his parents. Taylor is their grandbaby." She turned to me. "Katie, you're a lawyer, what do you think?"

"I'm sorry," I said. "I only learned enough about family law to pass the Texas bar exam. I have no idea, but I can look into it and research anything you guys need me to." I was practically worthless in this. A total legal loser.

"Teresa named me Taylor's godfather. That has to count for something," Nick said.

This was news to me, and a game changer. Nick was Taylor's godfather—not just his uncle, his *godfather*. In my mind, parents took care of children, so I had assumed until that very moment that Teresa's parents would take Teresa's child. But they wouldn't. Nick would. *We would.* My mind whirled with the impact on our lives, on me. On forever.

I swallowed hard and tried to contribute, pulling from the little family law I knew. "Derek is Taylor's father, so unless he signed away his parental rights, then his status as father may count more than Teresa's wishes."

Nick turned toward me. His eyes said, "Whose side are you on?" but his lips didn't move.

I yanked my eyes away. My mind raced back to me, me, me. I hadn't even had my time alone with Nick yet. When I married him, I hadn't imagined myself driving Taylor to kindergarten and packing his car to send him off to college. I had pictured big family Christmas gatherings where I was the special Aunt Katie, and Teresa was grateful and looked up to me like the big sister she never had.

It was a lot to take in.

The room was spinning around me. I tried to nod, but it came out as a jerk. I knew that I should put my arms around Nick and promise him I would love and support him no matter what, that I would gladly raise Taylor as my own. I felt peevish and small. I opened my mouth like a fish out of water, and a silent distance stretched between Nick and me. It grew wider with every second, and when I looked into the gap between us, the water was roiling with wide-mouthed sharks, their teeth gnashing. Wider, wider, wider it stretched. I braved looking up again and Nick's eyes bore into me.

And then the moment passed. The fish closed its mouth. My hands felt icy cold in my lap. Nick looked out the dark window at nothing.

I would tell him what he needed to hear soon. I would. But I couldn't do it now.

Chapter Thirty-one

The trip to Port Aransas, Texas, was an ordeal in a situation that was already difficult. Nick and Taylor, Kurt and Julie and I took one plane to San Juan, another to Dallas, another to Corpus Christi, then a ferry from the Texas mainland over to the island of Port A. It was a good warm-up for the next two difficult days of preparation, visitors, and Teresa's funeral itself. Not to mention the trip to D.C. we would make almost immediately afterwards for the burial in Arlington National Cemetery.

People poured into Nick's childhood home after the funeral to honor Teresa and her family. I was working in the kitchen, which overflowed with tuna casseroles, homemade breads, and jello-mold desserts we likely would never eat. I lifted a platter of deviled eggs off the yellowish-gold Formica counter and headed for the dining room.

On the way to the dining room, I stopped in the doorway to Julie's conservatory. It probably would have been a parlor in another home, but here she taught her students and displayed her instruments, from the piccolo to the trombone. Biographies of famous musicians and stacks of sheet music were scattered about. I wondered if anyone would miss me if I hid behind her timpani.

I turned into the navy and red dining room and squeezed the tray of eggs into a small open space between a plate of cold cuts and a plastic grocery-store tray of wilted broccoli. On the other side of the table were an ice bucket, liters of soft drinks and fruit juices, and an array of liquor bottles. The organist from the church was perusing the selection. She straightened her pillbox hat and looked around. No one but me. She grabbed a plastic cup and the ice tongs and fished for cubes. Her hands were shaking.

Mine started to shake, too. I could help her. "I think I'll have one of whatever you're having, ma'am," I would say, just to make her feel better. And then I would take only one tiny no-thank-you sip and pour the rest down the sink.

I turned away and closed my eyes. "No, Katie. No."

I started counting, my lips moving as I went through the numbers. One, two, three, four. I kept counting. I became aware of classical music playing over a sound system, a dour classical piece I didn't recognize. Slowly, the feverish yearning seeped out of my body. I counted higher. When I opened my eyes at fifty-seven, I was facing the china cabinet and its display of gold-rimmed plates with anchors in the centers. I had set my phone down on that cabinet earlier, and I reached around an enormous spray of lilies someone had brought from the funeral to grab it. Behind the lilies was a bouquet of roses in the darkest red I had ever seen. The name in block capitals on the card knocked the wind out of me: BART.

I yanked the card from its holder and ripped it into pieces. Why couldn't he just leave me alone? My phone was sitting on the sheet music for "That's All I Ask of You" from *Phantom of the Opera*. I picked it up and read my one message.

Ava: "Finish up your business and be back in time for Jump Up. Big things happening." Ava was referring to the monthly street festival, although I had no idea what she meant. I thumbed through the *Phantom* music while I tried to think of how to answer her. I decided it could wait and returned to the kitchen.

Nick was blocking the doorway. He was holding on to Taylor with one hand as he leaned in, deep in conversation with a gray-haired man a head shorter than him. He'd introduced him to me earlier as his junior high football coach. I touched him on the shoulder and he moved aside so I could get through.

I caught Taylor by the other hand and said, "I'll take him."

Nick smiled at me, a smile I didn't recognize and couldn't read. It made me feel sad. "Thanks."

I mustered a smile back, then swung Taylor in the air and caught a whiff. "Someone needs a new diaper."

I went back to Nick's old room to change Taylor on the bed. He looked up at Nick's old surfboard hanging on the ceiling as I pulled his elastic-waist pants off and tickled his belly. He laughed, so I did it again.

"Gonnagetcherbellybutton," I said.

Suddenly, I heard loud voices from the front of the house. I strained to listen and worked faster. Off with the old diaper. Wet wipes. Lots of them. My eyes watered as I bagged the mess and put on the new diaper. Taylor wriggled and chattered the entire time.

"Shhh, Taylor, let Katie hear."

Running footsteps approached and Julie burst in, her face pale. She whispered, "Katie, bring him into my bathroom and shut the door. Keep him quiet. Come on now—follow me quickly."

"What's wrong?" I asked.

She put her finger over her lips.

I grabbed Taylor and hurried down the hall behind her. I moved him farther down my body so my shoulder muffled his giggles. We slipped into the master bathroom and Julie closed the door behind us.

"Derek is here. He's demanding we give him the baby. Nick said he wasn't here, so we have to keep him quiet."

Fear wrapped icy fingers around my throat. "I've got it."

I remembered Derek's face, his scary voice and his knife, and I thought, Please, God, don't let him hurt Nick.

Julie squeezed my hand and left. I wanted to be out there with my husband. WWMD, WWMD, WWMD. I looked around for a quiet way to entertain the boy. I found a stack of magazines and fanned them out in front of him. He grabbed a worn copy of *Plane and Pilot* circa 2004 and used his whole hand to flip and mangle the pages. It would hold him for about two minutes, if I was lucky.

The bathroom door burst open and I jumped to my feet. It was Nick, looking like he was one small ignition source short of a big explosion. His pupils were dilated and his irises dark brown. His olive skin leaned toward the green end of the scale. The scent of his anger nearly overwhelmed me, like sweat but sharper, like a cornered alley cat. But he was my alley cat. I dove at him, and he wrapped his arms around me.

His voice was strained. "He's threatening to take Taylor. I want to kill him. I've never, ever hated anyone like I hate that *son of a bitch*." He spat out the last word forcefully and his whole body convulsed against me. He stepped back and handed me a card. "His so-called attorney."

"What did you say to him?" Taylor escaped the bathroom and ran back down the hall toward the sounds of people. I started to go after him until I heard Julie talking in her high-pitched grandma voice. He would be fine with her.

"I told him Teresa had appointed me as Taylor's guardian and godfather, and that I wouldn't hand Taylor over to him, now or ever. I don't get it, though. He doesn't even want a kid."

But I remembered the man I'd met outside Annalise, the one who was concerned about his son sleeping in a girly bed. "We have to get you a lawyer," I said. "I can help."

So for the next hour, I made calls. Teresa's burial in D.C. wasn't for three more days, so we scheduled an appointment for the next morning with an attorney in Corpus Christi. Game on, for better or worse.

The offices of Attorney Mary Posey were nice, but not as plush as those of my old Dallas firm, Hailey & Hart. That meant we wouldn't be paying for her image by the hour, which I appreciated. Her assistant, a squarish woman of indeterminate age, ushered us in with coffees, an air of competence, and a coloring book and crayons for Taylor.

Mary Posey said, "Derek's attorney, Albert Garcia, already called and said Derek wants the boy. But what I think he really wants is the money."

"What money?" Nick asked. "Teresa didn't have any."

"Teresa died while on active duty overseas for the Marines, so Taylor has a nice sum of money coming to him. At least the hundred thousand dollar death payment that Albert told me about. And there may be more."

"Oh my gosh," Julie whispered. Her hands gripped the purse on her knees.

Kurt pulled his lower lip.

"Let's make a few calls and see," Mary suggested.

Ten minutes later, Mary hung up the phone. "Taylor is the beneficiary of her SGLI policy. That's a Servicemembers Group Life Insurance policy, and he gets another four hundred thousand under that. That raises the stakes a bit."

Kurt spoke for the first time. "Derek's family has money, but they cut him off a few years ago."

Julie nodded. "Teresa said that was why he started selling drugs."

Nick snorted through his nose. "I think he could have found a few other ways to get by."

This was horrible. "His attorney could take his case on some kind of contingency fee basis," I said. "They both would have plenty of financial incentive to fight."

"While we pay by the hour until we run out of money," Nick said.

"Well, yes," Mary agreed. She ticked points off on her fingers. "When we talked on the phone yesterday, you said Derek's name was not on the birth certificate. He never filed for any type of parental rights, so Teresa never gave him any. He had no relationship with Taylor. He did time for a drug-related offense."

Nick growled, "He doesn't deserve to be a father."

Mary put both hands up and said, "I hear you, but he has points in his favor, too. We have to assume Derek truly is the father. The court will probably let him have visitation. I think they'll give him time to show he can be a good father and develop a relationship with Taylor."

Nick jumped up. "Visitation? That's bullshit."

"Maybe. But even if that's the direction the court goes, the good news is that you don't need to hand Taylor over to Derek unless and until a court orders you to do so."

My mind spun like the end of a spool of film.

Chapter Thirty-two

And all that explains why one short week later, I was back on St. Marcos, alone again in Annalise. Or it mostly explains it. But the rest of it was a natural result of all that happened before.

Derek's attorney filed for an emergency hearing while we were in D.C. The most honorable Judge Sylvia Nichols had no sympathy for our newlywed status. As she ruled that Taylor had to reside in Texas, the screen of my iPhone filled with Rashidi's picture. I hit Decline and heard the judge order Taylor to stay within a hundred miles of Corpus Christi until the attorneys had duked it all out. God, I hated lawyers.

"If you need to return to 'the islands' for your 'honeymoon' you could simply agree to hand Taylor over now and get on the next plane out," Judge Nichols said in a take-no-crap voice.

Ouch. I sat up straighter on the bench and tried not to look like a woman who was sad about canceling her trip to St. John. A series of texts from Rashidi hit my phone like torpedoes blowing holes below my waterline.

When I finally got to Rashidi's texts, I found that he'd stopped by Annalise and discovered fire damage and a broken window in the music room, apparently from an electrical short caused when a hole was drilled in the exterior wall. The shutters were in ashes.

His last message said, "Crazy can't help, I leaving. Sorry!" He'd be in San Juan for a month teaching in the master's botany program at the University of Puerto Rico. I was running out of options.

On the way out of the courtroom, Nick held my hand so tightly I imagined I could hear my bones cracking. I didn't pull away. I could be strong.

"Give us a minute," he said to his parents, and pulled me aside.

"We have to stay here, Katie, you know that, right?" He stroked my hand with his thumb.

"I do." I took a deep breath. "And it's only going to be for a few months. We lived apart for two months before."

Nick look confused. "What do you mean, live apart?"

I told him about Rashidi's news. "I have to get back and get repairs made. I can't leave her unsecured."

"*I?*"

"We, Nick, we. It's too risky. I need to be there."

His eyes darkened.

I tried again. "When the custody proceedings are over, you and Taylor can come back."

He pulled his hand away. "You can hire a house-sitter, Katie. They can oversee repairs." He ran his hand roughly through his hair, front to back.

"But it's not that easy. I poured every cent I had in Annalise, I gave up a successful career, and I invested *myself* in her as well. So, if I let Annalise go to hell, and oh yeah by the way meanwhile have no income, and you're hardly working while we rack up enormous legal bills . . . well, that's crazy."

"We just got married. We promised to be together. And we're supposed to be on our honeymoon," Nick countered.

"Yes, we're supposed to be on our honeymoon. But instead, we're packed in a tiny house with your parents, fighting a drug dealer for custody of your sister's kid. I fully support you, but I have obligations of my own. We can see each other every few weeks. Grown-ups do it all the time."

Nick turned up the heat but lowered his voice. "You know what, Katie? I think you're absolutely right. I'll stay here and fight for Taylor, and you go back and plant some flowers in the beds by the gate and sing karaoke with Ava."

My voice was loud and so shrill it hurt my own ears. "That's not what this is about! And if that's what you think of me, well then—" I sputtered out on that thought and launched recklessly into the next. "Real nice, Nick. I guess you are who I thought you were before. Cold. Heartless. Hurtful."

Nick's words came out in cracks like gunshots. "You're making a scene, in public, with my parents standing twenty feet away from us. Tamp down that Irish temper and quit making a fool of yourself and me."

And he walked away from me without another word. I was boiling, but there was nothing I could do but burn like an empty pot on a stove.

We spent a tense evening in the Kovacs' small house. Nick's parents' bedroom was on one side of us, and Taylor was in Teresa's on the other. He wouldn't talk to me and we went to bed angry. I lay awake all night, thinking that at some point he would put his arms around me and we would make it better. With every sleeping breath he drew measured against every moment I lay awake, I grew more upset. By morning I was fried. Nick woke up stiff and uncommunicative, and he didn't come around. I became aware that a dark place in me thought Taylor could stay with his parents and Nick could come back to St. Marcos with me.

I called for a taxi on the day I left. Nick walked me to the door.

"I need you, too, you know."

"You can handle Taylor with your parents' help."

"That's not what I meant," he said.

I knew it wasn't, but by then it didn't matter. Cinderella rode away from her prince in a pumpkin, alone.

Chapter Thirty-three

The morning after I got back to Annalise, I planted new bougainvillea by the gate under a brilliant pinkish-red sunrise unlike anything I had ever seen before. I stood back to see how the flowers looked. Wrong, I decided. They just looked wrong, nothing like what Nick and I had imagined.

I looked across the road at the deserted shantytown. Wrong there, too. Ever since I first saw Annalise, the shantytown had been home to multiple generations of a gentle Rastafarian family. They were gone now, and all that was left behind was a housedress flapping in the wind on a clothesline and the blackened carcass of a yellow school bus.

I headed back to the house. I was expecting the glass worker to arrive any minute to install the new window, then I wanted to drop in on Crazy on the way to pick up Ava. She was dragging me to Jump Up that night. I wasn't up for the crowds and street vendors, mocko jumbie dancers on stilts, or rum-fueled open houses at all the shops, but Ava had stressed the life or death nature of my presence, although she refused to tell me why.

I got to Crazy's just before the supper hour. The scrappy old man ignored my inquiries into his health, asking instead, "Where the boy and the mister?" through the left side of his mouth. He sounded stronger.

"Texas."

"So why you here, then?"

"It's a long story."

He chuptzed and said, "Red skies at morning," then shooed me with his left hand. "Lotta, I ready for my nap," he called.

As Lotta walked past me to put a pillow behind her husband's head, I whispered, "What did he mean about the red skies?"

She sniffed. "Red skies at morning, sailors take warning."

"Which means what?"

"He saying bad t'ings coming."

The things one doesn't learn growing up landlocked. I got back in my truck and put my face in my hands. I didn't want to see myself through Crazy's eyes. I didn't want to think about my mother giving up law school to raise my brother and me and telling everyone she met for the rest of her life she was the luckiest woman in the world. I wanted to think about the nights she cried because my father didn't come home from work. The times I heard her asking him why his job was more important than her. I didn't want to be my mother. I wanted to be the most important thing.

I pointed my truck toward Ava's. With each turn of the wheels, going with her seemed like a worse idea. We weren't even going to be performing. I pulled into her long driveway and rolled up to her house. I didn't even have time to put the truck in park before she had bounded out her door and across the grass.

She jumped in and said, "We late."

"Hello, Ava."

"We meeting Trevor at the Boardwalk before Jump Up. He said he have an offer for us."

I tried to care, I really did, but I couldn't. Nick had called us karaoke singers, and it still stung. Ava continued to tell me about Trevor and all he could do for us, but I tuned her out and concentrated on not thinking about Nick, which only made me think about him more. I wondered what he was doing, and if he was thinking about me, too. The next day was Derek's first visit with Taylor, and Nick had to be eaten up with worry. I was so lost in my reverie that I managed to make it all the way from Ava's through the excited throngs congregating in Town to the Boardwalk Bar without consciously interacting with her or taking any notice of the world outside my head.

Ava searched the bar for Trevor, who wasn't there. Surprise, surprise. I hadn't seen the man arrive anywhere yet when he said he would. I wasn't thirsty, but I armed myself with a sparkling water with cranberry and a lime. As soon as I turned away from the bar to rejoin Ava, Bart lurched into me. He grabbed my free arm as we collided. I held my bright drink high away from my blue linen shift. At least I wasn't wearing white.

"Katie, I was just coming to talk to you." He snuck under my raised arm and pulled my body to his in a tight hug, trapping my other arm against my side. I craned my head back to avoid his face and mouth and levered my elbow out with a sharp thrust to break his grip, then ducked out of his hold.

This wasn't the Bart I used to know. His eyes were bloodshot and he had lost a ton of weight. He had a seedy Don Johnson stubble going on, à la *Miami Vice*, and stringy hair. The only time I'd seen him like this while we were dating was when he was nursing the third day of a wicked hangover. It wasn't a healthy look then, and it sure wasn't now.

"Leave me alone, Bart," I said. I caught sight of Ava just fifteen feet away. She'd found Trevor and the flavor of the week and was deep in conversation. I started toward them.

"Stop," Bart said. "I need to tell you something."

"Can't it wait?" I said, closing my eyes. Nick was right. I should never have come back here without him. What was I thinking?

"I heard you left him." Bart reached a hand toward my face.

I blocked it. "Left him? You mean Nick? No, I didn't."

I stalked across the bar toward Ava. Her eyes widened at my glower and she clutched my arm hard and introduced me to a tall blonde who looked far too corn-fed for Trevor's taste. No leather or spandex, no stilettos, no slits up to there. Something about her seemed almost likeable, but it made me cringe at the same time.

Ava said, "Here she is. Katie, this is Trevor's friend Nancy. Nancy, Katie."

"Hello, Trevor. Nice to meet you, Nancy."

Nancy leaned toward me, her blue eyes eager. "You're the one Bart talks about?"

I closed my eyes and prayed for deliverance, then opened them and said, "It's possible."

She stepped closer and grabbed my arms. In a giddy voice, she said, "Bart is my brother!"

That could explain the cringe factor. I looked at Ava. Her mouth formed a perfect O.

Trevor said, "Nancy, why don't you let us talk business for a moment."

"I'll get us some fresh drinks," she said, and hurried off, quite the eager beaver.

Ava closed the gap left in the circle by Nancy's departure. "Trevor want us to come to his studio in New York and cut a demo."

Trevor sipped his drink, then said, "Your sound is unique. Great harmonies and the mixture of island and," he waved his drink at me, "not." Whatever that meant. "It would be better if you wrote your own songs, but I have a few I think you could do."

Nick writes music, I thought. Nick. Why did I feel like crying instead of cheering? I managed to say, "Wow, that's great."

Ava narrowed her eyes at me, but Trevor nodded, oblivious to my reaction.

"So we'll block a few days for you soon." To Ava he added, "I'll be in touch."

"Irie," Ava replied, which roughly translates to "everything is great" in proper English. Speak for yourself, I thought.

"Thank you," I added, but I was the odd man out, the one whose answer was irrelevant to the proceedings. I wanted to go home.

Nancy returned with a drink for Trevor, then turned back to me and in two steps had deftly separated me from the flock. I bumped into a chair behind me and realized I was trapped.

"So, you're dating my brother," she said, blasting me with a shot of rum breath.

"No. I'm married to Nick. I *used to* date your brother."

It took a moment to sink in. She brought her fist up to her mouth and pressed it against her lips. She shook her head. Her hand dropped. "Well, that changes things. My apologies. Can I ask you something?"

I tried to think of a polite way to say no, but she mistook my pause for a yes.

"Has Bart seemed OK to you? Like, I mean, oh, I don't know, has he acted normal?"

I was too late to hold in my guffaw. "Are you kidding me? He's completely different from the guy I met. Everything he's done in the last few months is strange. He needs a shower and a change of clothes, a haircut, a shave, a long nap, and possibly a trip to Betty Ford. His eyes are weird. He wrecked his car. He stole my phone. He shows up uninvited and stoned. I could go on. Is that enough?"

Nancy bit her fingernail and I saw that all her nails were quick-short and her cuticles red. "I thought so. He only got the trust money for his restaurant after he finished rehab at Promises last time, so I was worried this would happen again."

"Whoa, trust money? Rehab? I'm not in this loop."

She leaned so close our heads were almost touching. More fumes for me, goody. "Bart's always gotten by on his looks and charm, but when he got heavily into coke, my parents invoked a clause in our family trust that cut off his funds until he cleaned up." Almost as an aside she said, "Our grandparents were loaded." I nodded like I was in the know, but I was stunned. "He spent six weeks in rehab in Malibu. That's how he knows Trevor, because one of Trevor's musicians was there. That snake guy, Slither. As soon as Bart started getting checks again, he headed down here."

"Oh, my." I couldn't think of anything else to say.

She knocked back a slug of her drink. "Hey, here's my card. Call me if you need to, if, oh, I don't know, I just want someone down here to have it."

I took the card and stuck it in my handbag. "I will. Thanks."

"I love Bart to death, I really do. He's my big brother, what can I say? I came down a year ago, and it seemed like he really had it together. The restaurant was a huge success. Now I hear that people think someone was murdered at the restaurant. It's all gotten so seedy. He keeps telling me it's all still going great, but I don't believe him."

Her words were slurred, but the irony of her current state of intoxication while talking about her brother's addictions was lost on her.

"You shouldn't," I said. "Listen, Nancy, are you here with Trevor?"

Her eyes dulled with liquor and confusion. "I am. Sort of. Why?"

It was none of my business. She was a big girl. Trevor was about to possibly produce a record for Ava and me. Shut up, Katie, I thought.

"Just curious," I said. "But you should be careful in the islands. Being an outsider and all. Well, anyway, I have to run. Nice talking to you. Good luck with . . . everything."

She looked fragile suddenly, corruptible. She gulped from the glass in her hand. Rum punch of some sort, from the look of it. Painkiller, probably. And then something ugly and painful jolted me. I was looking at a vision of my old self. I wanted to tell her to run, but I had no idea where to send her to escape herself.

I needed more air than that dark, smoky bar could provide, even one open to the boardwalk on one whole side. Ava had decamped to parts unknown, but she would have to take care of herself. I all but sprinted out the door.

Chapter Thirty-four

I burst out of the Boardwalk Bar into the street, which was crowded with Jump Up revelers. I stepped off the curb and was swept into a torrent of humanity. I fought my way against the current, bumping into people, stepping on toes, apologizing to glaring faces. The stilt legs of a mocko jumbie dancer sliced by me and I looked up to see its masked face under a pointed hat staring down, judging me, finding me lacking.

Suddenly the crowd broke around two young men performing wildly, their legs sweeping, hands hitting the ground, their crazy dance much like the martial arts training of my childhood. I knew this dance. Capoeira. It was becoming something of a craze on island. The music from their boom box was fast and thumping and drowned out the crowd. I stood mesmerized for a few moments before the river pushed me onward.

The capoeira music faded and a thousand sounds competed for primacy in a dead heat.

"Cane, sweet sugar cane, get you sugar cane," a vendor yelled from beside a trailer loaded with a cane roller and a towering pile of sugar cane.

Sweaty bodies pressed into me, stole my air, robbed me of my line of sight. I panicked. This was a mob. I could die here without Nick even knowing where I was and how much I missed him. How sorry I was.

I broke free from the crowd and stumbled to my hands and knees on the grassy lawn of St. Ann's Catholic Church, beyond the reach of the melee and just inside the impenetrable darkness past the glow of the streetlight. I retched, but nothing came up. I couldn't remember if I'd eaten anything that day. I heard footsteps close by. A graveyard loomed between the church and me.

"You lost, miss?"

I gasped and scrambled to my feet to see a woman to my left, very close. She was tiny, barely five feet tall, and wrapped in layers of scarves. Her face peeked out, but in the dark I couldn't see it.

"Miss? I ask if you lost."

"I'm not sure."

"Come," she said, beckoning me, brusque and certain.

I followed, relieved to be told what to do. She led me down an alley toward a lighted side entrance to the building across from the church. The smell of overheated bodies was replaced with overripe garbage. She paused at the open door and light flickered through an orange beaded curtain.

"I help you find your way," she said, and pushed the beads aside just enough to slip her slight frame through them.

It crossed my mind for a split second that possibly this wasn't a good idea. I had just walked down a dark alley with a stranger to her mysterious lair. The woman weighed all of ninety-five pounds even with her scarves, though, and I *was* lost and I *did* need to find my way. No one else was offering to help. I'd just poke my head in, and if things didn't look kosher, I'd move along. And if I made the wrong call, well, I'd fought my way out of tighter spots before.

I parted the beads and entered. The room was low-ceilinged, or at least it felt that way with the billowing purple fabric tacked to the ceiling. The waves of purple continued down the walls and pooled at the chipped concrete floor. There were no other doors visible, although somehow it didn't feel closed off. I wondered if the fabric covered a door, or if it even covered walls at all or merely created the illusion of them. My tongue felt swollen and stuck to the roof of my mouth. I needed water, but something held me back from asking for it.

On a table in the center of the room were a pair of short, fat candles. Yellow wax pooled around their flames and spilled in slow waterfalls over their rims. They smelled of vanilla, patchouli, and coconut all at once, musky and sensual.

Really, what was Heather Connell's good Baptist daughter playing at here, anyway? I had taken leave of my sanity. I needed to make it through this politely and get out of there. I could get on my knees and ask God for forgiveness and answers at bedtime like my mama taught me.

"Sit," the woman said, her back still to me.

Or I could sit.

I looked at the thick wooden table, confused, then saw a stool tucked under it. I pulled it out and sat.

She turned and I saw her face for the first time. She was wizened like an orange left in the sun, its skin burnt and leathery. Her multicolored scarves obscured her hair like a nun's habit, but I imagined it wiry, sparse, and white. She pulled out her own stool and sat down across from me.

"I Tituba. I help them that lose their way."

"I'm Katie." And this is not *The Crucible*. Is it? I fought to stay on the right side of the line between reality and fantasy.

She reached across the table, her thin brown wrist exposed as the drape of gold fabric fell away. "Give me your hand."

I held out my hand as if to shake hers, and gasped when she grasped it. Her hands were sinewy and shockingly cold. She grunted and flipped my hand palm up with surprising strength and command, given that she was easily twice my age and half my size.

"Water hand," she said. She lifted eyes once brown but now hazy with the cataracts so prevalent in the people of the islands. "Things not always so easy for you."

I bit the edge of my bottom lip. Well, of course not. But were they for anyone? I started to ask what water hands meant, then caught myself.

Her frigid finger traced icy paths across my palm as she perused it, her lips parting and coming back together with little smacks and whistles of breath. I held mine, my heart thumping so loudly I was sure she could hear it.

"See this? This your heart line. You got a strong heart line."

"That's good, isn't it?"

She muttered as she continued to trace, but didn't answer. "You got a husband."

The wedding band was a dead giveaway. "Yes."

"And a baby."

"No." I started to change my answer, to explain about Taylor, but I didn't know how to explain it to myself, really, and by the time I found words, she had already moved on.

"You pregnant?"

"No."

She pursed her lips, puckering them like she was going to kiss a child. "Well, your heart line say you a nurturer."

I'd been called a lot of things in my time—the occupational hazard of being a female attorney—but never a nurturer. "What does that mean?"

"That you care for others. See how it curve up here toward your pointer finger?"

"It looks like a machete to me. Could it mean I'm a warrior?"

"No, child. It mean you take care of dem what need you."

Um, no I didn't. I'd never even wanted to, frightened by the trap of anti-quated notions of submission and gender roles. I made a D in home economics on purpose. I fought with my parents because I thought they treated Collin and me differently. I pursued a law degree, became an attorney, moved to the islands, and took on a major build-out by myself. Hell, I solved my own parents' murders and put their killer over the edge of a cliff. I took pride in my self-image: sharp angles and blunt force, not warm and nurturing.

So I answered her with great assurance. "Untrue. Even if it is true, it isn't—because I won't let it be. You need to do it again," I said.

"Your palm speak plain. But we read your cards and see what they say." She reached into a carpeted satchel at her feet and pulled out a deck of thick cards. They looked as old and worn as she was.

"I don't want to get into any kind of voodoo stuff," I said, but I knew those were funny words coming from the woman with the jumbie house.

She cackled, exposing more gums than teeth. "Wah, you think I'm gonna read your fortune in a vat of chicken blood?" She shuffled the cards, her gnarled fingers more deft than I expected. "Nah, these just tarot cards, play things of chirrun dem. We look at your past, present, and future, like a game."

She fanned the cards face down in front of me. Their backs looked like or-dinary blue and white playing cards, only they were bigger. I leaned in to get a closer look. The design was a repeating pattern of quarter moons.

"Pick three cards. Pull the first one forward with your fingers, put it on your left, then pull the next one by it, then the last one to the right. In a row, like."

I stared at the cards. This was a trap. I could feel the walls closing in around me, holding me in place while my mind screamed, "Lies and blasphemy! Run like the wind!" But instead of fleeing, I put my fingers on a card in the center of the deck and pulled it to my left like a zombie. I picked a card from the right and moved it to the center. I dragged a card from the left to my right. They were just cards. No biggie. But my pulse insisted otherwise.

The old woman pushed the other cards back in a pile and set them aside. She flipped over the card to my left. On its face was a very metrosexual angel standing sort of in or beside a stream and pouring liquid from one goblet to another. A two-fisted drinker.

"Your past," she said. "Temperance. Moderation something trouble you before, yes?"

Lack of moderation, more like it. The room was very quiet. Finally, I answered. "It's been a challenge of mine." But just because one card was right didn't mean anything. Lots of people struggle with balance and moderation. The odds were that the ancient crone could make any schmuck believe it fit. I wasn't going to be that schmuck.

"The present," she said, and she flipped the center card, revealing Adam and Eve as naked as the day God made them, with some sort of winged devil over their head. And of course the serpent and the fruit were behind Eve. Poor Eve never gets a break. What woman wants to be defined forevermore by her weakest moment?

"The Lovers," she continued. "Ah, I see."

"What do you see?"

"I see why you lost. You have a choice to make."

I felt the pull of the damn cards, their siren call. Yes. Lovers. A choice. Annalise's face, my own like a mirror, Nick's, Taylor's. That kind. I put my hands in my lap and they gripped each other fiercely, the fingers of my right hand closing over the blood-warmed gold band on my left.

She flipped the last card. "The future." She clucked. "The Empress."

The Empress?

I felt nauseous. The empress had become a joke between Nick and me. The butt-kicking empress of the St. Marcos rainforest, whose man worshipped her, as she well deserved. It had started with our crazy dreams at the same time, and—I made a strangled sound and choked back a sob—a palm reader who had called me an empress. I pinched my own hand, hard. Yes, I was still in the here and now. Or I was pinching myself in a dream.

I stared at the card. I studied its image. The empress sat in a throne in the middle of a field, a starred crown on her head, a scepter in one hand. She didn't look quite as ass-kicky as I would have wanted her to, but she wasn't bad.

Maybe there had been something to that dream, after all. The Empress. I could work with that.

"The empress mother, a creator, a nurturer," the seer announced. Then she smiled, and it was a smug one. "So, that your future, your path. At least it will be when you choose in the present. But you gotta let go of that anger and quit hiding what important."

I couldn't believe she'd sucked me into it. The Empress was the Nurturer? I rattled my last escape hatch. "I think you read them upside down."

"You know I didn't."

I stood up so fast my stool flipped over backwards. I grabbed the rest of the cards and the old woman didn't flinch. I ripped the top card off the deck and held it for her to see.

"Strength," she said.

"That would work."

"It not in your reading."

I pulled another.

"High Priestess."

"That's me."

She shook her head. "Not so, according to your cards."

I stood in that small room that was growing smaller by the second. When it started to spin, I knew it was time to go. "How much do I owe you?"

"No, child, you needed me. I cannot take your money."

"Thank you," I said automatically, because that's what I was raised to say. Inside was different. Thank you for messing with my head. Thank you for making me crazier than I already am. Thanks but no thanks, lady.

I took two sedate steps to the door, entered the dark world outside, and ran like the devil himself was on my heels. My blue shift rode up my thighs, my ballet flats slapped the pavement. The alley was longer than I remembered. I ran past a couple feeling each other up against a wall, the woman gasping but her eyes following me, the man groaning against her, oblivious. I ran past an old man on a pile of newspapers and gagged at his stench, then shuddered with guilt. I ran until I reached the safety of the thrashing crowd, and I threw myself into it headlong.

The crowd swept me along this time, and I bodysurfed through it. I needed to get home to Annalise. I needed Nick. I needed everything to be all right.

Chapter Thirty-five

I woke at noon the next day wearing the blue linen dress from the night before, lying atop my covers. Birds chirped. The sun shone. A soft breeze wafted through my southeastern windows. It was perfect, and it was awful. I missed Nick so much the floor of my heart was caving in and falling through the roof of my stomach. I texted him and told him so.

I changed into drawstring-waist navy gym shorts and a tank top and Oso and I trudged toward the gate to water the cursed new bougainvillea. On the horizon, the sky looked black. By the time we reached the gate, a stiff wind was blowing. I looked at my iPhone hoping to see Nick's name. I didn't. But I did see a message from Ava, who I'd found in the crowds and driven home the night before.

"Batten down the hatches, Empress," it read. "Big storm coming."

I stared at the fast-approaching darkness. She wasn't lying. "Oh, that's great." I said to Oso, who cocked his head and wagged his tail.

I shuffled back up to the sulking hulk of Annalise. When I'd first come back from Corpus Christi, I drove up the driveway in my big pickup and Annalise was sparkling. She'd radiated the energy of a child excited to see Daddy home from a business trip. Or maybe it was the sun in my eyes and the truck bouncing along the bumps, but whatever it was, the aura from Annalise was bright.

But quickly the mood in the house had fallen flat. When I pressed my face against her cool concrete walls and told her I was back to take care of her while Nick and Taylor were away, it grew quiet inside, the air heavy. I had yelled at her. "I'm the one you wanted, the one who saved you. What about me?" She had stayed in a funk ever since.

Now, I entered the somber house and checked the weather on my iPhone. Ava spoke true. Hurricane Ira was barreling toward St. Marcos and was expected to make landfall as a Category Four storm that very night. It was already nearly noon. "How could I have missed this?" I railed. But I knew the answer. I'd been in a self-absorbed stupor.

I checked the Saffir-Simpson storm rating system online and cringed. A Category Four meant sustained winds of 131–155 miles per hour, with wall and roof failures, signs blown down, and a high risk of damage from windblown debris. Alarm bells rang in my head.

I rifled through the stack of wedding cards and bills on the kitchen island for the hurricane checklist Nick and I made for his parents a few weeks before. I'd probably be without power and water for a few days, maybe even a few weeks, but we'd stocked the house and Rashidi had coached us on this. Time to set to it.

Lightning flashed outside. It smelled like gunpowder laced with the heavy scent of rain. It was preternaturally still for a moment, and then the heavens exploded downward.

If the cisterns weren't already full, the rain would soon top them off. I jammed on a rain hat and walked outside to check the diesel in the generator. The air was so heavy I almost needed to part it with my hands. The tank level read full. Good. I grabbed the clicker from my truck and walked to the end of the driveway to point it at the gate a football field away. I clicked it open so I could get out no matter what. Water was pouring off the sides of my hat. I shook it off and went back inside to verify my supply of candles and matches and fill the coolers with ice so the icemaker would make more.

Rashidi had stressed that the most important task was to protect the windows, because the only ones with hurricane glass were across the back of the great room and above the front door. So I jammed my rain hat back on and got out my ladders in the torrential downpour to survey the thirty-seven windows I'd have to barricade. I knew it would take several hours and require me to perch the ladder on the third-floor balconies to reach the highest windows.

"Son of a bitch!" I screamed. I needed my inner warrior, not my inner nurturer. I cursed the fortune-teller. Then I got to work. I decided to attack the highest, scariest windows first.

"You are not a human lightning rod," I lied aloud to myself. "You are grounded and safe." But doing this without Nick had left me anything but grounded. I was a literal and emotional lightning rod.

The wooden shutters were permanently attached to the house. When open, they latched to the outside wall. To close them, I had to climb up and unlatch the first side, then climb down and move the ladder, then climb back up and unlatch the other side, then climb down and move the ladder. Finally, I would climb back up and place a thick wooden beam in the slots on the outside of the closed shutters.

F-word. F-word, f-word, f-word. I swallowed the lump in my throat and put my foot on the first rung.

Over the next three hours, I climbed and re-climbed the slippery ladder steps, constantly wiping water from my eyes. More than once, I found myself facing a creature I didn't want to see: once a big centipede, another time a bat. I bit my lip and blinked back the tears. There would be time enough to cry later, and I promised myself one hell of a cry. I peered into the distance, hoping to see I don't know what, but the sky was too dark with clouds and rain to see anything farther than a few feet away. I felt more alone than I ever had in my life.

Finally, I dropped the beam across the last set of shutters on the ground floor. I shivered. The rain had soaked through me, and I was cold. As I walked back around to the garage, I remembered for the first time that there were no shutters on the music room's domed cathedral windows. And that there was still a big fat hole below one of them with exposed wiring. I stared at the windows and tried to process that. Finally I went into the garage and searched for extra shutters, although what I planned to do with them if I found any, I didn't know, because I had no clue how to install them.

I didn't find shutters, but I did find a piece of plywood. I ran to the laptop to get some information on how to use plywood to protect a window. There was no internet connection.

"Of course," I muttered.

I went and found my iPhone, which glared its bright red low-battery bar at me.

"Double crap," I said, and plugged it in. I started to go to the phone's internet browser and then noticed: no bars. No internet, no phone. I was by myself. I had hurried so fast to prepare Annalise that I hadn't let Nick know what was happening. The winds howled with me.

I looked for the biggest, toughest, thickest nails I could find and took them, a hammer, and the plywood outside to the window. I covered the windows and the hole below and sucked in the woody scent greedily, a smell I normally didn't like. I slammed the hammer against the nail heads with all my strength to get them through the plywood into the concrete. The complete darkness of a stormy night descended before I had finished. I had done the best I could, and I was out of time.

Through the blowing rain, headlights swept across my driveway and came at me up the drive. It was a really big SUV with dark windows. I shielded my eyes from the rain with my tented hand and tried to look strong and confident. Had opportunistic thugs already started preying on the helpless while the storm had barely started heating up?

Jacoby jumped out of the car, which he left running. Giddy relief surged through me. Not a thug! He leaned into the wind and made his way over to me, raising his deep voice over the gale. "I passing by from the West End station on the way back east to check out a tip on some funny business at Fortuna's."

"In this weather?" I yelled.

"Yah mon. The chief retiring soon, and Assistant Chief Tutein taking his place. I want to close a case up good for the old man." He sounded like he didn't want to do this. "You gonna be all right, Katie?"

I threw my arms around his solid body and he let me hug him. "Oh, Jacoby, I'm so glad to see a friendly face."

He leaned back and peered down at me like I'd said I lived on Saturn and ate breakfast at midnight wearing silk taffeta. "Nobody ever accuse me of that before," he said.

I let him go and laughed. "I'm going to be OK, but if you'd asked me an hour ago, I might have given you a different answer." I looked at his car, expecting to see his partner watching him in abject worship. "Where's Morris?"

"He got a wife and kids. Taking care of family dem."

Jacoby only had his grandmother. His brother Michael had drowned a year before. I nodded.

He started to walk away, then stopped and turned back to me. "Remember you ask me to look into the holes in your walls?"

"Yes." I held my wet hair back from my face with both hands.

"What I hear, the man that build your house die in prison. Before he die, he tell his cellmate that he put his treasures in the walls of Annalise. When he get free, the cellmate reach back to St. Marcos and he carry the story with him."

"You're kidding."

"Nope. For true." He grinned. "Seem Junior telling that story, anyway."

I wiped water from my face. "Now I just have to figure out how to make it stop."

"Good luck with that." He walked to my plywood shutter on the front corner of the house. He shook it and nodded, then stepped back, almost bumping into the flamboyant tree. Water coursed around its base, digging trenches through the now-exposed roots. "This rain too much." He chuptzed and shook his head. "Take care of yourself."

"You too. Thanks for coming by."

The black SUV drove off into the night.

It continued to rain for the next few hours, and then the wind showed me that it was playing to win, that its strength before was a mere warm-up. I gathered up the three flashlights I could find, checked their batteries, and stashed them carefully: one on the kitchen island, one in the great room, and one on my bedside table.

The power was still on, so although I didn't have internet, I had light. I sat on the great room sofa and wrote a letter to Nick the old-fashioned way, on a legal pad half-filled with notes I had made during the construction of Annalise. Just as I finished writing, a picture of Nick, Taylor, and me toppled over and crashed to the tile floor from the sturdy wooden coffee table. The ceramic frame and the glass shattered.

I held my breath and tested my senses. Not a single puff of wind was moving in the room. No tremors were shaking the house. Annalise stood silent and still.

But I sensed the presence of something else, of some*one* else. That part of me that connected to Nick, the part that had been disconnected for the last few days, responded as if he were there in the room. I could feel him.

"I am right here, my love," I whispered.

I folded my letter in thirds and stuck it in an envelope to address later. Off went the lights, and my heart lurched into my throat. The wind howled like a fiend. The clock on my laptop screen read straight-up midnight, the witching hour.

This is when the power has to go out?

The lights flickered back on as the generator powered up. I knew wind plus burning fuel is a dangerous mix. I needed to go outside and switch the automatic generator off, but when I opened the side door, the wind hit me with the force of a train, knocking me back into the house. I leaned forward, ready for it this time, and pushed my way out the door. The rain and wind pounded me and I started to shiver. It felt as if every light in the world had burned out.

Shit, I thought. I'd forgotten the flashlight. I thought about going back for it, but decided not to give up the ground I'd gained so far. Besides, I didn't really think it would do much good in that endless dark. I pressed on, dragging my hand along the house to stay oriented.

I walked up the driveway to the end of the house. I knew the generator was three feet directly in front of me, but I couldn't see it, and I couldn't hear it above the roar of the wind and rain. I took two giant steps forward into mud and ran into it. I felt along the upper front panel until I felt the lid to the control box. I put my face down to it until I could make out the lighted kill switch, then opened the cover and pressed the button.

I turned around and pressed the back of my legs against the generator. I moved a half step to my right then leaned forward and took two giant steps back to the house with my arms stretched out in front of me. There was nothing there. Panic flickered up hot from my center.

"Easy," I said out loud. "Annalise didn't blow away." Yet.

I took another side step, forward and to the right. My foot hit the house and as fast as I could, I walked hand over hand back to the metal door to the mudroom. I pulled it open and the wind flung it against the house. I stepped around the door and threw my weight into it, leaning and dragging it with me as I backed into the house until the door clicked shut.

The immediate break from the wind and noise was deafening. I could hear my teeth chattering as I threw the lock and crossed out of the mudroom. I closed that door behind me, too. I knew I would not leave the house again until the storm passed, whenever that was.

I walked carefully in the dark back into the great room from memory, toward the glow of my laptop. I lit the candelabra by its meager illumination and then shut the computer off to conserve the battery.

The wind screamed and the house creaked and groaned. Annalise had thick, strong walls, but what about the roof? What would I do if the wind found a weak spot in a corner and peeled it off like the pop-top of an old-fashioned Red Stripe can? What if I hadn't latched the shutters properly? I cut myself short. I had done all I could.

All around the island, I knew, people were mixing Hurricanes and riding out the storm. I had no doubt at that moment that if I had passion fruit juice, grenadine, and rum, it would all be over except for the hangover.

I picked up the candelabra and gravitated toward my grandmother's piano in the music room. The candlelight shone perfection against the aqua walls and bounced off the polished wood of the old upright piano. It was practically the only piece of furniture I'd moved from the states to St. Marcos, and I loved my memories of singing Christmas carols between my mom and her mother on the wooden bench. I turned toward the bookshelf and held the candles close to read the titles of my books of sheet music.

Thinking of my family led my thoughts to Nick and Taylor. A deep sadness started in my heart and slowly seeped all the way down to my toes. As I pulled down a book of famous tunes from musicals, a yellow sticky floated to the ground. I retrieved it and read the words, "Smile. You sing like an angel." I placed a hand on my heat-flooded cheek and knew that Nick was there with me.

The book opened as if of its own accord to "That's All I Ask of You." I had never played it, but I remembered seeing Julie's sheet music at the Kovacs' house. I heard the song in my head, the haunting melody building into an emotional crescendo. I set the book on the music stand and picked out the notes. Maybe they could take me back to Texas, to Port Aransas, to my family.

Slowly, I began to play the song recognizably as the winds rose around me. After half an hour, my back ached. My fingers were out of shape, and the underused ring and pinky fingers grew tired, but I didn't stop. I finally reached the point where my fingers were confident enough to allow my voice to join them. It cracked on the first words, so filled with longing, so fitting to this moment. I sang at the top of my lungs and played as loud as I could, and Oso joined me, cocking his head. Kitty, who almost never graced me with her presence and was only inside because of the storm, wandered into the room. Caught up in the music, I felt strangely at peace.

Then—wham!

I jerked my hands back, knocking my knees into the piano and the book off the stand. The candelabra wobbled. Oso jumped up and barked.

Wham!

Kitty ran out of the room to her hiding place under Taylor's bed.

Wham!

Wham!

Wham!

I ran into the kitchen in the dark. The noise had come from the hallway to the garage. I stepped closer and saw the mudroom door slamming repeatedly. What in the world would cause an interior door to come open? Oso crept in front of me, then stopped halfway between me and the mudroom, growling. I snatched my flashlight from the kitchen island and switched it on.

Wham!

Wham!

I had locked the outside dogs in the garage, and they were silent. So it wasn't as if it were something human or *alive* thumping the door. I told myself I had no reason to be afraid.

But rounding the corner into the hallway, my beam struck the whites of someone's eyes. I screamed and stopped within inches of my beautiful friend Annalise, her pupils stark against their whites and her black face almost hidden by the darkness. She didn't shy away from the glaring light, just nodded at me and stepped out of my way. I put my hand to my throat and faced the errant door, grasped its knob, and pulled it shut. When I turned to thank her, she was not there. While I was wondering if I'd just imagined her, I heard another noise, and that one terrified me.

It was the sound of wood cracking and a window shattering as if it were being pounded with a battering ram. The roar of the storm leapt through the window after it. Oso yelped and ran to the master bedroom and I wanted to follow him, but that was not a choice I could make.

Again, I made the long journey across the kitchen, following the flashlight's illumination back into the music room, which really wasn't much of a music room anymore. The plywood had disappeared. The lovely windows were strewn in tiny fragments across the floor. The giant, smooth tree trunk and wind-stripped branches of the flamboyant outside the window were now resting on the vestiges of my grandmother's piano. The book of sheet music lay soaked under the rubble. The candelabra topped the pile, its flames snuffed out.

The wind howled and buffeted me back, and the rain came from a thousand directions at once, like a tiny spin-off of the hurricane itself. I slid the bookshelf across the tile into the hallway, shut the door, and pushed the shelf against it. The storm had demolished the room and destroyed my piano, but it hadn't touched me.

"Thank you, Annalise," I whispered.

I lit more candles and walked with them to my room, then set them on the nightstand and crawled into bed. I pulled the covers up to my chin and let the candles burn down to nubs as I stared at the walls. The wind screamed and the rain pounded while I made plans to find my way back home to Nick.

Chapter Thirty-six

I lay in bed the next morning, my hot, sweaty body sticking to the sheets, and listened. The wind and rain were still beating mercilessly on the metal roof, although they sounded less pissed off. I stuffed my feet into a pair of Keds and padded into the great room. A meager light penetrated the hurricane-glass windows above the entryway and across the back of the house. Definitely an improvement.

By noon, the rain had stopped and the wind had calmed enough for me to go outside and survey the damage. The sky was an eerie green. The air felt thick with damp and the wind was barely beating down the quickly rising temperature, but it had stripped the land to sticks and dirt. Nothing green remained tethered to the earth as far as my eyes could see. I'd lost a few trees in addition to the flamboyant.

I walked around to the back of the house, my shoes making schlop schlop noises in the sticky, saturated ground. No exterior damage. Water was running across the patio, though, from the house. I looked up, expecting to see a waterfall of rainwater from a damaged catchment, but I didn't. The water was coming through broken panes in the basement's back doors.

I traversed the small river up to the doors and tried to open them, but they were locked. I pressed my nose to the glass to get a better view. There were ten inches of standing water in the downstairs living room. Had the Titanic struck an iceberg?

I ran back around to the open side door and grabbed my flashlight from the kitchen island. The basement had windows only on the west side, so it stayed dark down there. I stood at the top of the steps. I didn't want to go down there. The whole thing felt too much like my time in the cisterns. But finally I crept down the stairs from the main floor to the lower level and shone the flashlight around.

What I saw was mind-blowing. I had myself an indoor swimming pool. All I needed was a beach towel and a floatie, and I could have a grand time without ever going outside. Taylor's orange dump truck was floating lazily in the otherwise empty living room, but I thought of the brand-new mahogany bed in the room next to it and groaned.

"Shit!" I yelled. "Shit, shit, shit."

My voice echoed inside the water chamber. I took off my shoes and sloshed through the water to the back of the room. Had my water heater tank burst? I pried open the little closet under the stairs, but water seemed to flow into it, not out. Closing the door was much easier.

I worked the beam around the top of each wall. Maybe a catchment was dumping water into a wall from a roof leak. But I saw nothing coming from up high.

I moved the light down the walls, and when I saw it, I felt like a dolt. Of course. The water was gushing through the ruined patchwork over one of the many holes left by the treasure seekers. On the other side of this wall was the empty cistern I almost fell into. It took me another few beats to realize that the only reason it was leaking now was because Crazy's men had fixed the catchment. Once the cistern had filled, well, the result was obvious, and very wet.

It was a fixable problem to save for later. I splashed out of the basement. The only thing I could do about it now was isolate the power. I went to the breaker box in the garage and turned off the switches for the music room and the downstairs. Then I went outside to flip the generator on and listened to it fire up like an eighteen-wheeler. It smelled like one, too. I would run it just long enough to charge my laptop and iPhone and cool the refrigerator to make more ice and keep the freezer cold.

In the kitchen, I checked my devices. The iPhone still had no service. I switched on my computer and didn't have connectivity there, either. I decided to drive out and see if I could call Nick from the grocery store, but when I went out to the driveway, I found the road blocked by fallen trees in both directions outside my gate.

This was not good.

I walked back to the house to clear away debris and decided to try to patch my busted music room. I lugged out the chainsaw and tried in vain to operate it. It was like my inner warrior had given way to the empress. Either that or I just wasn't Paul Bunyan. I put it away before I hurt myself.

iPhone check: no service.

As awful as the night before had been, the weather that day brought even more misery. The sun broke through the clouds like it was trying to make up for lost time. Humidity stifled the air and a wind vacuum followed in the wake of the storm. The dogs had given up on finding cool spots on the tile patio and were lying in the dirt.

iPhone check: no service.

I used the rest of the day to open all the shutters. That, at least, I knew I could do. I needed air and light in my house. It took me far less time without the rain, but I finished the job with a wicked sunburn.

iPhone check: no service.

Dusk fell. Robotically, I fed the animals and myself. I remembered to eat only perishable food, a sort of post-hurricane food triage: thou shalt eat first the things that spoil fastest. Some last-week vintage lunchmeat already looked iffy.

"Here guys, treats!" I called to the dogs.

iPhone check: no service.

Time for a treat for me. I ran the generator so I could take a bath in my beloved tub. I filled it with bubbles and turned on the jets, and while the water ran, I straightened up the bathroom. I placed my hand on the bottle of Nick's stupid girly moisturizer that I had given him as a wedding present and my heart lurched.

When I settled in the bath, the water was too hot and the smell of the bubbles was cloying. Or maybe it was just time for that good cry. So I sobbed. Hysterically. Physically. Nose-blowing sobs. For as long as I could, plus a little.

Then I checked my iPhone and there was still no freaking service. It could go on like this for days. Weeks.

Sleeping would pass the time. I went out and turned off the generator, then came back in and stretched out on my bed, but sleep wouldn't take me. Hours later, in desperation, I found a bottle of Tylenol PM and popped two. I doused myself with mosquito spray and dropped the netting that up until then had just been for looks.

When I woke up again, it was late afternoon. I checked my watch. I had slept for eighteen hours. The open bottle of Tylenol PM glared accusingly from the bedside table and I had a vague memory of half-waking that morning and re-dosing. Foolish, I thought. Depressants are not my friend. I twisted my gold band around and around, trying to regain the use of my brain. I shoved my frizzy hair into a scrunchie from my nightstand, doubling it through until it had restrained my entire ponytail against my head. I checked for cell service and found that my iPhone was dead.

Crap!

I jumped out of bed and ran to plug it in. No power! I ran outside and threw on the generator switch, then sprinted back to the bedroom and stared at the phone until it gained enough juice to look for a signal.

No service.

Well, it was five o'clock, and it occurred to me that I needed to feed the poor dogs. I walked out to the garage and filled their bowls, then took them out to the driveway. A clopping sound made me look up. A horse and rider were approaching on my entrance road. Or I thought they were.

"That's what overdosing on Tylenol PM can do to you," I told myself. "Oso, what do you think, am I hallucinating?" He swept the ground with his tail. I looked back up, and I still saw a horse and rider. A big paint horse and a blond-haired man astride it.

Oh, no. Oh, please not that blond man.

Bart reined the horse to a stop by the downed flamboyant at the front corner of the house. He was listing to one side in his saddle and his eyes had that not-altogether-there look.

"What in the world are you doing?"

"I couldn't get through with my car, so I borrowed a horse," he said. Like it was completely normal for him to ride like a stoned Mad Max to visit me by horseback.

Objection; nonresponsive, I thought. God, I was delirious. "You shouldn't have come."

Bart ignored me. He swung out of the saddle and lowered himself to an unsteady but upright position. "Maybe I could help you."

"I don't need any help."

It was so wrong for him to be there. Had I been in the states and Nick on St. Marcos, I would have wanted Nick to send a helpful female interloper packing, times ten thousand if she were someone like Bart.

As if he read my mind, Bart said, "Your husband shouldn't have left you here all alone."

"That's none of your business."

"Well, I wouldn't have." He dug in a saddlebag. "I brought you something." He held out a cylindrical bottle of light Cruzan Rum.

My eyes burned and my mouth watered. I knew how much faster the days would pass in a blur of Painkillers. I had quit once before. I could quit again. If I just stretched my arm out toward him and grasped my fingers around the cool comfort of that bottle, peace would be mine.

Then I shuddered, and stared Bart down like Beelzebub.

"Get that away from me, and leave." I stomped through the garage into the kitchen, slamming the door behind me.

I pulled sandwich ingredients from the cooler and threw them out on the counter. Drawers banged and silverware rattled as I gathered up a spoon and table knife. I heard the side door open.

"I said LEAVE, not come in, Bart." I grabbed a butcher knife out of the block on the counter and waited for him to come in. But it looked too menacing in my hands. Besides, Bart was a wacked-up idiot, but he wasn't dangerous. I set it down.

Bart came into the kitchen, his face a storm. "What's wrong with you, Katie? I forgive you. I'm here for you. I'm ready to give you another chance." He was walking toward me, all six feet of him.

I really didn't have a choice. I grabbed the knife and thrust it between us. "Stop, Bart. You aren't welcome here. Leave now."

His eyes narrowed and he held up his hands, but he didn't stop. "Whoa, I'm not going to hurt you."

But suddenly I wasn't so sure. This was probably exactly the type of behavior his sister wanted me to report back to her, but there would be time for that later. I backed up to give myself room and I flexed my knees. I'd do better without the knife. But before I could make up my mind, the mayonnaise jar flew across the counter and shattered at Bart's feet. I didn't see it coming.

Bart jumped. "What was that?"

My voice gained strength from knowing I had supernatural backup. "Annalise isn't going to let you near me, so just leave."

And then another voice broke into our exchange. "And if the house doesn't kick your ass, I will."

My knife clattered to the floor.

Chapter Thirty-seven

It was my husband: sweaty, dirty, and holding seriously wilted flowers. Somehow, he was standing in our kitchen glaring at my ex-boyfriend when he was supposed to be two thousand miles away.

"Nick!" I screamed.

Nick was radiating fury. "Get away from her."

"What are you going to do, hit me?" Bart asked.

Yes, I thought, that's exactly what he is going to do. A thrill ran through me and I felt a flicker of guilt, but I didn't stop Nick. Bart more than had it coming.

Nick walked calmly across the kitchen. Without setting down the flowers in his left hand, he punched Bart in the face, his fist fast as a whip. "Yes," he said as Bart hit the floor.

Bart rolled onto his side. "Asshole," he said. He wiped blood from under his nose and looked down.

Nick's tone was menacingly calm. "I barely hit you. But if you want, I can try again."

"I'm going," Bart said. He looked from Nick to the broken mayo jar to me. His eyes were red-rimmed and slitted. He scrambled to his feet and walked rapidly toward the front entrance to the kitchen, breaking into a run and almost falling. He caught himself on the door, threw it open, and bolted out.

Nick walked after him as far as the doorway. "You'd better run," Nick called. "And if you ever come back, I promise, I'll kill you." He turned back toward me, looking like he meant it. "I may hunt him down and do it anyway."

I ran over the broken mayonnaisey glass and leapt into Nick's arms. I wrapped my legs around his waist and crossed my heavy work boots behind his back and started talking so fast that nothing I said made any sense. He kissed me all over my head, face, and ears while he stroked my Little Orphan Annie hair.

Within a few moments my babbling turned to tears and I let him rock me gently back and forth, the flowers tickling the back of my neck now.

"You did it again, you know," I said.

"What did I do, love?"

"You showed up on St. Marcos with no warning. This is the third time."
Hiccup.

"I'll quit if you want me to."

"Never."

"The way you're crying, you'd think this had been a Category Five storm.
Shoot, Katie, they say the sustained wind speed here never made it over a
hundred and forty-five miles per hour." He nuzzled me roughly against the side
of my head.

"Baby, it may have only been a Category Four hurricane, but it's definitely
been a Category Five month."

"Tell me about it."

"Oh, I'm going to, believe me, after I tell you what a terrible person I am,
and how sorry I am for leaving you in Corpus Christi."

"Shhhhh, don't be sorry. I'm sorry."

"No, we should be together, Nick. Nothing in the world is more important
to me than being with you."

He hugged me tight and set me on the counter but I kept my arms and legs
around him as he set the flowers down behind me. He said, "All I could think
about when I saw that storm was that I was a jackass, and I needed to get here
as fast as I could. But Mom and Dad had driven to San Antonio to the opera,
so I called Emily—"

"You called Emily? She's in Dallas!"

"I called Emily and she said if I could get Taylor to Dallas she would keep
him for the weekend."

"But you have a court order to keep him within a hundred miles of Corpus
Christi!"

"Are you going to let me tell this story or not?" Nick retorted, but he
smiled.

I made a zipping gesture over my lips and flapped my hand for him to con-
tinue.

"When I told her about the court order she said she'd be on the next plane
to Corpus. I made it to Puerto Rico, but not before they shut down the St.
Marcos airport."

"I could feel you getting closer!" I told him about the crashing picture frame.

He nodded. "I'm not surprised that you can feel me. I didn't know I could throw pictures off tables, though. I'm pretty awesome."

I socked his arm. "It was strangely comforting. But go on, tell your story."

He kissed me hard on the lips. "I searched for a helicopter pilot or a boat captain who could take me across, but I got nada. I decided to go down to a marina and look for a boat to charter. The first marina I tried, I went into the bar and started asking around. This guy turns around and says 'Nick Kovacs? Is that you?'"

"Oh my God! You're kidding!"

"I'm not. It was one of my surfing buddies from high school, Bill Thomas. He's even crazier now than he was then, and I tell him what I am trying to do, and he says no problem. He's the captain on the fishing boat of a dot-com millionaire who hightailed it to the states when the weather got bad."

I shook my head, and kept my mouth shut only by intense effort.

"I ran to buy you some flowers—which is a story in and of itself, finding flowers on the morning after a hurricane—and headed to bunk down on the boat. Meanwhile, Bill keeps drinking all day. About three in the morning, he wakes me up and says it's time to go."

"You left in the middle of the night on an ocean with hurricane-sized waves? Are you nuts?"

"I haven't gotten to that part yet."

He grinned like an upside-down rainbow. "We get out of the marina, and he's running without lights, because the Coast Guard isn't allowing boat travel yet. He keeps drinking; I get seasick. He's singing at the top of his lungs, and I am heaving up and down with the boat over the eight-foot waves, wondering if I have died and gone to hell. Twelve hours later, we tie up to the pier on the west end of St. Marcos. I don't have any food or liquid left in my body, but he's fit as a fiddle. I hop off the boat and look back to wave goodbye, and that's when I see the name of the boat for the first time."

He paused.

"And the name of the boat was?" I asked.

"The name of the boat was *My Wild Irish Kate*."

"No, it wasn't."

"Yes, it was. The boat's name was Kate."

We stared at each other, feeling it, the unexplainable power of our connection. You couldn't stop what was simply meant to be. I put my face on his chest and leaned into him. He looped his arms around the small of my back and finished his story.

"So it took me three hours to hike up to your place. The forest is naked, no vines, no bush. Animals are wandering around, all the fences are down. And when I got here, you had company," at this he kissed my nose, "but here you are, you and Annalise, and you did great."

I dropped my ear to his heart, speaking rapidly in time to its comforting beat. "Oh, Nick, I didn't do great. I was so scared, and a tree fell and bashed in the window where there were no shutters except I tried to put up plywood, and Annalise saved me by slamming the door, and I've been asleep for nearly two days, not to mention the voodoo palm reader telling me I'm the Empress, and all I could think about was that I was trapped here and I couldn't get to you, couldn't let you know I was alive, and that nothing was real anymore without you here."

Nick looked at me as if everything I had said made perfect sense. "I'm here now. Where's that smile?"

I gave him one, a real one, an "I'm so happy my husband is here" smile. He picked me up and carried me into our bedroom, and we spent the next few hours under the mosquito netting, finding the rest of the way back to each other.

We woke the next day to Queen's "Under Pressure."

I sat up in a panic. "What's that?"

"My new ring tone."

Apparently, cell service had been restored. Nick answered. It was his attorney, Mary, calling to let him know the court had issued some instructions. He put her on speakerphone. The news was not great.

"Judge Nichols has given Derek a six-month period to prove his fitness as a parent if he passes the paternity test."

"What do we do now?" Nick asked.

"You sit tight in Corpus Christi," Mary answered. Which was hard to do from St. Marcos, but I decided not to cloud the issue. "Any reason to doubt he'll pass the test?"

"Unfortunately, no," Nick said.

"Then expect to be in Corpus at least another six months, maybe longer. The court can decide to extend the evaluation period. It's even possible that at the end of the evaluation, you could win custody but Derek would have continued visitation."

"That's not even what he wants!" Nick exclaimed.

"Maybe for the right amount, Derek would give up his rights as a father permanently," Mary suggested.

Nick and I stared into each other's eyes. I said, "I'd hate to spend the money Teresa left for Taylor's future that way. The best thing for Taylor is for us to keep Derek from getting custody of him. But I think we'd spend far less money in six months than it would take now to make him go away."

Nick nodded. "The risk is worth it."

Mary said, "It's your call. There is a value, though, to avoiding the negative impact this will have on your life."

Man, she had that part right. But that was the impact on us, two grown-ups. We had to think about Taylor. I had to start thinking about Taylor.

I sucked in my bottom lip, then said, "We're OK, Mary."

We thanked her and said our goodbyes. Nick hung up the phone and gripped both of my hands. "Six months, Katie. That's a long time. If you need to stay here, we'll make it work."

I flicked my hair behind my shoulder. "Nick Kovacs, do you want me to be your wife or not?"

He frowned. "I thought you already were."

"Well, wives and husbands should live together." I took full credit for my change of heart and left out the "according to my new friend the psychic" part. "Let's get the hell out of here. I'll find a house sitter, and we'll put Annalise on the market."

Nick shook his head. "You don't need to sell her."

Truthfully, the thought of parting with Annalise made me feel sick, and I wasn't sure how much of that feeling was coming from me and how much from the jumbie. But I also wasn't a halfway kind of girl. Or woman. "We don't really know if we are ever going to be able to—or want to—come back. It could take a long time to find the right buyer. Let's plan for the worst and hope for the best."

Now Nick made my arguments from a week ago back to me. "But it's your house . . . it's more than that, it's *her* . . . and you worked so hard . . . you gave up your career . . . you moved halfway around the world . . . you spent so much of your *money* . . ."

I stuck my face up to his, almost nose to very prominent nose. "You are home to me. Annalise is a house, and money is only money."

His smile was as wide as the Gulf Coast, crooked and sure. "I love you." He pulled me into his lap in one swift motion.

I tried to ignore the sensation of dark, unhappy eyes watching us.

Chapter Thirty-eight

Despite our dramatic decision to depart, we didn't get anywhere in a hurry. Things started smoothly enough, though. We tackled the little issue of the tree in the music room early the next morning.

Nick operated the chainsaw and I removed the chunks. As we uncovered the window opening, I saw that the wind and tree had wrenched the window frame out. The exposed concrete blocks under the frame had crumbled.

"This is odd," I said when Nick turned off the saw. "I thought the whole house was made out of cinder block filled with poured concrete. These blocks aren't filled, here by the window." I pointed to pieces of pulverized block on the floor.

Nick looked down inside the block wall with me. "Sure enough."

I pushed on the edge of a block and it crumbled under my hand. Something glinted in the sunlight. "What's that?"

Nick had seen it, too. He took a closer look. "Rebar, maybe?"

"Too shiny." I stuck my hand into the opening, then thought better of it. Centipedes and all, ew. I went into the great room and retrieved the fireplace poker. I hadn't used it for a fire yet, but it seemed perfect for sticking down narrow dark holes. I inserted it and heard an intriguing clink.

"Not concrete, anyway," I said, and continued probing. I felt something loose, so I used the claw side of the poker and pried the edge of it up, then carefully dragged it out of the hole after a few false starts. A dirty round object tumbled over the top of the block and landed on the tile floor. I scooped it up in my hand. It was narrow, metallic, and seriously scratched up.

"I'm going to clean it," I told Nick.

He followed me into the kitchen, where I moistened a kitchen towel and scrubbed at the concrete dust and dirt. As the layers of yuck came off, I saw gold, a latch, and engraving. It was a pocket watch, and despite the grit and grime, it was newer than I would have guessed. Definitely not an antique. I couldn't get the latch to release, though.

"Let me try," Nick said.

I handed it to him, and he cleaned the concrete out of the cracks with the tip of a steak knife, then pried the two round sides away from each other. It opened slowly, a clamshell hiding its pearl.

Inside on the right was an exquisite clock face with roman numerals marking the 12, 3, 6, and 9. The time read 11:29, and the second hand was frozen in place. On the left was a picture. A remarkably well preserved picture, given that it had been buried inside a wall for ten years. A dark-skinned woman with straightened hair was posed for a studio portrait with two young girls wearing cornrow braids. One girl looked maybe ten, and the other five.

A slow smile stole up the corners of my mouth. "Nick, you are holding 'my treasures' in your hand."

"Meaning?" he asked, scraping more gunk out of the ridges and valleys of the pocket watch.

"Jacoby told me there was a rumor going around that the original owner buried his treasures in the walls of this house. He thinks we've been the victims of fortune hunters. But I don't think it was that kind of treasure at all." I took the watch from his hand and snapped it shut, and I rubbed my thumb across the engraved words on its front. My Treasures. I opened it to the picture.

He joined me now in the smile. "Somehow we need to get that word out on the criminal grapevine ASAP."

"Yah mon."

"It's a good-looking watch." He handed it to me.

"That it is. And just think, the fortune hunters were only one cinder block away from finding it on their last attempt. I'll be back in a moment." I went to my jewelry box in our bedroom and pulled out a jeweler case that held a brooch my Grandma Connell had given me. I nestled the watch in the satin lining beside the brooch and snapped the lid shut.

I rejoined Nick, and we finished up our work in the music room and set upon our next Herculean task: chainsawing our way out of the rainforest. It took the rest of a full and sweaty day. It wasn't an experience I would care to repeat, but we felt able to leap tall buildings in a single bound by the time we were through.

Afterwards, we drove to Ava's, passing plenty of houses that didn't have roofs anymore. A telephone pole had fallen through the roof of a house only a mile away from Ava's. Those that had roofs sometimes didn't have windows. Still others had lost trees. And everywhere, everywhere the brilliant colors of plant life had disappeared, as if the island had been scorched down to the bare brown earth.

When we arrived at Ava's, we found her grilling all the meat from her refrigerator and drinking piña coladas from a pitcher. "Everything spoil unless I use it up now," she explained. "I just got back from the funeral, and I need something to take my mind off things." She shook her small caramel fist at the innocent-looking night sky that was clear and twinkling with a million stars.

"Funeral? Whose?" I asked. She did look like she'd been crying.

"Oh, cheese and bread, you didn't know! That why you not there."

Foreboding crept over me. "What happened, Ava?"

Tears flooded her face, and she shook her head. She swallowed and said, "Jacoby. He die in the storm."

"That can't be! I saw him. He came by a few hours before it hit."

"They find his body by his car, outside the projects, where an apartment collapse. His door open, he lights dem on. Just like him, always helping people dem."

"But how did he die?"

She lifted her shoulders and let them drop. "It a hurricane. They say something knock him in the head."

"Oh Ava, I am so sorry. And so sad that I missed his service." I dropped into a lawn chair. Nick put his hands on my shoulders and kneaded them gently. "But why so quick?"

"That what his grandmother want. She the one who raise him and his brother. Now they both dead," she said. She slumped into a chair beside me.

The danger of the storm seemed more real to me now than it had since it hit Annalise. I began to worry about the rest of the people I loved on the island. At least Rashidi was on the western edge of Puerto Rico, out of the storm's path.

Finally, I braved the subject of our visit. "We're headed back to Texas. With Rashidi gone, I have to ask if you could house-sit for a while, take care of the hounds, and let the workers in and out?"

Nick added, "We'll pay you."

Ava tipped her wrist forward to signify that it was a small thing we asked. She started replaiting her long braids, then said, "Of course I help you. But Annalise not likely to make it easy on you."

I chose to ignore that. "Thanks, Ava," I said.

"Who look after things when I meet you in New York?"

"New York?" Nick asked.

"Um, I'll tell you about it on the drive, honey. Ava, we'll play that by ear." I didn't have the heart to break it to her. I wouldn't be going to New York. I'd tell her later.

Nick and I pulled to a stop outside the house Jacoby grew up in. I hoped we weren't coming over too late. Lights shone from inside the house, though, which was good, because this couldn't wait. Although I had only met his grandmother once, I knew I owed her a visit.

Her house was in the same neighborhood where Rashidi and I had spied on Junior and Pumpy. In the dark I couldn't tell how her house had withstood the storm. There was no doorbell, so I rapped my knuckles against the frame of the screen door.

"Ms. Jacoby?" I called.

In only seconds, a tiny woman came to the door. "Ain't no Ms. Jacoby here. I Ms. Edmonds. You wanting me, I expect."

She looked as I remembered her, and not unlike an unscarved version of my Jump Up psychic. She had on a Sunday go-to-church-type outfit, a black gabardine jacket and matching shirt with big brass buttons. Her posture was erect, but with a slight tremor.

"I'm Katie Kovacs, and this is my husband Nick. I knew Jacoby, ma'am, and I came to pay my respects."

"Nice to meet you, Ms. Edmonds," Nick said.

"Likewise. Katie, friend of Ava's?"

"Yes, ma'am."

"Well, you got good manners, Katie. Jacoby tell me about you. Tell me he didn't like you much at first, but that it turns out you saved Ava, that you good people."

A cloak of grief fell over my vision. "I felt the same about him." As I said the words, my eyes cleared. Oh, Jacoby.

She pursed her thin lips. "Sometimes it take someone from outside to see what those inside can't."

I nodded, unsure of what she meant.

"Come here, young lady." She led me into her dark, tiny kitchen. "When my grandson die, they bring me all his things, from he car and he pockets. Some make sense. Keys, wallet, phone."

She waited for a response from me, so I nodded again.

She opened her freezer and pulled out a large shrink-wrapped frozen fish. "But what you think of this? They say it from he truck, like he gone shopping before the storm."

"But Jacoby's allergic to fish, isn't he?" He'd told me so at our wedding.

Ms. Edmonds stabbed her index finger in the air triumphantly and placed the fish back in the freezer. "Deadly allergic. So why he carrying fish?"

"I have no idea."

"Me neither." She shook her head. "Something to think on, though." She looked at me, looked into me, and I squirmed.

"Absolutely. I will."

We left and I felt unsettled. It made sense that hurricane debris killed Jacoby. I didn't know how to reconcile his grandmother's words, though, or the fish. But what could I do about it from Texas? Sorrow clamped my heart like a fist and it struggled to beat.

I was failing Jacoby, but it was time to go. Being with Nick and Taylor was the right thing to do, the only thing I could do, and the one thing I could not fail at anymore.

Chapter Thirty-nine

The next morning I tried to book travel off island for us, but the airport was closed. I called Nick, who was in Town putting up fliers for our estate sale. We knew getting back to Texas was not going to be simple right after a hurricane, but I couldn't help but feel a flicker of panic.

"American won't even resume flights until their terminal is repaired, which could be months," I told him.

"We can try to hire a boat captain," Nick said. "I'd suggest we call Bill, but he told me he was taking the *Wild Irish Kate* straight up to Florida when he left here to pick up his boss."

By midday, we hadn't found any boat captains on St. Marcos willing to work during the post-hurricane bonus holiday. I tried some of the smaller airlines that flew from island to island, thinking that the damaged terminal might not affect them as much as it did the major airlines. And it really didn't matter where we flew to, as long as we could eventually get somewhere with a connecting flight to the states. By the third airline, a human answered the phone. LIAT, an airline Locals described as "Leave Islands Any Time they want to," was resuming flights the next day, assuming they still wanted to when tomorrow came. I crossed my fingers and booked us on a flight to Aruba with Oso. My protector and Taylor's BFF could not be left behind, but the rest of the pack would stay to guard Annalise.

As I hung up, the agent said, "Mind your dog don't weigh no more than a hunner pound with he kennel." We hung up.

"All set," I called from the kitchen to Nick in the garage. "You don't think Oso and his kennel are over one hundred pounds, do you?"

Nick walked into the kitchen. "About one twenty, I'd say. Why?"

"Oh, no! He's over the weight limit to fly." My heart sank from diaphragm to bellybutton level.

Nick shook his head. "Don't worry. I'll handle it."

"Really?" I couldn't bear leaving Oso there.

"No problem," he said, and swatted my behind. I could play that game. I popped him with a dishtowel and he chased me to the bedroom. I won.

All the next day, we prepared for our sale. The big house was far from full, but we'd been acquiring furniture at a fairly decent clip all summer long, in addition to what I'd brought from Texas. What we'd accumulated a little at a time had added up fast. Whatever we didn't sell or decide to take, we would leave with the house for a buyer to deal with—when we found one.

Cars were lined up at our gate at seven the next morning, honking. We had run an ad in the *St. Marcos Daily Source* announcing that the sale would begin at eight, but the people of St. Marcos love nothing more than a good estate sale. We ignored them as we did our last-minute preparations and slammed down King's coffee.

At seven forty-five we opened the gate to muttered complaints and long, drawn-out chuptzes, and the posturing and haggling began at once. I hated that part, but Nick loved it.

The sale went on for hours, and friends and acquaintances showed up, too. Egg even brought Crazy out to wish us well, but they couldn't stay. By midday the sale had become an impromptu pool party, and we finally shut the gate and counted our money.

"Ten thousand dollars? Not bad at all," I said. It helped that we'd sold all the office furniture and the mahogany bedroom set we got before the wedding. "How about we use our guests to help us clean out the refrigerator?"

"Good idea."

We carried a smorgasbord down to the pool, where a month before we'd been married. It was a bittersweet gathering. Some of our wedding guests were there again, although not Ava. She'd informed me that she would be taking Jacoby's grandmother to the doctor, and that she didn't do goodbyes. I missed Rashidi fiercely. I couldn't even think about Jacoby. It was just too much.

Ms. Ruthie made a brief appearance. "You tell that boy I love him," she said, her face tight and her tone stern. She embraced both of us and marched back to her golden car. I bit my lip.

Our mood grew increasingly somber and it spread to our friends, who packed up and began to take their leave. The goodbyes felt anticlimactic and mechanical, but I did my best.

Over the next few hours, Nick worked outside while I cleaned up the aftermath of the sale to the Dixie Chicks' mournful album *Home*. I played it over and over like a dirge for our life on the island.

"I'm going to miss you, Annalise. I'm really, really sorry about this," I said aloud.

The house remained still, silent, and morose, but I knew if she was going to mope, there was nothing I could do about it. I reminded myself for the zillionth time that I was doing the right thing.

Chapter Forty

Later that evening, while we had supper on the back patio, we watched the bats come out from under the eaves. Afterward, we threw away our paper plates and tidied up the kitchen for the last time. My pulse sounded in my ears and our feet echoed as we walked the long hall to the bedroom. I took a soak in the claw-footed tub, then put away everything but what I'd need in the morning. All our bags were packed and ready.

As we got into bed and turned out the lights, Nick brought up the cash from the sale.

"I'm a little concerned about the money. We did advertise in the paper, and we had a lot of people we didn't know up here," he said.

There were people on our quasi-third-world island who would go to great lengths for that kind of cash, and notice of an estate sale generally meant an untended house. Not only was the cash attractive, but the items left in the house would appeal to a certain class of person as well. And we weren't parting as friends with some of our neighbors, including Junior and Pumpy, Bart, the many friends of the crooked investigator I sent off Baptiste's Bluff in my old truck, and those of Jeffrey Bonds and Lisa Nesbitt, whom I'd helped land in jail for murder. Tonight was the last chance for some of them to bid us farewell in their own special ways.

"It hadn't occurred to me. And it's dark as pitch out there now." I thought for a minute. "Well, we've got the dogs and the flare gun." I wasn't so sure Annalise was on our side right then, so I left her off the list. "The gate is shut. We'll be fine, right?"

Nick nodded. "I'll hide the money in my closet. I didn't mean to scare you."

Right then, the quiet night vanished and a hot wind gusted through our open windows, whipping the curtains into a froth of seafoam-green gauze. I swallowed and looked at Nick in surprise. He gripped my hand and returned the expression.

We lay wide-eyed in the dark while the minute hand clicked forward as if through a vat of molasses. The wind grew stronger and built to a howl, but no rain came. Objects inside the house shifted, banged, and fell to the floor. We heard a thud in the living room and something crashed upstairs. I prayed the wind was the culprit. If it was anything else, the storm was blowing too loud for us to hear it.

The dogs howled, then barked, and finally started growling in a frenzy. Were they scared of the wind? Or was something out there? The night visits from the red Senepol cattle and the scrubby horses that roamed the hills didn't bother them anymore.

The bed felt like it was about to go airborne and the edges of the cotton sheets floated like poltergeists. I clutched at Nick's hand as if it would tether me down.

"Are you sure you locked up?" I asked for the sixth time.

"You know I am."

"Let's push the furniture against the door."

Nick sprang up to move the armoire. I fell in beside him and pushed with all my might, reassuring myself that no one could get to us through the windows, since our room was on the second floor. On a calm night, a determined house-breaker might climb a ladder to the balcony, but not in this wind. We blockaded the door to the hallway with two chests of drawers in front of the armoire and got back in bed. That was all we could do.

We must have fallen asleep, because I woke up in the middle of the night with my back against the headboard and my left hand holding Nick's right. Something was wrong. Nick woke, too.

"The lights," I said to him. "We left them on in the bathroom and now they're out. If we lost power, the generator should have come on."

"Do you want me to go outside and check it?" he asked.

"No! Let's stay here." We huddled close.

Many uneasy hours later, we awoke to a peaceful tropical morning that belied the night before. It was late. Neither of our phone's alarms had gone off, which I didn't understand, but I didn't have time to dwell on it. We had survived the night, we were relieved and exhausted, but if we were going to make our plane, we had to put it in high gear.

I went to turn on the bathroom light and nothing happened. Still no power. Great.

"Do you want me to see if I can fix it?" Nick asked.

"No time, I'll be fine," I said.

We threw on our clothes, grabbed our bags, and ran for the garage with Oso trotting behind us. I yanked open the door to the truck and cried out.

"What is it?" Nick called.

I scooped up a thorny pile of black roses and threw them to the floor behind me. One of the thorns dug into my thumb and a bright red drop of blood welled up. "Damn Bart left me a present and I cut my thumb on it. I'm OK." I stared at the blood for a second.

"It's a good thing we're leaving, Katie, because I swear to God I'd kill him, and you'd have to visit me in prison for the rest of our lives."

"I'd help you," I said.

I shoved Oso into the cab and went to say goodbye to the other dogs.

"I'm going to miss you guys."

They barely acknowledged me. They had worked hard all night long.

I climbed in the passenger side and Nick backed the truck down the driveway toward our lane, but then slammed on the brakes. All the construction scaffolding that had been carefully stacked against the house lay across the driveway, blocking our path.

We jumped out and Nick called me over to his side of the truck. He hefted a corner of the scaffolding platform and pointed at a machete, a patched Rasta cap, and a drying pool of what looked like blood on the ground.

"Holy Moses," I breathed.

"Annalise may not want us to go, but it looks like she isn't going to let anyone hurt us, either."

"The cap," I said. "It looks like Junior's."

"Maybe, although I've seen a lot that look just like that."

"Yeah, but not on the heads of people that hated me."

"Look," Nick said, holding up a severed electrical line that ran to the house.

I was pretty sure we'd find sabotage at the generator, too, but we were out of time. I ran back to the house and put my head against the cool yellow plaster like I had so many times before.

"I am so sorry, Annalise. I will find a good family to come live here with you. I promise."

Silence from the jumbie house. I couldn't wait for an answer. Nick and I dragged the scaffolding out of the way and got back in the truck. An ice pick of pain stabbed my heart as we went through the gate for the last time. It was done. We were leaving. Oso turned back toward the house and began barking madly, jangling my seriously frayed nerves.

"Wait!" I yelled. Nick slammed on the brakes and Oso yelped. I jumped out of the car and ran back toward the gate, snapping pictures as fast as my iPhone would let me: the lane, the gate, and the house standing serene amidst the ruins of the natural beauty that had been stripped off the island around her. Two wild horses had come up out of the bush and into the yard. I committed it all to memory, knowing I would probably not get another chance to soak in the house that I had brought back to life over the last year, and who had brought me back with her.

"Are you going to be all right?" Nick asked when I climbed back into the truck.

I nodded. "Drive."

He jammed the truck into gear and stomped on the accelerator, and we lurched forward. I scrolled through the pictures, squinting in the bright morning sunlight to drink them in, one by one. As I clicked to the last picture, something about the one just before it tugged at me, and I went back. A mare and foal were standing in front of Annalise, looking just as I'd seen them moments before, but there was something else. I held the phone farther from me, trying to bring it into focus. And then I saw her.

My hand opened and the iPhone clattered to the floor. Oso whined and shoved his nose under my elbow and my hand flew to my mouth. I turned to look back again at my house, to see what my eyes told me was true but my mind could not believe. Even stripped of leaves, the forest blocked my view.

"What's the matter?" Nick asked, his eyes on the road as he whipped around a narrow curve.

I picked up my phone again. On the front steps of my house stood a tall black woman in a white blouse and a loose, calf-length plaid skirt. A matching scarf was knotted over her hair. She was looking straight into the camera with somber eyes. One of the dogs was nuzzling her leg. In her right hand, she held

Junior's cap and machete, and in her left, his severed, bloody head by his dreadlocked hair.

I bit my lip and shook my head. My heart ached for the terrifying warrior goddess I had left behind. "Goodbye, Annalise," I whispered. Then I rolled down the passenger window and threw up.

Chapter Forty-one

Nick drove across the island like Mario Andretti in the Monaco Grand Prix, throwing caution and fears about flat tires and side-view mirrors to the wind. Ava was picking up our truck from the parking lot, and as late as we were, she might beat us there.

When we got to the airport, we went to the ticket counter to deal with Oso's departure. I raised my eyebrows when Nick put two twenty-dollar bills on top of the kennel. Oso's tail thumped against the inside of the kennel.

"Trust me," Nick whispered. And sure enough, Oso's kennel lost a few pounds in the transaction and we sailed through to baggage. But there, we had a problem.

"No way, mon, this kennel way too big," the baggage handler shouted. "This not me job to lift he."

Nick begged, pleaded, explained, and bribed. Cash changed hands, but the baggage handler still didn't budge.

"What's the problem over here?" a familiar voice inquired.

Nick turned and looked into the face of our favorite contractor.

"Hey, Egg," he exclaimed. "What are you doing here?"

"Working for the mon," he said, clasping hands with Nick.

"Can you help us get Oso on the plane?"

Egg grinned. "No problem." He turned to me and bowed. "Hate to see you go, miss."

I curtsied back. "I'll miss you, Egg."

Oso stuck his nose partway out the breathing slits and I stuck mine against it. Cold. I rubbed his nose with one finger. His eyes sparkled as Egg hauled his kennel away to the makeshift cargo bay. We could see his kennel from the temporary post-hurricane terminal, which was more like a cattle pen by the runway, and heard him barking at the chickens. They squawked and flapped their wings in their wooden crates, and feathers flew everywhere. It was hard to say whether the dog or the chickens would have the worst of it on the flight, but the passengers were bearing the worst of it at the gate between the racket and the smell of chickens and jet fuel.

Nick and I sat pressed together on a bench, our heads back against the wall, our fingers entwined. Almost on time, we got on our plane. As we taxied away, I looked out the window to soak in one more view of the island. The last thing I saw was my yellow house with her red roof, standing alone in a sea of brown.

Chapter Forty-two

And so the Nurturing Empress life foretold by my Jump Up psychic commenced. Sort of.

Nick and I crammed ourselves, Taylor, and Oso into a furnished apartment in Corpus Christi that reminded me of my first apartment in Dallas. Boxy and functional, but not much else to brag about, like Corpus itself. It was a far cry from the lifestyle I'd grown accustomed to. We weren't close enough to the ocean to smell it or hear it, much less see it. The walls were so thin we could hear the neighbors watching *Jersey Shore* and smell their garlicky spaghetti.

I wondered if they could hear me, too, each night at three a.m. when I started screaming. Nick sure could. The first time it had happened, I shot bolt upright in bed. It felt as if two giant hands had struck me hard in the chest. My hands flew to my chest and my heart beat so hard it felt it would break my ribs. I panted for breath.

"No!" I thought I heard Annalise say. But there was no one there.

Nick sat up and grabbed me by the arms and shook me once. "What is it? What's the matter?"

"Annalise is very upset with me."

He pulled me into him. The air vibrated as I whispered to Annalise.

"You love Taylor, too. You know I have to be here with him. We don't have a choice. You're upset now, but in the end, everything will be all right. Be mad at Derek, not at me. I love you." Eventually, Annalise released me and I fell back to sleep. But it happened almost every night at the same time from then on.

So, we had noisy neighbors, and vice versa. We missed Annalise. But on the other hand, we didn't have to deal with centipedes, hardly-working workers, or Bart anymore. I focused on the positives. Nick was steadily bringing in new clients and I picked up some contract legal work, which wasn't bad at all.

Oh, hell, who was I kidding? I hated writing discovery responses like an overpaid paralegal, and my sexy husband had attention deficit issues—mainly that he focused on the situation with Derek more than I wished. Money was tight and our problems were real, so I tried to keep a sock in it. I distracted myself by teaching classes to senior citizens at the neighborhood dojo while Taylor was at Mother's Day Out, the single greatest invention of all time. I could deliver vicious kicks and chops and no one had to know why.

When I wasn't quasi-lawyering or bludgeoning my issues into submission, Taylor, Oso, and I spent as much of the cooling fall days outside as we could. We enjoyed walking the boardwalk on top of the stone seawall. It had the best view in the city, not just of the water, but also of the beachside motels and the tallish buildings downtown. Being outside eased the pain of missing Annalise a little.

Colorless Corpus Christi was like the reverse image of shiny St. Marcos. But if I closed my eyes, breathed in salt air, and listened to the whoosh of the waves, I could almost see myself back in the beautiful blues, greens, pinks, oranges, and reds of the pre-hurricane islands. Almost. At least once Annalise sold, we could upgrade our living situation, maybe to a rental house with a big back yard and some trees.

I had a strong nibble on Annalise less than a week after we left. The St. Marcos realtor I had signed with showed her to a group of businessmen who wanted to share a house on the island. None of them planned to live on St. Marcos full time. None of them had kids. None of their spouses indicated any interest in spending time there. I had promised Annalise I would find her a family, and these guys seemed the furthest thing from it. Ava told me the men were arrogant and greasy when I called to see how the house-sitting was going.

"What do you mean, greasy?" I pictured them in need of a good shampoo, lank clumps of hair hanging over their pimply foreheads, smudgy spots on their glasses.

"They wheeler-dealers, and they slippery. I not the only one take a dislike to them. They opening cabinets and checking things out, and one of them look under the sink. The pipe bust and spray him good. I cheer Annalise on, let me tell you. Betsy all horrified, teetering around in heels, afraid she get water on her white skirt. White. Why she wear something like that up at Annalise, nobody know."

The realtor definitely lacked island sense, but I was looking for a Continental buyer. "You and Annalise be nice, now. We need a sale."

"We need to book our tickets to New York."

I still hadn't told her I wasn't going. I knew I owed it to her, but I couldn't muster enough courage. Ava could get righteously pissed, but I feared her sadness more than her anger. "Soon," I said, and changed the subject. "Anything new on Jacoby?"

"No. Should there be? People die in hurricanes. It sad, but it a fact. I do got news, though. Junior Nesbitt missing."

My hands turned icy. I had convinced myself I'd either dreamed up the picture on my iPhone or Annalise had conjured it to hurt me for leaving her. An image popped into my mind of a pool of blood on my driveway.

"Katie, you there?"

"Yes, sorry. What do you mean, he's missing?"

"Vanish. He s'posed to work and not show up."

"That's pretty normal for him."

"He not show up for a *week*. Even on the day he pay his men."

No contractor could stiff his workers and stay in business long. He really was missing. "Taylor is calling. So sorry. I have to run. Thanks, Ava." I hung up.

Nick was beside me on the sofa. He stared at me like my nose was growing. "What?" he prompted.

My mind scrambled for a plausible story without stopping to figure out why I felt the need to cover up for Annalise. "Junior disappeared. Ava thinks he ran off because he crossed the wrong person."

Nick's brow furrowed. He left the question of why that should bother me so much unspoken.

"Bad memories," I said into the silence, then quickly, "When is Taylor's next visit with Derek?"

Nick's eyes told me he wasn't buying it, but I could always count on Derek to take the spotlight off me. After the paternity tests had proven Derek was Taylor's dear old dad, their visits had become routine. And the routine was that Taylor went bananas every time he had to go, sometimes starting a couple days early.

"Monday," Nick answered. "We get the weekend off from Satan."

The weekend came and went, and Monday arrived.

"No go," Taylor informed me at breakfast.

I hadn't mentioned the visit with Derek yet. "No go where? The park? Don't you want to go to the park and go down the slide?"

This got an emphatic nod.

"The beach? Do you want to go play in the sand?"

Again, a happy nod of his head.

"With Mr. Derek?"

"No go! No go! No go!" Taylor yelled and kicked his heels against his high chair.

WWMD, I asked myself, and got no reply.

Nick walked into the kitchen. "What's the matter?" he asked.

"Taylor doesn't want to go with Derek."

Nick bent at the waist and pulled Taylor from his chair. He crouched down, setting the boy's feet on the floor but still holding him in place by the arms. "Why don't you want to go with Derek?"

Taylor squirmed away and ran off towards his bedroom. Nick's cell phone rang in harmony with the doorbell. The bell was bound to be the social worker to pick up Taylor.

He grimaced. "It's a scheduled client call. I really need to take it. Is that OK?"

I waved my hand in answer. I understood, but boy, did the universe have great timing.

I ushered Alice in and went to fetch Taylor. She had the joy of supervising the visits twice a week, and each time we handed Taylor off to her, it got worse. I hauled the struggling boy from his bedroom and followed Alice out to her car with him, talking up the outing as we went. "It will be fun, fun, fun!" My face almost cracked from the effort of my fake smile.

I wrestled Taylor into his car seat. The way he carried on, the neighbors would be calling the police for a domestic disturbance any moment. I was pretty sure I wouldn't do jail well. I shut his door and turned to Alice to confirm the logistics. They were meeting Derek at Chuck E. Cheese's, and the visit would last an hour. Then I told Alice about Taylor's resistance, as if she wasn't living through it herself right that moment.

"I'm really concerned about how badly it's going. It's not just when we give him to you. He starts resisting as soon as he senses a visit coming. I'm worried

Derek has done or said something that is making Taylor so," I searched for the right word, "distraught."

The heavyset young woman smoothed her skirt. "It's normal for a little boy his age to be scared of people that are new to him. And he could be picking up on how you and Mr. Kovacs feel. I'm with them every second, and I haven't seen anything to worry over. Give it some time."

Alice drove away with Taylor screaming and kicking in his car seat. I hoped she was right that nothing bad was happening, but I just didn't know what to think, and her answer was unsatisfying. WWMD, WWMD. I didn't know that either. She hadn't exactly faced this situation.

When I went back inside, Nick was off his call and wanted to know how it went.

"Awful," I said. "And she thinks everything is just fine."

Nick sat at the breakfast table, and I sat down in his lap. I leaned into him. He put his chin on my shoulder. "I think I should call our attorney," he said.

"I agree."

But when he did, Mary sang from the same hymnal. "Without proof or even a few details, we won't get anywhere with the court. It'll just drag this out further. And every report says Derek is still working at Chico's Shoes, meeting with his parole officer, and showing up on time and clean for his appointments. He's drug-tested once a week, and he's passed them all."

"What does she want us to do, just wait until all the damage is done?" Nick asked me after the call ended.

"I hate it, too, but I don't know what else to do."

Nick did, however. He scooched me off his lap and stood up. He looked taller than his six foot one. His eyes were burning with that dark intensity that made me want to climb up him and at the same time throw myself in front of him like a protester in front of a tank. "What good is it to be a PI if I don't use my skills and resources for my own family?" he asked.

Just because he was speaking logically and metaphorically didn't mean I was going to like where it went. "But what can you look into that the court doesn't already keep tabs on?"

"I don't know yet, but if I follow him for a few days, I might find out."

"Be careful, Nick. He scares me."

"He's a punk. But Teresa did tell me he had a habit of carrying a Beretta nine millimeter that he wasn't afraid to use." Or on St. Marcos, a switchblade, I remembered. "I promise, I'll be careful."

Now my phone rang. It was the realtor. I held up one finger to Nick, who nodded and walked back toward the office. Betsy told me to look for an offer on Annalise in my email.

I hung up. The email had already arrived. I opened the attachment and scanned it. The buyers were offering nearly one and a half times my asking price, as in half a million dollars extra. That was strange. No, it was unbelievable. I read further. It made no sense. I called Betsy back.

"What in the world is this?"

"I know, right? It's very unusual. These guys run a company that buys life insurance policies from terminally ill people. Then they make their company the beneficiary of the policies. The company keeps paying the premiums until the people die, and then they collect the payouts."

"What?! They get paid for people to die? That's morbid. Is it even legal?"

"Apparently so. The way they explained it to me, a lot of times when people get really sick, they can't work and they run up big medical bills, so they sell their life insurance policies to get the cash to live on until they die. They see themselves as helping people who are in distress."

I paced the confines of the apartment, walking as close to the cheap drywall walls as I could get, willing the space bigger, wishing it wasn't all painted utilitarian white. "They can see it however they want. It's still creepy."

"Yeah, but when you think about it, there are lots of businesses that profit from death. Funeral homes. Casket companies. Florists."

"I know, but these guys are sitting around waiting for *specific people* to die. They know their names. And I guess the faster they die, the better the rate of return on their investments."

"True. And yours, too, if you take the offer. They want to cover the purchase price by making you the beneficiary of policies whose payouts are one and a half times your purchase price. Think of the extra money as a prepayment of interest on the balance they owe you, since it will take a while for all the people to die."

"*Eww.* I'd feel like the Grim Reaper. Worse."

"You wouldn't have to get involved with the policies, though. It would be very arms-length. Their company would handle everything, make the premium payments, and arrange for you to be paid."

Ick. Ick to the max. Ick to the power of infinity. Ick to the hell no. Except that if I took the offer, I'd help us get out of that apartment and focus on being an empress instead of worrying about a big jumbie house two thousand miles away. All while dead bodies piled up around me to make it happen, and without even the consolation of a family for Annalise. It was a lot to think about. Better yet, not to think about.

"I'll have to get back to them."

"Make it fast. Their offer expires in forty-eight hours."

Chapter Forty-three

The morbid offer wigged Nick out, too. We talked in circles all afternoon but hadn't reached a decision by dinnertime. After we put Taylor to bed, we cleaned the small kitchen together and let the topic of dead people die. I tied the ends of the trash bag and hefted it from the can as Nick loaded the dishwasher. I hate touching dirty dishwater, and he knew it. He always picked that job. The man was twenty-four-karat.

"What are you going to do tomorrow?" I asked.

"You mean what are *we* doing."

"I do?"

"Yes, you do. My dad asked us to go deep-sea fishing with him and his buddy Nate."

Fishing is not my world-favorite activity. "I should work."

"You told me earlier you didn't have to."

Rats. I had. I played my trump card. "What about Taylor? I should stay with him. You guys just go have fun."

"Taylor is having a Grandma day. She can't wait."

"I could hang out with them."

"Come on, Katie, please? My dad really wants to spend time with us and get to know you better."

I tried to jive this with the taciturn father-in-law I knew, and failed. But Nick had said please. And a boat on the ocean is never a bad thing, right? "All right," I said.

Nick whooped, and we heard a yell from down the hall. He had woken Taylor up. And for some reason, we both laughed.

Nick had neglected to mention we'd take the five a.m. ferry to Port Aransas so we could be out on the water by six. He redeemed himself by bringing me fresh-ground King's coffee in my Baylor Bears mug. Taylor and I slept in our Tahoe on the crossing. He didn't wake up until we docked on the island and drove to the Kovacs house, where I handed him to Julie, who was standing alongside her tall, silent husband. I'd felt a little queasy getting off the ferry, and when I told her, she ran back into the house for a box of Dramamine.

I really liked my mother-in-law. One good thing about living in Corpus was that I would get to know her better. Well, today was get to know your father-in-law day, so maybe next time. Nick put his arm around me and whisked me back outside and into the white Lincoln Town Car, which Kurt already had in gear with the engine running.

It was only five minutes to Nate's place. He kept his boat, *The Juggerknot*, tied up in a slip outside his fantastic house on the point of Sandpiper Cove, overlooking the mouth of the port itself where it emptied out into the Gulf of Mexico. I walked sleepily from the car to the boat with a longing glance toward the house. It was tan stucco, Mediterranean style with a red tile roof, and it looked like a house that would have a lot of guest bedrooms for sleepy women who skipped fishing expeditions.

Nate was a hearty fellow, and he gave us a welcoming bellow.

"This is my wife, Katie," Nick said. "Katie, this is Nate."

"Nice to meet you, Katie." He stuck out a giant red paw and gave my palm a good loofah rub as we shook hands.

"And you as well, Nate," I said.

"The day's getting away from us, so we'll be pushing off," Nate said, despite the fact that the moon had not yet set. He climbed onto the boat and up to the flybridge. "Nick, untie the lines for me, son."

I scrambled aboard and the boat shifted slightly under my weight. I'd need to take the Dramamine pretty soon to give it time to work, but Nick had it and Nate had just commissioned him first mate.

Nick moved expertly around the boat, removing lines and pushing off. He threw his jacket down to me and worked in his shirtsleeves. I admired his arms and tried not to make it obvious that I was objectifying my husband. Kurt stood at the bow drinking his coffee, looking every inch the descendant of an Iroquois chief.

Nate backed us out of his slip and headed for the gap and out to sea. The brisk wind blew in my face and I was glad for my jacket, and Nick's too, which I slipped on over mine. I felt the boat move with the surging water and despite myself, I felt a frisson of excitement. I had missed the sea. As soon as we cleared the last of the buoys, Nick joined me.

My phone rang and I looked at the caller ID. Service on the high sea, go figure. It was Ava. Well, it was eight thirty there, but damn, that was early for her. Maybe it was an emergency.

"Ava, what's up? It's six thirty here."

"I had a bad dream," she said, "and I wake up with a bad feeling to match. You not going to New York with me to cut the demo with Trevor. I right?"

Crap. "Ava," I said.

"Just tell me yes or no."

"No, I'm not. I'm sorry. I have to be here." The wind was blowing and I couldn't tell whether she was being silent or I'd lost reception. "Ava? Are you there?"

"I here. When you gonna tell me?"

"Soon. Very soon."

"That crap. You don't go, no point I go. They don't want just me. You really gonna do this?"

I closed my eyes. It wasn't just a demo, it was all that came after if it went well, like more time in New York, far away from Nick and Taylor. Nick put his hand on my shoulder and I said, "I'm very, very sorry. I understand you're mad at me, and I hope you understand that I love you and I would do this for you if I could."

I heard her crying on the other end of the line. "I gotta go," Ava said. She hung up.

The waves had grown rougher, and I realized I was holding onto the side with one hand and bending my knees to absorb the shocks. A light smatter of water sprayed my hand. I turned toward Nick and he pulled me into his shoulder, where I laid my head. He rubbed the small of my back in slow circles.

I tilted my head up so my voice would carry to him. "I should take some Dramamine."

Nick didn't respond, so I repeated myself.

His head slumped forward. "Don't be mad," he said.

Nothing good comes after "don't be mad." Nothing. I tensed.

"I left the Dramamine in the car. But it's a calm day. You're going to be just fine."

Normally I would agree with him, but that day my stomach didn't. "Oh, Nick."

"You look great, really. Just focus on the horizon and keep your face in the wind."

He was probably right. I resolved to do just that. I loved being out on the water. I was with my gorgeous husband, and it was going to be a great day.

All of a sudden the boat lurched and the engines whined. Nick clutched me tighter and he and his father yelled up to Nate, "Whoa, whoa, whoa."

Nate cut the engines to neutral. The boat slumped into the water and started rolling with the waves. The wind created by our forward motion stilled.

Nick released me and walked to the back of the boat. "Am I going in?" he yelled up to Nate.

"Yah," Kurt said before Nate could answer.

"'Pears that way, son," Nate agreed. "Snorkel gear and knife are under the seat, there." He pointed to the bench seat in the stern.

The smell of diesel grew stronger. My mouth went dry. My ears started ringing. No, I thought. No, no, no. Look at the horizon. I tried to find it, but the boat's up and down motion made it impossible to hold it in my sight.

"What's going on?" I asked.

Nate turned the engines off.

Nick had retrieved the gear and stripped down to his skivvies, a sight I appreciated more when I felt better. "Got something in the propeller," Nick said. "I've got to cut it off." He slipped a knife holster over his ankle, donned the mask, kissed my cheek, climbed up on the side, and jumped in feet first.

"But what about sharks?" I yelled at him when he resurfaced, bobbing while he put on his fins and adjusted his snorkel.

He stuck the snorkel in his mouth and shot me a thumbs-up, then disappeared below the undulating surface of the water. I'd loved the clear, warm Caribbean ocean, but this was a different kettle of fish, a cold kettle you could pretty much call black. Long seconds ticked by. Didn't he have to come up to breathe?

"He's been down too long, don't you think?" I asked Kurt, who was sitting on the bench seat.

Kurt cocked his head like he was thinking, then he turned his face up toward Nate and spoke slowly, squeezing all the juice he could from each word. "How long he been down, Nate?"

Nate looked at his watch. "I wasn't timing him, but I'd say about a minute."

Kurt shook his head, then leaned it back into his hands. "Nah. He's got a lot left in him. He set a record for free diving when he was eighteen."

My father-in-law left a lot out between his sparse words. "And free diving is what?"

"Going down as far as you can on one breath, and coming back up. It's how deep you can go and how long you can hold your breath." He nodded, and almost smiled.

This was just about the longest speech I'd ever heard from him. I almost smiled back, except I felt too nauseous to do it without vomiting. Nick's head popped up.

"Fishing net. It's in there pretty good. Don't get in a hurry to go anywhere," he said. He sucked in a deep breath and disappeared again.

"Dammit," Nate said. "Nothing worse than that." He turned to me and said, "I carry nets, myself, but I don't ever let them loose in the water. They can do thousands of dollars of damage in an instant."

I managed a careful nod.

The boat rocked. The sun rose. The engines were completely off, but the smell of diesel seemed to grow stronger. I broke into a sweat and shed the jackets. Every few minutes, Nick would emerge for a breath, then dive again. Every time he did, I was breathing faster. My mouth watered. My eyes burned. And then it was no use fighting it any more. I ran to the side of the boat and heaved. Black coffee sprayed down toward the water. I was not too far gone to feel embarrassed.

"No vomiting allowed on my boat," Nate hollered, laughing. Then he reined himself in and said, "Go to the back. You're closer to the water there. Less to clean up later."

I stumbled to the back, which positioned me roughly above Nick. I looked back at Kurt.

"Don't worry about him. Just imagine what's already in that water," he advised.

I turned and spewed my breakfast into the water, then propped myself on the side of the boat, gasping. I hurled again as Nick came up for air. He got round two on his head.

"What the hell?" he said, then saw me hanging over the back. "Uh oh."

"I would be fine if I'd have had some Dramamine," I croaked.

He dove before I nailed him again.

Chapter Forty-four

The next morning a cold front blew in. What was a little frost in the air to me? I'd braved colder growing up in North Texas. I took Taylor and Oso for a walk every day at this time, and it guaranteed they would power nap afterwards, which kept me sane-ish. I bundled Taylor into a lined Dallas Cowboys windbreaker while he kept up a running dialogue about Oso and the park. He was easier to understand every day. It wouldn't be too long before his second birthday.

"Ma. Ma. Ma," he said.

I pointed at Teresa's picture. "Mama," I said. "That is Taylor's Mama. She is with God and the angels."

Taylor looked at Teresa's photograph from boot camp in San Diego. She was wearing her Marine fatigues. He turned and pointed at me. "Ma. Ma. Ma. Ma."

Something large swelled up in my throat and leaked out my eyes. Where would he get that? I had always been Kay Kay to him. Maybe he got it at Mother's Day Out, where he saw other kids and their mommies.

"Now's the time to ask me for a Porsche when you turn sixteen," I advised him.

I gathered him up in my arms and rained kisses on his face, which tasted syrupy. No wonder Oso rarely left his side. So much for my mothering skills, I thought. The kid needed a face-washing. I wetted a paper towel and gave him a quick one. Riding an emotional high, I grabbed Oso's leash and we headed out the door into the nippy exterior hallway. I pushed the stroller down the short sidewalk to street, then took a right instead of our usual left, feeling adventurous. I'd seen an elementary school just down the way. Elementary schools equal playgrounds.

We walked down a block of apartment buildings with narrow strips of grass and identical hedges, then came into a neighborhood with fall-brown front lawns and wider streets. My heart broke into song. I needed space to combat my cabin fever. I serenaded my boys with a few lines from Sheryl Crow's "Soak Up the Sun," missing Ava.

We passed a pretentious red-brick middle school with carefully cultivated ivy growing up its three-story façade. BMWs and Jaguars were delivering kids for an expensive day of private-school tutelage. Spoiled kids, I thought. My mother drove us to school in a wood-paneled station wagon.

Class hadn't started yet, and on the far end of the school kids had congregated. The smoking corner. I heard youthful voices—the girls giggly and high-pitched, the boys yelling instead of talking—but the kids' looks didn't match them. It was like a trashiest-outfit competition, with stretchy midriff-baring tops à la Miley Cyrus, outfits that would have earned me two weeks in Connell Solitary. The boys were a mixed lot. Some were still pre-growth-spurt-short, and skinny. A few of them had facial hair and grown-man musculature. I couldn't imagine Taylor at their age. Cigarette smoke wafted through the air, giving the corner a cheap pool-hall smell.

I averted my eyes and moved Taylor and Oso past as quickly as I could, but I watched through my peripheral vision. The action orbited around one boy in particular who was passing folded notes to some of the other kids. Or maybe they were packages.

And then it hit me. He was selling drugs. If I could see it, where were the cops? I leaned down and tipped the canopy of the stroller back and pressed my face into Taylor's soft hair, thinking that the world was a dangerous place for kids. I detoured around a block then hurried back in the direction we'd come, trying to outrun my fears. We visited a city park instead, and I let Oso and Taylor play for an hour while I bit my nails down to the quick.

When we got back to the apartment, I put Taylor down for his nap and dialed my realtor. All night the night before, after I had recovered from my seasickness, Nick and I had agonized over the offer on Annalise and its unsettling implications. But we decided that Annalise was a unique property in a unique location, and buyers weren't going to queue up at the gate bidding against each other.

Betsy answered.

"Tell the buyers yes," I said, hating myself.

"That's great," she said. "I'll get on it right now."

We hung up.

I put three hotdogs in a pan of water and set it on the stove, then emptied a can of Wolf Brand Chili into a saucepan over another burner and turned the knobs to medium-high, but nothing happened. I flipped a light switch. Nada. The power was out. I sighed. It was like being home at Annalise. It made me miss her, in a wacky kind of way. I'd have to call the power company.

I scraped the food into Tupperware and tried to run water into the pans, but nothing happened when I pushed back the lever.

"Nooooo."

It was ridiculous, like I had stepped through a time-space continuum into my rainforest kitchen. Next I'd have to kill a centipede.

My phone rang, playing the constant refrain of my life. It was Rashidi! I picked up.

"Rashidi?"

I heard static, then the call dropped. The universe had truly sent me back to the islands, through a wormhole to power outages, dropped calls, and empty cisterns.

The phone rang again, and I picked it up. "Rash?"

"Do I sound like Rashidi John to you?" Ava asked.

I couldn't believe it was her. Maybe she wasn't mad at me anymore. "Not so much."

"Good. I hear your news about the house selling. Now that settled, you can come to New York with me."

"Ava, it's not going to happen," I said.

The call ended. She was definitely still mad.

After Nick and I settled Taylor into bed that night, we finally had some us time. Nick lay on top of the covers in boxer briefs with stripes in the colors of a Tabasco bottle while I slipped on silky lavender pajama pants and a matching long-sleeved top with a pair of his tube socks. I flipped off the overhead light so the room was lit by the bedside lamp and plopped down facing him. I rested my head in my hand.

"Taylor called me Mama."

"Oh, baby, that's wonderful," Nick said. He rolled up on his elbow and faced me. He touched the space between my eyebrows. "Why the lines?"

"I'm worried that it's disrespectful to your sister."

"I don't think so. And he needs a real live mother. We won't let him forget Teresa."

"But what if the court rules against us?"

"It doesn't matter. Even if they do, it won't change anything."

I was going to have to wrap my head around it. I was Mama to Taylor. It felt pretty good.

Nick rolled onto his back again and patted his shoulder. I positioned my pillow in the spot he'd patted and put my head half on it and half on his chest. It wasn't just right yet, so I sat back up and repositioned it. It took three tries, but it was worth it. Nirvana.

"I love it when you do that," Nick said. He spread my hair across his chest.

I shook my head. "I'm like a dog arranging its bed, and you know it."

"A very beautiful dog that I love. Like an Irish setter."

"You're not supposed to agree with me."

"A Pekingese?"

I thumped him on the chest. "Did you get anywhere today with Derek?"

Nick rubbed his chin. He had forgotten to shave that morning and his five o'clock shadow had a ten o'clock look to it. "Nothing solid yet, and it's driving me crazy. I want to hurt him." I tensed, and he added, "I won't, of course, but I want to."

"I understand." I did, but I was still worried he might indulge in a little face-smashing if he got the chance. I told him about the kid I'd seen selling drugs to change the subject. "It's scary to think how young these kids go bad, and how dangerous it makes the schools."

"Very dangerous," Nick said. "If he's really selling, the supplier is probably lurking around, too." The thought chilled me, and I burrowed against him.

"Where was it?" he asked.

"Parker-Johnson Prep."

"You're kidding."

"No. Why?"

He sat up on his elbows so I had to scooch off of him. There went my perfect spot. "That's the school Derek's little brother goes to."

"I didn't know he had one."

"Yeah, he does. But Teresa said that when Derek's parents cut him off, they cut him off from the brother, too. So there may not be a relationship." He lay back down and I rooted around until I got comfortable on his shoulder again.

"Still, that's a really unpleasant coincidence. I think I'll scratch that route off our list."

He turned his face down into my hair. "Well, be careful. You're precious to me." He nudged my head in the other direction and nibbled at my neck. "You're delicious, too." He nibbled again. "Do you want me to shave?" He rubbed his stubble lightly against me.

"No, you're fine. Your fancy moisturizer softens the whiskers."

He rose up and turned off his lamp. "I really think we've talked enough for one night, don't you?" he asked.

I smiled in the dark. "It's OK when there's nothing more to say to me."

"What?" he asked, distracted by the serious business of liberating us from unnecessary clothing.

"Some song lyrics. You keep the world at bay for me."

He kissed his way downward from my neck. "Hmmm?"

"I said I love it when you do that."

I felt his lips curve upward against my skin. "That's music to my ears."

Chapter Forty-five

Over the next week, Nick tailed Derek as often as he could. I was a stake-out widow, but it gave me and my St. Marcos contractors time to get Annalise ready for the sale. I couldn't believe how much effort and money it was going to take to close the deal, but I had committed.

I did get something important in return for my concession to the buyers on their punch-list items: a quick close, only three weeks from the date of the contract. A sulky Ava arranged for packing, pick-up, and shipment of our last few household items. She called late Friday afternoon to let me know the pallets were on their way.

That night, I woke up screaming again. Middle-of-the-night, horror-movie, scream-your-throat-raw screaming. Or so Nick told me, because I didn't remember it.

"I grabbed you and you stopped, but you just stared out the window," he said the next morning. "You scared me to death."

"I'm so sorry," I said. "Was it at three o'clock?" I already knew the answer.

"That's the weird part. It was before midnight, eleven forty-seven, to be exact."

It didn't make sense. I would remember it if it had really happened, wouldn't I? I'd never sleepwalked or anything like that before, so I tried to convince myself Nick was wrong, that he'd just had a bad dream.

It didn't work.

Two days later, I got a call from Betsy, who had gone up to the house with the buyers and a contractor. "I don't know how to tell you this, but the house was vandalized and burglarized, Katie, completely stripped of every appliance on the premises."

"What? Burglarized? What do you mean?"

"Refrigerator, stove, microwave, washer, dryer, ovens, air conditioners, everything. They took hinges and doorknobs. They did serious damage to the cabinetry and countertops in the kitchen where they manhandled some of the stuff out, like the trash compactor and dishwasher. They left weird holes all through the house in the walls, too."

I had forgotten to talk to Crazy and Egg about busting up the treasure myth. Big mistake. "How could it all just be gone? Ava is house-sitting. This had to have taken a long time, maybe multiple trips."

"Ava left for New York on Friday after the shippers picked up your pallets. She drove out right behind the truck that was carrying your stuff. I thought you knew."

Oh, Ava, oh, Ava.

If the packers knew the house would be empty, they or anyone else they'd told about it on the island knew they could come back and take Annalise apart at their leisure.

Did Annalise even try to stop them? I wondered. I couldn't imagine that even a jumbie house could hold off determined thieves for long. And then it hit me like a fist to the throat: my screams the other night had come from Annalise. My poor Annalise. A teardrop fell into my lap. I touched my face. It was awash in them.

As for me, insurance would cover the loss—or most of it, I hoped—but it wasn't just about the cost of replacement and repair. Putting Humpty together again would be a long and difficult process. And the buyers had seen the horror firsthand.

"The buyers?" I choked out.

"I'm sorry, Katie, but they're pulling out of the deal. They know they'll forfeit their earnest money. I couldn't get them to change their minds."

I hung up and slumped into a kitchen chair and dropped my head into my hands. I had to call Nick. I dialed his number. He didn't answer, but a second later, my phone rang. I picked up and through gasping breaths told him what happened.

"Katie, I'm so sorry."

My breath stopped. Not Nick's voice. I held the phone away from me and checked the incoming number. It was from St. Marcos.

"Leave me alone, Bart."

"Wait. I know we didn't part on the best of terms, but I still care about you. I heard what happened up at Annalise, and I can help. I can house-sit, do construction, whatever you need. No strings attached."

"No, Bart. No, no, no."

"The last few times you saw me, I wasn't at my best, but I'm myself again. Really."

According to his sister, being himself would just be more of the same. "Absolutely not. I'm hanging up to call my husband now."

"I'll call you tomorrow, then."

"No. I'm going to be at my in-laws. Don't call. Not tomorrow, not ever." I clicked off, wishing for an old rotary phone so I could slam it down, maybe even do it over and over until it broke into a million pieces. I seethed. How great would that be, my phone ringing at the dining room table when I was with Nick and his parents, with Bart on the other end? Awesome. Just awesome.

How the hell had he even known about the burglary? Bad news traveled fast on that island. My phone rang again. This time I double-checked before I answered. It was Nick.

"Oh, baby," I said, then poured out the whole story again, this time with less wailing.

"I wish I was there," he said. "I'm turning around now. I'm so sorry, honey." He switched into fix-it mode. "But it's going to be OK. We'll get orders for new appliances put in right away. You know Crazy and Egg will help. I'm great on insurance issues."

I cut him short. "I don't care about any of that right now. I can figure out how to hire contractors. I've done it before. What I don't understand is how Ava could do this to us, to me. Why didn't she tell me so I could come down there or get another house sitter? She knew how important this was. Why, Nick, why did she do this?"

He was silent for a few seconds, then said in a gentle voice, "I don't know, and I'm mad at her, too. I'm sure she's pretty angry about New York. But, Katie, she wasn't the one who robbed the house."

I stopped him before his logic could get in the way of my righteous indignation. "It wouldn't have been robbed if she hadn't broadcast the opportunity to the movers! She might as well have put a sign in the yard! I didn't deserve that, even if she is mad at me."

"No, you didn't. But you know her, and Ava was just being Ava."

This explanation only made me feel guilty, and something just went off in me, something angry and raw. "So are you saying it's *my* fault that Annalise was raped and pillaged? Ava will be Ava, so Katie was wrong to ever trust her? Under your own rationale, I should never have left St. Marcos. Only I came here for you. I came here FOR YOU."

Nick didn't budge from his high ground. "You came here for us, yes, you did, and I am glad you did, and it was the right thing to do. I'm not blaming you. Maybe there's something we could have done differently. And maybe not. It doesn't matter." I started to interrupt him, but he stood his ground, firm but calm. "It doesn't matter whose fault it is, Katie, it really doesn't."

He was right, and I was spinning round like a record on a turntable with no needle. Dizzy. Frustrated. Completely ineffective. I wanted to hate him for being so damn logical. But I loved him for it. I loved him. And I wanted to kill Ava.

That night I called Rashidi, who had just returned from Puerto Rico. He pledged to be at Annalise before nightfall.

"I promise Jacoby's grandmother I look out for her. She make it OK without me a few nights, but best you look for someone who can stay there longer."

Another wave of guilt washed over me. Jacoby's grandmother had wanted my help, too—something about Jacoby's death hadn't felt right to her, and what had I done? Nothing. My own junk had cluttered my mind so badly that I couldn't even find the memory of *what* she had asked me to do.

Well, I could atone for that sin by getting Rashidi back to her place as fast as I could. Most of St. Marcos was chronically underemployed, so I put out the midnight bark for a project manager/house sitter. That was all I could do from Corpus at night. In the morning I'd tackle police reports, insurance, and reconstruction.

I crawled into bed with Nick without changing out of my gray sweatpants and sweatshirt. He wrapped his arms around me and locked his hands.

"I love you, Katie. Good night," he said, kissing me firmly on the lips.

"That's a tight hug," I replied.

He didn't answer, just checked his grip. Soon he was snoring rhythmically in my ear. I stayed awake. As the minutes dragged on with nothing to keep me from staring into the black pit of awful that the day had been, Ava's betrayal began to consume me. I'd called her all afternoon with no answer. I tried to get up, thinking I could make a few more calls. Someone would know how to reach her. And when I found her, well, Ava better be the one to bar the door.

Except I couldn't move. My husband had me trapped.

"Nick, are you awake?" I whispered.

No answer. But I knew better. And so, it appeared, did he.

Chapter Forty-six

When we awoke at six thirty the next morning, I stumbled straight to my laptop, straightening my sweatsuit while I booted up. Nick went to take care of Taylor. My stomach boiled, a cauldron of stress. Start-up seemed to take five times as long as normal, but finally I was on. I found an email from yugoslamerica@yahoo.com: "My friend tell me to contact you about house in rainforest. She say you need helper. Please call me. Stefania." Her number followed.

This was my first positive response about Annalise. At least I hoped it was positive. Her name wasn't Ava, so that was a good start. It was eight thirty on St. Marcos, a respectable time to call, especially since she'd sent the message earlier that morning. I grabbed my phone and coached myself to keep the desperation out of my voice. I dialed and someone picked up.

"Al-loh?" I heard. The accent sounded Eastern European and the voice female. Maybe the accent explained the funny email address.

"My name is Katie Kovacs. You emailed me about my rainforest house."

"Yah, I have friend who tell me you looking for help. What you need, and where you need it?"

"Well, we need someone to help us coordinate repairs up at our house at 18 Estate Annalise, in the rainforest."

"Ma sta ti hoces da ti radim u toj ludoj kuci?"

"Ummmm, excuse me, I didn't understand you?"

"Oh, sorry, sometimes I forget and talk in Yugoslavian. I asking what you need me to do. I know house, I think. The big one Locals call jumbie house?"

"I think so, but it's not a jumbie house. Well, not really, anyway."

"No, it is OK, really, it doesn't bother me. I just know which it is, I think."

"Yes, that's it. I'm looking for someone to live up there for a couple of months and manage the finish-out. It's a beautiful house, with a pool and lots of places to hike and bicycle."

"OK, I do it."

I was at a loss for words. I hadn't named a price, and I didn't know anything about this person. She might be a crook herself. She might not be capable of the things I needed her to do.

She said, "You on Facebook?"

"Yes," I said, although I found her question odd.

"I send you friend request right now. You see me. Maybe we have friends same, you know, for reference."

"That's a good idea."

I logged in. There it was. I clicked Accept and found myself staring at a picture of a nearly middle-aged Pippi Longstocking. For real? My long-lost Yugoslavian twin sister. Her name was Stefania Szvinyarovich, which I had zero idea how to say.

I sent messages to a few mutual friends for references. I had thrown out the chum, and now I would wait. But notifications popped up immediately, two bites within five minutes. Didn't people have anything better to do than Facebook? I squelched my inner critic, because if they did, I'd still be sitting there with nothing.

Both people claimed Stefania was a solid citizen and a serial house sitter who often did the legwork for off-island owners. One of our mutual friends described her as a Slavic female Clint Eastwood. That sounded fantastic, whatever it was.

"Thank you, God," I said, face upraised, eyes closed.

I emailed Stefania with a rate of pay, copying Betsy, and suggested that if Stefania found the pay acceptable, Betsy should get her a key ASAP. I attached a work list and clicked Send with a hopeful heart.

I turned away from the laptop. It was not yet eight a.m., but already music from the radio was filling our apartment. Nick. How could anyone stay in the dumps with him around? He was rolling around on the floor with Taylor, wrestling and being silly. Oso was prancing around them and whining, looking over at me for permission, but if he joined in the game, the TV in the small room was toast. I wasn't convinced Nick and Taylor wouldn't demolish it themselves.

"No roughhousing inside, boys," I said, then thought, I sound like my mother. WWMD, for real. I laughed and caught the lamp as it rocked off the sofa table. "Yo, Nick." I held it up.

Nick looked as tousled as his little wrestling partner. He stood up and said, "We have to stop, Taylor. We can't break things."

"And can you turn down the stereo a little while you're at it?" I asked. Now I sounded more like my grandmother than my mother.

"I'd be happy to turn this crap completely off," Nick said. "I've hated this band ever since Teresa came home starstruck when Derek met Slither in rehab. Like being pals with a famous heroin addict somehow made dealing drugs cooler."

We were going to Port A for the day to visit Kurt and Julie, and I needed to kick it into high gear. I scurried into the kitchen to pack drinks and snacks for Taylor, fighting a sudden attack of the barfies. I had not gotten near enough sleep and I needed to eat some breakfast soon. But first I needed a pair of jeans. I ran to the bedroom and change, then came back into the living room and announced, "Time to go visit Grammy and Grandpa!"

Taylor started running for the door.

"Wait for us," I called as Nick and I snatched up keys, bags, wallets, purse, and leash. I looked around, feeling like something was missing. What had we forgotten?

Oso wagged his tail. It made thump, thump, thump noises as it hit the coffee table. Ah, yes. The dog. I snapped the leash onto Oso, who now also tried to run for the door. It was pandemonium, in a not-so-bad way. Katie Kovacs, butt-kicking cat herder of Corpus Christi.

We drove onto the double-decker steel ferry in our sharesie blue Tahoe, pulling in tight like sardines in a can. Waves were crashing against the hull of the boat. It was windy and cloudy, common in the late fall there, I'd been told. I was thankful to be in our warm car.

Taylor was asleep in his car seat, snoring peacefully. A family trait. Nick leaned over and kissed the boy's head. When he sat up, he ran his hand through his hair.

Uh oh. My stomach tensed. But Nick's eyes were bright, not upset. He looked energized.

"I need to tell you what's going to happen while you're at my parents' house today."

You? I'd thought the visit to his parents was an us thing. "What's going on, Nick?"

"Remember the other day when you told me about the kid dealing drugs in front of Parker-Johnson?"

"Yes."

"I couldn't get that coincidence out of my mind, with Derek's younger brother going to school there."

I saw where he was going. "You thought the kid was Derek's little brother."

His eyes sparkled. "Right. And if he was Derek's brother, and if he was selling drugs," Nick paused, timing his lines, "then where was he getting them, and was it connected to Derek? I decided to check it out."

Everything made sense to me except the gap between when Nick had made these connections and now, the moment when he got around to telling me about them. The space was suddenly stuffy. I cracked my window. "Wait, when?" I asked.

He looked at me and lifted his shoulders in an I'm-busted-so-please-don't-hurt-me sort of way. "I've done some things I wouldn't normally do in the last few days to get to information. So, I've held back a little. I didn't want to get you in trouble along with me, in case I got caught."

"That's comforting," I said.

"C'mon, you're the one with a law license. I can't put you at risk. And I need to tell you about this now."

I swallowed my snarky response. This conversation was not helping my stomach. I took a deep breath of salty air through my nose. It smelled like fish and diesel. I raised the window back up. "Then tell me," I said.

"I went to the school, I saw what you saw, and it looked like this kid was selling." He pressed his lips together hard. "But after school, he walked to Chico's where Derek works, and estranged big brother gave him a ride back to his neighborhood, where Bobby—that's his name—walked the rest of the way home."

"So much for the parents cutting off their relationship." I was interested, even if I was concerned.

"I know. And this raised all kinds of questions. Why was Bobby coming to the store? Was it just brothers hanging out, or was he picking up drugs or dropping off money there? I'd already followed Derek. He wasn't meeting with suppliers. But maybe somebody else at the shop was helping them."

"Like who?"

"Well, not customers. I've been watching Derek at the store for weeks, and none of the customers seemed suspicious. But the shop has other employees, an owner, and regular service providers." Nick looked pleased with himself. Again, he paused.

"And you found out what?"

"The assistant manager and Derek go way, way back and run with the same crowd. He hasn't done time like Derek, but that could just mean he's smarter. So this guy Richie is the one I tail now."

Nick had changed to present tense. Hold on for the ride, I thought.

"I'd noticed before that he brings a bag in the store every morning, and it's empty when he leaves. I thought it was store business. But yesterday, I see him stop at an old warehouse. He comes out with crates of fruit. Way too much fruit for him and this girlfriend he lives with, and I know he's not selling it out of a fruit stand on the side of the road."

I tugged on my silver hoop earring and twisted it, dread building. "I don't like the thought of you following this guy. It doesn't sound good."

"Ah, but it is good. It is very good. But I decided rather than break into warehouses and houses in the middle of the night, I would turn it over to the authorities, so here's the best part: I called your brother."

"You called Collin?!" My mouth fell open and hung there.

"He did tell me to call if I ever needed anything."

"But why him?"

"Because he works anti-drug."

"In *New Mexico*."

"But he's family. So I called him yesterday morning, and I told him what I had. He was jacked up about it. He called the drug unit down here in Corpus, and the guy he talked to, Joe Fisher, was a few years behind me in high school in Port Aransas."

My jaw moved up and down to no effect. I was processing as fast as I could, but Nick stayed one step ahead of me.

"Collin sold it to Joe. Joe brought me in, I told my story, and they've been checking it out ever since then at top speed. Collin's flying in right now and the police are going after them at Chico's this afternoon."

I found my voice. "Stop there." I put the back of my hand against my hot forehead. "I'm not sure I understand. Collin's coming and there's going to be a raid today? *Today?*"

"Today. So it's great that we were already planning to come out to Port A. I can drop you and Taylor off, then pick Collin up from the airport in Corpus."

My stomach rolled. "Tell me you're not involved in this raid."

"Not really. But Collin is coming in kind of as a consultant, and he asked for my help."

"You can't do that!" Taylor made protesting noises but didn't wake up. I took it down a notch. "You aren't trained for this type of thing."

"It's OK. Collin and I will be in a communications van down the street. Way down the street. I'll help identify people the team captures on video feed, but I won't be anywhere I could be hurt." He put his hand on my arm. "Plus I'll be there to make sure Collin doesn't do anything stupid."

I spoke fast, through gritted teeth. "The stupid thing is for a desk jockey PI to be anywhere near a drug raid. The stupid thing is for the man who wants custody of Taylor to do something that could get him hurt or killed. The stupid thing is for my husband to care so little about me that he puts himself at risk unnecessarily." Then my chin dropped to my chest, my energy spent. He really could get himself killed. My stomach churned again. I still hadn't eaten the apple I'd brought to settle my stomach.

Taylor started to cry and I stroked his head. "Go to sleep, Taylor. We're still on the boat." He stopped crying, but he whimpered and kept his eyes open.

Nick sat very still. He bit down on his bottom lip, then exhaled. "We only have five or ten more minutes. It would be really nice not to fight with you. I love you. I love Taylor. Everything will be fine, I promise you, I will be smart.

But I have to do this. It's important to me, to us, and I need you to understand that, even if you don't like it."

I didn't like it. Not at all. Events were spinning out of my control. I was scared for him and what could happen. But I knew the part of Nick that needed to protect Taylor. To protect family. I felt the seconds ticking by, and I dug deep, then deeper still, looking for the supportiveness and serenity of the nurturing empress that damn fortuneteller had promised me. I got Taylor out of his car seat and pulled him into my lap. His little body was a space heater. I smoothed down his sweaty hair and rocked him back and forth.

I put my chin on his head and tried again. "I love you, too. I am going to pray for you to be safe. When you come to pick us up, I will be over this, because I do understand. I'm just not quite there yet." I turned my head and met Nick's eyes.

He leaned over and put his arms around both of us. "I'll take that." He pressed his face into my hair. "And when I come pick you up, we'll have Derek out of our lives."

The ferry bumped the dock. Nick released us and started the car.

My mind grabbed a line out of a song I used to sing as a kid, but changed up the lyrics to fit. *Over the ocean and through the town, to grandmother's house we go.*

Two of us, anyway.

Chapter Forty-seven

"It's so nice having you all close enough for a day visit," Julie said. "Although I hate that Nick got called back to work." She had pulled her short, dark hair back in a headband. Between that and the light in her eyes when she looked at her grandson, she looked forty instead of sixty. It was good that she'd bought Nick's excuse. I didn't want her to worry. I tried forcing myself to match her perkiness.

"Me, too!"

It was just us and Oso. Kurt was still on shift as chief pilot in the ship channel. Julie wasn't teaching that day, so there would be no students coming to the house. I wished there were, so I could relax.

The endless morning dragged by as Taylor and Oso played hide-and-go-seek and innumerable other games with Julie, and I tried to stay in the moment, or at least appear to. But I didn't do very well at it. Stress gnawed at me. I wanted to go to sleep and just have the entire day be over, but I didn't dare.

We ate an early lunch on the back porch that overlooked one of the canals that snake through the neighborhoods of Port Aransas, then I put Taylor down for his nap in Teresa's old room. This was the time I had dreaded. How could I hide my fears from Julie when all her attention was on me? But she announced that she needed to run some errands.

Perfect. "Can I use your desktop while you're out?"

"Of course. There's no password. Just turn it on and you'll be good to go. I'll be home by the time Taylor wakes up. Kurt's going to be late. There was a big drug bust in the harbor today, some South Americans smuggling cocaine in seafood, if you can believe, so the harbor got really backed up. He may beat me home, but if he does, it won't be by much."

I nodded. What was it with bad guys stuffing drugs into food? Something about the story niggled me, but I let it go. I set myself up at Julie's desk in Nick's old room and checked for messages on my phone while the computer booted up. One from Nick: "I have Collin with me. I love you."

I could pretend I didn't see it. I was still upset, but I'd done the run-off-and-pout thing in St. Marcos, and that hadn't worked out so well for me. I could evolve. Or try to.

"I love you, too. Please be careful." Then I sent one more. "Tell Collin he's in as much trouble as you."

I logged into my email, moving away from Nick troubles and onto the jumbie house that would not let me go. First, a reply from Stefania: we had a deal. She'd already driven over to Betsy's office and picked up the key. She, her laptop, and an overnight bag were on the way to Annalise. Could I call?

Yes. In twenty minutes on the phone, we sussed out the work list to get Annalise back in shape. Stefania was enthusiastic and bright. She radiated competence through the phone. I felt more optimistic about Annalise than I had in a long while. I'd take that as a good omen. I needed one.

Over the next hour, I called for a copy of the police report and figured out how to get it through Julie's fax machine, then scanned and emailed it to the insurance company. Next, I ordered replacement appliances. Stefania would focus on repairs to the cabinets and counters and replacing the missing hardware. Between the police, the insurance company, and Stefania, I managed to divert myself from worrying about Nick for an hour.

I decided to call Rashidi to thank him.

"You welcome. I at Ms. Edmonds and she say hi."

Jacoby's grandmother. I really needed to remember what it was she had wanted me to do for her.

"Tell her hi back for me."

My eyes landed on a picture of Nick and Teresa. He looked about nineteen or twenty. Teresa was awkward and full-faced, a tween. The camera had captured her mixed emotions about the fish she was holding. Pride and squeamishness. I wished I'd known her.

But that was it. Fish.

"Rashidi, can you run into the kitchen and pull something out of the freezer for me?"

"You a little far away to borrow something for supper," he replied.

"No, I want you to look at the fish the police gave Ms. Edmonds. It was in the back of Jacoby's SUV on the night he died. I want to know if there's anything odd about it."

"Hold on. Yep, I got it now. Only thing odd is you asking me. Otherwise, the fish I holding just a normal ole fish in a vacuum-sealed bag."

"OK."

"Except I don't know what Jacoby doing with a sea bass. Tuna or wahoo, maybe some mahimahi's what I'd expect."

"But why is that strange?"

"Because sea bass not from around here. This from South America, most likely. That's the closest place you find them."

Goosebumps raced up my arms. Rashidi sure knew his fish. South American sea bass. And Jacoby had told me he was meeting an informant who had information on shady dealings at Fortuna's, where the specialty was mango-infused Chilean sea bass. Could it be a coincidence? Or did Jacoby get the fish from his informant? I thought of my father-in-law, home late from work because of South American smugglers bringing drugs north in seafood.

"Rash, could you cut it open for me?"

"That a waste of a good fish."

"Please? I need to know if there's anything unusual about it."

"Hold the phone."

I paced around Nick's bedroom and heard a whoosh and an impressive thwack over the phone.

"I back," Rashidi said. "That fish frozen like a rock. I use my machete."

"Holy cow, Rashidi, is anything left of it?"

"Yah mon, I cut it clean in two." Now I heard his breath as he sucked it in and held it, then exhaled. "Well cheese-and-bread," he muttered.

"What?"

"There a bag in the gut of the fish. White powder. Cocaine, I think."

Drugs, in a fish that might have been bound for Fortuna's. What the hell was Bart mixed up in? Or maybe it wasn't him. Trevor owned a stake in the restaurant. Who was I kidding—if it was happening at Fortuna's, Bart was involved.

"Katie? You there?"

"Yeah, I'm here. Rashidi, I think you better call the police." An earnest face flashed in my mind. "Call Morris, Jacoby's partner. I think he's one of the good guys."

"For true, but tell me the rest of this story first."

I told Rashidi what I knew about Jacoby's ill-fated meeting with the Fortuna's informant, and when he had what he needed, he hung up to call Morris.

I heard the door to the garage open and shut. Kurt called out, "Anybody home?"

I checked the time on the monitor. It was two forty-five. Nick had said the raid was planned for three. It was about to go down. You will not think about it, I ordered myself.

"I'm in Nick's room," I called. "Julie's running errands and Taylor is asleep."

"G'anpa!" Taylor yelled.

"Was asleep," I amended.

I walked into the den and met Kurt halfway across it for a stiff but friendly hug, thinking that Nick really was the younger version of his rugged father. Kurt's skin was weathered from sun and wind, but it looked good on him. The fishing adventure seemed to have warmed things between us. Or maybe he just felt guilty because I'd puked my guts out.

The door opened and shut again. "I'm back," Julie announced.

"We're in the living room," I called.

"G'ama!" Taylor yelled from his crib.

When Julie walked in, Kurt leaned down to her and she stood on her tiptoes for a kiss.

"I'll go get him, if you don't mind." Kurt laid his big hand on my shoulder, and I realized he really wanted to.

"He'll need a change," I warned.

"I'll help," Julie said.

The two of them headed down the hall. Seconds later, I heard Taylor giggling. I went back to the computer and sat down, listening to Kurt's deep voice, then Taylor shouting "boat."

In my mind, crazy images suddenly lurched by of guns firing, men yelling, and tires squealing. I breathed in and out and told myself my mind was playing tricks on me. I ordered it to stop and focused on the screen. There was a surprise in my email.

To: katie18annalise@gmail.com

From: avavavoom@hotmail.com

Subject: I'm sorry

Oh Katie,

I heard what happened. I'm sorry for leaving without telling you. I was pretty mad at you, but that's no excuse. The demo in New York was a bust. I'm in Venezuela with a gorgeous man I met in the airport. I know you'll understand when I tell you I think he is the one. I probably won't see you for a very long time, and I will miss you.

Love,

Ava

P.S. I caught the packers drinking beer at your house. They wouldn't share with me, so I made them stop.

Huh, I thought. So Ava writes in proper English. It made sense, since she switched back and forth between island patois and Continental English seamlessly when she spoke.

And then I realized I was thinking about her grammar instead of her words.

Venezuela? Wow. I knew Nick would tell me it was pure Ava, saying what Ava would say, doing what Ava would do. I tested my emotions with a probe. I loved her, but I was still mad, mad enough that my only sadness about her departure was that it would be harder to find her and kill her for abandoning Annalise and me. I hoped I could find peace about it someday. Maybe if she was gone long enough. A twist of grief shot through me but I pushed it away. I just didn't have the bandwidth right then.

The time read 3:30. Why hadn't I heard from Nick? Surely the raid wouldn't take very long. It might already be over. Then I remembered that I'd promised to pray for him. I hoped I wasn't too late.

Please please please please please God, let Nick and Collin be safe. The prayer slipped through my silent lips over and over.

I opened my eyes and looked out the window into the front yard and panic washed over me, paralyzed me as I became sure that things had gone horribly wrong. I began to cry. No sobs, just tears, tears following tears, raining down my face. I didn't bother to wipe them away. What could I do? I was helpless. Marooned on the island of Port Aransas.

Not completely marooned, I realized after a minute. I could text Nick. He would have his phone on silent, but he might see it, and he could tell me he and Collin were fine. He would answer me, and it would all be better.

"Scared. Need update."

The back door burst open with the help of a powerful wind and a concussive blast of noise hit my ears. I jumped up and flew to the kitchen—and realized it was only Julie and Kurt taking Taylor into the backyard. Everything was all right. Except that it wasn't.

"Katie? Katie? Katie, what's wrong?" Julie asked.

She was in front of me, both hands on my arms, shaking me gently at first, and then much more forcefully, but I didn't speak. I couldn't. I opened my mouth, but still no sound came out. My mind was working, but my mouth wouldn't set the words free. I was trapped and screaming on the inside.

"Kurt, come here," Julie said in a bigger and sterner voice than I'd thought she was capable of. What was wrong with me? Why couldn't I answer her?

Now Kurt's big hands were grasping my arm and shoulder as he led me to a barstool. Julie whisked Taylor away from watching me go catatonic.

Kurt stood in front of me. Ah, Nick's face. "Katie, talk to me, tell me what's wrong," he said.

My fugue passed. I exhaled, I forced myself to speak. "Nick is involved in something crazy today."

"What kind of crazy?"

Nick was going to be mad, but I couldn't hold it in any longer. "He and my brother Collin are with the police in Corpus. They're doing a sting operation on the Chico's where Derek works, based on a lead Nick developed by tailing Derek. Nick thinks they're running drugs through there and using Derek's little brother to sell it at school."

"Huh," Kurt said. He pulled on his bottom lip. "Huh."

"Yeah," I replied. "It got the better of me for a minute. I think I'll feel better if I take a walk. I'll put Taylor in the stroller and push him down to see the boats at the marina."

Kurt nodded, but he looked doubtful. "Ah, yep. If you're sure you're OK."

"I'll be fine. I've just been feeling a little stressed." Which was the understatement of the year.

Five minutes later, I was pushing Taylor down the sidewalk from the Kovacs' house toward the port. I filled my lungs to capacity over and over, willing my heart to slow down and my mind to clear. The breathing helped. Taylor was singing "the wheels on the bus go round and round." That helped, too.

We reached the end of the block and I realized I'd forgotten to bring Oso. He would have enjoyed the jaunt. I thought about going back for him, but decided I didn't have time to do that and make it home for dinner like I'd promised Julie. She expected Nick to be home then. Which I would not think about.

Taylor stopped singing, so I took over. "Free your mind, and the rest will follow," I sang under my breath, keeping my steps in time to the beat in my head. Everything will be all right, I told myself.

Except that it didn't turn out that way.

Chapter Forty-eight

I'd had a gun pulled on me before, felt that cold, hard steel against my skin, but it was different this time because I didn't see it coming. Not one bit. A strong arm grabbed me around the waist and someone jammed the barrel of a pistol into my side under the loose edge of my shirt.

"Long time no see," an unforgettable voice said in my ear.

Derek. But Derek was supposed to be arrested by now. Something had gone very, very wrong.

"Keep walking, bitch," he sneered with a tightness and pitch that told me the guy had totally lost it. My heartbeat sounded like a racehorse in my ears, but as I listened to Derek, it slowed down, time slowed down, everything slowed down. I put one foot in front of the other and pushed Taylor's stroller several more yards until Derek said, "Stop here. Get in my truck."

His truck? If I hadn't known my truck was on St. Marcos, I'd have sworn the old red Ford was one and the same. I let go of the stroller and started to get in, hoping I could leave Taylor on the street, that Derek would just take me. Someone would come by and rescue the boy.

"Don't be cute. My boy, too."

I leaned in close to Taylor. His eyes were wide. "It's going to be just fine. Come here, sweets, come to Katie."

"Ma," he said. "Ma. Ma."

"That's right, darlin', come on now." I lifted him out and pressed him into my chest. He whipped his head around to stare at Derek.

"Doesn't say boo to his own father. Poisoned against me." Derek gestured with the gun. "Now."

I opened the door with one hand and clamped Taylor to my hip with the other. He was a good thirty pounds, but I barely felt his weight at that moment. Derek pointed the gun at us until we were in, then walked around to the driver's side. I reached out to blow the horn, but nothing happened. No power. No keys in the ignition. Shit.

Derek got in, reached under the steering wheel, and fiddled with the exposed wires. It wasn't his truck. I prayed someone would recognize it as stolen and call the cops. The engine roared to life and he made a U-turn.

"Anybody ever tell you I got a brother?" he asked me. "Bobby?"

I didn't see a way out of answering, and I didn't know what the right answer was, so I said, "Yes."

"I was at my job today—my worthless, stupid, insulting, pitiful job that I have to do so I can prove I'm a good daddy and deserve all of what is rightfully mine—when some unexpected customers arrived, only they weren't there to buy shoes so I could make my crappy commission. They busted in, front and back, weapons drawn, like sneaky pigs."

He spat on the floorboard and I jerked my feet away involuntarily, which made him laugh and do it again.

"I heard it all. I heard them scream at my brother and for everyone to freeze. But Bobby is young, he hasn't been through this kind of shit before, and he ran. The stupid little prick ran. And then, boom, boom, one of those pigs put a bullet in my brother."

My mouth went dry. I kept it shut.

"You're wondering right now, how can I be here with all that going down back at Chico's? Am I right?"

He didn't wait for an answer. He stopped at a red light and turned right.

"The pigs didn't know there's a space above the store where we keep inventory. I'd pretended to be a good employee and gone up to get some more shitty shoes right before they came, which is all for show anyway, since I really go up there because that's where we keep the special merchandise stashed for my brother to sell to his stupid friends."

Derek slowed down and turned left into the parking lot of the marina.

"So I'm up in the attic when I hear all this going down below me, and I decide it's time for me to get gone, so I did. Here's where it gets good. It's all one big attic stretching across the top of the stores on the block, with a window at the end. It was a long jump down. I'm not too happy about what it did to my nice work slacks." He motioned toward his knees. I couldn't help but look. His khakis were streaked with ground-in dirt. Derek pulled into a handicapped parking spot nearest the far line of boats.

"And then I walk down that street, nobody paying attention to me, and I walk away. A car door opens across the street, two doors open, and I see this muscly motherfucker, and I see your boy Nick."

He put the truck in park. "He took my woman, he took my son, he took my money, and now he took my brother. Did you know about this?"

I bit my lip, then shook my head no. But I did know. All of it.

"Bitch, you're lying."

His right arm shot out and slugged me in the jaw so fast I never saw it coming. I screamed, then bit down hard. My head literally rang. Taylor started to cry and I turned my face back toward Derek, angry now. He grinned, then reached down and disconnected the wires and the truck stopped.

"After I saw him, I ran like hell, lost 'em both. I am putting two and two together, so I jack a car and head for the marina. Now I'm in a real big hurry, so I skip the ferry and I hotwire one of those cigarette boats. I come across to Port A," he snapped his fingers, "just like that, I borrow this truck, and here we are. Now, time for a little joyride."

There was no doubt in my mind that I wasn't going anywhere with him. But something about what he said didn't make sense. "How did you know we were here?"

"You're supposed to be so smart, Ms. Attorney. Haven't you figured that out yet?"

And then I knew. Why I hadn't seen it before, I didn't know, because when the realization dawned, it was obvious. I just hadn't paid attention. My own husband had told me the answer that very morning. The damn rehab. Bart. Slither. Trevor. *Derek.*

He saw it on my face, I could tell. "All I had to do was ask Bart where I could find my kid today. Grandma's, he said. Hey, does your husband know how much you talk to your old boyfriend?"

Bart. You stupid, stupid man.

He reached out and tried to trace a finger across my lips, but I jerked my head away.

"We're going to have fun. Now get out. And remember I have a gun."

I needed to figure out a way out of this, and fast. We were running out of time. I opened the door and lowered myself to the pavement, keeping a tight grip on Taylor. His grip on me was even tighter. Derek made it around the truck in time to meet me with a gun to the ribs again.

"Walk. We're the first boat on the left."

I walked. All of the amazing moves I could have made to break free wouldn't work with a toddler in my arms. I knew all too well he couldn't swim, and I was sure he didn't repel bullets, either. I stopped at the first boat on the left.

"Hand me the kid," Derek said.

I clutched Taylor tighter. "Why?" I said. Then, "No."

"Do it, or I shoot him in the foot. He can always get a new one." He cocked the trigger.

Shit. He was insane. I pried Taylor away from me and he started to scream. I handed him to Derek and his screams intensified. Derek held him awkwardly and stepped onto the boat. When he put Taylor down, Taylor scuttled as fast as he could to the far side of the boat, howling.

As soon as Derek took Taylor, I reached into my pocket for my phone. I had to get a call off to Kurt and Julie. I tried to unlock the screen, but my fingers were wet with humidity. I tried again.

And then Derek's foot connected with my phone on its way into my chest. The iPhone flew from my hands and into the water, and I followed it in slow motion, tumbling backwards. I hit the water headfirst, and the shock of the cold felt like a mule kick. Water surged into my sinuses. My jeans and sweatshirt weighed me down and I flailed to find which way was up. There was no light on that dreary day, and all I could see was blackness.

An enormous rumbling started above me and to my left and I realized it was the boat's engine. That had to be the way up, but I needed to stay clear of the sound. I righted myself and kicked frantically. My hand broke the surface first, then my head, and I coughed and gasped.

Chapter Forty-nine

Derek had pulled the cigarette boat out of the slip, and it was gliding away from me. Taylor was screaming bloody murder beside him. Derek put the boat in idle and jerked Taylor off the seat.

"No," I yelled. Like he could hear me as I thrashed by the pier, trying to swim toward them in heavy, sodden clothes. I watched helplessly as Derek put an adult life jacket on Taylor's tiny body. His mop of brown hair was the only thing showing out the top. Then Derek grabbed a ski rope and threaded it through the arms of the life jacket.

What the hell was he doing? Was he going to drag Taylor behind the boat?

I was only marginally relieved when he sat Taylor roughly in the seat beside him and tied the rope around the seat. When he had him strapped in, he turned to me and yelled, "God, does he ever shut up? This is what happens when you don't raise a boy to be a man." He turned from me and put the boat back in gear. It eased forward.

My completely ineffectual attempt to swim had gotten me to the next boat, which had a swim platform on its stern. I hoisted myself onto it, crawled into the boat, ran to the bow, and jumped onto the pier. The marina was deserted. I could call the police if my iPhone wasn't at the bottom of the harbor. I didn't have my purse. I didn't have a car.

But Derek did. I ran across the parking lot and yanked open the truck's door and searched frantically for some form of electronic communication, crawling through the cab, rifling the glove box and cramming my hands under the bench seat. Nothing.

I was eye level with the steering wheel when the rainbow of electrical wires triggered an idea. The marina was less than five minutes from Kurt's friend Nate's house at the mouth of the harbor. Maybe I could get there before Derek did. I didn't know what I'd do then, but I'd figure it out on the way. For now, I just had to remember how to hotwire the damn truck.

"Red for power," I said.

I held up the red wire and started sticking its end against the ends of the other wires one at a time. Come on, dashboard lights. The horn honked. I tried another. Windshield wipers. Then I tried yellow and the dash lit up.

"Hell, yeah!" I yelled.

I twisted them together with damp fingers, ignoring the jolts of electricity.

"Green for go," I said.

I held the green wire to the jumble of red and yellow ones and the engine turned over. And turned and turned and turned.

"Come on, you piece of crap!"

The engine roared to life, and I dropped the green wire. I pulled myself onto the seat, slammed the door, and jammed the gearshift into drive with the accelerator nearly to the floor. I'd never peeled rubber before, never knew how satisfying the spin of the tires as they raced to grip the pavement could be, the jolt as they found traction, the squeal, and the wind in my face through the open windows. The truck rocketed out of the parking lot. I didn't let off the accelerator for the turn, and the tires squealed again. I ran the red light at the next corner, earning myself a middle-finger salute from an old lady who could barely see over her steering wheel. Now I had one mile of straightaway and I asked the truck for all it had. I prayed no one would pull out in front of me as the speedometer crept past ninety.

At the last turn, I slammed on the brakes and made a sliding left onto Nate's street. His house was only halfway down the block now. I drove straight through his side yard, laying on the horn all the way down to the water.

Nate jumped up from where he was working on his deck. "What the hell do you think you're doing?" he hollered.

I all but fell out of the truck as I propelled myself toward him. He met me halfway across the lawn.

"My baby, kidnapped, on a boat coming out of the harbor. Gotta stop them." I gasped for air.

"Katie Kovacs?"

"Yes, Nick's Katie. Help me. I need to stop a boat."

And then I saw her. I stopped and stared, stricken mute, at Annalise. She was standing on Nate's deck, holding up the end of a fishing net covered with orange balls that Nate had been working on. She gestured at me with it, then turned and pointed behind her to the mouth of the harbor. Approaching from a half mile away, moving slowly through the no-wake zone, was Derek's boat.

"What is it?" Nate asked. He was probably about two seconds away from calling the psych ward.

"Net!" I screamed. "Nets stop boat engines. Help me get a net across the harbor. He's taken our baby, and he's coming." I pointed.

Nate finally snapped to it. "Someone's got your kid in that boat? OK, I gotcha. I'll drag the net across the mouth of harbor. I think I've got just enough. Can you hold one end until I give you the signal?"

"Yes, go!" I screamed.

Nate turned and ran to the dock with me right behind him. He handed me one end of the net.

"I'll give you an OK sign when you need to let go, but you'll feel it because it's heavy and it'll get tight. Don't let it drag you in."

"Got it," I said.

He took the other end of the net onto the *Juggerknot* and tied it around a cleat on the back corner. He threw off the lines in seconds and clambered up to the flying bridge, started the engines, threw the boat into gear, and pushed the throttle forward, all with amazing speed and dexterity.

I carried the net to the end of the dock, looking at the orange baseball-sized Styrofoam floats and realizing that's what would keep the net at propeller level. I hadn't even thought about the net sinking. What luck.

I felt the pressure from the net almost immediately, and as I leaned back to steady myself, two black hands took position by mine. My friend's fingers were long and slender. Beautiful like her, but work-roughened. I snuck a glance at her face. Tears were running down her cheeks, and I realized that I was crying, too.

"Thank you," I said.

She nodded.

I turned back to watch the *Juggerknot* move directly into Derek's path. The speedboat was not far from him now. Nate shot me an OK sign.

"Now," I said to Annalise.

Our four hands released the net at once, just as another boat entered the harbor. The ferry. It was practically a traffic jam. I held my breath. Derek was steadily increasing speed. A hundred twenty-five feet. A hundred feet. My heart pounded in my throat. Seventy-five feet. Fifty feet. Please, God, I prayed, please. Twenty-five feet. And then Derek and his boat were passing the floating net.

My heart sank. It wasn't going to work. He was going to get away with Taylor.

I looked back at Annalise. She was gazing out into the harbor with a slow smile on her lips. I looked back at Derek's boat, which was still moving forward.

Until it wasn't.

Derek ran to the back of the boat, and I could see from a distance he was screaming, probably cursing Taylor's ears blue, for all the good it would do. No amount of screaming would move that boat forward.

But my elation was replaced by a fearful uncertainty. What now? We'd stopped him, but he still had Taylor, a lot of water around him, and a gun.

The ferry pulled through the inner mouth of the harbor, passing the *Juggerknot* on its port side. And then the ferry did the strangest thing. Instead of going into the marina, it cut its engines and floated up next to Derek's boat. I shielded my eyes against the dull glare off the midnight-blue water to try to see if the ferry was going to offer Derek a tow.

Two bodies jumped off the stern of the ferry as I watched. I waited for the splash, but it didn't come because they landed in the cigarette boat. In fact, it looked like one of them landed right on top of Derek, because Derek was down.

"Be careful of my son!" I cried into the sea wind.

Every passenger on the ferry had crowded against the railing to watch the drama. I heard the voice of the captain over a loudspeaker ordering them to return to the safety of their vehicles. But no one seemed to listen. Instead, as I gaped, a cheer went up on the deck. People raised their arms in air. I could hear whoops, hollers, and clapping.

And then the *Juggerknot* pulled up between me and the speedboat, completely blocking my view.

"No, no, no!"

Chapter Fifty

For five minutes I hopped and paced, trying to get a look to no avail. Then the *Juggerknot* started back toward its home slip, toward me. Could it go any slower?

Nate brought the *Juggerknot* around to back it up to the dock, and that's when I saw them. Nick, holding Taylor, and Collin holding onto the handcuffed wrists of Derek. I glanced back out to the harbor. Someone on the deck of the ferry was throwing a line to someone in the cigarette boat. But my interest wasn't out there anymore. I waved to Nick and Taylor, and Nick waved back.

It took everything I had not to jump for the boat. I looked behind me for Annalise, knowing she would be gone, but wishing she was still beside me. And, of course, she was gone. Maybe forever. But I couldn't think about that right then.

The *Juggerknot* bounced off the bumpers on the far side of the slip and eased toward me. "You've got him!" I yelled. The sound of the engines drowned my voice.

Nick walked toward me and shouted, "Wrap the lines around the cleats." He tossed me a line.

I caught it and wrapped it around the cleat nearest to me. It seemed to do the trick, enough that Nick leaned over and handed Taylor to me. I snatched him greedily and squeezed him tight while Nick redid my line and tied the others.

"I'll get off in a minute. I have to help Nate with the rest of the lines."

"OK," I shouted to Nick. Then I looked into Taylor's big, round eyes. Teardrops were clinging to his thick, dark lashes. I admired the little nose that looked nothing like the rest of his family yet. This child was beautiful. "Oh, Taylor, I am so glad to see you. You had a scary boat ride, but everything is going to be all right."

For once, he didn't struggle to get down, but laid his head into my shoulder. His soft curls tickled my neck, and my heart grew three sizes.

The *Juggerknot's* engines stopped and I backed up to let Collin by with Derek. I didn't trust Derek, even in handcuffs.

And it turned out that I was right not to, because when Derek stepped off the boat behind Collin, he barreled headfirst into him. Collin took a heavy step back, and one of the boards of the dock broke under his foot. His foot fell through, and his body followed, shades of Katie, backwards into the water.

Derek made a break toward the yard, but with his hands cuffed behind his back he wasn't very fast. I was the only one near him, so I took off after him. There was no way I was letting that asshole get away. As soon as I hit the grass, I set Taylor down, told him to sit still, and sprinted after Derek.

I could tackle an unarmed, handcuffed man. All I needed to do was slow him down. I pulled within two feet of him and grabbed the back of his collar. I pulled back on it and launched myself onto him. He didn't go down at once, and I rode his back awkwardly, like a really bad bull rider, or a monkey riding a dog's back. But I refused to let go.

Three steps later, he went to his knees. I ignored the shouting behind me. Hand-to-hand combat was my strong suit, thanks to the martial arts training my dad always thought I'd use to escape some jock in high school. I'd never had to, but I thought Dad would like this even better.

I changed my grip to a headlock, keeping my face safely away from the back of Derek's head. We lay entwined, intimate in a horrible way. He started to thrash, and I wrapped my legs around him so I could dig my heel into his crotch.

"Rot in hell, Derek," I whispered in his ear.

"Let go of him, Katie, and stand back," Nick said. It sounded like he was right next to me. I looked up to see him pointing Derek's nine millimeter at the ground.

"Move, Katie. I can't point it at him with you there."

I covered Derek with my body instinctively. No way in hell was I moving.

"Yo, brother-in-law, the suspect is in custody. Put your weapon away before we have any civilian injuries," a dripping wet Collin said as he came toward Nick.

Nick didn't seem to hear him. He was staring at Derek.

Derek took advantage of the diversion and used his weight against me to duck, twist, and roll his body over mine, exposing his torso to Nick. "Go ahead, coward. Shoot me," he yelled.

"NICK, NO!" I screamed. But I knew ordering him around wouldn't work. Softer, but just as firmly, I spoke again from under a hundred and seventy pounds of asshole. "We won. Please put down the gun."

Nick made no move to give up the gun. After several tense seconds he spat out, "I hate him, Katie. He doesn't deserve to live."

"No, but you do. And I deserve you."

He altered his gaze to meet my eyes. He sighed. "Can I at least shoot him in the knee or something?"

I looked at Collin and let go of Derek, and my brother pulled him off of me. "No, not even one little kneecap," I said. I crawled to my feet and brushed away grass and dirt as I made my way to my husband.

"It would make me feel so much better."

"So would putting your arms around me," I said. "The gun?"

He put the safety on and shoved it in the back of his waistband.

Nate walked up, beaming, with Taylor in his arms. "Good thing I radioed Kurt. I had a feeling he'd know who to call."

Apparently so.

Nick said, "I'm glad he didn't tell the ferry captain about Derek's gun, or Ole Cap might not have been so eager to pull alongside him."

It had taken all of us. Annalise's face flashed through my mind and I turned back to Nick. "You were right," I said.

"About what?"

"That by the time you picked me up, we'd have Derek out of our hair."

He kissed the tip of my nose. "I wish you would have let me shoot him."

I stood up on tiptoe and placed my smallish, pale freckled nose against his largish olive-skinned one.

"You, Nick Kovacs, are my hero because you didn't shoot him."

He harrumphed. "You, Katie Kovacs, are my hero, too." And then he smiled.

Chapter Fifty-One

Two weeks later, Nick and I got ready for court together in the tiny bathroom of our apartment. I massaged moisturizer into his face and snuck some down his neck. He kept his eyes closed and his face completely relaxed. I put my hands against both his cheeks for a few seconds, then said, "All done."

"Thanks, baby." He opened his eyes and the look in them was mischievous. He tucked a strand of hair behind my ear. "Well, I was going to wait until after the hearing today to give you something, because I didn't want to jinx it, but I've decided I can't hold out."

"Stop!" I broke in. "You can't risk it."

"All that voodoo stuff has gone to your head."

I had finally broken down and told Nick about my fear that Annalise killed Junior. For some crazy reason, it felt like confessing to the crime myself. The body still hadn't shown up. I just hoped that wherever she'd put him, he would never be found.

"Put this in your purse, then," Nick said, handing me an envelope, "and after we get our ruling, you can open it."

I stuck the envelope in the side pocket of my brown suede bag. "Well, just so you know, I have a little something for you in there, too."

"What?"

"I can't tell you. It'll jinx it."

"Argh," he said, and swatted my behind, which earned him a swat back.

Since we had already delivered Taylor to his Mothers' Day Out teacher's house for the day, we loaded ourselves into the Tahoe for the drive to the courthouse. We clasped hands during the walk from the car, but neither of us said a word.

When we were inside, Nick opened the courtroom door for me, and I entered for what I prayed was the last time. My husband followed me to the front row and I slid in next to my in-laws. I kissed Julie on the cheek and whispered hello to Kurt. Julie reached for my hand and gripped it tight as Mary turned around at the counsel table at the front of the courtroom. She waved and gave us a thumbs-up.

I wriggled in the wooden pew, which seemed even harder than usual. I hated being there. I hated courtrooms in general, except for maybe the one in St. Marcos where Bart and Trevor had been indicted on drug charges ten days before. Morris had come through for his partner Jacoby in a big way and busted Fortuna's new kitchen manager in their walk-in cooler with his hands wrist-deep in Chilean sea bass and vacuum-sealed bags of cocaine. Rashidi said the restaurant was boarded up tight. The police had reopened the investigations into Tarah's and Jacoby's "accidental" deaths. I just hoped some of it could be tied back to Derek and Slither, since their names were listed as officers on the company's official records alongside Bart's and Trevor's. It wouldn't bring Jacoby back, but justice still mattered.

"All rise," the bailiff said.

We got to our feet as Judge Nichols entered in a swirl of black robes. She sat, and the bailiff motioned for us to follow suit. I allowed myself a glance at Derek. As scary as he'd been in the Port Aransas marina, he looked far more malevolent that day, even shackled to a chair with his eyes fixed on the floor. He radiated hate. He sure didn't look like anybody's loving father to me.

He had accepted a plea bargain deal with the state, thirty-five years for first-degree kidnapping. Aggravated, since he'd used a gun on me. He got off easy, but the sentence still looked convincing to me of what a giant loser he was and the horrible impact it would have on Taylor for Derek to remain in his life in any capacity. I just hoped the judge agreed.

Judge Nichols went through the formal preliminaries, then got down to business in a *Law-and-Order*-type voice that rang throughout the courtroom, the kind of voice that makes me want to salute and put my hand over my heart. "This court loathes terminating parental rights, except in the most extreme circumstances. Had only one factor in the child's best interests supported termination, I would not have granted it. However, in this case, the respondent has made it difficult for the court *not* to find in favor of granting petitioner's request for termination; correction, the respondent has made it *impossible*."

The judge read off Derek's crimes and failings toward Taylor. It was a long list. I wanted to jump to my feet and pump my fist over my head, but I restrained myself.

"It is the ruling of this court that the respondent's parental rights be hereby and irrevocably terminated. Full custody is granted to the petitioner as requested by the deceased mother in her last will and testament, with named petitioner as guardian."

Basically, it was a whole lot of mumbo jumbo confirming that Derek was the cretin we all knew he was, and that Nick, my Nick, was forevermore Taylor's father. Making me, by virtue of the gold band on the third finger of my left hand, our vows, and our enthusiastic (and frequently repeated) consummation of the union, Taylor's mother.

Judge Nichols rapped her gavel. "Bailiff, call the next case."

I turned to Nick and he put his forehead against mine. I closed my eyes. It was official. We were three.

Mary whispered back at us, "You did it! Congratulations."

Nick and I pulled our foreheads apart, but we stayed nose to nose, looking into each other's eyes, holding the rest of the world out as long as we could. Kurt pushed his way down the row to hug Nick, and we allowed ourselves to be pulled away from each other. A little separation didn't stop the magic. And then we were all hugging each other and talking in excited whispers as the bailiff glowered.

I felt a coldness on the back of my head and I swiveled toward Derek. He was staring at me, smiling with his lips, his eyes flat and narrowed. It looked like a threat. It felt like a threat. Could he still hurt us while he was in jail? Derek had proved he had friends before, and we were on his turf. Hell, his little brother had survived the shooting and was growing up fast. It was a sobering thought. But I wouldn't let Derek see it. I forced myself to return his stare. I concentrated on sending him a silent message: Don't mess with me and my family ever again, you asshole.

Brave words, but I didn't speak them aloud, and the seed of worry planted itself deep inside me. Not just for Nick, Taylor, and me, but for Julie and Kurt, too. I had a lot to lose.

"What's the matter, baby?" Nick asked. His mouth touched my hair and ear, reassuringly close, his warm breath and the movement of his lips calming me in a way that no mere words could.

We had slipped into the stream of people making their quiet way toward the door, so I couldn't answer. The attorneys and parties for the next case were moving in the opposite direction. Nick stopped me before I could exit the courtroom.

He put a hand on each of my shoulders and I tried to mask my thoughts, fearful of ruining the moment for him. I wasn't fast enough.

"Are you going to tell me what's the matter?"

"Nothing." He shook his head at me. "Really," I insisted.

"Katie, don't close up on me. What's wrong?"

I was frustrated with myself. What was I afraid of? My pride was the only thing that had ever pushed Nick away. It was time to embrace a new, open Katie. It wasn't as easy as I'd hoped it would be. I took a long breath, sucking in air like helium from a balloon.

"I looked at Derek, and I had this flash of fear for what comes next. What if he doesn't let go? What if he sends someone after us or after your parents? I know I should enjoy the moment and be excited that we won. I know we can worry about all of this later. But, that's what I was thinking about."

He didn't look surprised. He looked something else. Mischievous again. "I understand. I think Derek is a very real threat. Collin and I have been talking about this a lot, actually." His dark eyes started to do their twinkling thing. "So we came up with a plan."

"Yours and Collin's plans scare the hell out of me." But the twinkling was infectious, and I could feel myself responding to it.

Like a game show host, he gestured toward my handbag and said, "The envelope, please."

How had I forgotten about the envelope? I retrieved it from my purse and tried to hand it to him.

"No, you open it," he said.

I carefully tore back the sticky flap. Inside it, Nick had block-printed SMILE and drawn a smiling stick-figure woman with long hair colored with red crayon. He would never be an artist, that was for sure. I stuck my fingers inside and felt a folded stack of papers. I shut my eyes and pulled it out.

Nick leaned in quickly and kissed one closed eyelid and then the other. I opened my eyes and looked up at him, at my husband, and I felt the rightness of things slipping into place without even knowing what I held in my hand.

Nick said, "I think we need to make it harder for Derek to do us any more damage. Something short of a formal witness protection program, more like the world's best home security system."

I allowed myself to peek down then and saw them, his gift: one-way tickets to St. Marcos. Home to Annalise. I sucked in my breath, and I felt the soundless hum from two thousand miles away that told me Nick's gift was well received indeed, back up in the rainforest.

"What do you say to letting the jumbie keep the bad guys away?" he asked.

"I think that's one of the best ideas you've ever had." I threw my arms around him. "I love you, Nick."

"I love you, too."

I leaned my head back. "Are you ready for your surprise now?"

"Hit me," he said.

I reached into my purse, my hand sliding against its silky lining, and retrieved the gold pocket watch we had found inside the crumbled wall of Annalise after the hurricane. "I had it fixed for you."

"Wow," he said. "Wow." He reached out for it, and I put it in his hand. He traced the engraving on the front and read it aloud. "*My Treasures*. I love it, Katie."

"Oh, but that's not all. Open the watch."

He flicked the clasp he'd had to pry open before, and it released perfectly. He parted the casing to reveal the functioning watch face on the right, and on the left, something more.

"What's that?" Nick asked.

"Haven't you ever seen a sonogram before?"

"Sonogram? You mean like a baby?"

I pointed at the picture once, then twice. "You could say that. Times two."

He threw back his head and laughed. "Two. Plus Taylor. Three." He pulled me back in to him and said, "Thank you, Katie." He rocked me back and forth.

"I hope you're OK, that you're as happy about this as me. It's been a lot, I know, and we haven't had any time just to be us."

I stopped him, shaking my head back and forth, my nose rubbing against his shoulder. "I don't need that as long as I'm your sun and moon." And as soon as I said it, I knew that it was true, and that being an empress beat the hell out of being a silly little princess seven days a week and twice on Sunday. "And as long as I know you'll have a sausage biscuit in my hand within the next five minutes."

Nick went for the accent and manner of an English manservant, which came off more like a cowboy with a really bad head cold. "Anything else you require, madame?"

We readjusted in sync like a ballroom dance team. Nick shifted one of his arms around my shoulders, and I kept one of mine around his waist.

I pulled myself up to the top of my height, feeling positively regal. Require? No. "That will be all, Kovacs." I had everything I needed, and, better yet, I wanted everything I had.

About the Author

Pamela Fagan Hutchins holds nothing back and writes award-winning and bestselling mysterious women's fiction and relationship humor, from Texas, where she lives with her husband Eric and their blended family of three dogs, one cat, and the youngest few of their five offspring. She is the author of many books, including *Saving Grace, Leaving Annalise, How To Screw Up Your Kids*, and *Hot Flashes and Half Ironmans*, to name just a few.

Pamela spends her non-writing time as a workplace investigator, employment attorney, and human resources professional, and she is the co-founder of a human resources consulting company. You can often find her hiking, running, bicycling, and enjoying the great outdoors.

For more information, visit http://pamelahutchins.com, or email her at pamela@pamelahutchins.com. To hear about new releases first, sign up for her newsletter at http://eepurl.com/iITR.

You can buy Pamela's books at most online retailers and "brick and mortar" stores. You can also order them directly from SkipJack Publishing: http://SkipJackPublishing.com. If your bookstore or library doesn't carry a book you want, by Pamela or any other author, ask them to order it for you.

Books By the Author

Fiction from SkipJack Publishing:
Saving Grace, SkipJack Publishing (Katie & Annalise #1)
Leaving Annalise, SkipJack Publishing (Katie & Annalise #2)
Missing Harmony, SkipJack Publishing (Katie & Annalise #3) (coming soon)

Nonfiction from SkipJack Publishing:
The Clark Kent Chronicles: A Mother's Tale Of Life With Her ADHD/Asperger's Son
Hot Flashes and Half Ironmans: Middle-Aged Endurance Athletics Meets the Hormonally Challenged
How to Screw Up Your Kids: Blended Families, Blendered Style
How to Screw Up Your Marriage: Do-Over Tips for First-Time Failures
Puppalicious and Beyond: Life Outside The Center Of The Universe
What kind of loser indie publishes? (coming soon)

Other Books By the Author:
OMG - That Woman! (anthology) Aakenbaaken & Kent
Ghosts (anthology), Aakenbaaken & Kent
Easy to Love, But Hard to Raise (2012) and *Easy to Love, But Hard to Teach* (coming soon) (anthologies), DRT Press, edited by Kay Marner & Adrienne Ehlert Bashista
Prevent Workplace Harassment, Prentice Hall, with the Employment Practices Solutions attorneys

CPSIA information can be obtained at www.ICGtesting.com
Printed in the USA
LVOW01s2030300514

387923LV00003B/3/P